Alan Mendelsohn, the Boy from Mars doesn't belong to you anymore. The book is mine; it kept me alive and sane all through high school. —*Zack Beyman*

My best friend and I read *Alan Mendelsohn* over and over again in the fourth grade. I consider it one of the three best books ever written (along with *Les Misérables* and *To Kill a Mockingbird*). —*Sarah Adams*

I am a twenty-three-year-old musician. Your slightly warped mind has greatly influenced my own slightly warped mind since elementary school. —*Christopher Bruzzi*

The Snarkout Boys and the Avocado of Death was an especially important book for me. I read it more often than I went to synagogue. —*Daniel Wabyick*

The truth is, everyone should Snark Out at one point or another. At the very least they should read the books.
—*Andrew Packer*

My thirteen-year-old son, Aaron, spends hours writing Kevin Shapiro stories. I just thought you should know.
—*Jessica Rubinstein*

Hello. I am a Japanese. In Japan your name isn't well known. But I could find *Doodle Flute* translated into Japanese by Shuntaro Tanikawa, a famous poet in Japan.
—*Nobuyasu Tsuge*

I hope, make that PLAN, to be a writer JUST LIKE YOU. I've been trying to achieve this goal by eating one-eighth of my weight in boiled pasta every day. I've gained 34 pounds so far, and it's only been two months! —*Jason Ward*

5 Novels

Alan Mendelsohn, the Boy from Mars · Slaves of
Spiegel · The Snarkout Boys and the Avocado
of Death · The Last Guru · Young Adult Novel

DANIEL PINKWATER

Foreword by Jules Feiffer

FARRAR STRAUS GIROUX · NEW YORK

Library of Congress Cataloging-in-Publication Data
Pinkwater, Daniel Manus, 1941–
    [Novels.   Selections]
    5 novels / Daniel Pinkwater ; foreword by Jules Feiffer.
        p.   cm.
    Contents: Alan Mendelsohn, the boy from Mars—Slaves
of Spiegel—The Snarkout boys and the avocado of death—
The last guru—Young adult novel.
    ISBN-13: 978-0-374-42329-2 (pbk.)
    ISBN-10: 0-374-42329-6 (pbk.)
    1. Children's stories, American.   2. Humorous stories,
American.   [1. Humorous stories.]   I. Title.
PZ7.P6335Aaf   1997
[Fic]—dc21   97-16939

Alan Mendelsohn, the Boy from Mars was first published in 1979 by E. P. Dutton. *Slaves of Spiegel* was first published in 1982 by Four Winds Press. *The Snarkout Boys and the Avocado of Death* was first published in 1982 by Lothrop, Lee & Shepard Books. *The Last Guru* was first published in 1978 by Dodd, Mead & Company. *Young Adult Novel* was first published in 1982 by Thomas Y. Crowell.

Contents

Foreword

I don't really know how Daniel Pinkwater writes his books, but I'll tell you what I think. He has an idea, or the germ of an idea, or, if not an idea, he has the name of a character. Whatever he has, he puts it down on paper and he looks at it, and it gives him a thought which connects to another thought which connects to another and another. Until he has a book, or what he calls a book.

Except it's not like any book you'd write or I'd write, because Daniel Pinkwater's thoughts don't connect like yours or mine. His tab A does not fit into slot A the way it's supposed to in a well-thought-out thought. More likely, his tab A will fit into slot 14 or slot X79, the kind of fit that might drive you or me crazy if we tried it, but when Pinkwater does it, you read it and say to yourself, "Why, of course. This is how it should be."

Pinkwater, like Alan Mendelsohn, one of his heroes, comes from outer space, but not from Mars, where Alan says he comes from. My guess is that Pinkwater lives in closer space, where he spies on what's going on down here. My guess is that he lives on the moon. Here's my proof: if you take a look at his picture on the cover of this book, and then look up at the moon when it's full, you can see a striking resemblance to the Man in the Moon. Of course, I have a good friend, Davis, who also resembles the Man in the Moon, but he doesn't write books. His wife, Betsy, does. But that doesn't get us anywhere.

From his own moon, Pinkwater sees how silly we are, how nasty we can be, how idiotic, how thoughtless, how unkind— and yet how funny, how genuine, how innocent, how human —that is, the good part, not the other parts of human.

Pinkwater's moon-view helps us to see ourselves his way, not ours, which is what always happens when you are in the hands of a good writer with a fresh way of seeing things. And it's this fresh vision that takes over our old tried-and-true and slightly boring vision. And we are braced by it, we are uplifted. We feel better about ourselves and the world, and how we are going to get along in the world.

What Daniel Pinkwater gives is pure Elixir of Man in the Moon medicine. But it only works if you take it in the prescribed dosage, one bookful at a time. Which is what you get in this volume. Don't be surprised if you find yourself coming back for refills.

Jules Feiffer

Alan Mendelsohn, the Boy from Mars

1

I got off to a bad start at Bat Masterson Junior High School. My family had moved from my old school district during the summer, and I didn't know a single kid at the school. On top of that, it turned out that kids at Bat Masterson put a lot of emphasis on how you look. This created a problem—I am a short, portly kid, and I wear glasses. Every other kid in the school was tall, had a suntan, and none of them wore glasses. Also clothes wrinkle up on me. I don't know why this should be—five minutes after I get dressed in the morning, everything is wrinkled. It looks like I slept in my clothes.

Not only did I not know anybody on my first day, not only did I find out that a short, portly, wrinkled kid with glasses is an outcast in that school, but I also sat down on somebody's half-finished Good Humor bar in the school yard. That reduced my confidence. Then it turned out that the school was not expecting me. My records, and grades, and whatever the old school was supposed to send, they had not sent—or they had sent them to the wrong place—or they had gotten lost.

So I had to sit on this bench in the office for most of the morning, sort of sticking to the bench because of the left-over Good Humor on the seat of my pants. Finally they gave me this big pile of cards to fill out. Then I had to run all over the school getting teachers to sign the cards. Three or four times I had to go back to the office with notes from teachers saying that their class was full, or it was the wrong class, or it conflicted with another class I was supposed to take.

And each time I entered a classroom, the class would giggle at me. Then the teacher would ask my name. It was written right at the top of every one of the cards—but the teacher would ask me to say it anyway. "Leonard Neeble," I would say, and the kids in the class would just go wild. I don't know why, but my name gets them every time.

At lunchtime I walked around the school yard. All the kids looked sort of grown-up and unwrinkled. Some of the girls even had lipstick on. The kids stood around in groups, talking and laughing. Some guys were showing off, walking on top of benches, and chasing each other, and hollering. Nobody looked at me or said anything to me. I had the feeling that if I tried to talk to anybody, they wouldn't have been able to hear me. I looked for a quiet spot to eat my tuna fish sandwich.

After lunch I went back to the office. The lady there had told me to come back at the beginning of each period. She looked at my cards and told me to go to gym class. I went. When I got to the gym, there was a bunch of kids sitting in rows on the floor. The teacher was standing on a bench. He was wearing sunglasses and had a whistle on a lanyard around his neck. He had white sneakers on. I went around the kids sitting on the floor and came up to him from the side, holding out the card he was supposed to sign. "You're late, boy!" he said. He had a very loud voice.

"The lady in the office . . . I'm supposed to . . . this card . . . you have to sign my . . ." The teacher cut me off.

"Nobody comes late to gym!" he shouted. He really scared me. I could see all his teeth. "Anybody comes late to gym, he does five laps! Now do five laps, chubby—work off some of that lard. And while you're running, listen to what I'm telling the class."

I started running, holding my stack of cards.

"You will get two pairs of gym shorts, green; two pairs of sweat socks, white; you will get a sweat shirt, gray." The gym teacher was shouting at the class. His name was Mr. Jerris. His voice was so loud it made my ears hurt, even when I was making my turn at the far end of the gym.

"That's five, fat boy; take a rest," Mr. Jerris said. "Now, since none of you have any equipment, you can spend the rest of the period horsing around, QUIETLY!" Mr. Jerris spun around, jumped off the bench, and walked through a little door at the back of the gym.

I was sweating and out of breath. I expected the other kids to start up with "fat boy" and "chubby," after Mr. Jerris had called me those things—which was unfair, since I am actually not fat but portly. That's what it says on the label when I get clothes in the department store: boy's portly. The other kids didn't tease me. They didn't pay any attention to me at all. They went right to work, fooling with the gym equipment, doing handstands, swinging from the rings, and stuff like that. I looked at the door Mr. Jerris had gone through. I wondered if I should go and knock on it. I just stood there, holding my cards, for a long time.

Mr. Jerris came back. "I said QUIETLY!" His voice made an echo. "Come here, fatty, I'll sign that." I started to walk toward him. "RUN!" I ran. Mr. Jerris signed my card. "Now, by tomorrow, make sure you have at least gym shoes. By the end of the week, I want you to have all your equipment, got that . . ."—he looked at my card— "Neeble?" Mr. Jerris went back through the little door.

The gym class was the high point of the day for sheer unpleasantness, but all the other classes I went to were more or less the same—the teachers seemed annoyed that I was there, making them sign one more thing or send for an extra textbook—and not one kid said anything to me, although quite a few giggled at my name. By the time school let out and I started walking home, I was totally miserable.

Our new house was almost a mile from school, and I didn't like it. There wasn't one kid my age in the neighborhood. Except for some very little kids, babies really, a couple of blocks away, there were no kids at all. About the only good thing that had happened since we moved out of our old apartment in the old neighborhood was that my parents let me have a dog. The dog's name was Melvin, a big brown dog we got at the pound. I had had him since the middle of the summer, and he hadn't been able to learn a single trick. I spent about two weeks trying to teach Melvin to fetch a ball. I couldn't even get him to look at it. About the only thing Melvin could do that was sort of unusual was walk in his sleep. Still, he seemed to like me, and would take naps in my room, snoring and mumbling while I read or worked on a model airplane.

When I got home, Melvin was sleeping in the front hall. He opened one eye to say hello, and then dozed off. My mother was in the kitchen, cooking liver for Melvin's supper. Cooked liver was all he would eat. I hate the smell of liver cooking. The whole house smelled of it.

Everything in the house was still sort of new. My parents had bought all new furniture when we moved. My mother had picked out a lot of stuff for my room so it would look like a picture she had seen in a magazine. I wasn't allowed to put any tacks in the walls because of the plaid wallpaper, which was very expensive, but just perfect for a boy's room—my mother said. So I couldn't put up any posters or pictures or anything. I flopped down on my bed, which had a plaid bedspread to match the wallpaper. "How do you like your new school?" my mother shouted from the kitchen. I told her it was fine—what else could I say?

Melvin wandered in with his eyes half-open, and sort of crashed down on his elbows next to my bed. In thirty seconds he was snoring. I closed my eyes and tried to pretend we were still living in the old apartment.

2

The old apartment was in a neighborhood where none of the houses had lawns, and backyards were either concrete or dirt. There were a lot of kids around, and you could get into a ball game or a conversation or trade comics, just by going outside. It didn't seem to matter to anybody that I was portly or wrinkled. The best thing about our old apartment was that my grandparents had an apartment in the same building. I used to spend a lot of time at their place.

My grandmother likes everyone to call her "Old One," and she's always saying things like, "Listen well, young one!" and "Mark well, my child!" She believes that everyone ought to eat only raw food, except meat, which she believes nobody should eat at all. She spends all her time grinding up nuts and wheat berries and soybeans, and mashing them together with honey and raisins and stuff. It tastes better than it sounds. My grandfather likes to be called "Grandfather." He has this parrot named Lucky, and he's always fooling with him—spraying him for mites, or bathing his feet, or just walking around with Lucky on his shoulder. Both my grandparents eat basically what Lucky eats.

There are some other people living in my grandparents' apartment. Madame Zelatnowa is a friend of my grandmother's. She is an anthropologist and she comes from Europe. She is studying the people of the Himalayas, especially their cooking. When my grandmother isn't dishing out her ground-up stuff, Madame Zelatnowa is making things like roasted barley floating in strong tea with melted butter and scallions. This stuff tastes worse than it sounds.

Some people come and go. Great-uncle Boris lives there in the wintertime. Uncle Boris is a movie nut. He takes 8-millimeter movies of clouds and squirrels in the park. Once he took a bus all over the country and took pictures of the sky in every state in the Union except Alaska and Hawaii.

I used to hang out in my grandparents' apartment as often as I could. The thing I liked about it was that everyone there didn't treat me in any special way. They were all sort of interested in various things, and they would talk to me about them in just the same way they would talk to anybody. Not being able to drop in at my grandparents' apartment was probably the worst thing about moving to the new house.

I was thinking about all this when I heard the electric radio-controlled garage door open. This was a special gadget of my father's. He had it installed the first week we had the new house. There was a button on the dashboard of his car. When he got within two blocks of the house, he'd push the button, and a little radio transmitter under the hood would start an electric motor in the garage that would open the door. When he got inside, he'd push the button again, and the door would close. Sometimes the door would open and close by itself, as trucks with two-way radios went by.

Melvin struggled to his feet and stumbled off to say hello to my father, yawning. My father always got a bigger welcome than I did. I heard the back door slam twice, and Melvin dragged himself back into my room, still yawning, and settled down to sleep again. I knew what had happened—my father had come out of the garage, stepped through the back door, kissed my mother, patted Melvin on the head, taken off his coat, and hung it on a hook, first taking his apron off the hook. The apron had WHAT'S COOKING? printed on the front, and a picture of a guy in a chef's hat standing in front of a barbecue with a big cloud of smoke coming up from it. Next, my father had gone outside (that was the second slam) and started building a fire in the portable barbecue. This had been going on all summer.

He would pour some charcoal out of a bag, spray about a gallon of starter fluid over it, and throw in a match. Then he would stand around for maybe an hour, watching to see that the fire didn't go out, and blowing on it once in a while to keep it hot.

Meanwhile, my mother would be in the kitchen, getting the meat ready—steaks or hamburgers or chicken. At the same time, Melvin's liver would be cooling on the counter. When the fire was ready, my father would holler to my mother, and my mother would holler to Melvin and me. While we were making our way to the table, she would run outside and give my father the hamburgers or whatever, and then she would run inside and put Melvin's dish of cool cooked liver down. Then she would run outside again and get the first of the hamburgers off the fire from my father. Then she would run in and give one to me. Then my father would come in, wearing his apron, with a big long fork in one hand and holding a platter with the rest of the hamburgers in the other, and we would all eat supper.

Besides the hamburgers or steak, we would have salad. My parents had been to a restaurant where they served this special salad with chopped hard-boiled egg on it, and anchovies, and all sorts of stuff. The waiter makes the salad at the table, and he has these oversized pepper mills and salt shakers made of wood, and he does a whole routine with the salad. Anyway, my father had gotten the same kind of wooden salt and pepper shakers and the same kind of big stainless steel salad bowl, and he would go through the whole routine every night. Before we moved to the new house I had always liked hamburgers and things like that. Now I was getting bored—my parents weren't, though.

"How do you like your new school, son?" my father asked.

"It's OK," I said.

"Have you made any new friends?"

"None of the kids will talk to me."

"Well, it's always hard the first day in a new school," my father said. "You'll make friends."

"I don't think so," I said.

"You say that none of the children will talk to you," my mother said. "Have you tried to talk to any of them?" I didn't say anything. I didn't know how to tell my mother the snotty kids at Bat Masterson Junior High School were sure to think I was a creep.

"To have a friend, be a friend," my mother said. "You just walk up to the other children and say, 'Hi! My name is Leonard Neeble,' and you'll see how quickly you'll get to know some very nice people." I could just imagine how that would go over. "Now, promise me you'll do that, Leonard," my mother said. "I don't want you to develop any complexes. You had lots of friends in the old neighborhood."

3

Walking to school the next day, I thought over my mother's suggestion. After all, the kids at Bat Masterson couldn't be all that bad. Maybe I just needed to give them a chance. Maybe I was being too sensitive. After all, only a few kids had giggled at me, not all of them. I decided I would try to be friendly.

I had been assigned to a homeroom, Room 107. Every day at the beginning and end of school I had to go to Room 107. There was a teacher there, Miss Steele. She would be my homeroom teacher all through junior high school. In our homeroom period, which was about fifteen minutes, Miss Steele would read us announcements and help us with our problems—that's what they told me in the office when I was filling out cards. I went to Room 107 and found a seat.

"That's my desk, little boy," someone said. It was a girl about six feet tall. "Now get out of here so I can sit with my friends."

Most of the girls were taller than me, but this one was really a giant. I thought I'd try out my friendly stuff. "Hi! My name is Leonard Neeble," I said. "I didn't know that seats had been assigned."

"Just get out of here, you little pimple," she said.

I took another seat in the back of the room. The giant girl sat down at the desk and leaned forward, talking to a bunch of other girls, all of whom were taller than me.

I watched kids drift into Room 107. They all seemed to know each other. They waved and smiled and changed seats so they could be near their friends. Obviously, seats had not been assigned. That big dopey girl could have just asked me to change seats. I was sitting in the last seat in the last row, so I could see everything that happened in the room.

A teacher came in. She was tall and sort of old. She smiled at the class with her lips pressed together. The bell rang.

"Class, come to order!" Miss Steele said. Everybody sort of shuffled around in their seats. "Now get ready for the P.A. announcements," Miss Steele said.

The door opened, and a little kid came in. He was a lot shorter than me, and was wearing brand-new blue jeans with the cuffs turned up about halfway to his knees. He had these real thick glasses that made his eyes look like fish in a bowl. He looked like he was about six years old.

Then I heard chimes—*bong, boing, boinng*—it was the P.A., the public-address system. There was a big loud-speaker on the wall of the classroom, up near the clock. "WELCOME TO YOUR SECOND DAY OF THE FALL TERM AT BAT MASTERSON JUNIOR HIGH SCHOOL," a voice said. "THIS IS MR. WINTER, YOUR PRINCIPAL. I TRUST YOU ARE ALL SETTLING

DOWN TO WORK IN YOUR CLASSES, AND I HOPE
WE CAN ALL ENJOY THIS TERM TOGETHER.
HOWEVER, NOBODY IS GOING TO ENJOY THIS
TERM IF WE HAVE THE SAME PROBLEM IN THE
SCHOOL YARD WITH WASTEPAPER AND CANDY
WRAPPERS THAT WE HAD LAST TERM. YOU
CHILDREN ARE PRIVILEGED TO LIVE IN THE
GREATEST COUNTRY IN THE WORLD, AND TO GO
TO A SCHOOL WHICH HAS A BEAUTIFUL CAMPUS
WHICH HAS JUST BEEN RESURFACED WITH
BLACKTOP. THERE ARE WASTEBASKETS EX-
ACTLY EVERY TWENTY FEET IN OUR LOVELY
LUNCH COURT, AND THERE ARE BENCHES, ALL
FRESHLY PAINTED, FOR YOU TO SIT ON IN THE
FINE WEATHER AND ENJOY YOUR LUNCH. THE
BENCHES ARE FOR SITTING—NOT FOR STAND-
ING ON, AND CERTAINLY NOT FOR CARVING
AND DEFACING. AND THE WASTEBASKETS ARE
FOR YOUR WASTEPAPER AND REFUSE. YOU WILL
SEE SOME OF YOUR FELLOW STUDENTS WEAR-
ING ARMBANDS IN ORANGE AND GREEN, OUR
SCHOOL COLORS.—THESE ARE LUNCH COURT
MONITORS, AND I EXPECT YOU TO LISTEN TO
THEM. IF A LUNCH COURT MONITOR TELLS YOU
TO PICK UP A CANDY WRAPPER, YOU WILL PICK
THAT CANDY WRAPPER UP! THE LUNCH COURT
MONITOR HAS THE AUTHORITY TO REPORT YOU
TO THE LUNCH COURT TEACHER, AND THE
LUNCH COURT TEACHER HAS THE AUTHORITY
TO SEND YOU TO MY OFFICE. NOW, MY OFFICE
IS OPEN TO ALL STUDENTS ALL THE TIME TO
DEAL WITH LEGITIMATE PROBLEMS, BUT I
DON'T WANT TO SEE ANY STUDENT IN MY OF-

FICE BECAUSE OF A VIOLATION OF THE LUNCH COURT CODE. . . ."

He went on like that. It was impossible to listen. Kids were talking to each other, and Miss Steele was writing in her attendance book. I decided to try out my friendliness on the little kid next to me. "Hi!" I said. "My name is Leonard Neeble."

"Yeah, I know," said the kid. "You're the weirdo. I saw you in gym class yesterday."

"You there! In the last seat! No talking! Stand up! What's your name?" Miss Steele was shouting at me.

My name got the usual laughs. Miss Steele went on about how we are all supposed to listen to the P.A. and did I think I was a special character. In the background, Mr. Winter was still booming away on the loudspeaker. ". . . WE ALWAYS SHOW CONSIDERATION FOR OTHERS BY KEEPING TO THE RIGHT WHEN PASS- ING THROUGH THE HALLS, AND WE DO NOT WEAR SHOES WITH METAL TAPS. ANY BOY WEARING SHOES WITH METAL TAPS MAY BE RE- PORTED BY THE HALL MONITOR, WHO WILL HAVE THE RIGHT TO SEND HIM TO MY OFFICE, WHICH IS ALWAYS OPEN TO ANY STUDENT WITH A LEGITIMATE PROBLEM, BUT I DON'T WANT TO SEE . . ." It went on until the bell rang.

I went to my first class, which was English. Apparently, the day before, when I hadn't been there, the teacher had the class write a composition on what they did on their summer vacation. Today she was going to have the kids read their papers. Since I didn't write one, I felt safe in my seat at the back of the room. Several kids were chosen to get up and read their papers. All of them had been somewhere. Some of them had been to summer camps, fancy ones that specialize in dance or tennis or horseback riding. One kid had gone to Europe on a tour for kids, and another one had gone with his folks.

The teacher's name was Miss Trumbull, and she seemed fairly nice. "We have one new boy in class," she said, "who hasn't written a paper, but maybe he'll tell us about his summer anyway. Leonard Neeble?"

There was the giggling. Kids swiveled around to see who Leonard Neeble was.

"Leonard, wouldn't you like to come to the front of the room and tell us about your summer vacation?" Miss Trumbull asked.

My face felt hot. I went to the front of the room. "Well, my parents and I moved to a new house," I said.

"That's very nice," Miss Trumbull said. "And what else happened to you over the summer?"

"I got a dog," I said.

"Oh, how lucky for you," Miss Trumbull said. "What kind of a dog is it, Leonard?"

"What kind?"

There was something creeping into Miss Trumbull's voice that told me she was getting the idea I was feeble-minded and needed to be helped along. "Is it a poodle or a dalmation or a scottie, Leonard?" she said.

"No, it's, he's just a big brown dog—we got him at the pound." There was silence. I couldn't see the kids in the class—I was looking at the floor.

"Don't mumble, Leonard," Miss Trumbull said. "Did anything else happen during the summer that you'd like to tell us?"

"Well, I worked," I said.

"Oh, you had a job. That's wonderful," Miss Trumbull said. "Would you like to tell us what sort of job it was?"

"Just helping my father in his business."

"And what sort of business is it, Leonard?" I had the feeling Miss Trumbull thought I didn't know how to talk, and she was going to teach me right then and there. Her voice was sort of extra sweet, and she was sort of leaning forward and bending around so she could stand behind me and look at my face at the same time.

"It's a rag business," I said. "Different peddlers bring rags, and my father buys them, and we weigh them and sort them, and pack them in bales, and sell them to factories and places." I was picking up speed. "I sort of liked working there, except a couple of times I got fleas."

"Thank you very much, Leonard, for telling us about your interesting summer. You may return to your seat." Miss Trumbull was standing a good way behind me. All the kids were scratching themselves, like they had fleas, and making chimpanzee faces as I walked to the back of the room.

I don't remember too much about the rest of the day. I gave up on trying to be a friend to have a friend, and spent the lunch period by myself. One kid did talk to me—a lunch court monitor made me pick up a Three Musketeers wrapper that wasn't mine. I didn't say anything to him. I just picked it up and carried it to one of the wire wastebaskets placed every twenty feet, and dropped it in.

After lunch I went to my gym class. As I walked through the door of the gym, I heard this terrifically loud voice shout, "FATSO, WHERE ARE YOUR GYM SHOES?"

4

Because I didn't have any gym shoes, I wasn't allowed to take part in the class. I had to sit on the bleachers at the end of the gym. Mr. Jerris ignored me, which was nice. The other kids all had to climb ropes. They had to shinny up these big fat ropes that hung down from the ceiling. They had to climb up about twenty feet, and then come down without sliding and getting rope burns on their legs. Some of them slid down too fast and got big red marks on the insides of their thighs. I decided to leave my brand-new gym shoes at home in my closet for as long as possible.

For a few days, Mr. Jerris would ask me where my gym shoes were. I would look at the floor and sort of shake my head, and look like I was really sad that I had forgotten my gym shoes. After a while, Mr. Jerris decided that I was stupid or feebleminded or something, and he quit asking me. When I came into the gym class, he would just nod in the direction of the bleachers, and I would climb up and sit down for the rest of the class. It was that way in all my classes. I found out if I acted dumb, pretty soon the teachers would leave me alone. I left all my books and stuff in my locker. When a teacher would ask me where my books were, I'd say I didn't know. Then they'd get me a new book, and I'd leave that in my locker too, and after a while, they just left me alone. After a couple of weeks of school, all I had to do was walk from class to class with nothing in my hands.

The only trouble was, it was boring. If I brought something to read, the teachers might have caught on that I wasn't really stupid. All I had to do was sit and think, and watch the other kids. I got to know a lot about them. I used to wonder what would happen to a kid who really was as dumb as I was pretending to be. Nobody would help him, and he would just sit there like I was doing.

The kids ignored me or maybe giggled at me. The teachers ignored me or just sort of smiled sweetly as if to say, "Leonard, if you will just sit still, and not make any noise, and not take up any of my valuable time, everything will be just fine." Bat Masterson was really a lousy school, even if most of the kids were rich and neat and unwrinkled and tall and didn't wear glasses.

There were a few kids who weren't really in much better shape than I was, like the small one whose name was Henry Bagel. Those kids got ignored and giggled at, and the teachers sort of overlooked them because they didn't look like Bat Masterson students—I mean, they were messy or freakish or smelly or twitchy. I thought at first that they would be willing to be friends with me—if nobody else was looking—but they all wanted to be regular Bat Masterson kids. They didn't want to be seen with me or any of the other weirdos, and they kept trying to be accepted by the real kids. I used to watch them in the lunch court. Each freak had picked out a little group to hang out with, and he would keep trailing after them and laughing at their jokes, and every once in a while he'd shout out something funny he'd been planning to say all week. Sometimes the older kids would stop ignoring Henry Bagel long enough to insult him or make fun of him—and I swear, Henry Bagel looked as though he liked it!

The strange thing was that Henry Bagel and the other weird kids all hated me. The real kids just didn't pay any attention to me, but the freaky kids that everybody played jokes on and punched around really hated me. I think it was because I was the only thing lower than they were. I used to spend time trying to pick the one who would be the lowest person in the school if I dropped dead.

After my boring day in school, I would take all my books home and read them. I am a good reader—since the first grade, when I bought a *Batman* comic and managed to read the whole thing, every word. I wanted to read it all because it was *my* book—I had paid for it. Also it was a lot more interesting than those dumb readers they gave us. Once I smashed my way through that *Batman*, I wasn't afraid to read anything. So I read whatever I wanted.

It only took me a couple of weeks to read all my textbooks. My social studies book I read in one night. In school, the kids had to read a chapter a week—or the teacher would say, "Tonight read pages 93 through 97 inclusive," and the kids would all go "Awwwwww," as though they had just been asked to crawl ten miles on their hands and knees. Then, the next day, the teacher would spend forty-five minutes trying to get the kids to explain what they had read. They could hardly do it. Almost all of them had a reading problem, and those that didn't hated reading because the other kids did.

Mostly what the teacher did was try to get some clue that the kids had read what they were supposed to, and that they understood it. "Who can tell me the name for the holy wars that the knights in the Middle Ages went to fight?" the teacher would ask. No hands. "Anybody?" Finally, a hand. Then the teacher would sort of move her lips silently, saying along with the kid, "Crusades?" Actually, I found that medieval stuff really interesting, and took a lot of books about it out of the public library. There was this good movie with Tony Curtis on TV, and then it turned out that it had been taken from a book, *Men of Iron,* which was even better. I found a lot of good stuff about knights and jousting and Crusades and all that. It was pretty exciting—but not to the kids at Bat Masterson. To them it was having to pick their way through pages 93 to 97, inclusive—Awwwwww.

The only class I went to where the kids enjoyed themselves—or admitted they were enjoying themselves—was Mr. Jerris's gym class. They sure loved to climb those ropes. Mr. Jerris told them one time that anybody who got an A in gym would be able to pass basic training in the Marine Corps. After that they went at those ropes like madmen. I guess they all wanted to be marines.

My parents are sort of dumb—I mean, I love them and all that, but they aren't very interesting. They are only interested in getting things for the house, and barbecuing, and that sort of thing. You can't talk to them the way you can talk to my grandparents. We'd go over there every week or so, and it was my only chance to enjoy some conversation.

Also, I could go outside and meet up with the kids in the old neighborhood. It wasn't the same as if I'd been going to school with them every day, but we could still hack around and tell jokes and throw a ball around. My former best friend, Charley Nastrovsky, had a new best friend, Billy O'Brian, who had been my second-best friend, which was only reasonable, because I wasn't there every day anymore—but it wasn't quite the same as it had been before we moved. I mean, they had special jokes about teachers I had never seen, and that sort of thing. Still, it was nice to be with people who liked me.

5

"Some school. You could cast a horror movie with some of the kids around here." Somebody was talking to me. I was sitting on my favorite bench at the far end of the lunch court. There wasn't anybody near me except this kid I'd never seen before. He had a beard! I don't mean he had a real beard like a hippie—but he had a heavy stubble like a grown man. He was wearing a green sweater with three yellow stripes around one arm and a big yellow letter *K* on the pocket. It was one of these sweaters that buttons down the front.

"Are you talking to me?" I asked. Nobody had talked to me for weeks.

"Yeah, how can you stand this place? Everybody is so snotty and stupid.—By the way, my name is Alan Mendelsohn."

"Leonard Neeble," I said.

"Glad to meet you, Leonard," Alan Mendelsohn said. I

noticed he was wearing black-and-white saddle shoes. I had never seen a real kid wearing those.—I only knew about them from old movies. He also had these weird plaid socks. I could see that Alan Mendelsohn wasn't going to fit in at Bat Masterson Junior High School. In his way he was as outlandish-looking as I was.

"I ought to tell you, I'm sort of a leper," I said. "If anybody sees you talking to me, people are going to treat you as if you had the plague."

That came from the stuff I had been reading about the Middle Ages. There were these lepers—they wore cloaks with hoods, and they had to ring a bell all the time. When anybody heard them coming, they'd get out of the way. I used to pretend that I was one of those lepers, that I had a bell, and that everybody stayed away from me because they were scared of catching leprosy. It was easy to pretend.—Except for the bell, things were just about like that.

"You mean these other slobs don't like you?" Alan Mendelsohn said. "Tell me what you did to get them that way, and I'll do it too."

"You have nothing to worry about," I said. "All you have to do is not look just like everybody else, and you're instant garbage."

"I figured something like that," Alan Mendelsohn said. "These kids have the mental power of a bunch of dandelions. We ought to be able to have some fun with them. Watch that guy walking across the yard."

Alan Mendelsohn pointed to a kid walking across the lunch court eating a sandwich. The waxed paper was sort of waving in his face. He was eating and walking fairly fast toward one of the garbage cans placed every twenty feet. Alan Mendelsohn put two fingers in his mouth, and just as the kid was about two paces away from the garbage can, Mendelsohn whistled. It was the loudest whistle I had ever heard. It traveled in the direction of the kid's head, as though Mendelsohn had thrown a hardball at him. I could almost see the whistle whiz across the lunch court at the kid. The kid looked around with his mouth full of peanut butter and jelly sandwich. He was still walking at the same rate. Turning in the direction of the whistle altered his course just enough to send him smack into the garbage can, which went over. The kid went with it, his legs tangling with the rolling can. He wound up sprawling in a heap of half-eaten sandwiches, wrappers, and banana peels.

"How did you do that?" I asked. The bell rang, ending lunch period.

"I'll show you tomorrow," Alan Mendelsohn said. "Meet you here." And he raced off, doing a neat hurdle over the kid who was still on his hands and knees amid the garbage.

It turned out that Alan Mendelsohn came from The Bronx, which is part of New York City. His father had been transferred to a new job in Hogboro, and Alan's family had moved into a house in the suburb of West Kangaroo Park, which is where Bat Masterson Junior High School is located. Alan Mendelsohn missed The Bronx in pretty much the same way that I missed the old neighborhood in Hogboro. We started meeting at lunchtime. Alan tried to teach me his special "missile whistle" but I wasn't too good at it. We started to hang out after school. We became friends.

Alan Mendelsohn was a lot less shy than me. Although, as I had predicted, all the Bat Masterson kids shunned him, Alan talked to them anyway. He got into a lot of fights. If someone said something that he thought was insulting, Alan might just top them with another insult—or he might haul off and hit them in the mouth. He knew about a hundred ways to trip people, or to distract them and make them trip themselves—on a bench, a garbage can, or another person. Certain kids who were easy to distract were Alan's special victims. Every time he saw them, he would trip them in a different way. One day he would use the "missile whistle," another day he'd call the kid's name, another day he'd just stick his foot out and trip the kid. He had a couple of trips that I wasn't able to figure out—he'd just walk alongside of a kid and then turn sharply away, and the kid would go over. A couple of kids got to be so scared of Alan Mendelsohn that they'd just trip all by themselves when they saw him coming.

People had looked down on me and ignored me. They started that way with Alan Mendelsohn, but it wasn't long before they hated and feared him. Also he was a good student. He refused to let the teachers ignore him. He talked a lot in class, and always got out of his seat and stood while answering a question or talking. The Bat Masterson kids didn't do that. If they were forced to talk in class, they did it sitting down. Sometimes Alan would pace up and down in the aisle when he was speaking, and once in a while he would even work his way to the front of the room, and pace up and down in between the teacher and the front row of seats. The teachers had to call on him all the time, because the other kids almost never put their hands up. In any class where Alan Mendelsohn was enrolled, you were sure to hear from him about as much as you heard from the teacher.

Another thing Alan did in classes was to find out weird things about the subject that the teacher never knew. Once he started talking about Benjamin Franklin's sex life, and when the teacher shut him up he brought in all these books the next day to prove that everything he had to say was true. There was a big shouting match between Alan and the teacher, and it ended with Alan being sent to the principal's office. He got sent there a lot.

I don't want to give the impression that Alan was mean or a bully. He was always friendly, even after he had beaten someone up. He thought most of the kids at Bat Masterson were stupid, and he liked to trip them and play tricks on them, but he never hated them the way they hated him.

Alan had a judo book, and most days after school we'd go to my house or his house, which was just like mine, and practice flipping each other. We also tried to teach Melvin to trip people, but it was no use.

Alan had over two thousand comic books. He kept them in a bunch of old wire milk-bottle cartons. He had a big notebook in which he wrote down all the numbers and titles of the comics he owned. Alan used to go to all sorts of secondhand bookstores when he lived in The Bronx. He'd pick up old comics and other books he liked. There weren't any secondhand bookstores in West Kangaroo Park, and Alan said he missed them. We planned a trip to Hogboro to look for bookstores.

I felt a lot better about things in the new school, now that I had a friend. Alan and I had saved up a few weeks' allowance and leftover lunch money for our book-buying trip. Then report cards came out. Mine came with a letter from Miss Steele, my homeroom teacher—it was to my parents. It seemed I was failing everything.

6

The next few days were full of trouble. My parents had to go to school and talk with Miss Steele and the school guidance counselor, a person I had never met. They decided to give me some tests to find out what variety of feeble-mindedness I had. The guidance counselor was named Mr. Heinz. He was a nice guy. He told me his whole story the first time I went to see him. It seems he had started out as the wood-shop teacher, but when Bat Masterson needed a guidance counselor, they picked him. So Mr. Heinz took all these courses in psychology and counseling. He took them by mail, from a correspondence school in Ohio.

Mr. Heinz had a lot of tests in his office. They were more like games than tests. He had blocks you put together while he timed you, and pictures of scenes that he would show you—and you had to make up a story about what's going on. He also gave me the inkblot test, which I had heard about, and a lot of other tests—me drawing pictures, and writing things, and filling in blanks. I was excused from classes four afternoons in a row, and every day I went down to Mr. Heinz's office to take tests. Mr. Heinz also gave me gum and candy when I was in his office.

After we had finished all the tests, Mr. Heinz said, "Well, I'm not supposed to tell you the results of the tests, but I will tell you that you are one hundred percent normal and average in every respect. Maybe you're a little bit brighter than average. I'll have a talk with your parents."

I was sorry the tests were over. It was the first time I hadn't been bored since I came to that school.

This is what my parents and Mr. Heinz decided: Since I wasn't feebleminded, and the psychological tests hadn't shown any signs that I was crazy, there was no reason that I should be failing all my subjects. Mr. Heinz said that there had to be something wrong with me, and since he couldn't find out what it was, my parents ought to send me to a child psychologist. Mr. Heinz said we were very lucky, because he could recommend someone really good. It seems the guy who had been his professor-by-mail when he was studying to be a guidance counselor had come to Hogboro and set up an office. He gave my parents the name and telephone number of the professor-by-mail, and they made an appointment for me.

The next Monday, I went to the office of Dr. Prince. It was in a big office building in Hogboro. I had to leave school early to catch the bus—Mr. Heinz had arranged it.

There was a newsstand in the lobby of the office building. I don't know why I did it, but before going up to Dr. Prince's office I bought a piece of bubble gum and a nickle cigar. Alan Mendelsohn had told me that if you chew bubble gum at the same time as smoking a cigar, it won't make you sick. I planned to go somewhere after my appointment with Dr. Prince and have a smoke.

Dr. Prince had this tweed suit that looked too big for him. He wore glasses. There were two big upholstered chairs in his office, the kind you sink into. He told me to sit in one. "You smoke, I suppose," he said. I said sure. "Well, you can smoke here. You can also say dirty words. Anything you say to me, I will never tell anyone. That's called confidentiality."

Actually, I had never smoked so far—the cigar was going to be my first attempt—but I wanted to get off on the right foot with Dr. Prince, so I popped the bubble gum in my mouth, and chewed it up for a while, and then got the cigar started. Mendelsohn was right as usual. I didn't get sick.

"Now suppose you tell me why you hate your parents," Dr. Prince said. As I mentioned before, my parents are sort of dumb, but totally loveable. I didn't hate them, and I told Dr. Prince so.

"Of course, I expected you to say that," Dr. Prince said. "You aren't willing to admit it now, but when you feel more comfortable with me, you will be able to say that you hate your parents." Dr. Prince seemed sort of disappointed. I didn't want to hurt his feelings—after all, he was letting me smoke my cigar, and he had told me that I could say dirty words. He was obviously trying very hard to get me to like him. I wanted to help him out.

"Well, I do feel sort of angry at my parents sometimes," I said.

"Aha! Now we're getting somewhere!" Dr. Prince said. "You're angry at them because they pay more attention to your little sister, right?"

"I don't have a little sister," I said.

"Little brother, then?"

"No. No little brother."

"Older brother? Older sister?"

"No."

"Twin?"

"No."

Dr. Prince looked puzzled. He had a big folder in his lap. I recognized some of the tests Mr. Heinz had given me. Dr. Prince thumbed through the papers in the folder. "I suppose you're upset because your parents drink so much," he said.

I told him that my parents hardly ever drink at all. Dr. Prince was silent for a long time. He stared at the pile of papers in his lap. Finally he said, "We won't get anywhere until you decide to cooperate. You can sit there smoking that cheap cigar and chewing bubble gum and resisting the therapy as long as you like—I don't care—I get paid just the same. But you are not going to be able to solve any of your problems unless you are willing to talk about them."

I started to tell Dr. Prince about how I was mad at my parents sometimes because I didn't like the new house or the new neighborhood or the new school, but he interrupted me.

"Don't rationalize. Right now you are feeling anger at me. It's perfectly normal. I have guessed your secrets, and naturally you want to cover up. You'll understand all this better later on. Now let's talk about something else. How did you feel about things in general when you were six months old?"

I told Dr. Prince that I couldn't remember anything about being six months old. He brightened up a bit when I said that, and he made some notes on a pad.

"Oh? Can't remember? Is that so? Well, don't worry, Leonard. You won't be having any more nightmares before very long. You're pretty confused, but it isn't too late to help you. Come again next Monday at the same time."

I don't think I've ever had a bad dream. When I dream about science-fiction monsters and things like that, I usually enjoy it. I had already caught on that it wouldn't do any good to tell that to Dr. Prince. He shook hands with me, and I went down in the elevator.

I bought another cigar and another piece of bubble gum at the newsstand in the lobby. When I got home, the charcoal in the barbecue was already red-hot. My mother wanted to know how my appointment with the doctor had gone.

"Dr. Prince says it's all right for me to smoke cigars," I said.

7

I listened in on the extension when my parents called Dr. Prince. "Your boy is flunking everything in school, and you're worried if he smokes a cigar?" Dr. Prince shouted. "Let him do what he wants—he's a seriously disturbed child. Just pray that I'm able to save him."

"But won't smoking stunt his growth?" my mother asked.

"Who knows?" Dr. Prince said. "But think about this— would you rather have him short or crazy? By the way, don't call me anymore—it undermines the boy's confidence in me. Get your own psychologist."

That settled the matter of smoking. The conditions were that I was allowed to smoke only in the house, and not in front of company. The next day after school, I invited Alan Mendelsohn over for milk and cookies and cigars. Alan was very impressed that I was seeing a shrink. He said he'd always wanted to go. There was a kid in his old school who went to a shrink. He could come in late, and leave early, and go to the nurse's office and take a nap, and skip gym, and nobody said a word. Alan's parents didn't believe in psychology. I told him that was too bad.

I thought about what Alan said about the kid in his old school. Mr. Heinz knew I was seeing Dr. Prince, and he would be sure to notify my teachers. I could see possibilities arising from seeing Dr. Prince.

My mother had been worried that the other kids would find out I was seeing a shrink and ostracize me. She still didn't understand that they couldn't ostracize me any more than they did already. *Ostracize* is a word I picked up from my social studies book. It seems that in ancient Greece, once a year, they would all drop pieces of broken pottery into a jar. The pieces of pottery were called *ostrakons*. If you didn't like somebody, you just wrote his name on your *ostrakon*. If he got enough votes, he'd be kicked out of town. The kids at Bat Masterson couldn't kick me out of town, but they could refuse to have anything to do with me—which is what *ostracize* means today. Besides, if they voted on anyone to ostracize it would have been Mendelsohn. He had started something new that seemed to annoy everyone.

It was in the week following my first visit to Dr. Prince that Alan Mendelsohn created his masterpiece. On Thursday he arrived at school very early, before anybody else. As each kid or group of kids arrived, Alan Mendelsohn approached them. "Did you know that I was a Martian?" he asked.

"Huh? What?" the kids would say.

"I'm a Martian—I mean, I'm not exactly a Martian, that is, I was born here on Earth, but my parents were born on Mars, and we go to Mars for our vacations, and someday we're going to move back to Mars to live." Then Alan Mendelsohn would turn and walk away. He kept this up until school started; then he'd catch people in the hall between classes. He'd fall in step with someone, take their arm, and say, "Did you know I was a Martian?"

"Huh? What?"

It went on all day. I hung around after school, waiting for Alan Mendelsohn to walk home with me. He kept starting to leave, but then he'd see another kid he hadn't talked to or didn't remember talking to, and he'd be off. "Say, did I ever tell you that I was a Martian?" I finally got tired of waiting and left. There were very few kids around the school. Alan Mendelsohn was sort of trotting from one kid to another, giving them his message.

That evening the telephone rang. It was Alan. "Say, Leonard, I'm sorry I didn't get a chance to talk to you in school today."

"Yes, well, you seemed pretty busy," I said.

"Indeed I was," Alan said. "I've decided that honesty is the best policy, and I've been letting everyone know who I am; that is, I've been explaining to people that I'm a Martian."

"I heard all about it," I said. "What's the point?"

"Well, Leonard, you see, I actually am a Martian—that is, I myself wasn't born on Mars, but my parents were born on Mars, and we go there all the time, and someday we're going to move back to Mars to live. . . ." Alan had remembered that he hadn't gotten around to me.

I wanted to change the subject. "Are we still going to Hogboro to look for comics and old books on Saturday?" I asked.

"As far as I know, Leonard," Alan Mendelsohn said.

"That is to say, if nothing special or catastrophic happens before then."

"I'll see you in school tomorrow," I said.

"Indubitably," Alan said. He had a bunch of books that he had gotten in a secondhand store in The Bronx. They were all about building a mighty vocabulary. Every now and then he would use a word like *indubitably*. We said good-bye and hung up.

I went out into the backyard. My father was hosing down the portable barbecue. "Did you know that Alan Mendelsohn's family are Martians?" I asked. I didn't know why I said that. It was just on my mind.

"I thought his people came from New York," my father said. "It will be too cold to barbecue outside soon, son. Maybe we ought to get one of those electric barbecues and set it up in the kitchen." I went inside the house to get a cigar and read a book on hypnotism that Alan Mendelsohn had loaned me.

The next day, Friday, when I arrived at school, a kid spoke to me, a big kid I had never seen before. "Do you believe?"

"What do you mean?"

"Do you believe he's a Martian?" the big kid asked.

"Sure," I said. The big kid hit me in the stomach and walked away. I felt like I was going to throw up. I sort of staggered over to the building and leaned against the wall, waiting to feel better. Not far away, another kid was approached by a kid carrying one of those green book bags. "Do you believe?" the kid with the book bag asked. "No!" said the other kid, and *BANG!* the kid swung his book bag and hit the other kid on top of the head.

There were confrontations of this kind going on all over

the place. Two kids would meet, exchange a few words, and one kid would bop the other, or they'd shake hands and walk away to find some other kids to question.

The bell rang before things could develop into a full-scale riot, but the kids were in an ugly mood as they crowded into the building, and girls and boys punched, pushed, and shoved one another.

Things were fairly quiet during the morning. There were three of four fistfights in the halls between classes—that was unusual—but nothing big happened. There was a kind of undercurrent of excitement building all morning. Everybody knew that lunchtime was going to be special.

When the bell rang for lunch, there was a loud cheer from all parts of the school. When I got to the lunch court, it was like a battlefield. Trash cans were over-turned, benches were lying every which way, garbage was everywhere. Quite a few kids had bloody noses and other minor injuries. Everywhere I heard the question "Do you believe?" "Yes." *POW!* "Do you believe?" "No!" *POW!* Henry Bagel, the smallest kid in our gym class, climbed up the body of Jeb Shore, the biggest kid in our gym class, and knocked him out cold. He had to be carried out on a stretcher by two lunch court monitors.

Girls participated too—in fact it was a girl who blacked my eye when I told here I wasn't sure if I believed or not. Some kids would hit you only if you believed—others hit you if you didn't believe—and some kids would hit you whatever you said.

"Believers over here!" someone shouted, and I was caught in a rushing mob of kids who believed. Someone threw a triple-decker tuna fish sandwich, which hit me in the back of the neck. I looked up and thought I saw Alan Mendelsohn hanging out a second-floor window. He seemed to be enjoying the whole scene.

"Death to the nonbelievers!" someone shouted. Soon a lot of people were shouting it. Across the court were a lot of kids shouting, "Death to the believers!" I was scared. I wanted to get out of there. Some nonbeliever was going to bash my head in a minute.

Then we heard sirens. Three police cars drove right into the lunch court. Other policemen were running from all directions. Mr. Winter, with a policeman on either side of him, was shouting through one of those electric bullhorns, "Go to your homerooms! This is an order! Any student not in his homeroom in five minutes will go to jail!"

School was let out early. Kids had to leave the building a homeroom at a time. There were policemen everywhere. You couldn't hang around the school building—you had to walk out of sight at once. There were squad cars and policemen on foot at every corner for blocks.

8

This is what happened when Alan Mendelsohn was sent to the principal's office after the riot:

"You started a riot!" Mr. Winter said.

"I never did!" Alan Mendelsohn said.

"It was all about you—all about whether you were a Martian or not!" Mr. Winter said.

"Still, I wasn't responsible," Alan Mendelsohn said, "and the disturbance, or riot, if you want to call it that, was about whether or not people believed I was a Martian."

"Just so," said Mr. Winter. "You convinced some of the students that you were a Martian in order to start a riot."

"I didn't convince them—I simply told them. I told them like this: I am a Martian. My parents were born on Mars. We go to Mars for our vacations, and we will someday go back to Mars to live permanently. What would your reaction be, Mr. Winter, if I had walked up to you and told you that? Would you believe it?"

"Of course I wouldn't believe it," Mr. Winter said.

"Well, neither would I," Alan Mendelsohn said, "so how can you accuse me of planning to start a riot between people who did and did not believe something which I never expected anyone to believe?"

"Why did you tell people you were a Martian in the first place?" Mr. Winter asked.

"Because it's true," Alan Mendelsohn said.

"You are suspended for five days, starting Monday," Mr. Winter said.

"That's fair," Alan Mendelsohn said.

9

Alan Mendelsohn apparently convinced his parents that the riot wasn't his fault—that is, he had them somewhat convinced. They still insisted that he stay in the house for the whole weekend. That put an end to our plans for a book-buying trip to Hogboro on Saturday. I went over to Alan's house and hung around for a while on Saturday morning. He said his parents hadn't put any restriction on where he went during his week of suspension. They figured that with me in school he wouldn't have any fun, since I was the only kid he went around with. He had mentioned to his mother that he might want to go to the museum in Hogboro to work on a science project. She said that would be OK. I said I wished I could be suspended with him. He said he wished I could too. Alan kept leafing through comic books, and there wasn't too much conversation. I told Alan I had to go to the library. He walked me to the door.

At the door, Alan said, "Leonard, I noticed that you were with the believers yesterday. Thanks, I appreciate that."

At the library I found a book in the children's section called *Psychiatry Made Simple for Younger Readers*. I checked it out. Also, I took out an adventure book called *Howard Goldberg, Frontiersman*. I got home in time for lunch. Grandfather and the Old One had been invited over to barbecue in the backyard. When I got there, they had already arrived. They were sitting in the house while my father stood over the portable barbecue wearing a plaid woolen lumber jacket over his apron. It was really getting kind of cold for cookouts.

"Leonard, are you crazy?" Grandfather asked me when I came through the door.

"No, I'm not crazy," I said.

"See?" the Old One shouted to my mother, who was in the kitchen. She was arranging some alfalfa sprouts the Old One had brought for us to eat. My father was barbecuing chicken for us, and nut cutlets for Grandfather and the Old One. "See, Louise? The boy says he's not crazy. So why are you sending him to a crazy-doctor?"

"He's not a crazy-doctor," my mother shouted back, "he's a child psychologist—and he's helping Leonard adjust so he can do well in school."

Melvin really loved Grandfather. He was sitting in front of him, three-quarters awake, drooling on his knee.

"Phooey!" Grandfather said. "Let the kid join the navy for a couple of years. A few months at sea, and he'll be fine."

"Leonard is only twelve years old," my mother said. "He can't join the navy."

"I was eleven years old when I joined the navy!"

Grandfather shouted. "No! Ten years old! I told them I was twenty-three. I had a beard and hair on my chest. I was six feet four inches tall, because I never ate meat, because I never ate chicken, and because I ate almost everything raw. You're cheating your son out of his birthright of good health!"

I wondered how Grandfather could have been six feet four inches tall when he was ten years old. He is about five feet one inch now.

My father came in with the chicken and nut cutlets. My grandparents didn't want to eat the nut cutlets because they were cooked. My father kept insisting. He wanted to show off how good he was at barbecuing.

"Just a few alfalfa sprouts for me," the Old One said, "and some raw potatoes and maybe a little yogurt." All through the meal my father kept trying to get her to taste the nut cutlets.

After lunch we all sat around and Grandfather talked about the Ituri Rain Forest Pygmies. He said they run everyplace, and clap their hands while they're running so they won't surprise a leopard. He also said that if you take Pygmies out of the forest and into the open grassland, they get confused. They aren't used to being able to see more than fifteen or twenty feet away. If they see a bunch of elephants a long way off, they will not think they are elephants that look tiny because they are far away, but little tiny elephants fifteen or twenty feet away. Grandfather said he always wanted to go and visit the pygmies. The Old One said she thought they were so small because of all the meat in their diet. The Old One wasn't much taller than a Pygmy herself—she came up to Grandfather's shoulder.

After a while, my parents took my grandparents home.

First, my father showed them how the radio-controlled electric garage-door opener worked. Then they drove off. I had decided not to go along for the ride. I wanted to read my book about psychiatry.

The book was sort of interesting. I read it all evening Saturday, and most of the day Sunday.

School on Monday was more or less back to normal. Mr. Winter made a long speech on the public-address system about how disgraceful everybody's conduct had been. He said the Bat Masterson students had a certain tradition to uphold. He said that for year and years, the Bat Masterson student had been a model to the world of good conduct, courtesy, and correct attire. He was ashamed of us all. And he was especially ashamed that a student who did not have the true Bat Masterson spirit had brought about such shameful behavior on the part of boys and girls who had been brought up to know better. He went on and on as usual. What really got me was that most of the kids acted as if they were really ashamed that they let good old Bat Masterson down.

I was let out early so I could go to my appointment with Dr. Prince. I caught the bus to Hogboro. Once again I bought a cigar at the newsstand in the lobby. This time I bought one called a Fargo Brothers Rum-Soaked Curley-Q. This was a great big cigar that had a wavy shape. It turned out to be a terrific smoke. I didn't even need the bubble gum. It was soaked in some kind of sweet sugary rum, and it made sparks every now and then when you smoked it.

"Well, Leonard, what kind of week have you had?" Dr. Prince asked me, once I was settled into the big chair, my Fargo Brothers Rum-Soaked Curley-Q sparking and burning away.

"I've had a lot of anxiety," I said. I picked this up from the psychiatry book I read over the weekend.

"Anxiety, eh?" Dr. Prince said, leaning forward in his chair. "Tell me more."

"Well, I have these dreams, and I wake up sweating, and sometimes, sometimes I can't tell if it's a dream or not," I said. This was all baloney. I had gotten it from the book too.

"Yes, yes, tell me about these dreams," Dr. Prince said. He was leaning way forward in his chair, he was puffing his pipe very fast, and he had his pen and pad poised, ready to write down whatever I said.

"Well, in these dreams I have missed school, and they come and get me, and it turns out that I wasn't really sick—that is, I didn't have a good excuse—and these people, teachers and principals, all say I have to be punished, and they take me to the electric chair. Then they strap me in, and my parents are there, crying, and the principal gives the order to throw the switch—then I wake up."

Dr. Prince was writing furiously. There were beads of sweat on his forehead. He was puffing his pipe so hard that little showers of sparks and ashes were flying all over the place, and landing in his lap. "So you think you'll be executed if you miss school, do you?" he asked.

"Well, no," I said, sort of hesitating, "I mean, they wouldn't kill me for missing school—would they?"

"Leonard, I want you to take a day off school," Dr. Prince said. "No—take the rest of the week off. Just stay home, or go to the movies, or do whatever you like. I will call Mr. Heinz, the guidance counselor, and explain everything, and he'll call your parents."

"You mean—you mean—not—not go to school?" I tried to sound frightened. "But what will they do to me? I mean, won't my parents, I mean, won't I be punished?"

"Nothing will happen to you, Leonard, my boy," Dr. Prince said. "Obviously, you are so tense about this, it is no wonder you are unable to do well in your classes. You just take the rest of the week off, and don't worry. You may feel a little nervous, but after you return to school and see that nothing happens to you, you will never have to be afraid again—and you won't have those dreams."

"Are you sure?" I said. "I mean, couldn't I just come in late—say five minutes?"

"Trust me, Leonard. Take the week off. It will be easy."

That night I called Alan Mendelsohn and told him I had the rest of the week off. We arranged to meet the next morning on the nine o'clock bus to Hogboro.

10

At eight o'clock the next morning the cow arrived. Actually it was a half-cow. My parents had bought this great big freezer—it had been delivered the week before. With the freezer, at no extra cost, they got a half-cow, butchered and wrapped in white paper packages with what part of the cow it was written on the outside.—For example, *Top round steak* and *Rib roast*. The writing was in black crayon. There were a lot of packages. It took two men a half hour to carry them all inside, and take them down to the basement, and stack them in the freezer.

When my parents told my grandparents about buying the freezer and the half-cow, my grandparents almost went wild. My grandfather wanted to know if my father was going to have the head of the cow stuffed and mounted on a plaque, and hung on the wall.

I wondered if all the meat that made up our half-cow actually came from one animal. If it did, it seemed to me that there might be a certain risk in buying so much meat all at once. I'm not sure if this is so, but it seems to me that all things being equal—such as what the cow was fed, age of cow, breed of cow, and so forth—some cows probably taste better than others. What would happen if you bought a whole half-cow and then found out that it tasted lousy? And what would happen if you went away on vacation, and a fuse blew, and the freezer went dead for two weeks? That actually did happen to us later on, before we were even a quarter of the way through our half-cow. Grandfather thought it was a big joke.

Having a half-cow's worth of beef in the freezer made me think more about the fact that all those white-paper-wrapped packages had been a real live animal, running around and enjoying itself. Before this, I had always thought of meat as something on a plate. I had been on a school trip to a farm once, and I remember that the cows had very nice eyes and tried to lick me with big slurpy tongues. I didn't like being licked, but there was no mistaking their good intentions. I had always thought of cows as nice animals that give milk—and meat as something your mother serves you. There hadn't been any connection before this. Watching the freezer fill up with meat made me realize that my grandparents at least had a point about being vegetarians—although I still couldn't understand why everything had to be raw.

I had a toasted corn muffin and a cup of half milk, half coffee. My mother was watching the men carry the meat to the basement, and checking off the number of parcels of each particular cut of meat on a checklist the freezer company had given her.

I went out to catch the Hogboro bus. Alan Mendelsohn had gotten on a few blocks earlier, near his house. "How come you don't have to go to school?" he asked. I told him that Dr. Prince had given me an excuse for the rest of the week. "God, I wish they'd let me have a psychologist" Alan Mendelsohn said.

It was the same bus I always took to go see Dr. Prince. It went right past Bat Masterson Junior High School. Alan and I punched each other as we rolled past the school. It felt good to be off on an adventure when all the other kids were listening to Mr. Winter on the loudspeaker. Alan was particularly friendly. He didn't say anything about it, but I suspected he'd had a boring time the day before, when he was the only kid out of school and not sick.

The bus ride only took about half an hour. We pulled into the Hogboro bus terminal. The first thing we did was look in the window of the tattoo place near the bus station. There were big sheets of paper with copies of the tattoos you could get. We discussed getting tattooed, but neither of use could find anything we absolutely would like to have on our skin. About the best one was Donald Duck, with the word *Mother* written underneath. We decided to give it more thought.

We walked uptown along Clarkle Street. We had looked in the Hogboro Yellow Pages, and there were a lot of bookstores on Clarkle Street. I had about fifteen dollars, and Alan had about the same. After a few blocks we saw four or five bookstores clustered together in the middle of the block. The biggest one had a vertical sign, as tall as the building. BOOKS, it said, in red block letters.

We went in. The bookstore had a funny smell—not bad, just funny. It was sort of a dry smell, like oatmeal before you cook it. There were bookshelves all the way to the ceiling, which was high, and tables piled with books, and books in stacks tied together with string, and a flight of stairs going up, with a big red arrow pointing straight up. On the arrow was a sign: More Books Upstairs— Comics and Periodicals—Third Floor.

We went up. The third floor was all magazines and comics. There were big tables covered with comics standing upright in long rows. A sign hanging from the ceiling said All Comics 5¢. We began to flip through the comics. Alan had a list with the titles and numbers of the comics he wanted. It was slow work. The only comic he found that was on his list of wants was a copy of *Action Comics* Number 1—but he didn't buy it because there was a corner torn off the cover. He said he only bought comics that were perfect.

I figure that there were about half a million comics in that place, and Alan went through about half of those. I was getting sort of bored. I was happy when Alan said he'd had enough of that place and why didn't we try somplace else. He had gathered together a stack of about fifty comics that he might just possibly consider buying if nothing more interesting turned up. He put them all together under a table, so no one else would be able to buy them until he made up his mind.

We went down the stairs and outside into the street. It seemed very noisy and lively in the street after the quiet of the bookstore.

There was a little bookstore next to the one we'd just come out of. The sign said SAMUEL KLUGARSH—OCCULT AND ORIENTAL BOOKS. Smaller signs said Meditation, Hypnosis, Magic, Outer Space, Ghosts, Mind Control, Healing, and Foot Reflexology. The signs were yellow with red letters, and they were stuck all over the front of the store. In the window there were books with pictures of flying saucers and weird guys with long white beards and Egyptian stuff on the covers. It was an interesting bookstore.

We started to go in, but the door was locked. There was a sign taped to the inside of the glass door; it said Gone to Bermuda Triangle—Leave Messages at Morrie's, Next Door.

Morrie's was another bookstore on the other side of Samuel Klugarsh's. It was very small, and the window was dirty, and there was a lot of dust on everything, and dead flies. We went inside. Morrie's Bookstore was sort of crummy. There were crude nailed-together tables along the walls, with a few beat-up books lying face up on them, and a metal book rack, with books on both sides of it, running down the middle of the room. The books had titles like *Accounting Made Simple* and *The 1952 Nafsu Oil Company Employees' Yearbook*—stuff nobody could possibly be interested in. At the back of the store was one of those redwood picnic tables with redwood benches. There were three chessboards with games in progress on the picnic table, but nobody playing—just an old hunchbacked guy, wearing a cap and steel-rimmed glasses, sleeping stretched over the table.

Near the back of the store, at another table, was a guy with the biggest beard I'd ever seen and one of those handlebar mustaches—the kind they wax—with the ends pointing up. The beard and mustache were all the more impressive because the guy's head was bald. He was wearing a green turtleneck sweater and he had what looked like a brass potato hanging around his neck on a leather thong.

The guy with the beard and bald head was sitting in front of an old typewriter. It was one of those big office machines, all black and shiny, with lots of little knobs and levers sticking out all over it. Next to the typewriter, on one side, was a stack of paper almost as high as the top of the machine. On the other side of the typewriter was another stack of paper about half as high.

The guy with the beard was typing. As we came in, he finished a page, and took it out of the machine, and put it on top of the tall stack. Then he took a sheet of paper from the small stack, and fed it into his machine, and continued typing. He must have had about two thousand pages typed already.

"Gentlemen, welcome to Morrie's Bookstore," the bald

beard said. "I am William Lloyd Floyd, resident philosopher. Is there anything I can do for you?"

"Well . . . uh . . . actually . . ." Alan Mendelsohn was a little uneasy for a change. "You see, we . . . we were going to go into Samuel Klugarsh's next door, but the sign on the door said come in here. . . . It said 'Gone to Bermuda Triangle,' so we . . . ah . . . came in here." I don't blame Alan Mendelsohn for being nervous; it was a weird place—not unfriendly or scary, just unlike any place we'd ever been before.

"That's the Bermuda Triangle Chili Parlor, around the corner," William Lloyd Floyd said. "Klugarsh is always eating there. He says their chili beans have sympathetic karma. Actually he's a calorie freak—eats about seven meals per day." William Lloyd Floyd was typing away fast and furious at the same time he was talking to us. "If you've got urgent business, you could go over to the chili parlor and join him. He likes to have company when he eats, although I personally haven't got the stomach to watch him. You aren't Mind Control students of his, are you?"

"No, we just wanted to look around the store," Alan Mendelsohn said.

"Oh, in that case, stick around," William Lloyd Floyd said. "Klugarsh will drop in here on his way back—he shouldn't be gone more than a few minutes." I had gotten close enough to see that William Lloyd Floyd was typing exactly what he had just been saying—also what we had said. The last line he had typed was—*he shouldn't be gone more than a few minutes.*

"Excuse me, Mr. Floyd," I began.

"Call me Bill."

"Excuse me, Bill," I said. "Do you mind if I ask you

what you're typing? It looks like a book. Is it?" William Lloyd Floyd typed while I talked—he had been typing the whole time we had been in Morrie's Bookstore.

"Yes, it's a book, all right," he said. I could see what he typed: *Yes, it's a book, all right..*

"What sort of a book is it?" I asked. "I notice you're typing everything we say."

"Just a second," William Lloyd Floyd said. He had come to the end of a page, whipped it out of the machine, and was putting another one in. "Not only have I typed everything we say," he said, typing it, "but everything anybody has said in here for weeks. Also, I'm typing everything I think, and whenever possible, whatever anybody else thinks when I'm feeling telepathic. In answer to your question about what sort of book this is, it is the ultimate work of fiction and philosophy. It includes everything that has ever happened to me, everything that has ever happened to anybody else that I know of, and everything that is happening right now." *Right now*, the machine clicked.

"How long have you been writing it?" I asked.

"Eight weeks now," William Lloyd Floyd said. "I thought I had it finished five or six times, but someone always comes in and starts saying or thinking something that hasn't been covered yet—and I have to go back to work. These aren't all the pages," he said, pointing at the tall stack next to the typewriter. "I have boxes more at home."

An alarm clock on the table went off. "Whew, I thought lunchtime would never come," William Lloyd Floyd said. "Will you join me for a snack?"

"We wouldn't want to impose," Alan Mendelsohn said.

"Oh, no imposition at all," William Lloyd Floyd said.

"I'm just going to send the Mad Guru out for some bread and cheese. Please join me—you're going to wait for Samuel Klugarsh anyway."

"Mad Guru?" Alan Mendelsohn said.

"That's right. My colleague. Oh, Guru! Lunchtime! Wake up!" William Lloyd Floyd shouted, and the old hunchbacked guy woke up.

"What will you be wanting, Chief? The usual?" the old guy asked.

"I think so," William Lloyd Floyd said, "and these two gentlemen will be joining us, so you'd better get the large size Wonder bread. Gentlemen, kindly give the Mad Guru a dollar each—you don't mind contributing toward lunch, do you?"

We each gave the Mad Guru a dollar, and he put on an old greasy raincoat and went out.

"How come you're not typing any of this?" Alan Mendelsohn asked.

"I'm on my lunch break," William Lloyd Floyd said. "Even a great artist has to relax once in a while. I've been working all morning, and I'm bushed."

The Mad Guru was back in just a couple of minutes with a brown paper bag. Out of the bag he took a family-sized loaf of Wonder bread and a chunk of blue cheese. There was a big electric coffeepot, and William Lloyd Floyd poured us cups of black coffee. It was a strange lunch. The coffee was strong, and the blue cheese with it made a funny feeling in the back of my throat. William Lloyd Floyd had turned his chair around and ate sitting near his typewriter. Alan Mendelsohn, the Mad Guru, and I ate at the picnic table with the chessboards.

"You're looking at my potato," William Lloyd Floyd said, fingering the brass lump hanging on the leather thong around his neck. "This is really rare. It's a petrified potato from the moon. I got it from the first man to ever go to the moon—this was years and years before the astronauts. This man was a master of teleportation—he could send himself places by thought, you know. He projected his thoughts to the moon one time and discovered the remains of a lost civilization. He brought back this petrified potato. I traded him a 1961 Volkswagen for it. He wanted to go to San Francisco, and I had this car, and well, there you are. Personally, I think he was a fool to part with this. The astronauts didn't find any potatoes, or if they did, they kept quiet about it. The thing must be worth a couple of million. You don't play chess, do you? It's twenty-five cents a game—seventy-five cents to play against me. The Mad Guru, who is an intergalactic Grand Master, will give you a chess lesson for a dollar and a half."

The skinniest man I ever saw in my life walked into Morrie's Bookstore. He had heavy tortoiseshell glasses and one of those crew cuts that are flat on top. He was wearing a green corduroy jacket and a pink bow tie.

"Ah, Klugarsh!" William Lloyd Floyd said. "These gentlemen have been waiting for you. Allow me to introduce . . . I didn't get your names. . . ."

We introduced ourselves. William Lloyd Floyd made a note in pencil in the margin of one of his typewritten pages. "You'll be in the index," he said.

"I hope you haven't been waiting long," Samuel Klugarsh said. "Please come with me, and we'll get started at once."

12

We followed Samuel Klugarsh out of Morrie's Bookstore. He unlocked the door to his shop, and we followed him in.

"Klugarsh is sorry you were kept waiting," he said. "You didn't make an appointment, so, of course, I wasn't expecting you."

"Actually, we just wanted to look around," Alan Mendelsohn said.

"That's perfectly all right," Samuel Klugarsh said. "Look at anything you like, while Klugarsh gets the equipment ready."

"Equipment?" I asked.

"The best equipment," Samuel Klugarsh said. "My method of Mind Control is the most scientifically advanced, technologically perfect, and generally successful system of accelerated human growth ever devised by man. . . . Now, where's that extension cord?"

Alan and I looked at each other. Samuel Klugarsh was rummaging around, dragging all sorts of machines, tangles of wire, and rolled-up sheets of paper from under tables. He set up a sort of easel, and dragged a bench into the middle of the room. All over the room there were signs like the ones on the outside of the store, yellow with red lettering. The signs all had slogans like Talk is Cheap—Action is Expensive; and Think Before You Think; and Today is the Yesterday You Won't Be Able To Remember Tomorrow.

Obviously, Samuel Klugarsh was setting up some sort of lecture or demonstration for us. "Mr. Klugarsh," I said, "we just came in to look at some books—we didn't plan to see your demonstration."

"How do you know that?" Samuel Klugarsh asked. "Do you know what I'm going to demonstrate?"

We admitted that we didn't.

"Well, then, how do you know you don't want to see it? Just look around and entertain yourselves—Klugarsh is almost ready," Samuel Klugarsh said.

There were books about all sorts of weird stuff I had never heard of—bean sprout therapy, messages from flying saucers, ancient health secrets of New Jersey, transcendental yoga, knee manipulation to increase brainpower. There were also a lot of books with pictures of strange-looking guys on the covers—a lot of them had beards—all of them were staring into the camera with this strange expression, eyes open very wide. They had titles like *Harold Platt, New-age Seer of Rochester*; and *Blong! You Are a Pickle! (The Blong-Pickle Master's Guide to Ego Submersion)*; and *Fred Watanabe—The Divine Inner Self*.

"Gentlemen, please take your seats. Klugarsh is ready to begin his presentation," Samuel Klugarsh announced.

Alan Mendelsohn and I sat down on the bench, facing Samuel Klugarsh, who was standing in front of the easel. On a table beside him were a bunch of odd-looking machines—square, and made of metal with black crackly paint on it. Some of them had tubes sticking out of the top and black dials with white numerals. On the easel was a great big drawing pad. The cover of the pad was turned back, and the first page showed a picture of what looked like an old-fashioned light bulb. Lettered above the light bulb were the words *Klugarsh Mind Control System.* Under the light bulb it said *Inc.*

"Gentlemen, what you are about to hear and see will be the most astounding and revolutionary set of ideas to which you have ever been exposed. You may not understand everything right away, some of these concepts are very deep. Klugarsh asks you to pay careful attention, and in the interests of time being saved, to please refrain from bursts of applause. Also, kindly try not to faint from astonishment. If you have any questions, Klugarsh will answer them at the end."

Samuel Klugarsh flipped over the page of the big drawing pad. There was a Magic Marker drawing of something that looked sort of like a cauliflower. "Gentlemen, the human brain—the most exquisite mechanism on earth," Samuel Klugarsh said. "This drawing is the result of intensive work by Klugarsh Research Associates, Incorporated. Together with the Klugarsh Foundation, our organization has delved deeper into the secrets of the brain than man has ever done before. It is well known that human beings make use of no more than ten percent of the potential power of the brain. If we were able to use twenty percent or even fifteen percent of our brainpower, we would all be geniuses and go down in history. There is no way to imagine what a human being would be able to do if he could utilize one hundred percent of his brain-power. Please keep this in mind during the rest of our little talk."

I couldn't understand why it took Klugarsh Research Associates and the Klugarsh Foundation such intensive work to make the Magic Marker cauliflower/brain drawing. It looked like an ordinary cartoon to me.

Samuel Klugarsh flipped the page. There was a complicated drawing with all sorts of funny symbols connected by lines. It looked sort of like a schematic diagram of a radio or stereo set. I had seen one of those—it came with the stereo that was also a bar that my parents had bought for the living room in the new house. It was like one of those old-fashioned globes of the world, a big one, that stands on the floor. You lifted the top half back on hinges, and there was your stereo, with AM and FM and a record player and an eight-track tape player; and around the inside edge of the globe were holes to put glasses and bottles into.

"This is a schematic diagram of a simple radio set," Samuel Klugarsh said, "a 1934 RCA Victor radio—this very radio, in fact." He pointed to one of the machines on the table. Old-time radios, that's what they were!

"It doesn't look much like the brain in the first drawing, does it? But in fact, it is very much like that brain—very much indeed. Look at this!" Samuel Klugarsh flipped to the next page, and there was another schematic diagram, only instead of being sort of squared-off, the lines, which were supposed to represent the wires in the radio, were curved. The whole picture had more or less the shape of a cauliflower. "Astounding, isn't it?" Samuel Klugarsh said with a triumphant smile. Samuel Klugarsh had a long wooden pointer, and he pointed to the various symbols in the radio-brain-cauliflower drawing. He didn't say what they were, though.

"Yes gentlemen, astounding . . . but not one-half, not one-tenth as astounding as what I'm going to tell you now. Having discovered the uncanny similarity between the human brain and radio receiving sets, I established the Klugarsh Psychical Phenomena Bureau. I began to collect little bits of information, piece things together, to study, study, study. I found out how to utilize the full one hundred percent of my brainpower. Now, this is the truly amazing part—right now, while we're talking, I'm in direct communication with people on Mars!"

Alan Mendelsohn had been sort of sitting bent over on the bench, with his elbows resting on his knees, during Samuel Klugarsh's lecture. Every now and then, when Samuel Klugarsh wasn't looking, he would poke me in the ribs. However, he was sitting up straight now.

"People on Mars?" he asked.

"Of course," said Samuel Klugarsh. "Long ago, I perfected the art of teleportation, or thought-travel. Then, adding a few little extra details of my own, I developed that art to the point where I am, in effect, in two places at once. In fact, while we are having our very pleasant conversation here on Earth, I am also sitting in the office of the Martian High Commissioner for Extra-Martian Transport, having a friendly chat with my old friend Rolzup, the Deputy High Commissioner. I am aware of my activities on Mars as I talk to you here, and I am aware of my activities on Earth as I sit sipping a cup of fleegix with my friend Rolzup."

"What is Rolzup saying?" Alan Mendelsohn wanted to know.

"I'm afraid I can't tell you that," Samuel Klugarsh said. "Not that it is anything private or secret or confidential—it's only that it just isn't the done thing to carry messages from one world to another. There are certain restrictions of usage that come with extraordinary powers. However, if you decide to learn Klugarsh Mind Control, it won't be very long before you can go to Mars yourself. Rolzup, who is one of my students, and therefore able to monitor our conversation, says it will be his pleasure to receive a visit from you both."

"You have students on Mars?" I asked.

"Oh, yes," Samuel Klugarsh laughed, "many thousands of students. You see, the civilization on Mars is far more advanced than ours. Therefore, they instantly recognized the value of Klugarsh Mind Control. Here on Earth, it's quite another matter. People just aren't ready for the next step forward in evolution. But let me get back to my explanation."

Samuel Klugarsh flipped the page of the big pad again. The next picture looked like a portable transistor radio with some wires coming out of it.

"This is the Klugarsh Mind Control Omega Meter," Samuel Klugarsh said. "Klugarsh has perfected this instrument to help Mind Control students all over this world and others. The principle of the Omega Meter is this: As you know, the brain is constantly putting out electrical impulses. You may have heard of alpha, beta, and theta waves—these are the only ones science has discovered in man, so far. That is, until Klugarsh discovered any number of other brain waves, the most important of all being the omega wave. The omega wave is produced in what I call 'state twenty-six,' which is an incredibly high state of creative consciousness, in which we utilize one hundred percent of our brainpower. The use of the Klugarsh Omega Meter is very simple. It is based on the principle of biofeedback. The meter makes a continuous buzzing noise, except when it receives omega waves. Then a tiny tape recording inside plays a few bars of 'Jingle Bells.' To activate the Omega Meter, we clip one of these wires to each of our earlobes, and meditate fiercely. The buzzing continues until we get to the point where we are producing omega waves. Then we hear the machine play 'Jingle Bells.'

"Once we are able to produce omega waves, we can then do things which we previously thought were impossible—for example, visit Mars. We can also read the thoughts of others, and we can control the actions of others. Of course, all of this takes practice, and you mustn't expect to be able to do it all at once. First you have to learn to make the Omega Meter play 'Jingle Bells.' Then you can learn to control the actions of others—that's the easiest thing. Somewhat later you can learn to read the thoughts of others; and later still, you can learn to do thought-traveling, to cause objects to move, to see into the past and the future, and to accurately predict the weather."

Samuel Klugarsh flipped the page again. The next pictures showed a man with a big smile on his face. "This is a picture of a man who has completed the Klugarsh Mind Control course. As you can see, he is totally happy. This concludes my remarks—now, I will be happy to answer three questions."

13

"Excuse me, Mr. Klugarsh," Alan Mendelsohn said, "but a lot of what you were saying didn't make sense."

"Klugarsh said three questions," Samuel Klugarsh said. "What you said wasn't a question. I'm not interested in your opinions. Try again."

"Excuse me, Mr. Klugarsh," Alan Mendelsohn said, "but a lot of what you said didn't make sense—did it?"

"That's better," Samuel Klugarsh said. "And the answer is no, it didn't make sense to you. That is because you are ignorant. For example, do either of you speak Turkish?"

We both said we didn't.

"*Waka waka. Needle noddle noo. Hoop waka dup dup. Baklava.* That's Turkish," said Samuel Klugarsh. "You didn't understand what I said because you're ignorant of the language. To you it just sounded like gibberish; to a Turk it's the pledge of allegiance—just a matter of point of view."

"I'm sorry," Alan Mendelsohn said, "I didn't mean to put you down."

"There's no need to be embarrassed, my boy," Samuel Klugarsh said. "Ignorance is nothing to be ashamed of—until you find out you've got it. Once you realize you're ignorant, if you don't do something about it, then you have the right to feel ashamed. So you mustn't feel bad that you have just told a great scientist and teacher that he doesn't make sense—twice. You mustn't feel bad because you were speaking out of ignorance. After all, this is America. In some countries, in Iceland for instance, things would be very different—but here we give people a chance!"

Samuel Klugarsh was very red in the face. He was shaking his finger at Alan Mendelsohn, and jumping up and down. We were a little scared of him. Alan kept glancing at me. He wasn't so fresh when he was outside of school. If a teacher had gotten that angry at him, Alan Mendelsohn would have enjoyed it.

"You little snot-noses!" Samuel Klugarsh shouted. "You come in here, and I give you the benefit of my years of study, I show you the exact same lecture that I gave to the president of the United States, and it isn't good enough for you. What kind of parents do you have to let you grow up so impudent? Sit still!"

Alan and I were both thinking about streaking out the door—but how did he know that? Neither of us had moved a muscle.

Samuel Klugarsh seemed to calm down a little. "Sorry I lost my temper, boys," he said, "but when you have devoted as many years as I have to a wonderful idea that is going to save mankind, and so many people don't even give you a chance to explain it to them, well, you get a little sensitive. Look, forget about the other two questions. You look like intelligent kids to me. Since you didn't understand my lecture, what I'll do is give you both the Klugarsh Mind Control course for half the usual price for one student. It usually costs twelve hundred dollars. I'll let you both take it for six hundred. That's three hundred apiece. Guaranteed. If you don't make it to Mars in five years, you get a portion of your money back.

"We don't have six hundred dollars," I said.

"No, I thought you didn't," Samuel Klugarsh said. "What do you say to a hundred and fifty? A hundred? Fifty?" Samuel Klugarsh could see from our faces that he was getting nowhere. "Look, how much can you kids spend?"

Alan and I both still had about fourteen dollars and change, some of which we needed to get back to West Kangaroo Park. "What about twenty-four dollars?" Alan asked.

"Twenty-four dollars? You insult Samuel Klugarsh," Samuel Klugarsh said. "However, I can do something for you for that price—although it isn't as good as taking the whole course. I will give you—*give* you, for twenty-four dollars, a portable Omega Meter and the first volume of the Klugarsh Mind Control course. This takes you through the basic Omega monitoring exercises, into making people do whatever you want. It doesn't deal with reading the thoughts of others or teleportation, and it isn't guaranteed. Still, the regular price is eighty-nine ninety-five—you're saving almost sixty-six dollars. And you can always sell the course to another seeker for forty bucks. What do you say?"

Samuel Klugarsh had dug out and was holding a little green plastic transistor radio with two wires hanging from it. At the end of each wire was a shiny alligator clip. In his other hand was a black plastic three-ring binder. Alan and I looked at each other. I decided I was going to do whatever he did. "We'll take it," Alan said.

Samuel Klugarsh handed us the transistor radio and the binder. The binder had a light bulb stamped in gold, like the one on the first page of the chart he had shown us. You could see where he had painted black over where it had said Hogboro Light and Power Co., and then in white paint had written *Klugarsh Mind Control System, Inc.*

"This Omega Meter is disguised as a transistor radio," Samuel Klugarsh said. "See, when you clip it to your ears and turn it on, you will hear a continuous buzzing." He clipped the alligator clips to my ears—it hurt—and turned it on. It buzzed. "When you get so that you can produce omega waves, it will play 'Jingle Bells,' " he said.

"Mr. Klugarsh, clip it on your ears, so we can hear it play 'Jingle Bells' now," said Alan Mendelsohn.

"I'm afraid I can't do that you little . . . fellow," Samuel Klugarsh said. "You see, my omega waves are so strong, they would throw the machine out of adjustment. However, I can show you on my stationary Omega Meter." Samuel Klugarsh pointed to another machine on the table, a big one with tubes and dials all over it. "This one is a little more complicated than yours," Samuel Klugarsh said. He slipped on a leather headband with wires—his machine didn't clip to the lobe of your ear—and pushed a button. The machine played 'Jingle Bells' until he pushed another button to stop it. "You see, I am always in a state of omega wave production," he said.

"Now about the book," Samuel Klugarsh went on, removing his Omega Meter headband. "It will tell you exactly how to use the Omega Meter, so I won't waste time on it now. The book is divided into two sections—Using Your Omega Meter, and and the second section, Controlling the Thoughts and Actions of Others. In connection with this, there is a formality of intergalactic law and usage that we must observe. When I point to you, say 'I swear.' Now, I promise never to use my power of mind control to steal money or overthrow the United States government." He pointed. We swore.

Samuel Klugarsh put our Omega Meter and Mind Control course into a brown paper bag, and we handed him our twenty-four dollars. It occurred to me that this was the biggest thing I had ever bought entirely on my own. I mean, my mother has been giving me money to buy my own clothes for a long time—but she tells me how much I can spend on, say a pair of shoes, and tells me what kind to get and where to get them. So things like that don't count. My half of the Omega Meter and Mind Control course, at twelve dollars, was the most expensive thing I had ever purchased by myself. We said good-bye to Mr. Klugarsh and started walking toward the bus terminal.

We were a couple of blocks away from Samuel Klugarsh's bookstore, carrying our package containing the Mind Control course and Omega Meter, when we saw a familiar hunched figure. It was the Mad Guru.

"Mornin' to ye, gentlemen, mornin'," the Mad Guru said, sort of touching his cap and walking sideways. "What bus take ye?"

"Take ye?" I asked—I didn't quite understand.

Alan Mendelsohn did, though. "We're taking the West Kangaroo Park bus," he said, "and where do you get this 'Good morning' stuff? It's two in the afternoon."

"Arrr, the West Kangaroo Park bus is it?" the Mad Guru said. "Waal, some speak of her as an evil bus. Some say that the driver is mad and searches for a white sixty-eight Chrysler. Some say that all who ride in her are doomed—but I say—Mornin' to ye, gentlemen. Mornin', mornin'." The Mad Guru half-backed, half-walked sideways around a corner and out of sight.

"That was spooky," I said.

"He doesn't scare me," Alan Mendelsohn said. "I've read *Moby Dick*."

14

On the bus to West Kangaroo Park, we took turns reading a page at a time of the Mind Control course to each other. The first part was just like the lecture Samuel Klugarsh had given us. There was the picture of the light bulb, the cauliflower-brain, the radio diagram, the radio diagram-cauliflower-brain, and the guy looking happy who had taken the Klugarsh Mind Control course. The book was all in capitals, set far apart, with big spaces between the lines. It was mimeographed in fuzzy purple letters. On every page there was a slogan like the ones on the signs in Samuel Klugarsh's bookstore:

> THINK BEFORE YOU ACT
> BEFORE YOU THINK
> BEFORE YOU ACT.

Or:

> NEVER PUT OFF UNTIL TOMORROW
> WHAT YOU CAN CAN DO YESTERDAY.

Even though there were a lot of pages in the book, there weren't many words, and the pages went by fairly fast. What with the big print, and the big spaces, and the slogans on every page, there wasn't much text. After we got through with the part that was just a repeat of Samuel Klugarsh's lecture, and all the pictures and diagrams, there were only a few pages left.

The section on how to use the Mind Control Omega Meter just said to clip the wires to your earlobes, and make yourself comfortable, and try to produce omega waves. It said that when you start putting out omega waves, the machine would automatically play "Jingle Bells." We already knew all that. The book also told how to change batteries.

The last section was about how to control the thoughts and actions of others. It said that after you've had some practice with the Omega Meter—when you can produce omega waves with pretty good regularity—then all you have to do is look at a person who isn't concentrating on anything in particular, and say to the person, mentally, "My will is stronger than yours. You must obey. My will is stronger than yours. You must obey." Then you tell the person what you want him to do, mentally, and he does it.

The book said that after you get real good at controlling the thoughts and actions of others, you don't even have to look at them. You just think—and they do whatever you tell them. Then the promise that any person who has the power of Klugarsh Mind Control will never use his power to steal money or overthrow the government was printed in a little box—and we were through with the book. We weren't even halfway home.

Alan Mendelsohn sort of leafed back and forth through the Mind Control course. He didn't say anything, and neither did I, but we were both feeling sort of uneasy about the whole thing. "You don't think Samuel Klugarsh cheated us, do you?" I wanted to ask him, but I didn't. I didn't say anything.

Then we got the Omega Meter out. We looked it over. It was a transistor radio—the cheap kind—the kind they sell in drugstores around the bus station in Hogboro for three dollars and nineteen cents. There was some red-label tape over the name of the radio. It said OMEGA METER—FOR KLUGARSH MIND CONTROL STU-DENTS ONLY. The volume sign and tuning knobs had big blobs of glue on them so you couldn't turn them, and a metal switch had been added—it stuck out of the middle of the radio. Two wires, about two feet long, came out of crude holes punched in the radio. They had clips on the ends.

Alan Mendelsohn flipped the switch. The Omega Meter buzzed. The two alligator clips accidentally touched and made a little yellow spark. He flipped the switch off.

"Do you think any of this is going to work?" I asked him.

"Of course it is," Alan Mendelsohn said. "Sure it works. I mean, we have twenty-four dollars invested in this setup. We ought to at least give it a real good try. It will work. Why shouldn't it work? Anyway, if it doesn't work, maybe we can find somebody to sell it to."

Alan put the Omega Meter and the Mind Control course back into the paper bag. Neither of us said anything for the rest of the ride. We got off the bus near Alan Mendelsohn's house. We decided to go there and practice with the Omega Meter. Nobody was home at Alan Mendelsohn's house. His father was at work and his mother had gone to her handwriting analysis class. She'd be gone for the rest of the afternoon. Alan made us each a peanut butter and banana sandwich and a glass of root beer, and we went into his room to work with the Omega Meter.

I tried it first. The alligator clips hurt, and after a while they made your earlobes all red. I tried to produce omega waves sitting, standing, and lying down. Nothing worked. The Omega Meter buzzed—my ears hurt—and no "Jingle Bells" played.

Then Alan Mendelsohn tried it. He sat down on the floor with his legs crossed. "This is called the lotus position," he said. "Swamis and yogis sit this way when they meditate."

Alan closed his eyes and breathed very deeply and noisily through his nose for a long time. "This is to make me calm," he said. Then he clipped the wires to his ears. The Omega Meter buzzed as it had for me. Alan Mendelsohn did not give up. He pressed his palms together and shut his eyes very tight. Beads of sweat started to appear on his forehead. Still the machine buzzed. He kept on meditating. The machine kept buzzing. After a while, he was meditating so hard that his hands were shaking. Still the machine buzzed.

"Let me try it again," I said.

"You might as well," Alan Mendelsohn said. "I'm getting tired, and my ears hurt."

We had another root beer before I took my turn. I was sort of impressed by Alan's meditating, and I decided I would try it too. I got a pillow from Alan's bed and sat cross-legged on it. I pressed my palms together and did deep breathing until I felt sort of dizzy. Then I clipped the wires to my ears and switched the machine on. It buzzed. I wasn't able to keep it up as long as Mendelsohn had. My back started to hurt as well as my ears.

"I want to try again," Alan Mendelsohn said. "This time I'm going to chant 'Om.' " Alan has this book, *Advanced Lessons in Yoga and Meditation*—that's where he learned all about the lotus position and chanting "Om."

"Ommmmmmmm," he hummed. "Ommmmmmmm, Ommmmmmmm, Ommmmmm, Ommmmmmmmmm." It sounded sort of nice. "Chant with me to help me get in the mood," he said.

"Ommmmmmmm," I hummed.

Alan clipped the wires to his ears.

"Ommmmmmmmmm," he chanted.

"Ommmmmmmmmm," I chanted.

He flipped the switch. *Buzzzzzzzz* went the Omega Meter.

We kept it up for as long as we could. Then we switched off the machine and looked at each other.

"Maybe there's something wrong with the machine," I said.

"We should have had it tested when we were at Samuel Klugarsh's bookstore," Alan Mendelsohn said.

"I have to go home soon," I said. "What do you think we should do with this machine?"

"Maybe we can return it to Samuel Klugarsh," Alan Mendelsohn said.

"Do you think he might give us our money back?"

"Maybe he'll let us trade it for books."

"Well, I'm going home," I said, not moving.

"Yeah, well, Leonard, see you tomorrow," Alan Mendelsohn said, not moving.

"Yeah, well."

"Yeah."

"Damn it, this machine is a fake," I said. "We got gypped. We wasted all our money that we were going to buy used comics and weird books with. What made you think that this would work? It's all your fault. I would never have bought this thing if you didn't want to." I was pretty mad at Mendelsohn all of a sudden.

"It wasn't my fault," Mendelsohn said. "You never said that you had any doubts. If you didn't want to spend your money on this, you should have said something."

"I guess we both got gypped," I said.

"I guess we did."

We both sat still for a long time. Neither one of us said anything. Then we both started to laugh. Alan Mendelsohn pushed me. I was still sitting in the lotus position, and I fell over on my back, my crossed legs in the air. I started laughing so hard that I couldn't get up or uncross my legs. "Klugarsh Mind Control," I howled, "Klugarsh, Klugarsh, Klugarsh!"

"I am Klugarsh, famous scientist and genius," Alan Mendelsohn said. "See this picture of a light bulb? See this picture of a silly idiot smiling? I can talk to people on Mars. Klugarsh Research Associates has developed this cheap transistor radio that talks to Mars."

I was laughing so hard that my eyes were wet with tears. Alan Mendelsohn was really funny.

"See, I clip these things to my ears, and throw the switch, and produce omega waves—then I talk to Mars," Alan Mendelsohn said. He clipped the wires of the Omega Meter to his ears and threw the switch. The machine buzzed. "Now I'm in the office of the Martian High Commissioner, drinking fleegix," Alan Mendelsohn said. Then he began to laugh so hard that he couldn't talk. Both of us were flat on our backs, laughing, with tears running down the sides of our faces and into our ears. The Omega Meter attached to Alan Mendelsohn's ears buzzed away.

We laughed and laughed until it hurt to laugh any more. Then we just lay there sighing. The Omega Meter buzzed.

"We're really suckers," Alan Mendelsohn said. "I'm supposed to be smart, but Samuel Klugarsh really made a monkey out of me." He was still sort of chuckling. "I give up."

We both lay there, getting over having laughed so much. We lay on the floor listening to the Omega Meter buzz. Alan Mendelsohn was apparently too weak from laughing to shut it off. For a long time we listened to it buzz. Then it stopped buzzing, and a set of silvery chimes played "Jingle Bells."

15

We were amazed, to say the least. The Omega Meter
played "Jingle Bells," beautifully, almost all the way
through. Then it started buzzing again, played a few more
notes of "Jingle Bells," and went back to buzzing. Alan
Mendelsohn and I stared at each other.

"How did you do that?" I asked him.

"I really don't know," Alan Mendelsohn said. "I was
just lying there—sort of knocked out—and it played 'Jingle Bells.' "

"But, in your head, how did you feel when it started
playing?"

"I don't know—good, I guess. I felt sort of good."

"Good? How good? Can you remember what you were
thinking?" I asked.

"I wasn't really thinking anything. We were just lying
there, remember? We were all tired out from laughing so
much. I was lying here like this. I wasn't thinking. I felt

tired and sort of good, and it started playing. I remember the last thing I said was 'I give up,' and . . ."

The machine started playing "Jingle Bells" again. It played it all the way through twice while we listened. Then it started buzzing again.

"Here, Leonard, you try it," Alan Mendelsohn said. "Put the wires on, and then sort of flop down and say, 'I give up.'"

I tried to remember the way we felt after all the laughing. I put the clips on my ears and flopped over backward. "I give up," I said. The machine played "Jingle Bells." I got it to play all the way through, and a little more, the very first time.

Then Mendelsohn wanted to try it again, and then I did. We traded it back and forth until my mother telephoned to ask if I was planning to ever come home for supper.

I left the Omega Meter at Alan Mendelsohn's house. He was supposed to come over to my house the next morning, and we'd practice together. I took the Mind Control course home with me to read over carefully, in case we'd missed anything—which didn't seem likely.

I got home. My father was waiting at the barbecue. It was starting to snow. Both my parents were sort of bugged about something. I could tell they wanted to talk to me. At the table it started.

"Leonard," my father said, "do you feel that Dr. Prince is helping you?"

"Sure," I said.

"Your mother is a little worried about his letting you take time off school like this," my father went on.

"It was his idea," I said. "I didn't want to take any days off—at first—but now I see that it was a good idea, and it's helping me make a better adjustment and become a better student."

"I don't see how taking days off school can make you a better student," my mother said. "You know I tried to call Dr. Prince on the telephone today, and he wouldn't talk to me. He said it would compromise his confidentiality if he spoke to me, and all he would say was that if I wanted a doctor of my own, he'd be happy to refer me to one. Why should he think I need to see a psychologist? Leonard, what sort of things have you been telling Dr. Prince about me—about us?"

I could see I was going to have to be careful with this. It was a lucky thing I had read that book about psychiatry. "I've been telling him that you're worried about me because I don't do well in school—and that upsets me and makes me worry about you, and that makes it even harder for me to do my schoolwork. I guess maybe Dr. Prince thought that you were so upset about me that you needed someone to talk to—I mean, you called him, didn't you?"

"Leonard, you don't have to worry about me," my mother said. "It's very kind of you, but I want you to concentrate on working with Dr. Prince and bringing your grades up. You're sure he's helping you?"

"Oh, yes," I said. "I'm not feeling nervous anymore, and I really feel sure that when I go back to school things are going to be very different."

"Well, that's all we wanted to know, son," my father said, "Would you like another piece of barbecued chicken?"

After supper I went to my room to study the Mind Control course. I lit up a cigar and started the book at page one. The only thing I hadn't really paid much attention to was the little slogan on every page. They seemed sort of sappy at first glance. I tried to figure out if maybe they contained some message I had missed the first time. They still seemed sort of sappy. For example:

FEELINGS ARE FACTS.
IF YOU FEEL A THING IS SO—
IT IS!

And:

DAMN THE TORPEDOES,
GRIDLEY—
FULL SPEED AHEAD!

And:

NEVER TRY
TO REASON WITH FEELINGS—
OBEY THEM!

I really couldn't make much sense out of the slogans. Finally, I put the book away and tried to practice my omega waves without the meter.

The practice paid off. When Alan Mendelsohn brought the Omega Meter over the next morning, I found I could get it to play "Jingle Bells" for ten or fifteen minutes at a stretch. Alan had stayed up late practicing with the Omega Meter, and he could do even better, but he couldn't tell when he was producing omega waves without the meter, and I could. We took turns all morning, and by lunchtime, had gotten so we could turn the omega waves on and off.

My mother made lunch for us: noodle soup and grilled cheese sandwiches. After lunch she asked us to take Melvin for a walk. We put on our coats, leashed up old Melvin, and went outside. It was cold and crisp. Melvin liked that kind of weather, and he was almost wide awake. We sort of strolled around the neighborhood, and Melvin lifted his leg on various things.

"Have you noticed that Melvin sort of favors his right leg?" Alan Mendelsohn asked. "Let's try using Mind Control to get him to use his left leg." We came to one of Melvin's regular stops, a lamppost around the corner from my house. We both went into state twenty-six and mentally commanded him, "My will is stronger than yours. You must obey. My will is stronger than yours. You must obey. Lift your left leg." Melvin lifted his right leg as he usually did.

"This may not work on dogs," I said. "Let's find a human who doesn't seem to be concentrating on anything in particular." There wasn't a soul on the street. This was one of the things I had first noticed about West Kangaroo Park. There were never any people walking around. In the old neighborhood there were always people walking, people standing and talking, people just standing, people leaning out of their windows. You never saw anybody in the new neighborhood.

"Let's go where there are some stores," Alan Mendelsohn said.

There weren't any stores at all near our house—another difference from the old neighborhood, where you could walk down to the corner and get a Fudgsicle or a comic book. It was a walk of about three-quarters of a mile to the street where all the stores were. They weren't really stores, in the sense of stores being little places that sold things. They were more like shopping centers—little bunches of stores clustered around a parking lot, and big bunches of stores spread out along a big parking lot. You were supposed to drive to them—you weren't supposed to walk. In fact, there weren't any sidewalks, and Alan Mendelsohn and Melvin and I had to walk in the gutter with cars whizzing by.

There weren't even any people to be found on the big shopping street. Everybody was either in the stores or in their cars.

"Where are we going to find some people to practice on?" I asked.

"There!" Alan Mendelsohn said. He pointed to a gas station on the next corner. There were four or five guys standing around, drinking soda pop and leaning on the fenders of cars. "These guys aren't concentrating on anything in particular," Alan Mendelsohn said. "Let's give them a try."

"What shall we tell them to do?" I asked.

"Let's pick one—that guy in the hat. Let's tell him to take off the hat and scratch his stomach."

We went into state twenty-six. "My will is stronger than yours. You must obey. My will is stronger than yours. You must obey. Take off the hat and scratch your stomach." Nothing happened. We tried it again. Nothing. And again. Nothing.

"Maybe we need to practice the omega waves a little more," Alan Mendelsohn said.

"Maybe we do," I said. "Are you looking at the guy?"

"Looking right at him," Alan Mendelsohn said.

"Well, I can't think what we're doing wrong," I said. "Maybe he's thinking."

"He doesn't look as though he's thinking," Mendelsohn said.

"No, he sure doesn't," I said. "He doesn't look as though he ever had a thought in his life."

The man slowly took off his hat with his right hand, and

with his left hand slowly scratched his stomach with a circular motion.

"It worked! It worked!" We jumped up and down.

"Tell him to bend over and bark like a dog," I said.

"Tell him to put his fingers in his ears," Alan Mendelsohn said.

"Tell him to dance," I shouted.

"Yes, tell him to dance!"

We went into state twenty-six. In a little while the guy in the hat was doing a private little dance, sort of a jig, shuffling his feet and bending his knees. When the other guys hanging around the gas station noticed the guy in the hat dancing, he looked sort of sheepish and embarrassed—as though he hadn't realized he was dancing—which, of course, he hadn't.

Alan Mendelsohn and I were hugging each other and dancing along with the guy in the hat.

"This thing has fabulous possibilities," Alan Mendelsohn said, "fabulous possibilities."

16

It turned out that the possibilities of Klugarsh Mind Control weren't as fabulous as Alan Mendelsohn had thought. For one thing, you needed to find someone who wasn't thinking anything in order to control them. People without a thought in their heads aren't as common as it would appear. Also, getting people to take off their hats or rub their bellies was about the best we could do. The guy in the gas station who did a little dance was our best subject all day.

We wandered around the shopping area of West Kangaroo Park, looking for subjects. The pickings were slim. We would do much better back at school—but we still had two more days of suspension/therapy and then the weekend before we could go back. Alan Mendelsohn had said he wondered how anyone could consider suspension from school as a punishment—especially suspension from a lousy school like Bat Masterson, but he was wishing we could be back. It's like this: As soon as you are locked out of a place and told that you can't come back in, you start thinking about getting back in. Even after we talked—even after we understood how it worked—we both would have been glad to get back into school a couple of days early.

We got cold looking for Mind Control subjects, and went back to my house. Melvin wasn't used to long walks, and he was exhausted. My mother was waiting for us to turn up.

"Alan, your mother has been calling. Your father is leaving on a trip, and you're supposed to go right home and say good-bye to him," my mother said. "Leonard," she said to me, "the Old One called to say that her vacuum cleaner is broken. Tomorrow, will you take our vacuum cleaner to her apartment, pick up her broken vacuum cleaner, and take it to the repair shop?"

All this made sense. The Old One needs a vacuum cleaner every day because of the piles of sunflower seed shells and other debris that the parrot leaves around. Not to mention Grandfather. Before he left, I asked Alan Mendelsohn if he'd like to come with me to my grandparents' apartment in the old neighborhood. He said that sounded fine—he'd call me on the telephone that night. I looked forward to showing him around.

Alan Mendelsohn called that night, as he said he would. It seems his father had to go to New York City, where his company had its headquarters, all of a sudden. Alan said it was no big deal, but there was this sort of tradition in his family, where, when the father goes on a trip, everybody has to gather around while he gives them advice before he goes—things like don't forget to feed the cat, and always turn off the taps after you're finished using the water. Alan said it was all right for him to go with me on my vacuum-cleaner delivering errand the next day.

When we got to the old neighborhood, Alan Mendelsohn got really excited. "This is like The Bronx! This is like The Bronx!" he kept shouting as we rode down streets of brick four-story apartment houses. When we got off the bus to walk to the Old One's apartment, he said, "This even smells like The Bronx!" He really liked the old neighborhood. I knew he would.

We stopped and looked in the window of the fish store. All the fish were lying dead on the crushed ice, except some crabs who were feebly waving their claws around. It smelled good. It was a good fish store. Everything was fresh. There was seaweed packed between some of the fish. People in West Kangaroo Park must think that fish come out of the sea frozen and packed in little square boxes.

Alan Mendelsohn was excited. There had been a fish store in The Bronx. I was sure there had been. And there had been a bakery where they actually baked things, as opposed to having them delivered in white cardboard boxes from a truck at eight o'clock in the morning. The bakery not only smelled good, but you could buy broken cookies for a nickel. We got a dime's worth, still hot, and ate them out of a white paper bag with little stripes, and a grease spot from the cookies. It felt good to be in the old neighborhood. It must have felt even better to Mendelsohn because he had no way of knowing such things existed outside of The Bronx.

Another thing they have in the old neighborhood is cobblestones and trolley tracks. The trolley doesn't run anymore, but the tracks are still there—and a lot of the streets have these yellowish, squarish stones that you can turn your ankle on. They don't have them anywhere but the old neighborhood—and The Bronx, as I found out from Alan Mendelsohn.

If being in the old neighborhood made Alan Mendelsohn excited, being in the Old One's apartment made him almost crazy. "My grandmother has an apartment just like this!" he shouted. It turned out that his grandmother even had a parrot. He was beside himself. He ate up the goop made of ground-up soybeans and raisins and honey as though it were the best stuff he'd ever eaten. He played with the parrot, he made conversation with the Old One, who didn't really want to talk—she was concentrating on catching up on her vacuuming. Mendelsohn even wanted to see Uncle Boris's movies. That was a fatal mistake.— Once Uncle Boris started showing movies, they went on and on until people started to scream and thrash about. I went out with the broken vacuum cleaner while Uncle Boris and Alan Mendelsohn set up the screen.

When I got back from the repair shop, where the man had said it would take eight months to fix the vacuum cleaner because they had to order parts from Romania, Alan Mendelsohn and Uncle Boris were talking and drinking tea out of glasses. They had already gotten through Uncle Boris's movie of the feet of everybody in the family, unto fourth and fifth cousins. Just the feet, you understand—no faces, no bodies—just feet. Also they had viewed Uncle Boris's zoological study of a squirrel in the park. This was a one-hour movie of a squirrel Uncle Boris liked—the squirrel running up a tree, the squirrel running from branch to branch, the squirrel sitting still, the squirrel eating a nut Uncle Boris had given it. It had taken me an hour and fifteen minutes to take the broken vacuum cleaner on the bus, drop it off at the repair shop, and come back.

"Hey, Old One," I shouted, "the man says it will take eight months to fix your vacuum cleaner!"

"I'm not surprised," the Old One answered. "They have to write to Romania to get parts."

I went into the dining room, where Uncle Boris and Alan Mendelsohn had set up their movie theater. They were talking about Samuel Klugarsh!

"Then I didn't see Klugarsh for some time," Uncle Boris was saying. "After the scandal over the Egyptian relics, he dropped out of sight, even though no one could prove he had any connection with the matter. Klugarsh reappeared some years later as a Chinese professor of mathematics named Yee Chi Poy. In that disguise he made some trips to Mexico, where he obtained a remarkable idol made of agate that had once belonged . . ."

"Excuse me," I said, "Is that *our* Samuel Klugarsh he's talking about?"

"Yes," Alan Mendelsohn said. "Uncle Boris has known Samuel Klugarsh off and on for twenty-five years. It seems that Klugarsh probably stole the basic principles of Mind Control, and a lot of other stuff, from an ancient brotherhood that had its headquarters in Mexico."

"That's right," Uncle Boris said. "The Order of the Laughing Alligator—a very old mystical brotherhood, said to have originated in Tibet or India or California, or one of those places. What Alan describes as Mind Control is probably something Klugarsh picked up from the brothers of the Laughing Alligator when he visited them in Mexico.

"Uncle Boris, do you think Samuel Klugarsh swindled us, or what?" I asked.

"Well, that would be hard to say," Uncle Boris said. "Samuel Klugarsh has always been regarded by some as a swindler. I myself have always thought of him as someone who sells people things they don't really need for more money than they're worth. If that's your definition of a swindler, then he is one. Of course, Mind Control does work, doesn't it?"

"Well, we can make people take off their hats and rub their bellies when we give them a mental command—and one guy did a dance," I said.

"I can't say that what you're describing is my idea of fun," Uncle Boris said, "but you have powers now that you didn't have before—even if they're boring powers. It seems to me that Samuel Klugarsh sold you something that's worth a bit less than you paid. But since you're interested in such things, I may as well show you my magic gem—more of a crystal, actually."

Uncle Boris wandered off to his room, apparently to get something.

"What's going on?" I asked Alan Mendelsohn.

"Somehow the subject of Samuel Klugarsh came up," Alan Mendelsohn said. "I don't remember how—or, yes I do. Your Uncle Boris had a picture of his feet. Apparently Samuel Klugarsh is a fifth cousin, once removed, of Uncle Boris. Anyway, he mentioned Samuel Klugarsh, and I said, 'That's the guy we bought the Mind Control course from!' And your uncle wanted to know about that, and I told him. Then he started in on all this history about Samuel Klugarsh. It seems that Samuel Klugarsh has been involved in all sorts of shady deals. He was telling me about it when you came in. Now he appears to have gone to get some sort of magic gem. Do you know anything about that?"

I told Alan Mendelsohn that I had never heard anything about a magic gem. This was the first I had ever heard about Uncle Boris having an interest in anything other than his movie camera, feet, clouds, and squirrels. Uncle Boris came back.

He had a little leather bag, tied at the top. "This is my magic gem," he said. "I started to tell you about a Mexican idol that Samuel Klugarsh brought back. Well, this was one of the eyes of that idol." Uncle Boris produced a dark green stone about the size of a marble, but not quite round. It had flecks of brown and blue in it. It was not clear, but looked like a little piece of earth that had gone all hard and shiny.

"It doesn't look magic, but it is," Uncle Boris said. "It is a sort of crystal—it vibrates at a certain frequency. When certain people hold it—well, give it a try." He handed me the stone. I felt it sort of wiggle in my hand. He gave it to Alan Mendelsohn. As soon as he took it, the stone began to give off a yellowish light.

17

"Well, well! My, my! Mercy, mercy!" Uncle Boris seemed to be very impressed by the fact that the magic gem had given off a yellow light when Alan Mendelsohn took hold of it.

"I never saw it do that before," Uncle Boris said. "It vibrates for certain people—that's supposed to show that you're psychically sensitive—but I never saw it light up before. You don't recall ever having heard anyone in your family mentioning that your ancestors came from a place called Mu? Lemuria? Anything like that?"

"The Ukraine?" Alan Mendelsohn asked. "That's where my great-grandfather came from."

"Mu and Lemuria and Atlantis are lost continents that are supposed to have existed a long time ago—and then sunk under the ocean. Samuel Klugarsh told me that this stone had originally come from some such place, and that it would light up if it were ever touched by a native of one of those lost continents. The thing about Klugarsh is that the stuff he sells is always real—but it isn't always what he says it is. He might sell you a real emerald, and tell you it was a rare Venusian green diamond. There's something special about this gem of mine, but I don't know if it really comes from Lemuria. For all I know it might come from the moon. Samuel Klugarsh used to have a brass potato that came from the moon—or so he said. At any rate, Leonard, your friend Alan Mendelsohn is a special sort of person, whether he's a Lemurian or not. The gem lit up like a little light bulb when he touched it, and it never did anything like that before."

Alan Mendelsohn was still holding the gem, and it was still giving off a definite yellow light.

On the bus back to West Kangaroo Park, we made a fellow take off his hat and rub his belly. We tried to make the same guy blink his eyes, stick his tongue out, and put his fingers in his ears—but all he did was take off his hat and rub his belly. We decided that Mind Control was boring, and that the next day we'd go back to Samuel Klugarsh's bookstore and try to get our twenty-four dollars back. What did we have to lose? We figured that even if he wouldn't return our money, maybe Samuel Klugarsh would let us trade the Omega Meter and the Mind Control course for something more interesting. I would have settled for one of those Lemurian gems—if it would light up for me the way it did for Alan Mendelsohn. We agreed to get up early and take the first bus into Hogboro. We were going to have breakfast at the Bermuda Triangle Chili Parlor.

18

It was just getting light—the sun wasn't up—when we got on the early bus for Hogboro. We had the Omega Meter and the Mind Control course in a brown paper bag. We had the leftover money we had not spent the last time we were in Hogboro, and a few additional dollars scraped from various secret savings. We had about a twenty dollars between us.

It was quiet and sort of deserted around the bus terminal. A few people were sleeping on the waiting room benches, and an old guy was mopping the floor. The rush hour wouldn't get started for almost an hour. Most of the stores were closed. There were sheets of newspaper covering the sample drawings in the window of the tattoo shop. We walked toward the Bermuda Triangle Chili Parlor. It was cold—the sidewalk was a funny gray color in the early morning light, and it bounced cold up at us. A few pigeons, looking ruffled and sleepy, walked around on

94

the pavement—trying to work up to the decision to fly. The wind whipped our ankles and up our trouser legs whenever we came to an intersection. Winter had arrived.

The windows of the Bermuda Triangle Chili Parlor were all steamy. We could smell coffee and hear cups and plates banging together. Through the steam we could see three—four—five yellow light bulbs. We went in.

The inside of the place smelled incredibly good. Fresh-baked corn muffins had just come out of the oven. I know what they smell like, because my mother gets these heat-'em-yourself frozen corn muffins that you make in the toaster. Even those smell all right—but this smell could only be the real thing. Besides, there they were, in a steaming pyramid on a big platter on the counter. We sat down on two stools, right in front of the corn muffins.

"Two corn muffins and two hot chocolates, am I right?" said the guy behind the counter. The hot chocolate was a great idea, and different from any I ever had before. I think it was made with milk instead of water. It was thick and foamy—and there was a marshmallow melting in the cup.

"Ah, the two scholars," a familiar voice said. It was Samuel Klugarsh. "Two corn muffins, heavy on the butter, and a hot chocolate with double marshmallows and whipped cream," he told the guy behind the counter.

"No eggs today, Mr. Klugarsh?" the counterman said.

"Not really hungry," said Samuel Klugarsh. "I had a late supper."

"We were going to come and see you after breakfast," Alan Mendelsohn said.

"See me now," Samuel Klugarsh said. "Bring your cups over to this table—have a refill of the hot chocolate, on me." Samuel Klugarsh gestured us toward one of the little black marble-topped tables in the place. He was wearing a red and white striped jacket with a pink shirt and a bright green bow tie. He had plaid trousers, and loafers made of bright orange-colored leather.

"You boys are working on interstellar telepathic communication, are you not?" Samuel Klugarsh asked.

"We bought a Mind Control course and an Omega Meter," Alan Mendelsohn said.

"Mind Control—of course," Samuel Klugarsh said. "I don't know what I was thinking of. Well, you can't expect results overnight. These powers don't come easily to humans—but I give you my solemn word, the machine *will* play 'Jingle Bells,' if you keep working at it."

"Oh, it plays 'Jingle Bells,' " I said. "It played 'Jingle Bells' the same day we got it from you."

"What?" Samuel Klugarsh looked very surprised. "I mean, of course it did. Klugarsh Mind Control is a scientifically designed course. It works. It always works. Maybe you'd like to write me a little letter saying how you're satisfied with your Omega Meter."

"Well, that's what we came to see you about," I said. "We really aren't satisfied. The Omega Meter works all right—it plays 'Jingle Bells,' and we followed the instructions and we can go into state twenty-six whenever we want to—but when we give mental commands, the only thing we can get people to do is take off their hats and rub their bellies, and once we got a guy to do a little dance."

"I don't believe you," Samuel Klugarsh said.

"No, really," Alan Mendelsohn said, "that's all we can get people to do. We read the book, and we've been practicing on people, on dogs, and that's all we can get anybody to do."

"That's *all?*" Samuel Klugarsh was pretty excited. "Show me. Show me right now."

We looked around for somebody who wasn't up to much mentally. There was a guy sitting at the counter, wearing one of those red hunting caps. He was pulling little pieces off a hard roll and popping them into his mouth. Then he'd spend a long time chewing each piece, all the time gazing at the coffee machine as though he were looking right through it and a hundred miles away.

"Watch that guy," we said. We both went into state twenty-six, and in a few seconds the guy was taking his hat off and rubbing his belly.

"Come with me," Samuel Klugarsh said. "I've got some machines in the bookstore that I want to use to test you guys. Put their stuff on my tab," he shouted to the counterman, and he hustled us out of the Bermuda Triangle Chili Parlor.

19

Samuel Klugarsh unlocked the door of his bookstore. He seemed to be really excited. "I've got a secret room in the back, where I keep all my really sophisticated instruments," he said. We walked past all the black boxes with wires and tubes and dials and switches, past the shelves of books on mystical subjects, to a locked door at the far end of the shop. Samuel Klugarsh unlocked the door, and we went into a small room. There was not much furniture in the room—a table and two or three folding chairs. There was something large covered with a sheet.

"I'll soon know for certain whether you're in state twenty-six," Samuel Klugarsh said. He whisked the sheet off what turned out to be the largest machine of all. It was painted in bright colors, mainly red. It sort of resembled a big refrigerator with a thing like a barber pole coming out the top of it. Written across the front of the refrigerator part of the machine was TEST YOUR BRAINPOWER in bright yellow letters about six inches high. The barber pole had a clear glass tube running up the outside. At the bottom it said Mental Midget; a little further up it said Sorta Stupid; a few inches higher it said Just About Normal; above that it said Smarty-pants; then it said Professor; then Wizard; then Genius; then Out of This World. Coming out of the front of the machine was a pair of heavy wires that were attached to something that looked like the stainless steel bowl that my father made salads in. The bowl had tubes and coils of wire coming out of the top. The whole thing had been sprayed with gold paint.

"This is the most advanced machine to test brain waves known to man," Samuel Klugarsh said. "It will take just a few minutes to warm up." Samuel Klugarsh threw a big switch. The machine hummed.

"This looks like one of those gadgets you see in carnivals," Alan Mendelsohn said.

"I know," Samuel Klugarsh said. "Isn't that incredible? The world's greatest expert on brain waves was a Tibetan lama and neurosurgeon, and when I met him he was operating an attraction in Atlantic City, New Jersey. He had designed and built this machine. I bought it from him and had it brought here. Out of This World corresponds to state twenty-six. When I put the Thought-Collector helmet on your heads, just do your Mind Control routine. A colored liquid will rise up that glass tube. If it gets as high as Out of This World, you will be the first humans to produce enough omega waves to be in state twenty-six. There was one person who did it while the machine was in Atlantic City—but he turned out to be a proven extraterrestrial."

"Can't you produce enough omega waves to be in state twenty-six?" I asked Samuel Klugarsh.

"Sadly, I cannot," Samuel Klugarsh said. "You see, when I was in the military, defending our country, I sustained a serious injury in the line of duty. As a result I have a silver plate in my skull, which creates an electromagnetic anomaly that prevents my participating in omega wave production. I'd appreciate it if this was kept confidential."

We promised we would never tell. Samuel Klugarsh said that the brain wave machine had warmed up enough, and would I be the first to be tested. I let him put the Thought-Collector helmet on my head. He told me to go into state twenty-six. I did. The brain wave machine made a whistling sound, and a column of red liquid rose in the tube past Mental Midget, Sorta Stupid, Just About Normal, Smarty-pants, past Professor, Wizard, and Genius. It stopped just short of Out of This World, and sort of bobbed up and down.

"Fantastic!" Samuel Klugarsh said. "And do you mean to tell me that you got to be able to do this just by reading my Mind Control course and practicing with the Omega Meter?"

We told him that we had.

"Let's try this helmet on the other gentleman," Samuel Klugarsh said. He put the helmet onto Alan Mendelsohn's head, and the red liquid shot all the way to the top of the tube—even quicker than it had when I had been tested.

"Excuse me," Samuel Klugarsh said. "I'm a little overwhelmed—you see, this is the greatest moment in the mental history of man. I need to sit down for a minute." Samuel Klugarsh staggered over to one of the folding chairs and slumped down into it, looking sort of sick. He sat there for a while, shaking his head slowly from side to side. Finally he spoke. "I want to thank you. I want to thank you for making my life worthwhile—you see, I never knew if I was on the right track until now. Now I know that Klugarsh Mind Control not only works, but is the ultimate development in the history of progress. This is a great moment, but I don't want to forget that you are my clients, and that I am here to serve you. Now what was it that you wanted to talk to me about?"

We couldn't tell Samuel Klugarsh that we thought Mind Control was boring. Not after his great excitement. Not after finding out how important it was to him that we could reach state twenty-six. We couldn't tell him that we wanted our money back. Samuel Klugarsh was looking at us with this strange expression—it was a little like the way Melvin looks at Grandfather, sort of like he expected us to scratch behind his ears or give him a biscuit. He was waiting to hear what it was that we wanted to talk to him about.

Alan Mendelsohn spoke. "We . . . uh . . . we . . . we wanted to know if we could trade in our Mind Control course and Omega Meter for a more advanced course."

That was quick thinking. There was no telling if the advanced course would be any better—but at least the boring Mind Control book and the Omega Meter would be off our hands.

"Of course you do," Samuel Klugarsh said. "I must have neglected to tell you about Klugarsh's trade-in policy. You can trade in any course or book you are dissatisfied with or, in your case, have gone completely beyond, for seventy-three percent of its current sale price, less a small handling charge, for any selected Klugarsh product or publication. Of course you want to trade in the Omega Meter—you gentlemen are ready for highly advanced work."

"Maybe we could sort of look around the store and pick out some books worth seventy-three percent of twenty-four dollars, minus a small handling charge," Alan Mendelsohn said.

"Oh, no, no, no," Samuel Klugarsh said. "Those books are not for talented people like you. Those books are for the—please pardon the expression—poor schnooks who go through life hoping that something will happen to them, like being able to achieve state twenty-six and make people take their hats off and rub their bellies at their command."

I couldn't imagine anyone going through life hoping to be able to make people take off their hats and rub their bellies.

"For people of real psychic prowess like yourselves, only the best, only Samuel Klugarsh publications and training devices are good enough. I will advise you. Now, what are your interests? Interstellar travel? Forecasting the future? Influencing inanimate objects? Reading the thoughts of others? Communing with lost civilizations—Mu, Atlantis, Lemuria?"

That rang a bell. Alan Mendelsohn and I both thought of Uncle Boris's magic gem from the lost continent. "What do you have in the way of lost continents?" Alan Mendelsohn asked.

"Lost continents? Certainly," Samuel Klugarsh said. "What you are asking for is the Klugarsh Mind Control Associates advanced course in Hyperstellar Archaeology. This will equip you to find the everyday clues to the existence of civilizations no longer with us." Samuel Klugarsh rummaged around in the back of a drawer in a file cabinet. He came out with a thick dusty-looking stack of papers. It was held together with three of those brass fasteners that look like a nail, except they are flat—you push them through the papers you want to fasten together, and then the flat part spreads out into two flat parts, and you fold them back, and you've got your papers fastened.

"Excuse me, there's a misprint," Samuel Klugarsh said, and he wrote something on the cover of the sheaf of papers. Then he handed it to us. It had said *Basic Lessons in Hyperstellar Archaeology*, but Samuel Klugarsh had crossed out the word *Basic*, and written the word *Advanced* above it, so the cover now read *Advanced Lessons in Hyperstellar Archaeology*.

"This normally costs one hundred and seventy-five dollars," Samuel Klugarsh said. "But since you are my favorite students, and including your Mind Control course as a trade-in—by the way, I'm allowing you the full price, and we'll forget about the handling charge—this will only come to eighteen dollars and fifty cents—and that's less than it cost me to produce. Fair enough?"

20

"Mr. Klugarsh, exactly what is Hyperstellar Archaeology?" Alan Mendelsohn asked.

"You know what archaeology is, don't you?" Samuel Klugarsh asked him.

"Sure," Alan Mendelsohn said. "Archaeology is the scientific study of the life and culture of ancient peoples, through the excavation of ancient cities, relics, artifacts, etcetera." Alan Mendelsohn was great at definitions, because of all his word-power books.

"That's almost right," Samuel Klugarsh said. "Close enough for purposes of our discussion." Alan Mendelsohn looked bugged. "Now," Samuel Klugarsh said, "Hyperstellar Archaeology differs from ordinary archaeology in two ways. Firstly, it concerns itself with the study of lost civilizations, such as Atlantis, Mu, or Lemuria—and the lesser-known lost civilizations such as Waka-Waka, Nafsulia, and Shabomm. The second way in which Hyperstellar

Archaeology differs from the regular kind is that instead of digging in the ground to find out about the ordinary life of these lost cultures, we look for clues to their existence in our everyday culture of the present. You see, in times past, beings from other planets came to Earth many times in order to study the activities of Earth life forms. Occasionally extraterrestrials took human form in order to study human activity without making anybody self-conscious. In some cases, the scholars from other planets left records, which Hyperstellar Archaeology decodes. I'll give you an easy example.—Nafsu Cola, which is about the third most popular soda pop in these parts, is made from an ancient formula salvaged from the lost city of Nafsulia. Walter C. Gull, the multimillionaire who developed Nafsu Cola, was a student of Hyperstellar Archaeology. He found the formula disguised in a coded document which appeared to be a list of outdated post office regulations. As a Hyperstellar Archaeologist, Gull instantly recognized the document as an encoding of Nafsulian material. He decoded it, decided to mix up a batch of the stuff, began to sell it, and the rest is history."

I had never tasted Nafsu Cola, although I knew that it existed. Every now and then you run across it in some out-of-the-way candy store, the sort of place that sells Moxie, and jelly beans by the scoop. I had no idea that it was the third most popular soft drink.

Samuel Klugarsh was talking. "Along with the course, I will include a copy of *Yojimbo's Japanese-English Dictionary*, vital for any student of Hyperstellar Archaeology, and one—no—two magic gems from the lost culture of Waka-Waka." He dug into the file cabinet and came up with two stones. They looked a lot like Uncle Boris's magic gem that had been the idol's eye.

"Those stones," I said, "they don't vibrate or light up or anything, do they?"

"Why bless your heart boy, of course they do," Samuel Klugarsh said. "Of course, we don't have the sophisticated energy sources they had in ancient Waka-Waka, so I've had these converted. You just unscrew them in the middle, like this, and drop in a one-point-three volt, H-C type hearing aid battery. In good old Waka-Waka, all you had to do was expose the magic gem to the great laser energy source in the middle of Waka-Waka city, and they'd have power for a year—but you'll find out more about that when you study your course. Shall I wrap it up? Oh, by the way, you get a specially fitted, red manila folder that holds the Hyperstellar Archaeology course, the magic gems, and *Yojimbo's Japanese-English Dictionary*, vital to the study of H.A. What do you say?"

I knew this wasn't a good deal. Alan Mendelsohn knew this wasn't a good deal. Neither one of us could ever say why, but we gave Samuel Klugarsh our eighteen dollars and fifty cents, and our Omega Meter and our Klugarsh Mind Control course. Samuel Klugarsh put the H.A. course, the Japanese-English dictionary, and the two magic gems into a perfectly ordinary red manila folder, the kind with the red ribbon stapled to it that ties around. We hadn't even bothered to ask why the Japanese-English dictionary. We figured it would all become more or less clear as time went by. Another thing that Alan Mendelsohn and I were feeling—we were not finished with Samuel Klugarsh. We would never be finished with Samuel Klugarsh.

As we left the store, he called out after us, "Don't forget—when you're through with that course, you can trade it in. It's worth thirteen fifty towards your next purchase—and you can keep the dictionary and the magic gems!"

There were a lot of pages in the Hyperstellar Archaeology course and, unlike the Mind Control course, they were filled with tiny, smudgy, mimeographed typing. Alan Mendelsohn and I spent the whole weekend either at his house or mine, reading the H.A. course. We'd take turns reading to each other, or just take turns reading a chapter silently while the other guy slept, or had something to eat, or played with the dog. By Sunday night, we had gotten most of the thing read, but not necessarily understood. There were lots of confusing things in the course.

A thing we did a lot of while we were reading the H.A. course was play with the magic gems. On close inspection, they seemed to be made of plastic rather than some kind of stone, but they were nice just the same. They buzzed and jumped and vibrated in our hands, and sometimes they would flicker or light up. The H.A. course didn't say anything about them, and we didn't have much of an idea what they were about. They were pretty, though.

The other thing that didn't make sense for a while was *Yojimbo's Japanese-English Dictionary*. We couldn't figure out what that had to do with Hyperstellar Archaeology for the longest time. We did though—when we were almost to the end of the course—but that came later.

The course, which was really just a book, told how there were clues to the existence of ancient civilizations all around us. It gave a lot of examples. It said that certain words in modern languages are really Lemurian or Atlantean words. It said that Haya and Doon were the two most important Nafsulian gods, and when people meet in

America and Australia and say "How're you doing?" they are actually repeating an ancient Nafsulian greeting.

The course also said that the native populations of North America and Australia both came from Nafsulia. It said that the potato was not a native crop to this planet, and that the people of Waka-Waka had introduced it when they migrated to Earth from their native planet of Haku-Hola.

The course was full of bits of information like that—but it didn't prove any of them. Alan Mendelsohn discussed whether anything in the course was true. It could have all been made up. The whole thing was written by a Professor Keith Brian Swerdlov of Miskatonic University. He could have been lying.

"I don't see where any of this is scientific," Alan Mendelsohn said. "Scientific means the theories in this book should be supported by experiments or tests that we can duplicate ourselves and see if they work. This book just says that kosher salami originally came from the planet Pluto with the people who colonized the ancient lost city of Shabomm. It doesn't say why we should think so, or even give us any idea whether Shabomm existed. As far as I can tell, the whole thing could be a fake."

Of course, we hadn't finished reading the course. It was before Sunday evening that we had these doubts. Still, we kept pushing on. We kept reading the thing. Even though it seemed to be one wild claim after another, for example—the book said that chickens were actually a degenerate form of an animal much smarter than humans, that had existed in Mu. It said that there are occasional throwback genius chickens about as intelligent as Einstein.

Then it would go on to something else equally weird, like saying that packaged chocolate pudding would turn into a deadly explosive if one easily obtainable ingredient were added. Naturally it didn't say what the easily obtainable ingredient was, and there were no cases of genius chickens as smart as Einstein listed, so someone could go and look them up.

It was a frustrating book. I would have quit plowing through the hard-to-read mimeographed typed pages if Alan Mendelsohn had said something—and I think if I had said something, he would have quit—but it had become one of those things that you finish because you *have* to finish it—because the other guy is going to finish it. It was a self-boring contest between Mendelsohn and me.

21

On Sunday evening the course got interesting. It got interesting when Alan Mendelsohn was taking his turn reading to me. He had just gotten through a long passage about how the custom of eating chopped liver is not of Earthly origin, but was picked up from interplanetary travelers by the residents of Atlantis. I must say the book was past the point of being boring, and had become totally ridiculous. Mendelsohn and I had laughed so much that we couldn't laugh any more; we just read on—reading the book because somehow we had made an unspoken pact to read our way through to the very end.

Mendelsohn had gotten through the part about chopped liver. Now he was into a section of Lemurian prophecies. It seems the Lemurian wise men had predicted the Civil War, the airplane, the automobile, sliced bread, Frisbees, and the Hong Kong flu. So what? Anybody can say he predicted anything. I could say that I predicted that men would go to the moon. Unless I had some proof that I said it a long time before anybody went there, or looked like they'd go there, it wouldn't mean a thing. Then Alan Mendelsohn got to the interesting part.

" 'Also,' he read, 'the Lemurian sages predicted that one day accounts of their deeds would be read by two boys named Alan Mendelsohn and Leonard Neeble.' " I thought he was just fooling around—making it up. His surprised expression and sort of sputtering, pointing, poking at the book, I took to be acting. Good acting, but not real—how could it be real? How could our names be in the book? Alan showed me. In the same smudgy little mimeographed typing, there they were, our names. How was this possible? Was it some trick of Samuel Klugarsh? We didn't put anything past him, but how would he have done it?

Samuel Klugarsh didn't know we were coming. We had run into him at the Bermuda Triangle Chili Parlor. He hadn't been out of our sight the whole time we'd been with him. In order to insert our names, he would have had to type the whole page on a mimeograph stencil, and then run it off, and insert it in the book. Alan Mendelsohn had worked on the school newspaper in The Bronx and had used a mimeograph machine. He said it would have taken at least fifteen minutes, if Samuel Klugarsh was a fast typist and mimeographist. Of course, if Samuel Klugarsh had known in some way that we would be coming back, he could have prepared the Hyperstellar Archaeology course with our names in it—but how could he know we'd be back in only a couple of days—and how could he know that we would want to trade in our Klugarsh Mind Control course and Omega Meter? What's more, neither of us could remember having told Samuel

Klugarsh our names. He usually called us "Gentlemen."

If there was a trick in it somewhere, we couldn't figure it out. Of course, if it wasn't a trick—at least not a trick of Samuel Klugarsh—if it was a trick of the ancient Lemurian sages, then it put the whole book in a different light. Then it meant that all the stuff about the origins of eating chopped liver, and packaged chocolate pudding being a deadly explosive with one ingredient missing, and superintelligent chickens—it might all be true. We had been making jokes and playing a dumb game with a book that might be true!

Right after the book mentioned our names, it went on to something totally unrelated, which seemed to be the style of the thing. It went on to talk about how rubber automobile tires are actually living beings, and have feelings and memories and personalities. When they get flat, it means they're dead.

We were confused. First the book had gone on and on with all sorts of weird, unproven statements, one after another—with no rhyme or reason. Then it mentioned us both by name! Then it went back to strange little snippets of information.

> *Yojimbo's Japanese-English Dictionary* was compiled by Clarence Yojimbo, a beloved Japanese scholar, who was actually a beloved Venusian scholar in disguise. Since Venusians live upward of three thousand years, Clarence Yojimbo had the opportunity to reside both in Lemuria in its Golden Age and, much later, in Japan during the late Tokugawa period. Yojimbo compiled a much-respected Japanese-English dictionary for the use of merchants doing business in Yokohama. What is singular about the dictionary is that when read backwards, noting only the second word in English in each entry, it is found to contain another book—a key to ancient Lemurian Mind Con-

trol methods, rediscovered briefly, and then lost again by the Order of the Laughing Alligator, of which Yojimbo was a member.

We got the Japanese-English dictionary out of the red manila folder. We turned to the last entry.

> **zū-zū-shii** [zu'u-] 図々しい Impudent; audacious; bold; cheeky; saucy; un- blushing; shameless; brazen-faced; lost to a sense of shame.

So the second word in English was *audacious*. The next to last entry in the dictionary was *zuzuki*, meaning *pushing one's opponent on the chest with one's head*. The second word in the English part was *one's*, but it was mis- printed with no apostrophe. So far we had "audacious ones . . ." We went up the page, writing down the sec- ond English word in each entry. Soon it began to make a sentence—then two:

> *Audacious ones push straight to the center. In order to ad- vance mental power show caution and courage daring and patience.*

It made sense. We didn't understand it, but it made sense. We read on. Alan Mendelsohn read aloud—read- ing the second word in English from each entry, going from the back of the book to the front. It made sentences all right—but they were very hard to understand. Obs- cure, Alan Mendelsohn said.

> *A short song effortless. A single monorail charged with coal syrup. The metalworker's steel prospect imparts a candid lump of airworthiness to the short dandelion. Mark a post an object with wood screws of tacit approval. Aim silent mental wooden drum at Buddhist temple. Win (lose) by ten crosses. Profit net proceeds of one thousand yen. Turn a book upside down.*

Most of the sentences seemed to us to be saying something, but we couldn't figure out what. Sometimes it was a little easier:

> *To send thoughts mentally without speaking directly by special means telegraphically radio telegraphy it is best to use made of metal an antenna a fence a gate a sword a thing silver·copper steel. To receive same similar procedure good.*

That seemed to us to be fairly clear. It was saying that to send or receive thoughts, like radio waves, you need an antenna.

We went through the dictionary slowly, backwards, writing down a word at a time, and puzzling over the groups of words, trying to see them as sentences. It was slow work. We hadn't covered very much of the dictionary by the time Alan's mother called on the telephone and said for him to come home at once.

Alan asked me if I'd mind if he took the dictonary home with him. He said he would stay up late and copy out some more stuff, and maybe recopy the parts that made sense into a notebook. I told him to go ahead. We'd talk about it more in school, the next day.

22

At school, the next day, Alan Mendelsohn had a notebook with a bunch of words copied backwards out of *Yojimbo's Japanese-English Dictionary* in it. He hadn't had time to organize them into sentences—he just copied as many as he could before going to sleep. We met before school to discuss our Mind Control program for the day.

I had a metal ruler. We tried it out as an antenna. There was some debate at first as to where it would be best to put the antenna. Alan Mendelsohn thought that it would work best if it were attached to the head in some way, held in the teeth, or balanced on top of the head, or maybe just Scotch-taped to the head. I thought it would work best if it was hand-held and maybe pointed at the subject. We tried it my way. It worked. Soon, just about every kid in the school yard had been zapped with a mental command. One by one, they removed their hats, if any, and rubbed their bellies, and in some cases, danced.

All I had to do was point at the kid in question with the ruler, think my command, and off they'd go, uncapping, rubbing, and dancing.

Alan Mendelsohn and I were delighted. *Yojimbo's Japanese-English Dictionary* was definitely a source of good advice. We had enough time before the bell to try to figure out some more sentences from Alan Mendelsohn's notebook. He had copied the words in neat columns on the left-hand side of each page. He had about ten pages of words. We went down the column, pointing with a pencil:

> *Cost expenditure outlay employment casual hired (in the air)*

We included parenthetical expressions as one word.

> *(brown-eared) chicken rich lovers conditions. Petition the Emperor. Conceal pyramid mark object thus (decide upon a matter) hand a definite answer. Interesting framework construction (be imposing in appearance).*

None of this made any sense to us. It was too obscure, as Alan Mendelsohn liked to say. Then we came to some clearer parts.

> *Best way get results. Have mental picture illustration sketch example before requesting order to send to transmit to give an order. Execute an order. Do one's bidding. First see it, then send it.*

We thought that over. I pointed the ruler at a kid, closed my eyes and tried to see the kid walking with his arms stretched out to the sides, putting one foot directly in front of the other, sort of waving his arms up and down, first one, then the other—a picture of a kid walking a tightrope. I gave the mental command. I opened my eyes. The kid was doing a perfect imitation of a tightrope walker. It was beautiful.

Alan Mendelsohn wanted to try it. He had something special in mind. He picked out a kid, pointed the ruler at him and closed his eyes. He opened his eyes, the kid stepped on his own foot, made circles in the air with his arms, and collapsed forward in a shower of schoolbooks, pencils, blue-lined three-hole notebook paper, and the contents of his lunch bag.

"This is it," Alan Mendelsohn said. "The ultimate trip. The Remote-control Trip. This is the culmination of my career as a tripper. This will be my masterpiece. Leonard, let me borrow the metal ruler until lunchtime"—there was still time before the bell rang to start school. I told Alan sure—he could borrow the ruler. The bell rang and we went to our classes.

I wondered what it would be like, coming back to school after all those days off. It wasn't like anything. Nobody paid any special attention to me. It was evident that nobody had noticed I hadn't been there.

The next bell rang. "Take your seats and get ready for the P.A. announcements," Miss Steele said.

I unscrewed the top of my ball-point pen and took out the little brass refill. I pointed it at Miss Steele. I closed my eyes and got hold of a mental picture. Then I gave the command and opened my eyes. Miss Steele was looking very uncomfortable. I had picked a tricky mental picture, but apparently it worked—I had imagined a smoker going crazy for a cigarette. I had seen Miss Steele lighting up outside the building on the way to her car, and I figured she had a pretty serious habit. She was starting to sweat. Finally she said, "I'll be gone for just a moment—Robert Robinson, will you please take charge of the class while I'm gone?" She left. I made a mental note to quit fooling with cigars before I got hooked.

Robert Robinson was perhaps the most obnoxious kid in

the school. He was big and had muscles, and wavy hair, and no pimples, and was handsome in a sort of simpy way. He spent all his time looking at the backs of his hands, or combing his hair, or making his muscles twitch. He was Mr. Jerris's favorite kid. He could climb those ropes just like a cockroach.

I pointed the ball-point refill at him. It was working out just fine as a short-range antenna. I worked up a better mental image for Robert Robinson than I had for Miss Steele—it was someone who has to go to the bathroom but can't leave the place he's been assigned to stay. This was perfect for Robinson. Ordinarily, he would be clowning, and sort of looking handsome for the girls, and doing cool things like putting one foot on the front desk in a row, and sort of leaning forward and twitching his muscles. Now he had to concentrate on not wetting his pants, and that made it impossible to be funny or act cool, or crack jokes, or do much of anything but shift from foot to foot, and try, unsuccessfully, to look casual while doing it.

I had seen a detective program on television in which the crime had been solved on the basis of the fact that the detective knew that it takes seven and a half minutes to smoke a cigarette. Miss Steele was not going to come back without smoking her cigarette all the way down. The class was going wild, and Robert Robinson had nothing to do but rock from foot to foot and try to hold on. He was too dumb to simply walk out of the classroom, go to the bathroom, and come back in the hope that Miss Steele wouldn't have come back before him. Even if she had, he could have just told her that he had an emergency—or if he was too shy to say that, he could say he went out to look for her, or anything. But he was too dumb. She had told him to stay, and he just stayed—like a trained dog.

The P.A. started up. Mr. Winter said, "GOOD MORN——WHEN THE SURF'S UP IN OLD CALIFORNIA, THERE'S JUST OLD PAINT AND ME; JUST A BOY AND HIS HORSE ON A SURFBOARD, WHERE THE WIND AND THE WAVES ARE FREE. SURFIN', SURFIN', SURFIN' WITH MY HORSE; SURFIN', SURFIN' WITH MY HORSE, DOO WAH, DOO WAH." He was singing. This was obviously Alan Mendelsohn's work. I waited until Mr. Winter finished his song. He was sort of sputtering around, trying to make sense out of what he had just done. I pointed my ballpoint refill at the loudspeaker. I made a mental image of a sound—that was obviously how Mendelsohn had done it.

"I WILL NOW GIVE THE CORRECT TIME," Mr. Winter said, "CUCKOO—CUCKOO—CUCKOO—CUCKOO—CUCKOO—CUCKOO—CUCKOO—CUCKOO—CUCKOO." The whole school was laughing. This didn't make things any easier for Robert Robinson.

There was a loud click. Mr. Winter had switched off the P.A. Miss Steele came back into the room. Robert Robinson ran out without a word as soon as he saw her. It took her until the bell rang to get things quieted down.

At lunchtime, Alan Mendelsohn and I met for a discussion of strategy. We agreed to cool it for the rest of the day. We had done so much Mind Controlling that we were getting dizzy. Also, we didn't want to create a full-scale riot like the time Alan had told everyone that he was a Martian. Between the opening bell of the day and the start of lunch period, we had caused people to be rooted to the spot, bark like dogs, have uncontrollable urges to do various things that they simply couldn't do with people watching. We had done a lot of tripping and a good deal of making people think that a notebook or a pencil weighed a hundred pounds. The whole school was like a circus, and we were the audience.

But it wasn't as much fun as we thought it would be. For one thing, part of the fun of the circus is the big crowd of people you're watching it with—that's why circuses are no good on television. With only Alan and me in on the joke, it wasn't all that entertaining to get people to do funny things. Also, those kids who weren't too stupid to realize that something strange was going on were getting scared. A couple of kids had even cried when Mr. Winter was cuckooing. People get scared when they think other people are going crazy.

We had decided to cool it. We wouldn't do any more tricks on people that day—and we would plan something really big for our new power. There was another sentence Alan Mendelsohn had found in the dictionary the night before:

> To control minds (of) other people is good trick, but to control objects is great trick. Can a stone fly?

We picked up a small pebble and went to work on it. It didn't budge. We tried again and got it to move, so slightly that we couldn't be sure it had moved. It took the rest of the lunch period to move it an inch.

23

We had agreed to knock off Mind Control tricks for the rest of the day—at least big tricks that might get people stirred up. I did manage to knock twenty-two minutes off the school day by speeding up the master clock that controlled all the clocks in the classrooms. As we were leaving school, it occurred to me that everybody was going to be twenty-two minutes late in the morning. Except Mendelsohn and me. Later, Alan Mendelsohn persuaded me that we'd better be late too, so as not to arouse suspicion.

Alan Mendelsohn had a lot of junk in his room. He liked to pick up all sorts of things in the street and in empty lots. He had lots of wire and odd pieces of metal that came off cars and machinery. We headed for his house to see if we could work out a better type of antenna. On the way there, we picked up a brick from a place where they were building a house. That was going to be our test Mind Control subject. The idea was to try the different antennas on the brick—giving it the same mental command each time. The best antenna would get the best performance.

We set the brick in the middle of the floor of Alan Mendelsohn's room. Then we took turns giving it commands to rise into the air—without using any antenna at all. It didn't budge. Then we both commanded it at once. No results. Then we pointed the metal ruler and the ballpoint pen refill at it and gave simultaneous commands. No soap. Alan got a big coil spring. He put that against his forehead and commanded the brick to rise. It wobbled a little. We tried loops of wire, half an army bayonet, a metal tennis racquet, a boy scout trumpet, and various odd bits of metal—we didn't know what they were. Nothing made the brick rise or do anything more than vibrate slightly, the way it might if a heavy truck went by.

Mendelsohn dug around in his closet, which was very full of all sorts of odd junk, and came up with something that looked really promising. It was a rabbit-ears television antenna, but not the ordinary kind. This one had knobs on it and eight rusty brass-plated hoops encircling the base, in addition to the two rabbit ears, each of which had a little crystal cylinder about halfway up with a coil of copper wire inside. Super Signal Booster it said on the plastic base in letters of tarnished gold. This definitely looked like it would do the job.

There were two wires coming out of the base of the Super Signal Booster, and we each took one of them and pressed the little brass horseshoes at the end to our foreheads. We gave the command, "Rise, rise!" The brick shot up to the ceiling and made a large dent.

Alan Mendelsohn and I looked at each other. This antenna really worked. We tried again. "Rise slowly!" The brick floated up to the ceiling like a balloon, and bounced gently against it. "Descend!" We forgot to say slowly. The brick fell—like a brick—and made another big dent in Alan's floor.

"We need to practice with this," Alan Mendelsohn said.

"This antenna certainly has possibilities," I said.

"With this antenna and a little practice," Alan Mendelsohn said, "we could . . ." his voice trailed off.

"We could make the school float," I said.

"Yes, we could!" Alan Mendelsohn said. "We could levitate it!"

"Levitate?"

"Yes, that's what it's called when you cause something to float in the air. That's what we just did with this brick. It's just about the hardest thing to do in all magic. You almost never see it."

Alan Mendelsohn was really excited at the prospect of making Bat Masterson Junior High School float in the air.

"You don't think we could make it float away altogether?" I asked.

"We'd have to practice a lot first," Alan Mendelsohn said. "Just getting it off the ground is going to be no easy feat. What's more, we have to decide if we want to send it up empty or with everybody on board. If we send the school up loaded, we have to be very sure we can set it down again gently, or we'll wind up killing everybody."

Alan Mendelsohn had a point—in fact he had a number of them. Mind Control was one thing when you were dealing with a pebble, or even a brick—but when you started sending buildings up into the air, you had to know what you were doing. We needed to do a lot of practicing if we were going to get it right.

The workmen at the construction site had gone home.

We went back to practice lifting bricks. Behind the place where they were building, there was a grassy hill. We went there and sat down with the Super Signal Booster pointing at the big square pile of bricks. The brick pile was forty bricks long and twelve bricks across; it was twenty bricks high. So there were four hundred eighty bricks to a level and a total of nine thousand six hundred bricks in the pile.

We commanded one brick to rise—just an inch—we didn't want to attract any attention. It rose up an inch, and then we commanded it to set itself down. Then we had two bricks rise an inch and set down again. That worked. Three bricks. Four bricks. Five. Six. Seven. Ten. Fifteen. Twenty. Twenty-five—and the twenty-five bricks dropped with a loud crash, landing slightly out of line, instead of settling neatly into rows as they had when we tried the same trick with a smaller number of bricks. A couple of the bricks even cracked when they fell.

"I was afraid of that," Alan Mendelsohn said. "We don't have enough power."

Just then an exterminator's truck came past. DR. KILZUM it said on the side of the truck, ALL HIS PATIENTS DIE. There was a picture of a cartoon guy in a doctor's suit. He had a bag full of carpenter's tools and was holding a Flit gun. For some reason I thought of Dr. Prince.

"Holy cow!" I said, "I've got an appointment in Hogboro with my psychologist in less than half an hour. I'm going to be late for sure."

"I'll ride into Hogboro with you," Alan Mendelsohn said. "I've got nothing to do."

We ran for the bus. We were lucky. One was just coming when we got to the bus stop. If we ran from the bus terminal to the office building, I'd only be late five minutes, or a little more.

We were sweating when we arrived at the building where Dr. Prince had his office. Alan rode up in the elevator with me. People stared at us—I guess we looked strange to them, two sweating kids in tennis shoes in a fancy office building in downtown Hogboro.

"Doctor Prince, this is my friend Alan Mendelsohn. Is it OK if he waits here for me?" I asked.

"Of course it's all right," Dr. Prince said. "You're more than five minutes late. You must be full of aggression. That's a good sign. Come in, Leonard, my boy."

I went into Dr. Prince's office. He seemed very happy that I had come in late. Psychologists are strange people.

"Well, Leonard," Dr. Prince said, "tell me what happened when you came back to school after being absent for four days."

"Nothing happened," I said.

"Nothing! See? What did I tell you?" Dr. Prince seemed really happy. I guess he was a nice guy—just misguided. "And you came here late," he went on. "You weren't afraid to be late. I'm really pleased with your progress, Leonard."

I decided to tell Dr. Prince about Klugarsh Mind Control, and Hyperstellar Archaeology, and making bricks rise into the air. He seemed to want so much for me to confide in him—it wasn't his fault that he was a psychologist and got things mixed up. I told him about going to Samuel Klugarsh's bookstore and everything that happened since. He made a note in his little book when I told him about the fresh corn muffins at the Bermuda Triangle Chili Parlor, and he wanted to know the address.

When I got through telling Dr. Prince all about my new

powers, he said, "Leonard, I can't tell you how pleased I am that you trust me enough to share your psychotic fantasies with me. Now we'll really make some progress."

"They're not psychotic fantasies," I said, "I'm telling you the truth."

"You'll have to prove that to me," Dr. Prince said, rubbing his belly and removing an imaginary hat.

I had left my metal ruler and ball-point pen at Alan Mendelsohn's house, and we had hidden the Super Signal Booster in the bushes when we ran for the Hogboro bus. So all I could have done to prove my powers would have been to make Dr. Prince rub his belly and remove his hat—which he was already doing. Besides, I didn't really feel like proving anything to him. I was sort of mad at him for making fun of me. Let him believe whatever he wanted to.

24

Dr. Prince walked me to the door of his office. Alan Mendelsohn was sitting in the waiting room, reading a copy of *Psychology Today*. On the cover was a picture of the Mad Hatter from *Alice in Wonderland*, and written across the cover, diagonally, in yellow block letters, it said, HOW TO TELL IF YOU HALLUCINATE.

"I'm glad to see you're making friends, Leonard," Dr. Prince said. Alan Mendelsohn put down his magazine, and we both moved toward the outer door. Dr. Prince followed us. "Don't worry about a thing," he shouted down the hall as we headed for the elevator, "I've cured people twice as crazy as you!"

Alan and I rode down in the elevator. The people in business suits and high heels all looked at us again. The elevator filled up. "So the doctor says there's no hope for you?" Alan Mendelsohn asked me.

"No, he says it's incurable," I answered. The people in

the elevator all looked at me. "The lucky thing is there isn't a leper law in this state, so I can live at home if I want to."

"Yeah, that's good," Alan Mendelsohn said, "otherwise you'd have to go to that place in Hawaii."

Somebody pushed the button, and the elevator emptied out on the seventh floor.

We were alone in the elevator. "Look," Alan Mendelsohn said, "have you got any money on you?" I had about four dollars. Mendelsohn had about six. "Let's have supper in the Bermuda Triangle Chili Parlor. I'll call my mother and tell her I'm eating at your house, and you can call home and say you're eating at mine. There shouldn't be any problem."

It was a good idea. We found telephone booths in the lobby of Dr. Prince's office building and made our calls.

The rush hour was almost over. The streets of downtown Hogboro were nearly empty. A few late workers rushed to catch buses and trains. The stores were closing. It was just about dark. Alan Mendelsohn and I set out for the Bermuda Triangle Chili Parlor, our Fargo Brothers Rum-Soaked Curley-Q's glowing red in the chilly wind.

As we got away from the downtown business district, the streets got quieter and emptier. We moved away from the warmth and bustle around the bus station and into colder darker streets. We zipped up our jackets and walked fast, puffing our cigars. A motorcycle club roared past us. KNIGHTS OF POWER it said on the backs of their jackets. Bunched together, the motorcycles made a noise like running a ruler along an iron fence or a radiator—only much louder. We watched the red taillights get smaller and smaller in the distance.

It was just a little bit scary. All the buildings around us

were dark. They weren't office buildings. They contained little factories, tailor shops, wholesalers, and warehouses. They were all dark. There wasn't anyone on the street but us.

The lights of the Bermuda Triangle Chili Parlor, two blocks away, made a welcome sight. As we got closer, we saw that the storefront was surrounded by a little puddle of brightness made by the light bulbs behind the steamy window and the red neon sign which said EAT. Parked outside the Bermuda Triangle Chili Parlor were six or seven motorcycles—shiny ones, with all sorts of gadgets and decorations on them. Each of the motorcycles had a fancy dragon or alligator either painted in gold on the gas tank or worked into a fancy chrome backrest. We figured they belonged to the motorcycle club that had passed us earlier.

By this time, we could smell all sorts of good cooking smells and hear the faint clinking of dishes and silverware. When we opened the door, a blast of noise, warmth, and the most incredible smell of chili hit us. Now up to that time, my only experience with chili was stuff out of a can and stuff they served in the cafeteria in my old school. Right away, just from my first whiff, I could tell that this stuff was very different from the chili I had run across so far. When my glasses unfogged a little, I could see a sign hanging behind the counter. It said Chili—one dollar; Regular, H-Bomb, Green Death. The guy behind the counter was serving up the chili in white bowls. It seemed like everybody in the place was eating chili. The Knights of Power motorcycle club had pushed two tables together—they were eating the Green Death chili. I could tell because it was green. All the other chili was regular chili color.

"What's yours, boys?" the guy behind the counter asked. We played it safe and ordered the Regular chili. He handed us bowls of the stuff, a spoon apiece, and a stack of crackers, and we carried our stuff over to an empty table.

The chili tasted great. It was hot, too. Alan Mendelsohn said that he thought he could have handled at least the H-Bomb variety. I couldn't have—the Regular chili made me sweat and see little spots before my eyes. There was a sort of serve-yourself stainless steel sink, with racks of water glasses over it. You press the glass up against this metal horseshoe-thing with little rubber tips, and the glass fills up with cold water. We made quite a few trips to get water.

We liked the Bermuda Triangle Chili Parlor. It was warm and cozy and friendly. The motorcycle guys didn't seem sinister, or bad, or anything like that. They just ate their Green Death chili and talked quietly among themselves. In the kitchen, a radio was playing—some kind of foreign music I'd never heard before—it sounded like something between banjos and bells. It was nice.

Samuel Klugarsh walked in. He saw us and walked over. "Hello, students," he said. "Mind if I join you?" He went to the counter and came back with two bowls of Green Death. Then he went back to the counter again and returned with an enormous stack of crackers and a mug of hot chocolate with double marshmallows and whipped cream. I couldn't for the life of me figure out why this guy wasn't fat. Samuel Klugarsh crumbled the crackers into his two bowls of Green Death chili. "How are you doing with the Hypersteller Archaeology?" he asked us.

One of the Knights of Power spun around and glowered

at us for a moment. He had a big bushy mustache. Then he turned back to his friends and his chili. The motorcycle guy had distracted me. Samuel Klugarsh spoke again, "It was Hyperstellar Archaeology, wasn't it? Mu and Lemuria and Atlantis, and all that?"

"It's been very interesting, Mr. Klugarsh," Alan Mendelsohn said. "At first we couldn't understand the book at all—it just seemed to be full of all sorts of whacky facts. Then the Hyperstellar Archaeology course actually mentioned us by name."

"You're putting me on," Samuel Klugarsh said.

"No, no—it's the truth," I said. "The book said that the ancient Lemurian sages had predicted that one day two boys named Leonard Neeble and Alan Mendelsohn— that's us—would read an account of their deeds."

Samuel Klugarsh looked stunned. "Are you actually sure this happened?" he asked.

"It was right there in black and white, Mr. Klugarsh— actually blue and white, since it was mimeographed," Alan Mendelsohn said.

The biker with the bushy mustache—the one who had turned around and looked at us—was obviously listening in. He was leaning back in his chair so he could hear what we were saying. I never know what to do in situations like that—I mean, it's worse when you're the one listening and you can't help it. Sometimes people have family fights in restaurants, or holler at their kids, or talk about all kinds of personal stuff—and there you are, sitting right next to them. I didn't really care if the guy in the Knights of Power jacket listened or not, I decided. There was no way he was going to know what we were talking about anyway.

"If I hadn't actually seen proof that you guys could attain state twenty-six, I'd never believe this for a minute," Samuel Klugarsh said. "As it is, I have another copy of the course at my shop. I've never read it—that is to say, I've never read it for a long time—but I'll have a look at it. Where exactly did it mention you guys by name?"

"It was just before the part where it talks about *Yojimbo's Japanese-English Dictionary*," I said.

The motorcycle rider—the one who'd been eavesdropping—had a coughing fit. Samuel Klugarsh turned around and pounded him on the back. "What's the matter, buddy, did something go down the wrong way?" he said. "You've got to go slow with that Green Death if you're not used to it." He turned back to us. "Eating hot chili is an art," Samuel Klugarsh said. "The first thing you have to learn is to ignore the pain. You see, pain is your body's way of warning you that something is happening to it that is harmful—for example, if you put your finger in a candle flame, the pain tells you to take it out before it gets burned to a crisp. Now in the case of eating hot chili, the peppers give the illusion of pain. But in this case, it isn't harmful—there's nothing better for you than hot chili—so you just have to say to yourself that this isn't going to harm you." Samuel Klugarsh stopped talking to swallow a big spoonful of the Green Death. I could have sworn I saw blue sparks jumping when he dug into it. Then he covered his mouth with his fingertips and gave a modest burp.

Dr. Prince walked in. He was holding a slip of paper. I guessed it was the page from his notebook on which he had noted the address of the Bermuda Triangle Chili Parlor. His glasses were all fogged up.

"Look!" I said, "There's my psychologist!"

Dr. Prince had gotten into an argument with the guy

behind the counter. It seems they only made corn muffins in the morning, and were usually all out of them by evening. Dr. Prince had come in for corn muffins, and corn muffins he wanted. He was giving the guy a hard time.

Dr. Prince saw us and came over. "Oh, hello, Leonard," he said. "I thought you told me this place had the best corn muffins in town. Now I come in here, and they won't sell me any. I'm most upset."

Samuel Klugarsh stood up. "Our young colleague is correct about the corn muffins," he said, "but he neglected to tell you that what this place is really famous for is the Green Death chili, a secret recipe of the owner. I advise you to try it. By the way, I am Professor Samuel Klugarsh, Fellow of the Royal Astromental Society." He shook hands with Dr. Prince and then took him by the arm to the counter. The two men came back to the table with a bowl of Green Death apiece. It was Klugarsh's third!

"Excuse me just for a moment," Samuel Klugarsh said, and returned to the counter.

"Ah, Leonard," Dr. Prince said, "you must excuse my perturbed state a moment ago. I become unreasonable when I am denied gratification I have been anticipating. This is your young friend . . ."

"Alan Mendelsohn," I supplied the name.

"Ah, yes, and is the other gentleman, Professor Klugarsh, the one you were telling me about? The one who sold you the course in Hyper . . . Hyper . . ."

"Hyperstellar Archaeology," Samuel Klugarsh said. He had returned to the table balancing four cups of hot chocolate with double marshmallows and whipped cream. Out of his pockets he took a great many saltines and deposited them on the table. "A fascinating topic, Hyperstellar Archaeology. We'll have a good old scientific discussion in a bit—but first, enjoy your meal, Doctor. I'm curious to know what you think of the Green Death chili.

Dr. Prince scooped up a big spoonful of the stuff. At first, after he had popped it into his mouth, he had a sort of musing expression; then he looked pleased; then he looked surprised; then he got very red; then he grabbed handfuls of saltines and stuffed them into his mouth—by this time he was sweating freely—then he ran to the stainless steel water dispenser and gulped three glasses of water. When he came back to the table, tears were streaming down his face. He loosened his collar and sat down. "Without a doubt, the best chili I've ever tasted," he said to Samuel Klugarsh.

Samuel Klugarsh leaned across the table and clapped Dr. Prince on the shoulder. "A gentleman and a scholar!" he said. "Now, eat up. If you don't go into shock from the first spoonful it's clear sailing after that. Eat up now. Then we'll have a good chat.

25

I was getting sort of angry at Dr. Prince. When I had told him all about Hyperstellar Archaeology and Lemurian Mind Control methods, he thought it was fantasy. Now, Samuel Klugarsh, who, by his own admission couldn't even attain state twenty-six, was telling him the same stuff, and Dr. Prince was listening politely—just because Samuel Klugarsh was an adult. It bugged me.

"And of greatest importance," Samuel Klugarsh was saying, "is *Yojimbo's Japanese-English Dictionary*, which is actually a secret key to . . . Tell Doctor Prince what *Yojimbo's Japanese-English Dictionary* is a secret key to, lads."

Alan Mendelsohn took up the story. "You see, *Yojimbo's Japanese-English Dictionary* was compiled by Clarence Yojimbo, who was not really Japanese, but a Venusian, who had lived a long time in Lemuria. If you read the book backwards, counting only the second word in English in each entry, it makes a book of instructions in ancient Lemurian Mind Control methods."

"And what are those?" Dr. Prince asked.

"Well, it tells you how to control people and then objects, with your thoughts. That's as far as Leonard and I have gotten. We're learning to move objects by mental commands. That's what Lemurian Mind Control is all about."

"That is utter nonsense!" someone said. It was the biker—the motorcycle guy who had been listening during our whole conversation. "In fact," he said, "I've never heard anyone get anything so utterly turned around. You're as wrong as you can be."

Samuel Klugarsh turned in his chair. "And what do you know of such matters, you ruffian?"

"I know a great deal about such matters," the biker said. "In fact, I probably know more about these things than any person alive."

"Sir," said Samuel Klugarsh, "you evidently do not know to whom you are speaking. I have devoted half my life to the study of the lost and obscure arts and sciences, the civilizations of the vanished continents—Mu, Atlantis, Lemuria, Waka-Waka, and so forth—and especially the study of hitherto concealed and unknown powers of the mind. My name is Professor Samuel Klugarsh."

"And my name," said the motorcyclist, "is Clarence Yojimbo."

There was a silence. Alan Mendelsohn and I stared at the biker. There was something strange about his appearance. It was nothing obvious, but somehow he didn't look like anyone we had ever seen before. His hair and skin were almost the same color, a sort of bronze color. He was very big, and there was something strange about his eyes.

It was hard to pin down—he looked like an ordinary person, and he didn't.

"You'll have to prove that to me," Samuel Klugarsh finally said.

"You have sixteen dollars and forty-two cents in your pocket," the biker said. "Your underwear is blue with white stripes. There's a hole in your left sock, at the toe. In your refrigerator at home, there are six slices of garden variety pizza, which you intend to eat cold before you go to bed. The book you are reading every night in bed is called *Confessions of a Yugoslavian Streetcar Conductor*; you have gotten up to page 42. Tomorrow morning you plan to open your shop late, because you have to stop by the Motor Vehicle Bureau and pay a traffic fine for a ticket you got last April when you double-parked outside a doughnut shop. You own a cat named Willy, who happens to have four ears. You found him in an alley in Durham, North Carolina, but you tell people he's a Martian space-cat. Is any of this information incorrect?"

Samuel Klugarsh really looked astounded. "No," he stammered, "every word you've said is absolutely correct."

"And, have you ever seen me before in your life?" the biker asked.

"Never," Samuel Klugarsh said.

The biker bowed from his chair to the Knights of Power motorcycle club, who had been listening to this whole exchange. The bikers burst into applause, whistling and cheering. Clarence Yojimbo gestured for them to stop. "Thank you, gentlemen, thank you."

"Wait a minute," Dr. Prince said. "All you have proven is that you are a remarkable mind reader. Not that I doubt your word—if you say you're Clarence Yojimbo, I have no reason to doubt you—but, surprising as your mental feats may be, they don't prove you are who you say you are."

"A reasonable objection," Clarence Yojimbo said. "I will now put your doubts completely to rest." He pointed to the pocket of his motorcycle jacket. Spelled out in little metal studs was the name Clarence.

"Bravo! Bravo!" shouted the Knights of Power.

"And now . . ." Clarence Yojimbo said, and with a flourish, pulled out and flipped open his wallet. In a little plastic window was a driver's license. "Note the name," he said, and passed the open wallet around. The license was made out in the name of Clarence Yojimbo.

"Brilliant! Brilliant!" said the motorcycle club.

"But are you *the* Clarence Yojimbo? The one we've been reading about?" Alan Mendelsohn asked.

"I am that most excellent person," Clarence Yojimbo said.

"Then . . . then you're a Venusian!" I said.

"Not so loud! Not so loud!" Clarence Yojimbo said. "That's not something to shout about in a public restaurant."

"Shhhhh!" said the motorcycle club.

"Ordinarily, I'd never reveal myself like this," Clarence Yojimbo said. "The only reason I'm doing so is that I couldn't help overhearing your conversation—and you people have got everything so badly mixed up that I really had to take charge of the situation before you get into serious trouble. Besides, I've known that I was going to have to deal with these two boys since the old days in Lemuria."

"That's right!" Alan Mendelsohn said. "The book said that the ancient Lemurian sages predicted that Leonard and I were going to read about their deeds!"

"Read about them, and a good deal more," Clarence Yojimbo said. "But for now, let me clear up a few things. First of all, I will introduce my companions." He gestured to the motorcyclists, who had turned their attention to their bowls of Green Death chili again. "These good men are the last surviving members of the ancient Order of the Laughing Alligator. For the past few thousand years, that brotherhood has guarded the extraterrestrial secrets which all of you seem so interested in. These last surviving brothers—none of them under eight hundred years old—have been my constant companions and friends for the past few centuries." The Laughing Alligator brothers looked up from their chili and winked at us.

"Now, let's correct a few things," Clarence Yojimbo said. "Professor Klugarsh, the Hyperstellar Archaeology course was sold to you by an individual named Rodni Rubenstein, am I not correct?"

"Well, yes," Samuel Klugarsh said. "Ordinarily, I do my own research, but in this case . . ."

At this point, it suddenly started to sink in that we were sitting around talking to a Venusian. I felt the hair on the back of my neck stand up. My skin felt all tingly. I guess the Bermuda Triangle Chili Parlor, the Green Death chili, and everything were so unfamiliar that the addition of a supposed Venusian didn't really stand out as something exceptional right away. It seemed that the situation had crept up on everyone in the same way, because Dr. Prince was listening quietly, smoking his pipe, while Samuel Klugarsh and Clarence Yojimbo talked. Alan Mendelsohn was looking a little pale, but I couldn't tell if it was the combination of the Regular chili and the second half of the cigar he had started before the meal, or if the fact of Clarence Yojimbo's otherworldliness had finally hit him.

"You see," Clarence Yojimbo was saying, "Rodni Rubenstein is perhaps one of the most annoying investigators of extraterrestrial phenomena—along with Erik VonDankninny, who's just as bad. These fellows have almost the right idea, but they go about it all wrong. Rodni Rubenstein has the awful habit of tinkering around with the material he gets ahold of in order to make his arguments more convincing. What he did to my dictionary is just a shame."

"You mean that what these boys told me is false?" Samuel Klugarsh asked. "Do you mean that you cannot, by reading *Yojimbo's Japanese-English Dictionary* backwards, noting only the second word in English in each entry, discover the ancient thought control methods of old Lemuria?"

"Of course you can," said Clarence Yojimbo. "And if you multiply the area of the base of the Great Pyramid of Cheops by your grandmother's height in centimeters, add two, and take away today's market price of chopped liver, you'll get either pi or the distance from the earth to the sun—I forget which. It doesn't prove a thing. You can't use Earth methods to solve unEarthly problems. It's like trying to fix an automobile engine by giving it an aspirin—although there are some rare cases where that will work—anyway, you see what I mean."

"I see what's happening," Dr. Prince said.

It's about time, I thought.

Dr. Prince was staring at the steamy window. He had a funny expression—sort of a bitter smile. "I've lost my mind. It's strange that I didn't notice it coming on. Here I am, smoking my pipe and listening to a fellow have a conversation with a Venusian motorcyclist, just as though it were the most natural thing in the world. Here I am, sitting in a place where I've just eaten something called Green Death chili, with one of my patients who has classic paranoid fantasies, and I'm just going along with the whole thing as if it were all true. It even makes sense to me. I'm a very sick man."

It was obvious that Dr. Prince wasn't talking to any of us. He was just staring at the window, out of which you couldn't see a thing, and babbling on.

"I assure you, you're imagining none of this," Clarence Yojimbo said.

"Why should I believe you?" Dr. Prince said. "You're a figment of the imagination. You're not even a figment of my imagination. You're a figment of Leonard's imagination. Why should I believe a figment?" Dr. Prince was starting to cry.

"I think our colleague is a little upset," Samuel Klugarsh said.

"I agree," said Clarence Yojimbo. "Perhaps we should bring this evening's discussion to an end. I'll see to it that Doctor Prince gets home all right, and I'll administer a Lemurian substance that will cause him to forget everything he's heard. We can meet again at your shop tomorrow. There are some things we really have to clear up."

The brothers of the Laughing Alligator escorted Dr. Prince, who kept saying "Crazy as a coot! Crazy as a coot!" out of the Bermuda Triangle Chili Parlor. They hoisted him onto a motorcycle and roared off into the darkness. Samuel Klugarsh arranged with Alan Mendelsohn and me to meet at his book shop the following day, right after school.

Alan Mendelsohn and I walked back to the bus station. We didn't say much. Seeing Dr. Prince go nuts was a little upsetting for both of us.

We were in luck—a bus for West Kangaroo Park was just about to leave. It was getting pretty late, and we were afraid that our parents might have telephoned each other and discovered we were missing. As it turned out, we got back just in time. Both mothers said that they were just about to telephone.

I had a hard time getting to sleep that night. I kept going over the things that had happened in the Bermuda Triangle Chili Parlor.

In the morning, I got a telephone call from Dr. Prince before I left for school. "Leonard, I just wanted to let you know that I won't be able to meet with you next week," he said.

"Is anything wrong?" I asked.

"No, no, nothing is wrong. I just want to take some time off. I'm going to visit my sister in Lemuria—I mean Bermuda—I mean San Diego. I've been working too hard and I need a rest."

"Have a nice trip, Doctor Prince," I said.

"Waka Waka," Dr. Prince said.

26

We were the first kids out of Bat Masterson Junior High School when the bell rang. The bus rolled up, and we got on.

We half-walked, half-trotted from the bus station to Samuel Klugarsh's shop. The Laughing Alligator motorcycles were parked outside. In the front part of the shop, the brothers of the Laughing Alligator were leafing through the books and giggling. They winked and nodded to us as we came in. In the back of the shop, Samuel Klugarsh and Clarence Yojimbo were sitting on folding chairs. They were drinking hot chocolate with double marshmallows and whipped cream from paper containers. Apparently they had sent out to the Bermuda Triangle Chili Parlor.

"Ah, there you are, boys," Samuel Klugarsh said. "Clarence Yojimbo has only been here a little while. Your hot chocolate is still hot, although, I'm afraid the marshmallows have completely melted by this time." He offered us two of the cardboard containers.

I noticed that the cover was off the Test Your Brainpower machine. Apparently, Samuel Klugarsh had been testing Clarence Yojimbo's brainpower before we arrived. The tube in which the red liquid rose to show you how advanced you were had melted, and the red stuff had dribbled all over the front of the machine.

The file cabinet drawers were open, and Samuel Klugarsh's mimeographed courses were all over the place. Also, the old-time radios and other scientific equipment looked as though they had been given a workout. Samuel Klugarsh's polka-dot bow tie was crooked, and he had spilled some hot chocolate on his pink shirt.

"We've been going over some of Mr. Klugarsh's research and educational material," Clarence Yojimbo said. "I was able to point out quite a few things that will have to be corrected immediately, isn't that right, Sam?"

"Absolutely, yes sir, this very day, sir," Samuel Klugarsh said. "Can I run out and get you some more hot chocolate? A cheeseburger? The contents of my savings account? Havana cigars?"

"Thank you," Clarence Yojimbo said, "I don't require anything at this time. Why don't you just take a chair and rest? I have to discuss a few things with Alan and Leonard."

"Yes, sir. Thank you. I'll sit down, now. Thank you," Samuel Klugarsh said. He seemed to be trying very hard to be extra polite to Clarence Yojimbo.

"Now, boys, let me bring you up to date. It seems that our friend, Mr. Klugarsh, has made somewhat the same error as that of Rodni Rubenstein, and other psychic and extraterrestrial scholars. He's become aware of certain things, but doesn't understand their use or significance. It's a little like this: Suppose there was no such thing as an automobile, and you came upon a good-as-new 1961 Studebaker Lark, all gassed up and ready to go. You'd call everybody to come and marvel at your discovery—but instead of realizing that it was a machine which had the power to carry people from place to place, suppose you and everyone else thought the purpose of that 1961 Studebaker Lark was to sit in the front seat and play the radio. You'd have pretty much missed the point, don't you agree?"

"Sure," we said.

"Thank you for referring to me as your friend," Samuel Klugarsh said.

"Well this is what has happened to students of strange phenomena," Clarence Yojimbo said. "Erik VonDankninny somehow guessed that persons from other planets have been visiting the earth for many thousands of years—but then he mixes us up with pyramids, and cave paintings, and, of all things, the history of religion. Utter nonsense. And Rodni Rubenstein seems to have found out that in some places, large rocks, and so forth, can be moved by mental power—and he makes the assumption that this is something that Earth people should be able to do as well. Then he goes ahead and doctors certain books, like my dictionary, to support his ideas. All very shocking."

"Shocking," Samuel Klugarsh said.

"And our friend, Mr. Klugarsh . . ."

"Thank you," said Samuel Klugarsh.

". . . packages the stuff and sells it to people—believing, of course, that he is doing nothing wrong."

"I swear," said Samuel Klugarsh.

"But, you see, it is very wrong. It would only be foolish to discover a brand-new 1961 Studebaker Lark and mistake it for a machine for listening to the radio—but to encourage people to do Mind Control stunts is much more than foolish. It is very dangerous."

"Dangerous," said Samuel Klugarsh. "Now you boys listen to Mr. Yojimbo."

"But we didn't do anything evil," Alan Mendelsohn said.

"That's right," I said, "we were just having fun. We wouldn't have used our powers to hurt anyone."

"Except yourselves," Clarence Yojimbo said. "If you got the idea that all these powers were good for was tricks, then you'd be limited forever from ever finding out what their real uses were. You'd end up like . . ." He looked at Samuel Klugarsh, "like Rodni Rubenstein."

"Mr. Yojimbo, is that chair comfortable?" Samuel Klugarsh asked. "I have a nice easy chair at home. I could get it."

"I'm fine just like this," Clarence Yojimbo said. "Now I want to explain everything to these boys. You see, you are the first people, regular Earth people, ever to attain what Mr. Klugarsh calls state twenty-six at will. Other people have attained it, but only at certain moments, and by accident. Somehow, from Klugarsh's moronic instructions, you've learned how to turn it on and off like a light switch. Now, while it's perfectly true that a person in state twenty-six can, to some extent, transmit his thoughts, and get people and even objects to do his bidding, that's not really what state twenty-six is good for. The point of state twenty-six is not to make yourself into a radio transmitter—but to make yourself into a radio receiver. In other words, instead of trying to put out messages, you should be picking them up. It's much more useful, and much more interesting."

"Well, we had sort of begun to get bored with giving people commands," Alan Mendelsohn said.

"That's when we got into levitating bricks and such," I put in.

"And you would have gotten bored with levitating bricks, and even whole houses soon," Clarence Yojimbo said. "Some people never get bored with stupid games—but usually when a person gets to be able to do something pointless, like transmit his thoughts, he soon realizes just how dull it is. Now tell me the truth: Except for some boorish mischief, can you think of any good use for sending mental commands?"

We couldn't.

"But what about moving objects by mental power?" I asked. "That could be useful for putting up buildings and things like that, couldn't it?"

"Why do you suppose God gave us hands, and brains that can figure out how to do things?" the Venusian said. "You know, there are people who believe that the pyramids and the Easter Island statues were erected by some kind of magic power that the ancient people learned from extraterrestrials. The reason they think this is because it hurts their pride that they can't figure out how it was done. They don't want to believe that some ancient Easter Islander knew as much about engineering as they do. But none of that stuff about spacemen building the great monuments of the ancient world is true. All those things were done by humans using their human gifts—including, but not depending on, moments of inspiration or intuition, or state twenty-six as Sam here calls it."

"Now, I want to explain about Mu, and Atlantis, and

Lemuria, and Nafsulia, and Waka-Waka—all those lost continents. This is going to be a little tricky to understand, so feel free to ask questions as I go along. None of them were ever lost."

"You mean none of them ever existed?" I asked.

"All of them existed, and still do. They aren't exactly continents—but they exist. Oh, they're not called Waka-Waka or Atlantis—those are just made-up names for them—but they're real."

"Where are they?" Alan Mendelsohn asked.

"Here," Clarence Yojimbo said, "right here."

He was right. It was tricky to understand, and we said so.

"I'll explain. Maybe you've read about excavations of ancient cities—like Troy. After the archaeologists dig down and find the ancient city, sometimes they find that there's another still more ancient city underneath. Then they find that there's another city underneath that one— even more ancient. They find layers, levels. The so-called lost continents, or lost societies, are a little like that."

"Do you mean that if we dug straight down, we'd find Atlantis?" Alan Mendelsohn asked.

"If you dug straight down, you'd find the Hogboro Municipal Sewer," Clarence Yojimbo said. "To find Atlantis, you'd have to dig straight down within yourself."

"So Atlantis exists in our imagination—our memory?" I asked.

"If you like," Clarence Yojimbo said. "I prefer to believe that it exists outside us, but we can only find it by going inside."

"I'm getting confused," Alan Mendelsohn said.

"So am I," I said.

"I've been confused since last night," Samuel Klugarsh

said. "How about we break for a snack? I can run around the corner for some frozen yogurt for us and the Laughing Alligator brothers—by the way, how are they doing out there?"

We peeked into the front of the store. The brothers of the Laughing Alligator were taking turns reading a Scientology book to each other and cracking up laughing.

"Reynold and Hamilton will go with you to help bring back the yogurt," Clarence Yojimbo said. "It's a good idea—I'm getting dry from all this talking."

27

While Samuel Klugarsh was gone, Clarence Yojimbo went around the room tapping all the scientific gadgets. He seemed to be listening to the taps—he'd keep tapping until he was satisfied, and then move on to another machine. I couldn't hear any difference between the taps.

"Most of your instruments were out of adjustment," he said to Samuel Klugarsh when he returned. "I've got them pretty well tuned up for you. Just try not to move them around too much—they're pretty primitive and delicate.

"Now," Clarence Yojimbo continued, between bites of yogurt, "I'm going to explain to all of you about the so-called lost continents. It seems we weren't making much progress before, so I'm going to try to just blast right along, and maybe you'll get a general idea. People tend to believe only what they can see—that's perfectly natural and reasonable. But what if everybody saw in black and white and you could see colors? Chances are, no one would believe that colors existed. They might think you were crazy if you kept talking about colors. But the colors would exist just the same, even if not everybody could see them. Everybody with me so far?"

We were.

"Suppose I told you that I could see something that you couldn't see? Taking into account that I'm a Venusian, and have already demonstrated that I am able to know things which I have no way of knowing—like that fact that today Samuel Klugarsh's undershorts are white with little red hearts on them . . ."

"That's absolutely right!" Samuel Klugarsh said.

". . . would you be willing to concede, just for the sake of argument, that I can see things which ordinary Earth people can't see?"

"Yes."

"OK"

"That's reasonable."

"OK," Clarence Yojimbo continued. "Having granted that I am able to see things that you can't, and having noticed that I am really a nice guy, besides which, I have no reason to lie to you, are you willing to believe that, in addition to us four, there are others in this room?"

For some reason this idea struck me as sort of scary. I felt a shiver.

"In fact," Clarence Yojimbo said, "there are a whole lot of people in this room. There are some people about nine feet tall, sitting around and drinking cups of fleegix. There are also some people walking through here on their way to someplace else. There are also some people cooking. There are also some people making tables and chairs out of wood. There are also some people sleeping.

What's more, the people drinking fleegix can't see us or the people walking, the people cooking, the people working, or the people sleeping. The people walking can't see us or the people drinking fleegix, or the people cooking, or the people working, or the people sleeping. Are you starting to get the picture?"

"What's fleegix?" Alan Mendelsohn asked.

"It's a hot drink, similar to hot chocolate, usually served in a cup with two marshmallows and whipped cream," Clarence Yojimbo said. "But that's not the point. The point is that in the same space, there are at least six different bunches of people—or beings—doing different things, and not interfering with any of the other bunches of people—or beings."

"What has this got to do with lost continents?" Samuel Klugarsh wanted to know.

"Wait a minute!" Alan Mendelsohn said. "I think I've got it! Those places where the others are—drinking fleegix, walking, working, and so forth—those *are* the lost continents!"

"You've got it," Clarence Yojimbo said.

"But continents are places," Samuel Klugarsh said. "I've got at least fifteen books in the front of the shop that tell how there's proof that these continents used to exist. How did all those people get into that ghostlike state? Did they die, or what?"

"One of the reasons," Clarence Yojimbo said, "that you haven't got a bigger, more successful, mystical, occult book shop, is that you read all the books. What makes you think that the people I'm telling you about are in a ghostlike state, in limbo? What do you suppose they'd say if I appeared before them and told them that the three of you are sitting here, in the back of a book shop?"

"They'd think we were like ghosts?" Samuel Klugarsh said.

"Of course they would," Clarence Yojimbo said. "They can't see you; they can't hear you; they can't feel, smell, or taste you. If I could persuade them to take my word for your being here at all, the best they could do would be to assume that you were insubstantial, like spirits—but you're not, are you?"

Samuel Klugarsh scratched his head, "No, I'm really here."

"And they're really there," Clarence Yojimbo said. "If you go to some tribe in the Amazon River jungle and tell them all about Los Angeles, California, they're going to have a hard time believing you. Even if you show them pictures, the best they're going to be able to do is fix up their idea of Los Angeles, California, so that it fits in with their everyday experience."

"Mr. Yojimbo," Alan Mendelsohn said, "how come you can see all this stuff? Is it because you are a Venusian?"

"That's right," Clarence Yojimbo said. "Obviously, people from other planets are going to have extra powers that Earth people don't have. Anybody who has ever watched television knows that. But—and this is interesting—there has always been contact between these different, let's call them planes of existence. That's where all the stories about Atlantis and Mu and Lemuria and Nafsulia and Waka-Waka came from in the first place. People from this plane of existence have stumbled on information from one or more of the other ones. Sometimes they even get a quick look."

"How does that happen?" I asked.

"Well, it's like this," Clarence Yojimbo said. "Right now, I'm sort of tuned in on Nafsulia; that's the plane I described on which people are walking from one place to another. It so happens that this room is right in the middle of the main street of Nafsu City. It's four o'clock in the afternoon on a business day—the Nafsulians have the same sort of time sequences as you do—so hundreds and thousands of people have passed through this room all day long. Not one of them has noticed that he or she is walking through a room. Maybe one in five thousand will have a funny sensation, just for a second, while walking through here. Maybe one in ten thousand will have a funny sensation and pay any attention to it. Maybe one in a hundred thousand will suspect they have come into contact with something not visible in their ordinary world—but they won't quite know what it is. One in a million, or fewer, will actually have a pretty good idea of what's going on when they walk through this room—and maybe one in ten million, at the most, will actually get a glimpse of us. And that one in ten million won't be able to glimpse us every time he comes this way. It will just happen at random, maybe a few times in his life. Now, one Nafsulian in a hundred million will be able to really see what's going on here, just as clearly as I can see all of them. If that Nafsulian tells the other Nafsulians what he's seen, they'll take him to the booby hatch. He's a pretty intelligent fellow, so he doesn't say anything.

"Now that intelligent Nafsulian gets a look, one day, at—let's say, the Bermuda Triangle Chili Parlor. Chili is unknown in Nafsulia, although they have all the ingredients to make it. He watches the owner of the Bermuda Triangle Chili Parlor make up a batch of Green Death chili. He sees how it's done, and he makes some too. The other Nafsulians love it. But they also know that nothing of the kind has ever existed or been thought of in Nafsulia. They want to know how the fellow who made it got the idea. He tells them they made chili like that in Hogboro. Where's Hogboro? It isn't on any Nafsulian map. Nobody ever heard of it. Yet there's the chili. It had to come from somewhere. Are you getting the picture?"

"Yes," I said. "The Nafsulians assume that if Hogboro doesn't exist now, it must have existed in the past. Since it doesn't exist anymore, something must have happened to it."

"So they make up a story," Alan Mendelsohn broke in, "about how Hogboro used to be a mighty continent, but it sank into the ocean."

"That's it exactly!" Clarence Yojimbo said. "Now, why am I bothering to tell you all this?"

"Because you like us?" Samuel Klugarsh said.

"Because I like you, and something more important," Clarence Yojimbo said. "A while ago, I told Alan and Leonard that they were the first Earth people ever to be able to turn what you call state twenty-six on and off at will. I also told them that using that power to do simple tricks was wrong because it would cause them to be unable to find out what that power was really good for.

"What that power is good for is to enable a person to see and hear what is happening on the other planes of existence. That's how Venusians do it. Any person equipped with what you call state twenty-six can learn to travel in and out of the various parallel planes of existence. Remember, I said that some people have always been able to experience state twenty-six at random moments. Those are the people who get little blips from the other planes of existence. Even the guy who discovered Green Death chili couldn't do such a thing at will. But these two boys can learn to do it just the way I do."

"By the way, Mr. Yojimbo," Alan Mendelsohn asked, "how exactly did you get to Earth?"

"A good question," Clarence Yojimbo said. "I come from the sixth existential plane on Venus. To get from the sixth existential plane on Venus to the Waka-Waka plane on Earth is as easy as taking a bus to West Kangaroo Park where you guys live. Then equipped with what you call state twenty-six, I can come from the Waka-Waka plane directly to this one. If I want to, I can get back to my home plane on Venus in about an hour and twenty minutes—which I don't want to do, because they're having a terrific snowstorm there right now."

"Do you mean to say we can do that too?" I asked.

"When you learn how," Clarence Yojimbo said.

"How do we learn how?"

"Read my book."

28

"Your book? Do you mean *Yojimbo's Japanese-English Dictionary*?" Alan Mendelsohn asked.

"That's the only book I ever wrote," Clarence Yojimbo said. "It explains, step by step, how to observe and even visit other planes of existence."

"But you said that following the instructions in the book was wrong," I said.

"It's wrong if you read the book backwards, noting only the second word in English in each entry," Clarence Yojimbo said. "That was the idea of that so-called scholar, Rodni Rubenstein. The right way to read the book is front to back, using The Key—then you get the instructions in Interplanar Existential Communication."

"Good Lord, how I admire this man!" Samuel Klugarsh said.

"The Key?" Alan Mendelsohn and I asked.

"The Key that comes with the book. Didn't you sell

157

them a copy of The Key with the book?" Clarence Yojimbo asked Samuel Klugarsh.

"I never heard of The Key," Samuel Klugarsh said. "All
I ever saw was the dictionary. That's all Mr. Rubenstein
sold me along with the course in Hyperstellar Archaeology."

"Well, you've got to have a Key—otherwise, the book is
no good," Clarence Yojimbo said.

"Where can we get a Key?" Alan Mendelsohn asked.

"It so happens, I've got one with me," Clarence Yojimbo said. "I'd really like to give it to you, but they're
very expensive to produce. The Laughing Alligator
brothers and I have expenses to meet, you see—I mean,
even a Venusian needs money to get around. There's gas
for the motorcycles, and food, and all sorts of things."

"Could you sell us The Key?" Alan Mendelsohn asked.

"Well, yes," Clarence Yojimbo said. "That hadn't occurred to me—I mean, I'm really interested in your de-
veloping your powers to their highest potential—but that
would be the best way."

"How much would you want for The Key?" I asked.
There was something strangely familiar about all this.

"Let's see," Clarence Yojimbo said. "The last time I
sold a copy of The Key, it was to Rodni Rubenstein. I
charged him, now let me see . . ." Clarence Yojimbo
took a little notebook out of his jacket pocket and
thumbed through it. "Ah! Here it is. I sold him the dictionary and The Key for six thousand dollars."

"We could never pay six thousand dollars," I said.

"Of course not," Clarence Yojimbo said, "and this is entirely different. All I want from you boys is enough for the
Laughing Alligators and me to get to New York City—you
probably didn't know that we've got a folk-singing group.

We sing Venusian and Waka-Wakian folk songs, and we've got an offer to do a week at a folk club in New York. All we'll need, is, let me see . . ." He dug a pencil out of his pocket and did some figuring in his notebook. "One hundred forty-two dollars and fifty cents—how's that sound?"

"Like six thousand," I said.

"Really, I couldn't do it for a penny less," Clarence Yojimbo said. "What's more, we have to start out tomorrow if we're going to get to New York in time. I was planning to maybe go back to the sixth existential plane of Venus tonight, and see if I could borrow the money from my brother—but I really don't want to, with the snowstorm and all. Besides, my brother is mad at me because I haven't paid him back the money I borrowed for the motorcycles."

"I just don't know where we'd get a hundred and forty-two fifty," I said.

"My comic collection is worth a lot more than that," Alan Mendelsohn said, "but I don't know where I could sell it fast."

"William Lloyd Floyd at Morrie's Bookstore buys comics," Samuel Klugarsh said. "Maybe he would be willing to make a fast deal."

"I'll tell you what," Clarence Yojimbo said, "I'll take a chance. I won't go to the sixth existential plane of Venus tonight. Instead, I'll wait until tomorrow, and meet you here at two o'clock sharp. Then, if you've been able to raise the money, we'll leave for New York straight from here. If you can't do it, I'll go to see my brother, and we'll just have to break the speed laws getting to New York the following day. Fair enough?"

We said we guessed so.

"OK, we'll meet tomorrow," Clarence Yojimbo said. "Now I've got to go and rehearse with the Laughing Alligators." He headed for the door. "Waka Waka!" he said.

"Waka Waka," we all replied.

29

Something I had never done before was cut school. It was easier than I had ever suspected. At lunchtime, we just walked out. I figured none of my teachers would report me absent, since they never noticed me anyway. In Alan's case, they would be so grateful he wasn't there, they weren't likely to look into the matter. In any event, even if we got into trouble later, this was important.

The tricky part was sneaking into Alan Mendelsohn's basement, where he had his treasured comic collection stuffed into two big cartons, waiting by the door. His mother was home, so we had to sneak by her. Luckily, she was vacuuming, and the noise covered any sounds we might have made. The cartons were large and very heavy. I could hardly walk with mine. Each of them contained over a thousand comics. By the time we hoisted them onto the Hogboro bus and flopped into our seats, we were sweating and out of breath.

I felt sort of bad that Alan Mendelsohn was putting up all the money for The Key to *Yojimbo's Japanese-English Dictionary*. He said that this was no time to quibble over details—besides, he thought that after we had gotten good at traveling to other existential planes, we could sell the whole works to Samuel Klugarsh. And he made me promise to go around with him and help him rebuild his collection when we had some time. I told him I would be happy to do that.

When the bus pulled into Hogboro, we dragged our cartons off and started out for Morrie's Bookstore. It was hard work. The cartons were too big to get a good hold of, and Alan Mendelsohn kept telling me not to let my carton drop—he didn't want any of the comics to get crumpled. We had to stop and rest twice in every block.

We finally got to Morrie's Bookstore. We opened the door and pushed the cartons of comics across the floor to William Lloyd Floyd's desk.

"What are those, comics?" he said.

"Yeah," Alan Mendelsohn panted. "We heard that you buy collections."

"I love comics!" William Lloyd Floyd said. "Let me see them!"

He dove at the cartons hungrily. He pulled out handfuls of comic books, and whistled, and hummed, and talked to himself. "Wow! *Fantastic Eleven* Number 6—I've always wanted that one! Hey, you've got a complete run of *The Avenging Chicken*, including Number 1. This is a great collection! Oh look! *Bloody War Stories!* That's really great!"

I never really understood why some people get so excited about comics. I mean, they're all right when there's nothing else, but William Lloyd Floyd was really going out of his mind over Alan Mendelsohn's collection.

"Oooo! Ooo! *Superduck!* I love *Superduck!* These for sale? Tell you what—I'll give you ten dollars for each box, OK?"

Alan Mendelsohn didn't say anything.

"Oh! Oh! *The Avenging Chipmunk!* I've never seen *The Avenging Chipmunk*; it's really rare. Oh! I've got to have this."

William Lloyd Floyd was sitting on the floor pulling handfuls of comics out of the two cartons. Alan Mendelsohn looked completely cool. I was sweating. I was wondering how Alan Mendelsohn would get the price from ten dollars for each carton to one hundred forty-two fifty.

"Oh! *Dr. Unpleasant!*" William Lloyd Floyd shouted. "You've got every issue of *Dr. Unpleasant!* Oh, I really have to have this!"

At the picnic table in the back of the store, the Mad Guru was playing three simultaneous games of chess against himself. Alan Mendelsohn was totally relaxed. William Lloyd Floyd was nearly crazy.

"Would you sell me just the series of *Dr. Unpleasant?*" he asked.

"The whole thing," Alan Mendelsohn said.

"OK, the whole thing," William Lloyd Floyd said. "Oh look! *The Mad Goon! Nobody* has *The Mad Goon!* If I give you two and a half cents per book, there's about two thousand here—how about fifty bucks?"

"No," Alan Mendelsohn said.

"OK, a hundred," William Lloyd Floyd said.

"Did you notice that I've got *Roosman the Barbarian,* Numbers 1 through 12?" Alan Mendelsohn asked.

"One hundred and ten dollars, and that's my final offer!" William Lloyd Floyd said.

"Let's go, Leonard," Alan Mendelsohn said, and he began gathering up the comics.

"Wait!" William Lloyd Floyd shouted. I'll give you my top price, nine and one-quarter cents a book—that comes to a hundred and eighty-five dollars. I haven't got a cent more than that to my name."

"Throw in the potato?" Alan Mendelsohn asked.

"What? My brass potato from the moon? It's worth millions!"

"I've also got here, *Wonder Wombat* from the nineteen thirties, in perfect condition," Alan Mendelsohn said.

"*Wonder Wombat?*" William Lloyd Floyd shouted. "Show me."

Alan Mendelsohn dug out a copy of an old comic in a plastic envelope. "It's the first issue," he said, showing it to William Lloyd Floyd.

"Take the potato!" William Lloyd Floyd said, and he slipped the leather thong off his neck. He rummaged around in his desk drawer and pants pockets, and borrowed six dollars from the Mad Guru, finally coming up with one hundred and eighty-five dollars.

Alan Mendelsohn and I walked out of the store with enough to pay for The Key to Interplanar Existential Communication, with forty-two fifty left over and a brass potato from the moon.

"The difference between that man and me," Alan Mendelsohn said, "is that I am a connoisseur, and he is a fanatic."

30

"Hey! Alan and Leonard!" Clarence Yojimbo seemed glad to see us. "We were worried you wouldn't . . . I mean . . . I'm glad to see that you . . . uh, did you get the money?"

"Sure," Alan Mendelsohn said.

"See?" Clarence Yojimbo shouted to the Laughing Alligators, who were milling around inside Samuel Klugarsh's bookstore. "What did I tell you?"

We noticed a bunch of bags, suitcases, and things that looked like they might contain guitars and banjos, piled just inside the door of the bookstore.

"The Laughing Alligator brothers were worried that we might not be able to go to New York," Clarence Yojimbo said. "See, you guys? It's all right. I told you so," he shouted to the bikers.

"Mr. Yojimbo, about The Key," Alan Mendelsohn said.

"Oh, yes—The Key—I've got it right here." Clarence Yojimbo pulled a thick manila envelope out of his leather jacket. "That will be one hundred forty-two dollars and fifty cents," he said. "We'll forget about the Venusian sales tax."

Clarence Yojimbo handed Alan Mendelsohn the envelope, and Alan Mendelsohn handed him one hundred forty-two dollars and fifty cents.

"Well, that's that," the Venusian said. "Look, I hate long good-byes. Me and the Laughing Alligators will just split, OK?" He started for the door.

"Wait!" I shouted. "How do we use this Key?"

"All the instructions are in the envelope," Clarence Yojimbo said. "Bye." He went through the door, followed by the brothers of the Laughing Alligator.

All this time, Samuel Klugarsh hadn't said anything. He had just stood around in various corners. Now he stepped forward. "Do you boys mind if I have a look at The Key?" he said.

The front door opened, and Clarence Yojimbo stuck his head in. "And don't show that thing to Samuel Klugarsh," he said. "Don't even open it here. Just get it home where it will be safe. Bye again!" and he was gone.

"Just a peek," Samuel Klugarsh said.

"We've got to be going now, Mr. Klugarsh," I said.

"Just let me feel it," Samuel Klugarsh said.

"Let's get out of here," Alan Mendelsohn said.

When we got out into the street, we could still hear the roar of the motorcycles of the Laughing Alligators and Clarence Yojimbo, and Venusian, and we could still see the blue smoke from their engines as they headed for the interstate highway.

We headed straight for the bus station. Neither of us spoke until we were locked in Alan Mendelsohn's bedroom.

Alan Mendelsohn put the manila envelope on his desk and flopped on his bed. I sat down in Alan's desk chair, having pulled it back so both of us could look at the envelope. Neither of us talked for a long time.

"Well, we've got The Key," I said, finally.

"Yes, it's right there in that envelope," Alan Mendelsohn said.

"Communicating with other planes of existence should be very exciting," I said.

"Yes," Alan Mendelsohn said.

"It sure cost a lot of money," I said.

"Sure did," Alan Mendelsohn said.

"Do you think it's going to work?" I asked.

"There's only one way to find out," Alan Mendelsohn said.

"Right," I said. "Go ahead. Open it."

"No. You," Alan Mendelsohn said.

"You paid for it," I said.

"You open it," Alan Mendelsohn said.

There was something heavy and stiff inside the envelope. I carefully undid the little metal clasp and peeled back the glued flap. Then I slid out a whole bunch of sheets of smooth, thin brown cardboard with lots of little rectangular slits cut in them. There was a typewritten sheet too:

INSTRUCTIONS

In this envelope you will find a whole bunch of sheets of smooth, thin brown cardboard with lots of little rectangular slits in them. This is The Key to *Yojimbo's Japanese-English Dictionary*. You will notice that each sheet has two numbers on it—one red and one black. The black number tells you in what order to use the sheet—1, 2, 3, 4, 5, 6, and so forth. The red number tells you which page in the dictionary the sheet corresponds to—for example, page 146 (the red number) corresponds to sheet 1 (the black number).

The sheets are exactly the same size as the pages of the dictionary. Place the appropriate sheet carefully over the page, with the numbers facing you, and certain words and phrases will appear in the slits. Copy these down in a notebook—this will create your copy of The Key. Be sure to hide the sheets and the dictionary in separate places, so no one can decipher the secret message in the dictionary, even if they find one or the other. Also, guard the notebook with the deciphered Key with your life. Best of luck. Burn this.

"Well, let's get started," Alan Mendelsohn said. He got a fresh notebook. "You read, and I'll write," he said.

I put sheet number 1 (the black number) carefully over page 146 (the red number) and read off the words visible through the slits to Alan Mendelsohn, who copied them down in the notebook. We went fairly fast, not really paying too much attention to what we were reading and copying. When we were all done, Alan Mendelsohn turned to the beginning of his notebook and read aloud.

31

THE KEY TO INTERPLANAR EXISTENTIAL COMMUNICATION

For centuries people have believed that once there existed continents, places, and whole civilizations, now lost through natural catastrophe or intervention from inhabitants of other planets. This is not so.

In fact there are a number of parallel planes of existence, which are happening right now under, over, and around us—but we can't see them. Only in moments of especially high intuition, or inspiration, can we be aware of these planes of existence—which, for purposes of reference, we will call by the names of the traditional lost continents: Atlantis, Mu, Lemuria, Nafsulia, Waka-Waka, and so forth.

The special mental attitude, or state of intuition, is sometimes called state twenty-six by modern psychic researchers—so we will use that term as well.

Ordinary people cannot experience state twenty-six just by wishing to do so. It is something that just happens at random—and sometimes, when it happens, we get a glimpse of one of the "lost continents" of extraplanar existence.

What this key, or guide, cannot do is tell anyone how to achieve state twenty-six. All that can be done is to point out the fact that there are certain physical places on this Earth where it appears to be easier to make contact (state twenty-six being present) with the other planes. There follows a list of such places. The experimenter is advised to go to one or all of them—and wait for state twenty-six to happen. Good Luck—Clarence Yojimbo, Venusian and folk singer.

32

"That's it? That's it? That's all it says for my one hundred and forty-two dollars? We've been swindled again!" Alan Mendelsohn was really worked up.

"Look," I said, "It might not be so bad. After all, Clarence Yojimbo said that we're the first people ever to be able to go in and out of state twenty-six at will. The least we should do is try it out."

"Well, I don't see that we've got much choice," Alan Mendelsohn said. "I mean, he's got my money, and he's on his way to New York with his motorcycling folk singers—but, boy this has me mad—this isn't even as interesting as those courses Klugarsh sold us."

"Which taught us to get into state twenty-six," I reminded Alan Mendelsohn, "and to transmit our thoughts."

"You may be right," Alan Mendelsohn said. "Let's have a look at the list."

The list was on a single page of the notebook. It said:

PLACES SUITABLE FOR INTERPLANAR CONTACT

Giant rock, Muhu, Estonia
Rampa's Kosher Deli, Heiho, Tibet
Mukerjee's Shoe Shop, Nainpur, India
Paleolithic formation, Tjidjulang, Java
Dead Flamingo Lake, Loitokitok, Kenya
Public library, Popovo, Bulgaria
42 Wishnik Street, Krasnik, Poland
Central sewer, Gruben, Switzerland
MacTavish's Fast Food and Opticians,
    Findhorn, Scotland
Akanakuji Temple, Ichikawa, Japan
Hergeschleimer's Oriental Gardens,
    Hogboro, United States
Meteor crater, Fort Simpson,
    Northwest Territories

"We appear to be in luck," Alan Mendelsohn said. "The only location in the United States is right here in Hogboro."

"That's right," I said. "The next closest spot is the meteor crater in Fort Simpson, Northwest Territories, Canada."

"Where is this Hergeschleimer's Oriental Gardens?" Alan Mendelsohn wanted to know.

"Search me. I've never heard of it," I said. "How about checking the telephone book?"

We looked for Hergeschleimer's Oriental Gardens in the Hogboro telephone directory. There was nothing under *Hergeschleimer*, *Gardens*, or *Oriental* in the yellow or white pages.

"It could be Hergeschleimer's Oriental Gardens doesn't have a phone," I said.

Alan Mendelsohn remembered a book he'd bought in a bookstore in The Bronx when he heard his family was moving to Hogboro. He dug out a cardboard carton from the back of his closet, and rummaged around in it. He came up with a tattered old paperback. "This is a tourist guide to Hogboro," he said, "published in 1932. Let's see if it mentions Hergeschleimer's Oriental Gardens." We looked in the index and table of contents. We looked at the map of Hogboro with little pictures of monuments and places of interest. There was nothing about Hergeschleimer's Oriental Gardens.

Alan Mendelsohn tossed the book onto my lap. "I'm really disgusted," he said. "There's no such place as Hergeschleimer's Oriental Gardens."

I looked at the book. The cover was printed in yellow and black. *Tourist Guide to Hogboro*, it said. The rest of the cover was taken up with a picture of a bunch of postcards. The postcards were all together in a pile, and you could only really make out four or five of them—the rest were covered by other postcards. At the bottom of each postcard, in the narrow white margin, was printed whatever the postcard showed, the War Memorial, City Hall, Fleegle Street at Night, and one of the partially covered postcards bore the lettering ——hleimer's Oriental Gardens.

"Hey, look at this!" I shouted.

Alan Mendelsohn looked at the cover. He scrunched up his face and peered at it from one inch away. There wasn't much doubt that ——hleimer's Oriental Gardens would say Hergeschleimer's Oriental Gardens, if the postcard covering it were moved away.

"So it does exist!" Alan Mendelsohn shouted. "But why doesn't the book mention it? It's on the cover."

We went through the book again, page by page. Nowhere was there any mention of Hergeschleimer's Oriental Gardens.

"Look at this," Alan Mendelsohn said, pointing to the copyright page. "This book was first printed in 1932, and reprinted in 1951. If you look closely at the pictures of postcards on the cover, you'll notice that all the cars are old-time nineteen twenties types."

"So you think that Hergeschleimer's Oriental Gardens may have ceased to exist sometime between 1932 and 1951?" I asked.

"It looks that way," Alan Mendelsohn said, "but the *place* is still there. My guess is that it's the place that makes the interplanar communication possible—not what's in the place. We have to find out where Hergeschleimer's Oriental Gardens *were*!

He was starting to cheer up and get interested again, now that we had some detective work to do.

The following day was spent trying to find out where Hergeschleimer's Oriental Gardens (whatever they were) had been. None of our teachers knew anything about them. My parents didn't remember ever having heard of them. The school library was no help, and neither was the branch of the public library. We called the *Hogboro Tribune*—they didn't know either. We were stuck. Then my father had a good suggestion. "Why don't you ask Uncle Boris?"

Uncle Boris had been a taxi driver once, and he was a sort of amateur Hogboro historian. He was more likely to know about Hergeschleimer's Oriental Gardens than anybody.

I phoned Alan Mendelsohn, and told him that I was going to arrange for us to eat supper at my grandparents' house the next night. There was no point to telephoning Uncle Boris to ask about Hergeschleimer's Oriental Gardens, because he had a terror of telephones. You had to see him in person.

33

Eating supper at my grandparents' house is a unique experience. First of all, the Old One believes that people shouldn't eat regular meals three times a day. She thinks that's unhealthy. She thinks you should eat something whenever you're hungry. This means that the people who live in the apartment just wander into the kitchen whenever they want, and take some food, and eat it there, or eat it while walking around, or settle down someplace and eat. The Old One is almost constantly in the kitchen, which is surprising when you consider that she believes everything ought to be eaten raw—so there's no actual cooking. I don't think she even has a stove—I know I've never seen one in use in her kitchen. But she has blenders, juicers, mixers, a grain mill, and two refrigerators. When she has all the electric equipment going at once, and the two refrigerators humming, it sounds like a shipyard, and the lights flicker throughout the rest of the apartment house.

She had a really interesting soup the night Alan Mendelsohn and I came for supper. It had ground-up cherries, and celery, and raw buckwheat groats in it, and a lot of other stuff I couldn't figure out. She also gave us something called tsampa that Madame Zelatnowa had made. It was OK. As usual there was a salad with everything in the world in it, and big gobs of homemade yogurt on top. She also served bean sprouts with sesame seeds and garlic and vinegar. Alan Mendelsohn liked that best. I'm not saying that I'd like to eat at the Old One's house every day—but it isn't bad—and I do feel sort of good for hours after I've eaten every time I go there. Alan Mendelsohn had three helpings of everything.

Just as we were having our dessert of unbaked sesame, honey, coconut, carob, vegetable-protein cookies and cranberry juice, Uncle Boris walked in. He helped himself to a big bowl of raw oats with cashew nuts and carrot syrup and sat down at the kitchen table with us. "Hello boys," he said. "How's the psychic investigation?"

"That's what we came to talk to you about," I said. "You see, we met this Venusian . . ."

"No kidding!" Uncle Boris said. "A Venusian! That's really interesting. I met a Saturnian once, but we never got to be friends. He kept trying to eat my wristwatch. Was this Venusian friendly?"

"He was very friendly," I said. "He sold us a Key to *Yojimbo's Japanese-English Dictionary* that decodes instructions for getting in touch with parallel planes of existence—like invisible worlds. In order to make contact, we have to find a place called Hergeschleimer's Oriental Gardens, but it seems to have vanished. We can't find anyone who knows where it is, or was. We were hoping you'd be able to help us."

"Sure, I remember Hergeschleimer's Oriental Gardens," Uncle Boris said.

Alan Mendelsohn and I couldn't help jumping up and down in our chairs, like little kids.

"I used to go there a lot, years ago," my uncle continued. "It was really nice. You see, Lance Hergeschleimer was a fine man. He was a traveler and a botanist and a collector of wonderful things. His garden was a combination park, museum of rare tropical and Asiatic plants, and a nice place to have tea. He must have been very rich, because the place went on and on, and he had planted big trees, full-grown ones, from all sorts of distant places. Just getting them here alive and well must have cost a fortune. There were statues made of bronze and stone too—Buddhas and scenes of Asian village life. He had Japanese sand gardens and little teahouses and pagodas. Oh, it was a wonderful place to go for a walk, years ago. You know, I made a movie of that place. Would you like to see it?"

We said we would like to see it very much, but did Uncle Boris happen to remember where Hergeschleimer's Oriental Gardens had been?

"You know, I've been trying to remember that," he said. "It wasn't right in town—but somewhere out in the country—you had to take a long, long streetcar ride to get there. Maybe it will come back to me when we're watching the film."

We followed Uncle Boris to his bedroom, which looked more like a storeroom. There were stacks and piles and mounds of all sorts of things—books, geological specimens, camera equipment, stuffed birds, hiking equipment, bundles of letters, clothing, paintings, tools, everything. Uncle Boris began dragging large cardboard cartons out of his closet. They were full of reels of movie film. On the side of each carton, Uncle Boris had written in black crayon the titles of the films in the box. He dragged out five or six cartons, and finally found the one with a film called *Hergeschleimer's Oriental Gardens, 1939.*

Uncle Boris was pretty old. He wasn't my regular uncle—like my father's brother or my mother's brother. I think he was the Old One's brother—or maybe he was the Old One's uncle. She called him Uncle Boris. He talked with an accent.

"Now," he said, "let's get the projector set up in the dining room, and we'll have a look at this film."

The very first shot in the film was a picture of a street sign. You could read the names of both cross streets, Nussbaum Street and Utopia Avenue.

"Those are out near my house!" I shouted.

"Well, I told you Hergeschleimer's Oriental Gardens were out in the country," Uncle Boris said. "When this film was taken, West Kangaroo Park did not exist. It was all woods and dairy farms and Hergeschleimer's Oriental Gardens—now watch the film."

The camera panned from the street sign to a big neon sign on a tall post. The sign wasn't turned on—it was daytime, but there were painted letters behind the neon tubes, HERGESCHLEIMER'S ORIENTAL GARDENS. There was no doubt—we now knew where the Oriental Gardens were located.

Then we saw pictures of beautiful trees and flowering plants. There were neat gravel paths leading among the wonderful trees and bushes. Then we saw Uncle Boris, looking a lot younger, dressed in light brown suit with a straw hat, one of those flat ones, and spats! He had to explain to us about spats—they're like leggings, only they cover just part of your shoe. That didn't make any sense to us. Uncle Boris said they were snappy. He also had a tie with a palm tree on it. He said it was hand painted. Uncle Boris, in his suit and straw hat and spats and hand-painted tie, walked straight toward the camera, which didn't move. The last thing you saw was his nose. Then the movie showed more of the beautiful plants, and a pond. Then you saw Uncle Boris again, this time in a light blue suit, with different spats and a different hand-painted tie—same straw hat—walking into the camera again. Then you saw the gardens. Then you saw a black-and-white photograph in a little golden frame hanging in the leaves of some strange plant. You couldn't see what the picture was of because of the reflections in the glass—it looked like a person, or people. Then you saw Uncle Boris, in still another suit, spats, and hand-painted tie, walking into the camera. Then foliage. Then another black-and-white photograph hanging among the leaves. You still couldn't see what the picture showed, but you could see it was different from the first. Then Uncle Boris. Then foliage. Then a statue of a Buddha. Then foliage. Then black-and-white photos in little golden frames. Then foliage. It went on and on. It was strangely interesting. Well, it wasn't interesting—but it was nice to look at. It was restful. Uncle Boris wouldn't explain why the different suits or what was in the black-and-white photos. "It's a work of art," he said. "You don't have to know what it means."

34

It was Saturday morning—the next day. Alan Mendelsohn and I started off on foot for Nussbaum Street and Utopia Avenue, right after breakfast. It was a long walk—it took almost an hour to get there.

Utopia Avenue is one of those big streets—a highway almost. Cars travel fairly fast, and the sides of the road are lined with chain stores and discount houses—Shoe Monster, MacTavish's Pickle-Burgers, Do-it-Yourself Swimming Pools, Intergalactic House of Waffles, and lots of gas stations. No sidewalks, of course—we walked along in the gutter with cars zooming past us.

At the intersection, we found a deserted diner, an auto muffler place, a gas station, and a little junkyard. None of it looked anything like Uncle Boris's movie. In the film, the whole area had been green and countrylike. Now it was all built up and dirty and noisy and smelling of automobile exhaust.

There was a tangle of old trees and bushes behind the junkyard—most of them looked dead.

"Do you suppose that could have been Hergeschleimer's Oriental Gardens?" I asked Alan Mendelsohn.

"It looks like our best bet," he said. "Let's go over and find out."

We crossed the road—that was hairy, with all the cars whizzing by. As we entered the junkyard gate, a very old German shepherd walked stiffly over to us and barked. It was more like a cough. We could see that he had very few teeth.

"Pretend you're afraid of him!" someone shouted. We saw that it was a little fat guy who had just come out of a little shack. "Please, otherwise his feelings will be hurt."

"Pretend we're afraid?" I asked.

"C'mon, do it," said the little fat guy. "It'll make him feel good."

I felt a little silly. "Oh, please don't bite me!" I said to the dog, who was yawning.

"Hey mister, call off this vicious dog!" Alan Mendelsohn said.

"That's enough, Fafner," the little fat guy called out. "Let them come in."

The dog staggered back to the car seat he'd been sleeping on, and crashed down onto it.

"Thanks for cooperating," the little fat guy said. "Fafner is pretty old, but I don't want him to feel useless. My name is Noel Wallaby. What can I do for you?"

"We wanted to know if this place was ever Hergeschleimer's Oriental Gardens," I said.

"My goodness," Noel Wallaby said, "I didn't think anybody remembered Hergeschleimer's Oriental Gardens—especially not anybody your age. Yes, this was where the teahouse stood, and behind us, where you see that sort of jungle-looking place, that was where the gardens began."

"His uncle has a movie of the gardens," Alan Mendelsohn said. "Whatever happened to them?"

"Well, this part of town started to get developed," Noel Wallaby said, "lots of cars and houses and factories—and airplanes flying overhead. They all created pollution, and a lot of the plants and trees, which were tropical and sort of delicate, just died. Then Mr. Hergeschleimer disappeared, and the place just sort of fell apart. You can still follow some of the paths, and some of the trees are still alive, though not at this time of the year. Do you boys want to go over the back fence and walk around?"

We did.

"OK, just be careful back there. If you get lost, holler for Fafner. He'll come back there and lead you out. And be sure to be back by 1 P.M.—that's when I close on Saturdays."

Alan Mendelsohn and I climbed over the fence at the back of the junkyard and into the ruins of Hergeschleimer's Oriental Gardens. Just after the fence there were a lot of beaten-up bushes and garbage, tall grass and dead weeds. We had a little trouble crashing through all that. Then things opened up a bit, although the grass and weeds were still pretty high. We found a gravel path and followed it.

"This must have been great once," Alan Mendelsohn said.

We followed the path through avenues of huge trees. Some of the trees were dead, and some of them had fallen. A few lay across the path, and we had to scramble over them. We came upon little clearings. In one of them a stone statue of a Buddha was almost hidden by weeds.

We found a little lake where a few wild geese that still hadn't flown south were swimming.

We went a long way. The noise of cars on Utopia Avenue was far behind us, barely heard.

We really liked Hergeschleimer's Oriental Gardens—or what remained of them. For a while, we actually forgot all about what we had come for, all about making contact with a parallel plane of existence. The ruined gardens were so interesting that we just wanted to walk around and enjoy them. We sat on a big rock and watched the Canada geese for a long time.

"Well, we're here," I said.

"Yeah," Alan Mendelsohn said.

"This is supposed to be a place where we can make contact with another plane of existence," I said.

"If we go into state twenty-six," Alan Mendelsohn said.

"Yeah," I said.

"Well, do you want to do it?"

"We might as well—I mean, that's what we came here for."

"Do you want to do this one at a time, so the other one can sort of watch out for you, or both at once?"

I thought it over. "Both at once," I said.

We closed our eyes and went into state twenty-six. When we opened our eyes, everything was the same. We were still sitting on that same rock, the geese were still swimming around in the little lake. The trees rustled over our heads.

"Nothing happened?" I said.

"No. Well, maybe. I mean, I'm not sure," Alan Mendelsohn said.

I knew what he meant. Everything was the same—but it wasn't. I don't know exactly what we expected. I wasn't sure if I felt anything out of the ordinary. It seemed awfully quiet.

There was something different about the light. It was sort of pink. The geese were the same geese we'd been watching before we went into state twenty-six, but there was something special about them now. They were—this is hard to explain—more real.

"Are you in state twenty-six now?" Alan Mendelsohn asked.

"I'm not sure. Are you?"

"I can't tell either."

We sat on the rock for a few minutes—it seemed like a long time. Both of us were trying to sense if anything had happened. Finally, Alan Mendelsohn spoke.

"There shouldn't be so many leaves on the trees at this time of year," he said.

"And they shouldn't be green," I said.

"Can you see leaves on the trees?" Alan Mendelsohn asked.

"Yes. No. I mean, yes and no. I can see the leaves, and I can see the trees bare—both at the same time."

"Yeah, me too," Alan Mendelsohn said. "Do those geese look different to you?"

"Yes and no."

"That's right," Alan Mendelsohn said. "I feel weird. I feel split up. It's like I'm in two places at once—one as real as the other."

"That's how I feel too," I said. "I'm in a place that's cold and a place that's warm—and they're both this place."

"That's it!" Alan Mendelsohn said. "That's why there are certain places where you can make contact with parallel planes! This place exists in both planes! Or there are two places just alike, one on top of the other, and both in the same spot. We've done it! We're in touch with a parallel existential plane!"

"Do you really think so?" I asked. This was getting exciting.

"It has to be," Alan Mendelsohn said. "How else could we be cold and warm? How else could the trees be bare and leafy? And what in the world is the Mad Guru doing here?"

35

It was true. There he was, the Mad Guru, the guy who hung out in William Lloyd Floyd's bookstore, picking his way through the underbrush.

"Well, well," the Mad Guru said as he approached us, "Where in Waka-Waka did you two come from?"

We had both realized by this time that the Mad Guru was not visible in both the almost identical worlds we could see. This may be hard to understand, but we were both getting used to looking at two worlds at once. It was as though someone had drawn a picture of a tree in winter on a piece of thin paper, and then traced the picture of the tree and added leaves—as if it were summer. Then, imagine holding one picture over the other—but not exactly lined up—and holding them both up to the light. We could see the ruins of Hergeschleimer's Oriental Gardens in winter—which was what we would have expected to see—and at the same time, we could see Hergeschleimer's Oriental Gardens in full summer foliage. We could see these things at the same time, and we could see both of them separately. It was confusing—but not as confusing as you might think. It was like looking at one thing and listening to another at the same time.

What was surprising about the Mad Guru was that he was in the summertime picture—the parallel plane of existence—not in our everyday world where we were used to seeing him.

"What are you doing here?" we both asked at once.

"That's what I asked you," the Mad Guru said. "I don't recall ever seeing you before."

"Sure you have," Alan Mendelsohn said. "We met you at William Lloyd Floyd's bookstore. We had lunch together. And we met in the street once; and then we saw you when I sold my comic books."

"Are you sure?" the Mad Guru asked. "I think you may have gotten me mixed up with somebody else."

"Aren't you the Mad Guru?" I asked.

"No. My brother Arnie is the Mad Guru. My name is Lance Hergeschleimer."

"Wait a minute," Alan Mendelsohn said. "Are you the Lance Hergeschleimer who used to own Hergeschleimer's Oriental Gardens?"

"I still own them," the man said.

"And disappeared a long time ago?" Alan Mendelsohn went on.

"Do I look as if I had disappeared?" the man said. "Although I suppose when you go from one place, or plane, to another, you could be said to have disappeared from the place where you used to be. But, one never thinks of oneself as having disappeared, because one is always right there, if you know what I mean. I didn't disappear so much as leave. What I did was leave the city of Hogboro, in the United States of America, in whatever plane of reality those places exist, to come and live here in Waka-Waka, just as you have."

"This is Waka-Waka?" I asked.

"It is," Lance Hergeschleimer said.

"And you came here?" Alan Mendelsohn asked.

"I did."

"How?"

"State twenty-six, same as anybody who comes to live here—same as you."

"But we thought we were the first Earth people ever to attain state twenty-six by our own will," Alan Mendelsohn said.

"Nonsense," Lance Hergeschleimer said. "Where'd you get a strange idea like that?"

"Clarence Yojimbo. . . ."

"Clarence Yojimbo, the Venusian hippie?" Lance Hergeschleimer exclaimed. "He's madder than my brother Arnie! He was here a few months ago with a bunch of eight-hundred-year-old men on motorcycles—folk singers they were. He's wrong about state twenty-six. That's how I got here. That's how lots of people get here who want to live in Waka-Waka instead of their old world."

"We didn't come to live here," I said. I was getting a little nervous.

"Of course you did, boy," Lance Hergeschleimer said. "Nobody ever goes back."

This worried me quite a bit. I hadn't counted on going to live in Waka-Waka. I didn't even know if I liked it. And besides, there were my parents, and Melvin, the dog, and Grandfather and the Old One. They wouldn't know where I was.

Obviously, Alan Mendelsohn was worried too, by Lance Hergeschleimer's insistence that nobody ever goes back. "Mr. Hergeschleimer," he asked, "is it warm or cold?"

"Why, it's warm," Lance Hergeschleimer said. "It's always warm, or at least mild, in Waka-Waka."

"Do you see any leaves on the trees?" I asked.

"Excuse me, young fellows, but I think you're asking me silly questions," Lance Hergeschleimer said. "Is there any point to all this?"

"Yes there is," Alan Mendelsohn said. "We'll explain in a moment, but first please answer the question. Do the trees have leaves?"

"Of course the trees have leaves," Lance Hergeschleimer said impatiently. "It's the middle of summer. It's been the middle of summer for twenty-five years—that's how the seasons are here. Every tree has leaves."

"None of them are bare?" I asked.

"Not one," Lance Hergeschleimer said. "Now what's this all about?"

"One more question," Alan Mendelsohn said. "Hogboro—the place you used to live—can you see it now?"

"Certainly not," Lance Hergeschleimer said. "I'm here, not there."

"Well, you see, Mr. Hergeschleimer," Alan Mendelsohn said, "I think Leonard and I—by the way, this is my friend, Leonard Neeble, and I am Alan Mendelsohn. . . ."

"Glad to meet you," Lance Hergeschleimer said.

". . . I think that we are here *and* there. I'll explain. Right now, it's the beginning of winter in Hogboro. All the leaves have fallen. The trees are bare. The weather is fairly cold. We can see and feel that. At the same time, we can see and feel summer in Waka-Waka. We can see you—but only in the Waka-Waka summer. In the Hogboro winter, you do not exist."

"Well! If that is true, it's really something out of the ordinary!" Lance Hergeschleimer said. "I thought only extraterrestrials could go back and forth between planes like that. My goodness!"

"Well, that's how it is," Alan Mendelsohn said.

"If that's the case, I'll bet you could take a message to my brother Arnie, the Mad Guru," Lance Hergeschleimer said. "He's probably still wondering what happened to me. But you'll be wanting to learn more about Waka-Waka—it's an ideal society."

I was just getting ready to ask Lance Hergeschleimer some questions about the ideal society of Waka-Waka, when he suddenly grabbed Alan Mendelsohn and me by the shoulders, and pushed us down behind a bush. "Duck! Duck!" Lance Hergeschleimer said. "And don't make a sound if you value your lives!"

Lance Hergeschleimer crouched with us behind the bush. He was sweating. It was easy to see that he was really scared. Alan Mendelsohn and I were scared too. We couldn't see or hear anything out of the ordinary. We wondered what it was that Lance Hergeschleimer had noticed to frighten him so.

After a while, Lance Hergeschleimer seemed to relax. "That was a close one," he sighed.

"A close one?" I asked.

"A close call," Lance Hergeschleimer said. "It almost got us that time."

"What did?" Alan Mendelsohn asked.

"What did?" Lance Hergeschleimer repeated. "The thing without a name—the accursed thing—the unspeakable awfulness. It does *their* bidding."

"*Their* bidding? Who are *they*?" Alan Mendelsohn asked.

"Not now, boy—I'll explain it later," Lance Hergeschleimer said, raising one finger.

"But Mr. Hergeschleimer," I said, "I didn't see or hear anything."

"Then it's lucky you were with me," Lance Hergeschleimer said. "I'm especially good at sensing the presence of the unseen attacker—the invisible antagonist—the ineffable ickiness. I know when it's near. That's why I can walk around like this, in the open, with relative safety. You boys are all right as long as you're with me. When I say duck—you duck."

"Wait a minute," Alan Mendelsohn said. "What exactly is this terrible monster?"

"That's good," Lance Hergeschleimer said, "the terrible monster—the terrific molester—the terrorist mangler—that's very good."

"Well, what's it all about?" I asked, "and who are *they*?"

"I told you—later," Lance Hergeschleimer said. "Now I can continue to show you around the ideal society without trouble—the intangible trouncer seldom appears more than once in a day."

"Some ideal society," Alan Mendelsohn whispered to me.

Lance Hergeschleimer overheard him. "Everything is relative," he said. "When you've seen the benefits of Waka-Waka, you'll realize that the unexampled eviscerator is a minor inconvenience by comparison."

"This I've got to see," Alan Mendelsohn said, and we followed Lance Hergeschleimer through the Oriental Gardens which bore his name.

36

Lance Hergeschleimer led us along the paths of Hergeschleimer's Oriental Gardens, back toward the junkyard. When we got to the tangled bushes and the wire fence, we ran into a little trouble.

While we were inside the gardens, the matter of being in two places—or existential planes—at once wasn't too difficult. After all, it was the same place in both worlds, and all we had to deal with was two versions—two seasons, really—of Hergeschleimer's Oriental Gardens, sort of superimposed. From the edge of the Gardens, we could see two *different* worlds, and that was altogether another sort of thing.

We could see the junkyard and the little shack where Noel Wallaby stayed, but in more or less the same place was the big teahouse, the one we had seen glimpses of in Uncle Boris's film, the one that didn't exist anymore—in our world. There was the highway—and there was a big Waka-Wakian forest, growing right through the highway.

There was a sort of path through the forest, which ran right through Noel Wallaby's shack, which seemed just as solid as the Waka-Wakian trees around it. I felt—well, sort of carsick, dizzy.

"Right this way, boys," Lance Hergeschleimer said.

If we had followed him, we would have had to walk through the solid walls of Noel Wallaby's junkyard shack and then out into the highway, where solid cars would mow us down.

"Just a minute, Mr. Hergeschleimer," Alan Mendelsohn said. "We have a little problem here."

"What do you suppose we ought to do?" I asked.

"I'm not sure," Alan Mendelsohn said.

He touched the wire fence which existed only in the Hogboro plane. Then he touched a wooden railing that existed only in the Waka-Waka plane. "They're both solid," he said.

"Do you realize something?" I asked.

"What?"

"We're not in two existential planes at once—we're trapped *between* two existential planes."

"This may be serious," Alan Mendelsohn said.

"What seems to be the trouble?" Lance Hergeschleimer wanted to know.

We explained it to him.

"That really is a problem," Lance Hergeschleimer said. "Under ordinary circumstances, we don't feel, see, hear, smell, or taste anything from another plane of existence— maybe once in a while we get a sort of faint impression, but that's all. Still, at the same time, activity in the other planes is going on all around, and even through us. When you boys came here, you probably walked right through Waka-Wakian trees and buildings, and didn't even know it. Now, everything feels solid, am I right?"

"Yes," Alan Mendelsohn said. "What do you think we should do?"

"I haven't the faintest idea," Lance Hergeschleimer said. "Of course, you two seem to be especially good at state twenty-six. Maybe you could try using it to work this problem out—if not, I'll have to say good-bye. I can't be late for lunch, and we don't have very much time."

It was certainly worth a try. We didn't like the idea of being left by Lance Hergeschleimer, trapped between two existential planes—and the accursed thing, or whatever it was, apt to turn up at any moment. We went into state twenty-six and experimented with the solidity of objects. It didn't take very long to get results. We found we could tune ourselves like the fine-tuning knob on a television set. We could tune Waka-Waka down until it was almost invisible—just like a ghost in a TV picture. When we did that, the Waka-Waka wooden railing, which could hardly be seen, was as insubstantial as air. When we tuned down Hogboro, the wire fence gradually dissolved, until it was just a vague smudge before our eyes, and then we could pass our hands right through it. It took a few minutes to get used to doing this. Then Alan Mendelsohn thought of something.

"Mr. Hergeschleimer, when we tune out Waka-Waka, do we become invisible?"

"I was just remarking to myself about that," Lance Hergeschleimer said. "You don't become entirely invisible—if I try real hard, I can just make out your outlines—but if I wasn't sure you were there, I'd pay no attention to you. You just become sort of thick places in the air."

"This may come in handy later," Alan Mendelsohn said to me.

We surprised Noel Wallaby by appearing and vanishing before his eyes. When we invisibly left his junkyard, he was cleaning his eyeglasses with the tail of his shirt and talking excitedly to his dog, Fafner.

The forest through which Alan Mendelsohn and I followed Lance Hergeschleimer was not open and parklike, like Hergeschleimer's Oriental Gardens. It was sort of dark. The trees were tall and grew close together. The forest floor was all tangled roots and rotten leaves, and wherever there was dirt it was black and slippery and smelled funny. There was a cold wind blowing through the forest. Sometimes it was so dark we could hardly see where to put our feet. I fell down a few times, and so did Alan Mendelsohn.

"This place is called Moo-Shu Forest," Lance Hergeschleimer said. "It got its name from a Chinese restaurant that existed here a long time ago. Nobody remembers the name of the Chinese restaurant, but Moo-Shu pork was one of the dishes they served there."

"There was a Chinese restaurant in the middle of a forest?" Alan Mendelsohn asked.

"Oh, there's quite a bit in this forest, as you'll see later on," Lance Hergeschleimer said. "It's a nice place, really; cool in summer, easy to hide in, and the dreadful destroyer doesn't come here very often—it doesn't like dim places, just bright sun and . . . total darkness." When Lance Hergeschleimer said the word *darkness*, he sort of shuddered.

"About this dreadful destroyer," I said.

"Yes, the demon of darkness," Lance Hergeschleimer interrupted. "I'd prefer that we not discuss that particular topic right now—later, if you don't mind."

"Well, will you tell us this," Alan Mendelsohn asked.

"Does everybody live out here in the woods? Don't you have any cities?"

"Oh ho. Ha ha. Hoo hoo," Lance Hergeschleimer said. "Don't we have any cities? Hee hee. Hoo hah. Ho ho." He didn't sound as though he was laughing—he just said the words *ho ho*, and so forth. "We have a city. We have the greatest city in this or any other world. We have a city—Lenny. Lenny the great. Lenny the rich. Lenny the beautiful."

"The city is named Lenny?" I asked.

"Yes," Lance Hergeschleimer said. "You think that's funny? You think that's a funny name for a city? And I suppose you think Chicago is a pretty name. Lenny is the name of our great city. It is named after the bravest man ever to live in Waka-Waka."

"Are you taking us to the city? To Lenny?" I asked.

"Well, actually, almost nobody ever goes to Lenny any-more—unless they have to. People live—sort of—in the suburbs now."

"Well, where are you taking us?" Alan Mendelsohn asked.

"I'm taking you to my cave," Lance Hergeschleimer said. "I share a cave with a lot of other people. They're very nice—you'll see. We're almost there now."

For some time I had been pretty sure that pairs of eyes were watching us through the heavy underbrush. Once or twice I thought I saw someone—or something—darting through the forest ahead of us. This had me worried, especially until Lance Hergeschleimer told us that the dismal dreadfulness, or whatever they called it, didn't like the forest. But someone was watching us. I was sure of that when I saw Lance Hergeschleimer disappear into a pit someone had dug in the forest path and then carefully covered with leaves.

37

"Let me out! Let me out!" Lance Hergeschleimer shouted. "It's me, you fools! It's Lance Hergeschleimer!"

There wasn't a sound in the forest—other than Lance Hergeschleimer's shouting. Alan Mendelsohn and I stepped, carefully, closer to the edge of the pit.

"Are you boys still up there?" Lance Hergeschleimer was sitting in a puddle of muddy water, about ten feet down. "Stand where they can see you," he said. "If they just hear me shouting, they may think it's the horrendous horror trying to trick them."

We stood around, not too close to the edge of the pit. Without a rope, there was no way to get Lance Hergeschleimer out.

"It's me!" he shouted, every few minutes. "They'll be along soon," he said to us. "They're watching.—Just as soon as they're sure this isn't a trick, they'll come and get me out. It's this one fellow, Eugene, you see—he keeps setting traps for the maniacal marauder, and then forgetting to tell the rest of us where they are. I've been caught this way five or six times—we all have. Once, I was caught in a rope snare, and dangled from a tree by my right foot for half an hour. It's me! It's Lance Hergeschleimer, your friend! Get me out of here, you imbeciles!"

We stood around, feeling sort of useless and a little scared, while Lance Hergeschleimer bellowed from the bottom of the pit.

"What do we do if the horrible you-know-what turns up?" I whispered to Alan Mendelsohn.

"Well," he whispered back, "if the thing doesn't take us totally by surprise, I suppose the best thing to do would be to go into state twenty-six and tune ourselves back to the Hogboro plane. If it doesn't turn out that we're standing in the middle of a highway, that should get us away from here safely."

We heard a rustling in the bushes, got scared, and involuntarily went half-invisible, before we saw that the noise was caused by a bunch of ordinary-looking people carrying a long ladder. They lowered the ladder into Lance Hergeschleimer's pit, and he clambered out.

"Well, you certainly took your time!" Lance Hergeschleimer said.

"We had to be sure it was you, Lance," one of the people who had brought the ladder said. "We had to be sure it wasn't the dreadful dreariness, trying to trick us."

Lance Hergeschleimer looked at us. "See? What did I tell you?" He was trying to brush off his trousers, which were hopelessly muddy. "At least, no harm was done— thanks for asking," he said, "but I've forgotten to introduce our guests. Leonard and Alan, these are the people I live with—my cave-mates." Then Lance Hergeschleimer reeled off a bunch of names. I hate it when people do that—I can never remember who is who. I caught a few names: Clara, Walter, Helena, Raymond— but the only name I was able to connect with a person was Eugene. He was the guy who had dug the pit that Lance Hergeschleimer had fallen into. Eugene looked embarrassed.

After Lance Hergeschleimer had introduced us to everybody—and, except for Eugene, I didn't have any idea of who was who—the group of people led us off to their cave, which wasn't far away. As we walked, Lance Hergeschleimer's cave-mates all fussed about the fact that, at the time of his falling into the pit and making a commotion, he was already seven minutes late for lunch, and everyone was getting very upset. They went on and on about this—how Lance Hergeschleimer was late for lunch, and how they didn't know what to do, and how there were now two extra people to feed, and luckily there was enough food, but what if there hadn't been— and on and on and on.

Each person repeated the whole thing about how Lance Hergeschleimer had been seven minutes late, and how this upset everyone—and then they'd repeat it again. It was about the dumbest thing I'd ever heard. Nobody paid any attention to Alan Mendelsohn and me. We just walked along with this gang of complaining people because there wasn't any place to go, short of giving up on the whole adventure and going back to the Hogboro plane.

The cave itself was sort of neat. You had to crawl through a narrow, low, tunnellike doorway, and then you were in a very big room carved out of solid rock. Opening off the big central room were little rooms, or sets of rooms—the apartments where the people who shared the cave lived. The central room had a big table, all set for lunch. There must have been places for twenty or thirty people.

Everybody went straight to the table, carrying on all the time about lunch having never been this late before, and how they hoped nothing was spoiled. Nothing was, it turned out, but you couldn't have told from my experience. It was, without a doubt, the worst-tasting food I've ever eaten. They served something that looked like a dead alley cat, and tasted worse. It turned out to be made of roots and bark. Now, with my grandmother being who she is, I've had a lot of experience with weird-tasting food—so when I say that this dead alley cat made of roots and bark tasted terrible, I mean terrible! There were a few other things, but I didn't even try them. Alan Mendelsohn tasted a couple of the other dishes and said the dead alley cat was the best part of the meal. Lance Hergeschleimer and his friends ate just as though everything was all right.

At the end of the meal, Lance Hergeschleimer told us that because they had guests, the cave people were going to serve a special treat—a drink called fleegix. Alan Mendelsohn and I were interested in that, because we'd heard of fleegix before—once when Samuel Klugarsh was telling us about the Martian High Commissioner, Rolzup, and once when Clarence Yojimbo mentioned it to us.

"Isn't fleegix sort of like hot chocolate?" I asked Lance Hergeschleimer.

"Only much, much better," he said, "but where did you ever hear about fleegix?"

We told him about Clarence Yojimbo and the Martian High Commissioner.

"Do you know Rolzup?" Lance Hergeschleimer asked.

"No," I said, "we just heard about him—why?"

"Because he's coming here," Lance Hergeschleimer said, "in response to our urgent plea for help in dealing with *them* and the unapparent antagonist."

"Really?" Alan Mendelsohn asked. "Could we meet him?" He was really excited. I never knew he was so interested in meeting celebrities.

I had a question of my own, which just couldn't wait any longer. "Who," I asked Lance Hergeschleimer, "are *they*, and what is this unseen thing you're all so scared of."

"Yes," Lance Hergeschleimer said, "I did promise to tell you about the situation with *them* and *it*. Now is a good time to tell the whole story without interruption. While the fleegix is being prepared, I'll tell you everything."

38

"Civilization in Waka-Waka is very old," Lance Herge-schleimer said, "much older than it is in the plane of existence from which we came—the world which contains Hogboro. A long time ago, all the problems which afflict your world were solved here. People learned to get along without war, crime, and confusion. Also, all problems of survival were solved a long time ago. There were food and fleegix enough for everyone. Everyone understood his role in society, and everyone was content. For a long time, once things had progressed to the point where nobody had to work for a living, there was intense activity in the arts.

"That was the period during which our great city, Lenny, was built and adorned. Wonderful buildings were designed and constructed; people worked to make beautiful paintings and sculpture; works of music involving thousands of fine musicians were composed and performed every day. Science and engineering also flourished, and everything imaginable was done to make life a pure pleasure.

"This went on for a very long time—so long that nobody can quite remember how long. After a while, it seemed that everything that could possibly be done, had been done—and the happy people of Waka-Waka left off creating new pleasures, and settled down to enjoy the ones they already had.

Little by little, the people forgot how to make amazing buildings, how to paint pictures, make statues, compose music—but it didn't matter, because there was already so much to enjoy in those areas.

"So the people became specialists in enjoying the fine things they already had. Everyone spent most of the time quietly admiring the great accomplishments of Waka-Waka's splendid past.

"Little by little, people began to lose interest in the buildings, the paintings, the music, and so forth. The people having learned to truly appreciate aesthetic experiences, the experiences themselves got smaller and smaller. People were satisfied to spend a whole day looking at a single flower, or even a weed, and maybe drinking a cup of fleegix. Little by little, the thing of beauty they were experiencing grew less and less important; the important thing was the ritual of experiencing it—and the cup of fleegix.

"Finally, the whole cultural life of Waka-Waka was based on drinking fleegix. Since there had been no political life or economic life for a long time—and Waka-Wakians never had much in the way of religion—there wasn't really anything to do but enjoy the drinking of fleegix."

Alan Mendelsohn interrupted. "You mean, that's all you do—just sit around and drink fleegix?"

"Oh, it's hard to understand if you haven't really experienced it fully," Lance Hergeschleimer said. "It isn't just sitting around and sipping something hot—although that's part of it. You see, all the experience of life has been, as it were, boiled down to fleegix drinking. Contained within the subtle and complicated ritual of drinking fleegix is all that is, or ever was, good or beautiful in the life of Waka-Waka. It's like baseball, television, art museums, and presidential elections, all rolled into one. It's all a Waka-Wakian needs to be happy.

"Now, I said that Waka-Waka had no political or economic life. That isn't precisely true—the one industry that flourished after everything else was finished was the manufacturing of fleegix, and the making of beautiful cups and other things used in the fleegix drinking ceremony. We also exported fleegix to some other planes of existence in which fleegix is popular—although nothing like it is here. Our main customer was the twelfth existential plane on Mars, where they like fleegix very much. In return for the fleegix we exported, the Martians would send us the little plant called *Zigismunda formosa*. We encase these little plants in the Lucite handles of our fleegix cups—it's a very important part of the fleegix ritual. It's a sort of holdover from the days when Waka-Wakians liked to spend the whole day looking at a flower or a weed while drinking their fleegix."

"Excuse me, Mr. Hergeschleimer," I said, "this is very . . . well, sort of . . . interesting—but I thought you were going to tell us about *them* and *it*."

"I was just coming to that," Lance Hergeschleimer said. "After nobody knows how many hundreds of years of living in perfect peace and tranquility, enjoying good relations with our neighbors, our life was totally uprooted by *them*.

"First, I have to explain to you that our great city, Lenny, is built on the sides of a mountain. The city goes almost to the top—in fact, the city looks like a mountain made of buildings. At the very top of the mountain-city grows a variety of bush found nowhere else in Waka-Waka. It is called the zitzkis, and it produces a berry which is utterly essential to the successful making of fleegix.

"There are only four zitzkis bushes, and each of them bears only a few berries each year—but one berry can impart its special flavor to over six thousand pounds of unbrewed fleegix. The zitzkis bush, as I mentioned, grows nowhere else but the summit of the mountain-city of Lenny. It can't be cultivated—it just grows wild. During the period of artistic and scientific activity in Waka-Waka, our chemists did practically nothing but try to find a synthetic substitute for the zitzkis berry. Without it, fleegix smells and tastes like spoiled fish. The attempts to find a substitute for the zitzkis berry failed. The best synthetic fleegix tasted like month-old flat root beer. All of Waka-Waka depended on those four bushes at the summit of Lenny.

"Then *they* came and took over: first the top of the mountain, where our zitzkis bushes grow—then they took over the top half of the city of Lenny—and finally, the whole thing. And of course, they have *it*, the unspeakable beast, to do their bidding and terrorize the people. That's why we all moved out of Lenny and into the forest."

"But who *are* they, and what *is* it?" Alan Mendelsohn and I shouted.

"Yes, yes, I'm coming to that," Lance Hergeschleimer said. "But I see that our fleegix is ready. Let's stop for now and enjoy it. I need to calm down a bit before telling you the rest of the story."

39

The fleegix tasted lousy. I wasn't surprised. It tasted worse than the watery hot chocolate my mother makes. The stuff they serve at the Bermuda Triangle Chili Parlor is ten thousand times better.

Lance Hergeschleimer and his friends made a big deal about drinking the fleegix. This didn't surprise me either. After all, from what Lance Hergeschleimer had just told us, it was all they had in the way of entertainment. Nobody made a sound while they handed around the cups of fleegix. The cups were made of plastic. They were like some cups my parents have for drinking coffee and stuff outdoors—they're called thermo-cups, or something like that, and they have double walls, with an air space beween—they're supposed to keep your drink hot longer than an ordinary cup. It doesn't work. The handles of the cups were made of transparent plastic, and inside each handle was a little sprig of weed. I supposed that was the

Zigismunda formosa Lance Hergeschleimer had told us about.

Once the cups of fleegix were distributed (they were about one-third full, which I wasn't sorry about) everybody sat around with closed eyes, taking a little sip now and then. I tried to get into it, closing my eyes and taking little sips—but it just tasted like watery hot chocolate to me. I could see that Alan Mendelsohn wasn't too excited by the fleegix either. The fleegix-drinking ceremony went on and on. It seemed like it was going to last forever.

Since everybody's eyes were closed, it seemed like it might be a good time to slip away and have a private conversation with Alan Mendelsohn. I poked him in the ribs and held up two fingers, and then six. Alan Mendelsohn nodded, and we both went into state twenty-six, and tuned ourselves out of the Waka-Waka plane and back to Hogboro. It turned out we were sitting in the front yard of a house in West Kangaroo Park—about six blocks from where I lived.

"What do you think?" I asked Alan Mendelsohn.

"About the doings in Waka-Waka?" he asked. "So far, I'm really sorry that I sold my comic books. Still, I'd like to hear about *them* and *it*, if Lance Hergeschleimer ever finishes his story; and I would like to meet Rolzup, if we get the chance."

"But mostly, it is sort of boring," I said.

"For sure," Alan Mendelsohn said. "It *would* be our luck that we get to visit another plane of existence, and it turns out to be the dullest place in creation—and that fleegix—yuck!"

"Well, let's give it a few more hours," I said. "It's still early, and things may pick up."

"Sure," Alan Mendelsohn said. "I've got nothing else to

do—and besides, I've got an idea we may be able to help those dullards out with their problem. They're not mean or evil—just *so* uninteresting."

We tuned ourselves back to Waka-Waka. Everybody was still sitting around contemplating their fleegix. I guessed that the whole business took half an hour.

Finally, the Waka-Wakians started to wake up, and blink, and look around. They all looked very contented.

"There!" Lance Hergeschleimer said. "Wasn't that beautiful?"

"Oh, yes—beautiful," Alan Mendelsohn and I said.

"I'm glad we had a little fleegix on hand so you could have this rich experience," Lance Hergeschleimer said. "*They* only gave us enough so that we don't go crazy and revolt. Often we don't have any fleegix for days at a time."

The other Waka-Wakian cave people were drifting away, cleaning up the fleegix things, and wandering off to their little rooms.

"Mr. Hergeschleimer," I said, "about *them*—you were going to tell us about *them* and *it*."

"Oh, yes," Lance Hergeschleimer said. "I was so transported from ugly reality by the fleegix experience that it completely slipped my mind. Thanks for reminding me." Then he fell silent.

"Yes?" Alan Mendelsohn said.

"Yes?" answered Lance Hergeschleimer.

"About *them*," I reminded him.

"Oh, yes. *Them*. Where did I leave off?"

I hoped this was going to be worth the effort. "They came," I said, "and took over the zitzkis bushes and half the city of Lenny, and then *they* kicked everybody out of the city of Lenny. Who are *they*?"

"*They*," said Lance Hergeschleimer, "are three Nafsulian freebooters—pirates, plunderers—known as Manny, Moe and Jack. Somehow they managed to cross the interplanar barrier, just as you did. Upon arriving here they looked around for our most valuable commodity to steal. Naturally, in our fleegix culture, the most valuable things we have are the zitzkis bushes, so they took those over. Since they couldn't take them away with them, they stayed here and set up a sort of pirate empire. They export our zitzkis berries at cutthroat prices, and give us just enough berries to make a tiny quantity of fleegix for our own use."

"But if there are only three of them, why didn't you all just kick them out?" Alan Mendelsohn asked.

"Well, my boy," Lance Hergeschleimer said, "we can't do that for two reasons—first, we have such a highly evolved and peaceful civilization, that it's been centuries and centuries since we had any sort of police or army or tough guys. There's nobody here who would know just how to go about kicking them out. They're very scary, you know. Second, they have *it*—the unspeakable beast—the hateful thing—the malicious monster—The Wozzle."

"The Wozzle?"

"That's its proper name," Lance Hergeschleimer said. "We're so scared of it, we don't even like to say the word. Oh, it's a fearful thing, boys, and invisible. You never know when it's lurking about, ready to bite, and scratch, and thump you to death."

"Has it killed anybody recently?" Alan Mendelsohn wanted to know.

"No, not lately," Lance Hergeschleimer said. "We've learned to avoid it—to sense its presence—and we've learned to stay in the dimly lit places, where it doesn't like to come. At night, we hide in our caves."

"When was the last time it killed anybody?" Alan Mendelsohn asked.

"Oh, a very long time ago," Lance Hergeschleimer said. "I don't exactly remember when it was."

"Who did it kill?" Alan Mendelsohn asked.

"Who? Oh—somebody—I think—it was . . . actually, I don't really remember who got killed," Lance Hergeschleimer said.

"I'd really like to know who got killed, and when," Alan Mendelsohn said. "Could you ask the others?"

Lance Hergeschleimer called out to his cave-mates, who gradually straggled out of their little cells and gathered in the big room. "I'm explaining to these newcomers about . . . you know . . . *it*. . . ."

"The Wozzle," Alan Mendelsohn interrupted.

"Yes . . . that," Lance Hergeschleimer said. "Alan is very much interested in knowing who the last person it happened to kill might have been, and when this tragedy took place. Will someone please tell him?"

There was a lot of confused muttering and arguing among the cave people. It soon became clear that none of them knew who The Wozzle had killed or when.

"Well, let me ask you this," Alan Mendelsohn said. "When was the last time anyone has suffered any violence at all from The Wozzle, and who was it that was attacked?"

"I can answer that," Eugene said. "It was me. Not six years ago, I was standing on the edge of the forest, taking some sun, and something crept up behind me and gave me a terrible kick in the seat of the pants. It was the . . . you know . . . for sure, and it would have done worse, but I ran into the shadows, where it couldn't follow."

"Anyone else?" Alan Mendelsohn asked. There were no

other firsthand experiences of The Wozzle. "Now, has anyone ever seen Manny, Moe and Jack?" Alan Mendelsohn asked.

"Oh, yes," Lance Hergeschleimer answered. "We've seen them many times. We see them when we have to go to the city of Lenny to collect our zitzkis berry rations—and sometimes they call us together and holler at us and frighten us."

"What do they look like?" Alan Mendelsohn asked.

"Oh, horrible!" Lance Hergeschleimer said. All the other cave dwellers nodded agreement. "They have mean faces, and they have strange, scary eyes. They're small, but wiry and hairy, and they have long, strange noses."

"Can anyone go to see them?" Alan Mendelsohn asked.

"Nobody would go to see them unless they're sent for," Lance Hergeschleimer said. "Why go looking for trouble?"

"When they do send for you, what happens?" Alan Mendelsohn asked.

"Well, first they sound this huge electric horn—you can hear it all over the countryside. That's our signal that they want us to come. Then we all gather on the steps of the Palace of Culture, the biggest building in the city. After a while, the three bandits come out and stand at the top of the steps, and call us names, and make faces at us. They they go inside and send *it*. . . ."

"The Wozzle?"

"Yes, the . . . that thing, out to chase us away."

"What does The Wozzle do when it comes out?" Alan Mendelsohn asked.

"We don't wait to find out," Lance Hergeschleimer said. "The second they go inside, we all run away."

"This is very interesting, isn't it, Leonard?" Alan Mendelsohn said. "Now, tell us something about Nafsulia," he said to Lance Hergeschleimer.

"Well, there isn't much to tell," Lance Hergeschleimer said. "Nafsulia is all the things Waka-Waka is not. There's no order in Nafsulia, no culture, no government, no morality. We tried to contact some kind of government in Nafsulia, through our friend Rolzup, to see if we could get some help in stopping this tyranny—but Rolzup couldn't find any government in Nafsulia."

"Is Rolzup nearby?" Alan Mendelsohn wanted to know.

"Yes," Lance Hergeschleimer said.

"We may want to see him later," Alan Mendelsohn said, "but first, I'd like to have a talk with my friend, Leonard. If you'll excuse us, we'll go out into the forest for a while. When we come back, we may have an interesting proposition for you."

40

"What's this all about?" I asked Alan Mendelsohn, when we were out of the cave and in the forest.

"Do you feel like taking a chance?" Alan Mendelsohn asked me.

"What do you mean?"

"I've got a feeling about The Wozzle and the Nafsulian pirates, Manny, Moe, and Jack," he said. "I think we may be able to straighten out this whole thing for the Waka-Wakians—but if I'm wrong, there may be some danger. Are you interested?"

"Well . . . sure," I said, "anything to make this adventure a little more interesting."

"Great," Alan Mendelsohn said. "Now, we've got to work fast. I'd like to get this whole thing wound up today. First, let's find a patch of sun in this forest."

We found a spot where the sun was shining through the trees and making a bright place on the forest floor. Alan

214

Mendelsohn stood in the middle of the patch of sunlight. "I'm going to tune back to Hogboro, count to thirty, and then rematerialize here," he said. "Keep your eyes on the spot, and after I come back, tell me exactly what you saw."

Alan Mendelsohn faded away, and I was alone in the forest—it was eerie. I counted to thirty in my head, and at the count of thirty, Alan Mendelsohn began to reappear in the sunny spot.

"How was that?" he asked.

"Just fine," I said. "You vanished and reappeared."

"Now," Alan Mendelsohn said, "I'm going to try the same thing while standing in the shadows. Watch closely."

Alan Mendelsohn stepped into a shady place, and faded, and returned.

"Well," he said, "what did you see this time?"

"You didn't vanish completely," I said. "I could sort of see your outline if I squinted a little."

"Just as I thought," Alan Mendelsohn said. "Now we know why The Wozzle doesn't like shadowy places. This invisibility thing only works in bright light or total darkness. Remember, in Hergeschleimer's Oriental Gardens? Lance Hergeschleimer said he could still see us when we tuned ourselves into the Hogboro plane—he said we were like thick places in the air."

"Does this mean that there are sort of ghost images of us walking around Hogboro," I asked, "and do you think that's permanent? I mean, when we go home, will there be ghosts of us here in Waka-Waka?"

"I think we aren't really altogether in either place," Alan Mendelsohn said. "When we get ready to go home, I think we have to go to Hergeschleimer's Oriental Gardens in order to get all the way back into the Hogboro plane—

the same way we got here. We can't get totally into Waka-Waka because we really belong in the Hogboro plane."

"But Lance Hergeschleimer is from the Hogboro plane, and he's totally here, and he can't get back," I said.

"Yes," Alan Mendelsohn said, "and that worries me. I wouldn't want to get stuck here, with the stupid fleegix, and all that. Maybe Rolzup will be able to tell us something about that."

"Rolzup?" I asked.

"Yes, that's the next step," Alan Mendelsohn said. "I'm going to talk with Rolzup. He may help us. He and I are both Martians, after all."

That was one of the things I liked about Alan Mendelsohn—you never knew what he was going to come up with next.

We went back into the cave. Alan Mendelsohn asked Lance Hergeschleimer to call all his cave-mates together.

"Look," Alan Mendelsohn said, "if The Wozzle were taken care of, do you think you could handle Manny, Moe and Jack?"

"I don't know," Lance Hergeschleimer said. "Nafsulians are pretty tough. They never give up—even when they pretend to surrender, they still have a lot of fight left in them. There's only one way to be sure that a Nafsulian is finished."

"And what's that?" Alan Mendelsohn asked.

"Well, there's one ultimate Nafsulian gesture of surrender," Lance Hergeschleimer said. "If a Nafsulian removes and replaces his hat continuously, while rubbing his belly with a circular motion, that is a gesture of surrender which no Nafsulian can retract."

Alan Mendelsohn and I looked at each other. "I can just about promise you a complete, unconditional surrender if you will just cooperate," Alan Mendelsohn said. "Now, how many Waka-Wakians live in this forest?"

"Oh, I'd say about twenty thousand," Lance Hergeschleimer said.

"Can you spread a message to all of them?" Alan Mendelsohn asked.

"Yes, we could do that," Lance Hergeschleimer said.

"OK," Alan Mendelsohn said. "Tell everybody to get a piece of wood suitable for making a torch. When you hear the electric horn calling you to the city of Lenny, everybody has to turn up with a burning torch. Tell everybody to pick up the rottenest, smokiest wood they can find. Will you do it?"

"How do we know this will work?" Lance Hergeschleimer asked.

"Because Rolzup, the Martian High Commissioner, is going to give my plan his full approval," Alan Mendelsohn said, "if someone will just take me to him now."

Apparently, I wasn't supposed to go with Alan Mendelsohn to see Rolzup. This bugged me a little bit. I thought he was carrying this bit about being a Martian too far. I would have liked to see the Martian High Commissioner too. As it was, Alan Mendelsohn was led off by Lance Hergeschleimer and some other Waka-Wakians to the cave where Rolzup was staying. The rest of the people from Lance Hergeschleimer's cave hurried off to spread the word through the forest. I kept myself busy collecting torch wood.

I was on my own for about an hour. After I got the torch wood collected, I turned back to Hogboro, just to see what was happening. It wasn't any more interesting there, and besides, it was cold, so I tuned back to Waka-Waka and just hung around the cave.

Finally, I heard voices and people crashing through the undergrowth, and Alan Mendelsohn, Lance Hergeschleimer, Eugene, and some other Waka-Wakians came into view.

"It was interesting," Alan Mendelsohn said. "I learned a lot. I had a private audience with Rolzup. Nobody else was allowed in—so you wouldn't have been able to see him, if you'd come along." It was nice of Alan Mendelsohn to at least mention that. I got over feeling mad at him for not taking me with him.

"Rolzup is all for my plan, and he's going to help us. Also I found out something even more important," Alan Mendelsohn said. "If anybody comes to Waka-Waka and stays a certain number of hours—he gets stuck here."

"How many hours?" I asked.

"Rolzup isn't sure," Alan Mendelsohn said. "He's been here before and stayed up to eight hours—then you have to stay away for at least a year and sort of build up an immunity—so I guess we can figure that up to eight hours is safe—at least for Rolzup and me. I don't know if it's the same for an Earth person. Maybe you should go back now, and I'll try to bring off my plan without you."

"Why don't you cut out that Martian stuff?" I said. "This is no time for it."

"Thanks, Leonard," Alan Mendelsohn said. "You're a brave kid. We've been here for about five hours, so we'd better wind things up in a hurry so we can get home. By the way," Alan Mendelsohn smiled, "Rolzup and I took care of some personal business too."

The truth is, I hadn't always known what Alan Mendelsohn was talking about. Sometimes, I thought he was a little crazy—for example, with his business about being a Martian—but he was my friend, and I usually just went along with whatever he wanted to do.

"Now, here's the plan," Alan Mendelsohn said. "By this time everybody has got their torches and instructions. Right now, the word is spreading that Rolzup has approved my plan—they all respect him a lot. I think they'll go through with it. Even though they're frightened of Manny, Moe and Jack, the Nafsulian bandits, they're really sick and tired of getting pushed around and not having all the fleegix they want. I'm sure you realized that we can get Manny, Moe and Jack to make the Nafsulian gesture of surrender—taking off their hats and rubbing their bellies—by using Klugarsh Mind Control."

"Sure. I realized that," I said.

"Well, Rolzup says that once we get them to surrender, he can transport them out of here and back to their own existential plane."

"I thought if you stayed here more than eight hours, you couldn't get out."

"That's Martians and Earth people—Nafsulians can go anywhere," Alan Mendelsohn said. "All we have to do is get Manny, Moe and Jack to summon all the people of Waka-Waka to the city of Lenny—then we neutralize the Wozzle, get them to surrender by using Klugarsh Mind Control, and the whole thing is wrapped up."

"Wait a minute!" I said. "How are we going to do all those things? How will we get them to summon all the people? And what if we can't get them to surrender by Klugarsh Mind Control? We don't know if it works on Nafsulians. And what if The Wozzle doesn't want to be neutralized?"

"If any of those things happen, we just have to tune ourselves back to the Hogboro plane, and never come back here again—because if I'm wrong about any of this, and any of the Waka-Wakians survive, they'll never get over being mad at us."

"Look," I said, "I think we'd better talk this over some more."

"There's no time," Alan Mendelsohn said. "We've only got three hours to get this done—then we have to get back to Hergeschleimer's Oriental Gardens to make the complete return to our own existential plane—and it's a good half hour walk to Lenny, so we'd better start moving right now."

41

As we walked through the forest, I wondered if maybe
Alan Mendelsohn wasn't really seriously crazy. If it took
us a half hour to get to the city of Lenny, then it was
going to take at least that long for the Waka-Wakians to
get there with their torches. (I still didn't know what the
torches were for—maybe Alan Mendelsohn was planning
to burn down the city.) That meant that we'd be alone in
the city of Lenny with Manny, Moe and Jack, the Nafsulian bad guys, and their terrible beast for at least a half
hour after the electric horn was sounded. This didn't
make me feel too comfortable, especially since I didn't
know what Alan Mendelsohn's plan was, and he apparently wasn't going to take the time to tell me.

Alan Mendelsohn had a little map Rolzup had sketched
for him, and he was constantly checking it and looking for
landmarks as we made our way cross-country toward the
city of Lenny. He didn't seem to be interested in talking
as we walked.

The city of Lenny was pretty impressive. Just as Lance Hergeschleimer had described it, it looked like a mountain made of buildings. There was a highway leading up to a gate, and after that, an incredibly long and wide flight of steps leading up to a big building that looked a little like the Hogboro Museum. Alan Mendelsohn and I stepped onto the road and walked up to the gate.

"Who goes there? Who trespasses on the city of Manny, Moe and Jack?" a voice boomed.

"Pay no attention," Alan Mendelsohn said. "It's a recording—Rolzup told me about it."

"Halt, Interlopers!" The voice was even louder.

"Still a recording," Alan Mendelsohn said. "Don't worry about it."

We started climbing up the steps.

"BEWARE! THIS IS YOUR LAST WARNING!" The voice was *really* loud.

"Pay no attention, and keep climbing," Alan Mendelsohn said. "It's just a mechanical burglar alarm to alert Manny, Moe and Jack that someone is coming."

Ahead and above us, I could see the doors of the big building slowly opening. I couldn't see any people.

"PREPARE TO DIE!" the voice said—louder yet.

"Let's go, Alan," I said. "It's obvious we aren't wanted here."

"Don't worry," Alan Mendelsohn said. "They're just trying to scare us."

"Well, it's working," I said.

"Look!" Alan Mendelsohn said, pointing. "Manny, Moe and Jack!"

Three little men appeared. None of them could have been taller than five feet. They all had thick horn-rimmed eyeglasses, and they were wearing plaid sport jackets. Except for their greenish color, they could have been anybody. They didn't look pleasant, but they didn't look especially scary.

"Who dares?" one of them shouted in a thin, squeaky voice. He cupped his hand in front of his straw snap-brim hat so he could see us—the sun was behind us.

"To violate," another of the three Nafsulians squeaked.

"The sacred city of Manny, Moe and Jack?" the third said.

Alan Mendelsohn's reply surprised me. "We are emissaries of the Martian High Commissioner Rolzup—here to discuss matters concerning the zitzkis berry trade."

"Oh, wait a minute," said one of the Nafsulians. They went into a huddle. "You may approach," they said, "but no tricks—or we will send our pet out to deal with you."

We approached. "We have been sent to find out," Alan Mendelsohn said as we got near the top step, "why you are charging us twelve Martian klatchniks per zitzkis berry, while the People's Zitzkis Berry Collective of Waka-Waka is able to offer them for three Martian klatchniks apiece."

"What?" Manny, Moe and Jack shouted. "What's that you say? Three klatchniks? That's impossible! Unless . . . unless the Waka-Wakians have a secret store of zitzkis berries . . . unless they've been saving zitzkis berries out of the generous free gifts of zitzkis berries we present to them. Treachery! The ingrates are trying to undermine our enterprise! Sound the alarm!"

One of the Nafsulian pirates ran inside the big building and apparently threw a switch, because the loudest electric horn I ever heard began to sound. "It worked," Alan Mendelsohn whispered to me.

By this time we were already at the top of the stairs.

The three Nafsulians had brought out chairs and set them in a circle on the wide, flat place in front of the building. There was also a little table with cups of fleegix. Ugh! I thought to myself.

"I am Manny," one of the Nafsulians said, "and this is Moe, and this is Jack. Kindly sit down and have a cup of fleegix with us. A large portion of the Waka-Wakian populace will soon be here, and this misunderstanding will be cleared up. I'm afraid the reason you were offered those zitzkis berries at such an unconventional price is that they are, or were, purloined zitzkis berries. The ones who offered them to you had no right to do so. We control all zitzkis berries in Waka-Waka and the universe, and we set the price. It will all be cleared up in a very short time."

We sat through our second fleegix ritual of the day. This one was more interesting, because at least we had the green Nafsulians to look at. It was also fortunate that the pirates had adopted the Waka-Waka fleegix ritual, because it meant a half hour during which we wouldn't have to answer any questions. I was afraid they would ask me something about the twelfth existential plane on Mars.

As it was, the fleegix ritual didn't last long enough. The Nafsulian pirates came out of their aesthetic trance before anyone from the forest had arrived with a flaming torch. Manny, Moe, and Jack didn't come out of their period of fleegix contemplation all fuzzy-headed and peaceful, like the Waka-Wakians—they seemed sort of sharp and suspicious. "How is it that our usual contacts, Doldup and Weezup weren't sent with this message?" Moe wanted to know.

"Doldup and Weezup are on vacation," Alan Mendelsohn said.

"That's odd," Jack said. "I've never heard of a Martian official taking a vacation."

"I can see that you're a Martian," Manny said to Alan Mendelsohn, "but your colleague . . . I didn't catch the name. . . ."

"Leonard," I blurted out.

"Leonard?" Manny said. "That's not a very Martian-sounding name. He doesn't look like any Martian I've ever seen."

"He's from the seventh existential plane," Alan Mendelsohn said. "He's just with our department temporarily—sort of an exchange program."

"People from the seventh existential plane on Mars ought to have gills," Manny said, "since everything there is under water."

"Look!" Alan Mendelsohn shouted, and pointed to a column of smoke rising near the gate to the city.

42

"What's that?" said Manny.

"It's the Waka-Wakian peasants, bearing torches," said Moe.

"Why are they carrying torches?" asked Jack.

"Who cares?" Manny said. "It's probably some weak trick of theirs to distract us so we won't ask them who's been stealing our zitzkis berries. They can't do any harm with those torches—the city is made entirely of stone."

The Waka-Waka populace was arriving in large groups and gathering on the wide steps of the Palace of Culture. Each Waka-Wakian carried a burning, smoking torch.

When all the Waka-Wakians had gathered on the steps, the three Nafsulians addressed them. "Miserable citizens of Waka-Waka," they began, "it has come to our attention that some of you have been offering *our* zitzkis berries to our Martian neighbors at a reduced price. We want the ringleaders. We will give five zitzkis berries to anyone who comes forward with information."

"Phooey!" someone in the crowd shouted.

"Banana oil!" shouted another.

"Your grandmother's mustache!" someone else said.

The Waka-Wakians weren't particularly original in their insults, but they were showing a lot of courage. I felt sort of proud of them.

"We will not waste any more time," the Nafsulians said. "We have important Martian guests to attend to." It was Moe who said this. I was glad they hadn't figured out that we were fakes. They were so excited by our story of zitzkis berries being sold without their knowledge, that they didn't even try to find out if it was true or not. Alan Mendelsohn told me later that this is called the "big lie" technique. You start off with a whopper, and try to spring it on your victim all of a sudden—and he'll be too excited to do much thinking. It's like this: someone rushes in and shouts, "YOUR GRANDMOTHER'S HOUSE IS ON FIRE—COME AND SAVE HER!" You might be six blocks away when you realize that your grandmother lives in a mobile home in Nefesh Park, Florida. The Nafsulians were just too greedy to stop and think when someone told them that their stolen zitzkis berries were being stolen from them. They just reacted.

"If someone doesn't talk right now, we'll just go inside and send out our little pet. He'll take care of you—if you know what we mean." The Nafsulians all laughed nasty laughs.

This was going to be the test of Waka-Wakian courage. I knew that Alan Mendelsohn had passed the word not to run away, even if the unfathomable evilness was sent for—but I also knew that the Waka-Wakians were deathly afraid of the monster, and usually ran the moment the Nafsulians threatened them with it. There was a wave of terror that went through the crowd—it was noticeable—

but nobody ran. They all wanted to run—you could feel that too.

"Anybody feel like talking?" the pirates said.

Nobody made a sound or said a word. They just stood there, holding their torches.

"All right—you've brought this on yourselves," the Nafsulians said. "And just for fun, we've pushed the button that electrically locks the city gate—this time you can't run away from our pet."

There were some whimpers of fear from the crowd. It's one thing to make up your mind not to run away from a dreadful monster—it's something else entirely to find out you have no choice in the matter.

"Last chance," the Nafsulians said.

The three Nafsulian bandits went inside the doors of the Palace of Culture. There were a few scattered screams from the crowd. I had been feeling so sorry for the frightened Waka-Wakians that I forgot all about the fact that I was standing not twenty feet from the door out of which the intolerable abomination was going to appear any moment. All of a sudden I remembered that. I also realized that I was so scared and excited that I probably wasn't going to be able to go into state twenty-six if things went wrong. There were, maybe, five terrible seconds—the Waka-Wakians' torches wavered—the thick, choking black smoke made the whole city seem as dim as the forest—my heart was pounding.

Then something appeared in the doorway! The Wozzle! I felt sick and scared. It was as big as three men—three little men. Wait a minute! The Wozzle was supposed to be invisible—and yet, I could see something. In the dim light caused by the smoke from the torches I could see that the Wozzle—the invisible terror—was actually

Manny, Moe and Jack, the three Nafsulian bandits! *They* were The Wozzle!

The Waka-Wakian populace caught on just a few seconds after I did. First there was some giggling—then some loud laughter—then a deafening roar. Manny, Moe, and Jack looked confused. Twenty thousand Waka-Wakians, who were supposed to be scared silly, were pointing at them and laughing.

"Now!" Alan Mendelsohn whispered in my ear, "while they're still confused! Let's command them to surrender!" I went into state twenty-six with Alan Mendelsohn, and we commanded the three Nafsulians to remove and replace their little straw hats continuously, while rubbing their bellies with a circular motion—the old Klugarsh Mind Control trick.

It worked! The Nafsulians gradually became more visible, looking at each other with amazed expressions, as they continued to rub their bellies and remove their hats in the classic Nafsulian gesture of complete surrender. The crowd was cheering. "THEY'VE SURRENDERED! THEY'VE SURRENDERED!" Then the crowd began to call for the Martian High Commissioner. "ROLZUP! ROLZUP!" they shouted. People stepped to the side to make a little path through the crowd, and up the steps came a very dignified-looking man. He was wearing a sort of green-and-white sweater, and black-and-white shoes with plaid socks.

"I am Rolzup, High Commissioner of the twelfth existential plane on Mars," the dignified man in the sweater said. "I am here to officially acknowledge that you have made the ultimate gesture of surrender—which no Nafsulian can ever retract—and to offer, as the representative of a neutral government, to provide you with safe conduct and *make sure* you get home." The Nafsulians looked as though they were afraid of Rolzup. "We'll be starting out for the Nafsulian plane of existence almost at once," he said. And then he said to us, "I'd start out for home without hesitating, if I were you. I don't think you can stay here safely for much more than an hour—you don't want to get stuck in Waka-Waka." Then he waved to the cheering crowd of Waka-Wakians, and he and the three Nafsulians faded and vanished before our eyes.

Lance Hergeschleimer rushed up to us. "You boys are great Waka-Wakian heroes!" he said. "We want to honor you, and also celebrate our return to complete liberty, with an all-night fleegix ceremony beginning in one hour." There was wild cheering from the crowd. You couldn't hear yourself think. Alan Mendelsohn and I went into state twenty-six and tuned ourselves back to Hogboro.

43

We were across the street from Bat Masterson Junior High School. Although we had tuned ourselves as far as we could back to the Hogboro plane, we could still hear the faint cheering of the Waka-Wakian crowd. "We're not entirely here," I said.

"No, we're not," Alan Mendelsohn said. "We have to get to Hergeschleimer's Oriental Gardens in under an hour, or we're going to wind up stuck between Waka-Waka and whatever plane Hogboro exists in—or worse."

"You mean, if we don't go to Hergeschleimer's Oriental Gardens, tune ourselves to Waka-Waka, and then tune ourselves back to Hogboro, we might wind up sort of fading into Waka-Waka and staying there?"

"It's a possibility," Alan Mendelsohn said.

"Well, let's go," I said. "I don't want to spend the rest of my life drinking fleegix."

It was a long walk to Hergeschleimer's Oriental Gardens. We could just do it in under an hour, if we went fast the whole way and didn't stop. Of course, we weren't sure if an hour was all we had—it was just an educated guess of Rolzup's—but we didn't feel like taking any chances. We started walking, and went as fast as we could, not talking, sweating.

When we arrived at Noel Wallaby's junkyard, he had gone home. The gate was locked. There was barbed wire at the top of the fence. Fafner was there, but he didn't seem so old and harmless as before. Also, he didn't seem to recognize us. I had the feeling that he'd bite us with as many teeth as he had, if we got inside the fence.

"Without getting inside the junkyard, there's no way to get inside Hergeschleimer's Oriental Gardens," I said.

"I know," Alan Mendelsohn said. "I'm trying to think." He was all out of breath from the fast walk.

"We're wasting valuable time," I said.

"I know," Alan Mendelsohn said. "There's a way to get in there, but I can't think of it."

"Wait a minute!" I shouted. "I've got it! We tune ourselves to Waka-Waka here, and walk right into the Gardens, and then tune ourselves back to Hogboro!"

"That's it!" Alan Mendelsohn said. "I don't know why I couldn't think of it—I'm tired, I guess."

We went into state twenty-six, tuned out of Hogboro and into Waka-Waka, and walked into the Gardens. We had to pick our way along the paths—it was pretty nearly dark, but we found our way to the little lake where we had first made contact with the Waka-Waka plane of existence. We sat down in the same spot and went into state twenty-six. Something was wrong!

"This isn't working," I said.

"I know. Try again," Alan Mendelsohn said.

We weren't quite making contact. We'd get almost all the way into the Hogboro plane, but not quite—there would still be a little contact with Waka-Waka left.

"It's too late," I said. I was starting to get really scared.

"We have to keep trying," Alan Mendelsohn said.

We tried again and again. Each time we nearly made it, but not quite.

"We're stuck," I said.

"We can't be," Alan Mendelsohn said. "We must be doing something wrong. Look! Let's do it once more—but this time don't try—just do it—like the time we made the Omega Meter play 'Jingle Bells'!"

It worked! We got through. We both knew that we were in Hogboro, one hundred percent. We collapsed on the ground.

"Now we face the problem of getting *out* of Noel Wallaby's junkyard," Alan Mendelsohn said.

"That's right!" I said. "I hadn't thought of that. We might wind up locked up in here for the whole weekend." Somehow, that didn't worry me so much now that we had escaped from Waka-Waka and were securely back in good old Hogboro.

"Of course, the problem is different when viewed from the inside," Alan Mendelsohn said. "When we were out there, we just had our bodies. Inside there are tools, ladders, and everything we need. The only question is, will Fafner be friendly or not?"

It turned out that Fafner was only programmed to act fierce if you approached the junkyard from the street side. He was not very interested in us at all when we approached from the tangle of foliage that marked the edge of what was left (in our plane) of Hergeschleimer's Oriental Gardens. In Noel Wallaby's shack we found a big rusty pair of pliers, and there were lots of old ladders. It was perfectly easy to break out of the junkyard. We didn't cut the barbed wire—just unhooked it at one point, and we used two ladders, one on each side of the fence. When we were over, Alan Mendelsohn repaired the barbed wire, and we sort of slid the second ladder back into the junkyard, so nobody else would be able to break in.

We were both late for supper, and so tired on the way back from Noel Wallaby's junkyard that we didn't say a word to one another.

"Alan, tomorrow I want to ask you a whole bunch of questions," I said.

"OK, tomorrow," he said, as he dropped me off at my house.

44

I never saw Alan Mendelsohn again. It's funny, I had a sort of feeling that I would never see him again when he dropped me off outside my house that night, after we got back from our adventure in the Waka-Waka plane of existence.

When I got home, I thought I was going to drop right into bed—but I got a sort of second wind. I ate my supper, listened to my parents holler at me for staying out too late, and then I felt wide awake. There was nothing in particular I wanted to do—I just sort of ran over the details of my adventure with Alan Mendelsohn and watched television with my family. On Saturday nights I am allowed to stay up late, so I got to watch the late news.

It was some late news! It seems that in the course of the evening *hundreds* and *thousands* of people had called the television station, the police, the air force, the mayor, the White House, and each other to report UFO sightings.

Now these were not your usual lights in the sky—this was a real spaceship! They could see the rivets in the hull, scratches in the metal; they could even see into the windows—they could see guys wearing green sweaters inside, working the controls! Lots of people had snapped pictures of the spaceship, which had hovered over the housetops of Hogboro and West Kangaroo Park for almost an hour. A couple of times the spaceship had seemed to land! The whole news program was about the UFO sighting, with interviews of the mayor, the chief of police, some science-fiction writer who was visiting Hogboro, people who had seen the spaceship—everybody!

My mother was scared. My father thought it was a publicity stunt for some movie. I thought it was real—just a spaceship visiting Hogboro. We had a big discussion about it. In the end, my father convinced my mother—which was good for me, because at one point she had made up her mind not to let me go out of the house anymore. I didn't convince anybody. My father said that if the spaceship were real it would belong to the good old United States, and when the White House was called, the President would have explained the whole thing. He was absolutely sure that the whole thing was just a promotion for some space movie that would be coming to the local theaters in a week or two. It was nice to have a family discussion—even if my parents were completely wrong about everything. We usually didn't have anything to talk about.

In the morning, I wanted to hear what Alan Mendelsohn would have to say about the spaceship—although, as I said, I had this funny feeling that Alan Mendelsohn was gone. It was just a feeling, though—I didn't have any reason to believe it was true.

When I got to Alan Mendelsohn's house, it was obvious

that the whole family had gone. The windows of the house were dark, the Sunday paper was lying on the porch, the comic section sort of flapping in the wind. There was a big burned spot in the middle of the front lawn—as though there had been a campfire there the night before—only there were no ashes, just burnt grass.

I had a heavy feeling in my stomach as I stepped onto the porch. I rang the bell, but I knew nobody was going to answer. I could hear the chimes making a hollow sound inside the house. I peeked in the window. The house was completely empty. There wasn't a single piece of furniture, a rug; even the place where the telephone had been was just a bunch of wires coming out of the wall. Alan Mendelsohn and his family were totally, completely, and forever gone!

Pinned next to the front door was a lumpy brown manila envelope. Written across it was my name, *Leonard.* Inside was the brass potato from the moon that Alan Mendelsohn had gotten from William Lloyd Floyd, and a note to me.

Dear Leonard,

I had to leave with my family. We're going back to"The Bronx," if you know what I mean. I'm sorry to leave like this, without giving you any warning, but I had to promise a certain person that I wouldn't tell anybody about this, not even my best friend—and that's you. The certain person—I had to promise not to mention his name, but he's a sort of high commissioner of a certain place—you've seen him.

I'll try to get a note to you sometime, but it isn't easy to get mail from "The Bronx" to this place. In the meantime, please don't forget about your old friend,

Alan Mendelsohn

P.S. The fleegix is much better where I'm going!

So he really was a—no, it could have been just another joke. I mean, if Alan Mendelsohn was really from . . . why didn't he ever tell me? But of course, he had told me—he had told everybody. I just couldn't tell what was true. And I didn't care. All I knew was that my only friend had left and I was miserable.

45

I just dragged myself around all day Sunday. I really missed Alan Mendelsohn. I was mad at him for a while, for leaving and not telling me anything about it. But, really, it wasn't his fault if he promised Rolzup that he wouldn't tell anybody he was going back to Mars—or The Bronx. I couldn't make up my mind if the whole thing about being from Mars was a put-on or not. I hung around the house, watching television and looking at my brass moon-potato.

Another thing which bugged me was that I wanted to ask Alan Mendlsohn a lot of questions about what had happened in Waka-Waka. I wanted to know how he guessed that The Wozzle was really Manny, Moe and Jack. I wanted to ask him what he and Rolzup had talked about—although I now had a pretty good idea of that. They had talked about Alan Mendelsohn and his family getting a ride home to Mars on a UFO—that is, if the

Mars story was true. Something else I'd never be able to find out.

Dr. Prince telephoned to tell me that he was back from his trip, and expected to see me in his office the following afternoon. I figured I might as well go—Dr. Prince was sort of a jerk, but at least he was somebody to talk to, and it meant I would get out of school early.

Something funny happened at school the next day. I was sort of depressed at first, and then I got angry. I felt impatient with everybody. I did something I had never done before—I tripped a kid. It wasn't as good as one of Alan Mendelsohn's trips, but it was pretty good. It had some style.

"Did you trip me?" the kid asked.

"Yes, featherbrain," I said. "Care to make something of it?"

The kid I tripped was a lot bigger than me—but I didn't care. If he wanted to fight, I'd be only too glad. I really felt like getting into a fight. The kid didn't want to fight, though—he just walked away. I was disappointed.

In my social studies class, they were talking about the Crusades. The teacher was talking about how the Crusaders were these real brave romantic types, who were models of morality and all that.

"Except they never took a bath," I heard myself say.

"What's that you said . . . Leonard?" The teacher was sort of surprised to hear my voice. I guess I hadn't said anything in that class before.

"They never washed. They stank. They used to douse themselves with perfume so they could stand being around each other—and they all had fleas," I said. I was really enjoying myself.

"Leonard," the teacher said, "I don't know where you

got such a disgusting idea. I know there's nothing about this in our social studies textbook."

"They were dirty and smelly and flea-bitten," I said, "and they pushed people around and stole stuff. I've got a couple of books all about the Crusades at home. I'll bring them in tomorrow and read to everybody about what slobs the Crusaders were."

"I'm sure that won't be necessary, Leonard," the teacher said.

"Oh, it won't be any trouble," I said. "I'll bring the books in tomorrow, for sure." I was out of my seat and pacing up and down in the aisle. The teacher had this horrified expression. She was hoping I wouldn't bring in my books that told about the filthy personal habits of the Crusaders. I was going to, though.

I was starting to feel very light and happy. My next class was gym. This was the one class I really had been afraid of. Most of the time, Mr. Jerris just ignored me, but at least once a week he'd chew me out. I don't think it was anything personal—there were quite a few kids who didn't like gym, and Mr. Jerris would abuse all of them. Every so often, it was my turn. I was always afraid that each time I went into the gym class, it would be my turn. I always felt sick on my way to gym. This time I didn't.

I wandered in a couple of minutes late. I was late sort of on purpose. I had made a point of taking the longest way possible to the gymnasium.

"Well, well, we're glad to have you with us, fatso," Mr. Jerris said.

I walked up to the front of the class, which was all spread out for calisthenics. "Mr. Jerris," I said, "the next time you call me fatso or tubby or lard-butt, or anything like that, you're going to find yourself meeting with the principal, the PTA, and maybe appearing in a court of law, with that stupid whistle in your mouth. My only regret is that my father, Judge Neeble, will have to disqualify himself, because I'm his son—but I'm sure you'll get a fair trial before a judge who will listen to all the arguments before he convicts you of verbally abusing me, fines you, gets your teaching certificate revoked, and maybe throws you in jail."

Actually, my father has a rag business—but Mr. Jerris didn't know that. "Neeble, come to my office," Mr. Jerris said. He didn't roar it in his usual way. He almost sounded like a regular human being. I followed him to his office.

"Leonard," Mr. Jerris said, when we went in his office, "we've started a corrective gym class. It's for kids there's something wrong with—bad posture, fallen arches, and kids who aren't regular—like you—I mean—no offense, Leonard, but you don't really want to climb ropes, and get into the Marine Corps, and kill your country's enemies, do you?"

I said that it wasn't one of the big goals of my life.

"Well, maybe you'd like me to get you into this corrective gym class, where you can study toe dancing, and grow up to be a little Commie, sissy boy," Mr. Jerris said.

I told him I'd like that just fine, and it would solve the problem of Mr. Jerris having to appear in court to explain why he was insulting, stupid, and ignorant.

He sent me over to the corrective gym class right away. He said he'd take care of the paper work later.

The corrective gym teacher was Mr. Winkle. He told us later that he never wanted to be a gym teacher, but there was a job open, so he took it. The class met in an empty classroom, not a regular gym. Mr. Winkle said he didn't care if we got any exercise or not. He said we could play chess or read comics, if we didn't feel like participating in the class. For kids who didn't know how to play chess, he suggested that those of us who knew could teach the others. He said after everybody knew how to play, he'd give a five-minute chess lesson at the beginning of each period. For the gym part of the class, Mr. Winkle said he would teach us yoga. He had a paperback book called *Yoga Made Simple*. He said he didn't know anything about yoga himself, and he'd be learning right along with us.

Most of the kids decided to give yoga a try. The exercises were easy—most of the beginning ones could be done sitting or lying on the floor. Mr. Winkle's paperback said that by the end of the book, anyone who did the exercises would be really supple and strong. I liked the idea that Mr. Winkle was doing the exercises right along with us. Gym went from being my least favorite part of school to the class I liked best, in ten minutes.

The corrective gym class was made up of all the weird kids—Henry Bagel, and all those kids that everybody who was regular picked on—the ones who had picked on me before Alan Mendelsohn turned up. I was ready to start tripping kids and offering to fight—but everybody was sort of nice to me. It seems that when there weren't any of the regular kids around, the weirdos didn't mind each other's company so much. Also, we knew we were the weirdo gym class—there was no point in pretending anything else.

Even Mr. Winkle looked like he had been a weirdo when he was a kid. I sort of liked him. We all did.

The gym class made me feel kind of good, and for the rest of the day I didn't trip anybody or pick on any teachers. I left school early, with permission, so I could go to my appointment with Dr. Prince.

I had already decided not to bother Dr. Prince with the

story of what had happened in Waka-Waka. I just was going to tell him regular everyday stuff. Dr. Prince had a suntan, and he kept jumping and looking around, as though he expected something to be hiding behind his chair. Except for that, he seemed to have recovered nicely from going crazy in the Bermuda Triangle Chili Parlor. I told him how I tripped a kid and talked back to my teachers. He seemed really happy about that. He said I was getting my aggression out in the open. Dr. Prince was a little slow on the uptake, but I guess his heart was in the right place.

When I got home I was still sad about not having a best friend anymore, but I was feeling sort of good about school. I did a lot of extra homework. I was planning to do a lot of talking in class the next day.

46

What was happening was that I was taking over Alan
Mendelsohn's old job at Bat Masterson Junior High
School. It made me miss him less to do the sort of things
he used to do. I drove teachers crazy by bringing up all
sorts of weird stuff in classes. In order to get away with it,
I had to be sure I was ahead of the class so I wouldn't get
shot down on tests. Then I'd have to do a lot of outside
reading in order to come up with little-known, but absolutely authentic, facts to throw at the teacher. There's a
gentle art to bugging teachers. You have to sort of pace
yourself, or you'll spoil it. Sometimes, I'd be quiet for a
week or more—this was to lull the teacher into a false
sense of security—then I'd spring the results of my latest
research, and take over the class for a day or two. By ro-
tating classes, I was able to create an explosion in one
class or another once or twice a week.

I started out to develop a tripping program like Alan's,

and even spent some time trying to develop a "missile whistle" like his—but I wasn't really able to get into it. Besides, I found that I didn't hate all the kids in school as much as I thought I did. Part of that had to do with the corrective gym class. After the first few days, the kids in the class started to eat lunch together. At first, the other kids called us names, like "the awkward squad," and "the freak show." Then we started practicing our yoga exercises during lunch. Even after only two weeks, most of us could get into some positions that would really hurt you if you were tense or didn't know what you were doing. Some of the regular kids found this out when they tried to imitate what we were doing. One kid sprained his ankle trying to imitate the Dying Chicken posture. You have to know what you're doing or you can really get hurt doing yoga.

I turned out to be the best chess player in the corrective gym class. Anytime we felt tired or not interested, Mr. Winkle would let us knock off the yoga and play chess, provided that we didn't make noise and disturb the other kids. Also, we found out that Mr. Winkle came to school a half hour early and did some jogging around the track. We asked him if we could come and jog with him. He said OK, and after that some of us—whoever felt like it—would show up just about every morning.

A lot of the kids in the corrective gym class were good students. Some of them were in the same classes with me. They liked the Alan Mendelsohn imitation I was doing, and sometimes they would back me up. After a while, some of us started to team up on research projects so we could really confound our teachers.

So the next time grades came out, I discovered I was getting all A's—even in gym! My parents were pleased,

and so was Dr. Prince, who took all the credit for everything. My parents wanted to give me a present for
straightening out, and getting good grades, and not being
crazy anymore. I told them I wanted to throw a party.
They said OK, and I wound up taking the whole corrective gym class and Mr. Winkle out for a meal at the Bermuda Triangle Chili Parlor. I hadn't been there since Alan
Mendelsohn disappeared. I thought it would depress me
too much, but I felt like taking all my friends there. I considered inviting Dr. Prince too, but I remembered the
bad experience he'd had there, and decided not to even
mention it to him.

So there we were, enjoying our second helpings of
Green Death Chili, when who should walk in but Samuel
Klugarsh!

"Leonard! My old pupil!" Samuel Klugarsh shouted.
"Where have you been all these weeks?"

"I've been meaning to come and see you, Mr.
Klugarsh," I said. "I've got a message for the Mad Guru.
Will you tell him that his brother, Lance Hergeschleimer,
is alive and well, and living in Waka-Waka?"

"We know all about it," Samuel Klugarsh said.
"Klugarsh Extraplanar Scientific Associates has been getting a lot of brand-new information of late—but I'm so
glad to see you. I've got a message for you too. Clarence
Yojimbo was here a few weeks ago and wanted to get in
touch with you, but I never did know where you lived.
The folk-singing thing in New York didn't work out, you
know. Poor fellow—he was very disappointed. Wants to
go into the health food business in the fourteenth existential plane of Saturn."

"What did Clarence Yojimbo want to see me about?" I
asked.

"He wanted to give you something," Samuel Klugarsh said. "In fact, he left it with me. If you like, I'll just nip around to the shop and get it. Then I'll come back and you can introduce me to your friends, and we'll have three or four bowls of Green Death together."

Samuel Klugarsh rushed out of the Bermuda Triangle Chili Parlor. He was back in two minutes with a strange metallic envelope in his hand. I opened it. Inside was a note on a sheet of something that looked like metal, but felt like plastic. It was from Alan Mendelsohn! It said:

> Dear Leonard,
>
> My parents want you to ask your parents if it would be OK for you to spend your summer vacation with me, here in "The Bronx" (if you know what I mean). If they say yes, our friend Rolzup will be able to arrange all the details.
>
> Your friend,
> Alan Mendelsohn

Slaves of Spiegel

Part 1
ON THE PLANET
OF THE
FAT MEN

IT IS SPACE. DESOLATE, WILD, BOUND-less, huge. In a far distant corner of the uni-verse, in an unnamed galaxy, in an unimpor-tant solar system, a small untidy planet hurtles through time.

Candy wrappers from a million stars, printed in a million languages, tumble across the arid ground. Soft drink cans, of every imaginable shape and size, rattle and click together in the solar wind. Here is a half-eaten taco from the planet Glupso in the Mouse Nebula. Here is a Styrofoam box which once contained a deluxe cheeseburger from Earth.

Here and there, a circle of rocky outcrop-pings conceals the landing place of a giant spaceburger, one of those dreaded pirate ships of the cosmos. Here and there, in the shadows, a dark round form can be seen—a fat space pirate, standing guard.

This place is Spiegel, home of the feared and hated Fat Men, whose raids have depleted much of the junk food in the universe. This is Spiegel the notorious, known on a thousand thousand worlds as the sugar vampire, the grease magnet, and the home of the fat guys.

It is here on Spiegel, that Sargon the Magnificent, Sargon the Merciless, Emperor of Everything, and leader of the space pirates has called a meeting of all his men.

For scorching Spiegelian days and freezing Spiegelian nights, spaceburgers from every point in the known and unknown universe have been landing on the fearsome sphere. Space pirates in their most splendid finery: Blue leisure suits, shirts with tiny polka-dots, and perforated white plastic shoes are seen everywhere. They are waiting for their leader, Sargon the Incredible, Sargon the Insufferable, to make his appearance.

Finally, when every pirate has left off plundering in the far reaches of creation, and returned to Spiegel; when every spaceburger, filled to brimming with calorific spoils of conquest, has come home; the Fat Men gather under the twelve green moons of Grabowsky to greet their leader, Sargon the Fortunate,

Sargon the Fantastic, Sargon the Fattest of the Fat.

In Wimpy, the great crater of Spiegel, all the pirates have assembled. Ten million Fat Men, round and sleek and heavy, stand shoulder to shoulder and belly to rump, awaiting the coming of the Great One, Sargon. The ground beneath their feet groans at their combined weight of more than three billion earth pounds, and the planet wobbles on its axis.

Sargon appears atop the great natural rock formation, known as the White Tower. He raises his hand and speaks. "My mighty men— pirates all—I greet you!"

Ten million pudgy hands are raised in greeting. Ten million digital watches and pinky rings catch the light of the twelve green moons. Ten million voices are raised in a mighty cheer.

"All hail our leader, Sargon!" the pirates shout. "All hail the sacred potato pancake of the universe!"

"My brave pirates," Sargon says. "In the past years, decades, centuries, and millennia, we have made the name of Spiegel feared on every world. Our raids have been successful, and our underground vaults are utterly full of potato pancakes—all of which belong to me by royal right—cheeseburgers, pizzas, cupcakes, and every sort of sugary, starchy, greasy, sticky thing. And now, because it is the birthday of my illustrious father, Roosman the Hungry, I invite you all to join in a gigantic planetary pig-out!"

Ten million shouts of joy respond from Wimpy's walls. Ten million pairs of perforated white plastic shoes shake the ground as the pirates jump up and down.

"Bring on the food!" shouts Sargon.

Gigantic underground vaults are opened. Huge elevators, laden with snacks of every kind, rise to the surface. Thousands upon thousands of hamburgers or their equivalent, from every inhabited planet, are passed from hand-to-hand. Congealed and dripping pizzas, made of everything from wheat flour to aluminum, are torn to bits and stuffed into the greedy faces of the pirates. The dreaded deep-fried cherry pies in little cardboard boxes from Earth are popped into pirate mouths. Vast kegs containing mixtures of colas, root beers, and myriad other kinds of soda are tapped. Frozen bagels, hush puppies, Venusian packaged cookies, French-fried meteorites, and the highly popular Milky Way bars, both frozen and toasted, are greedily gobbled by the pudgy pirates.

Atop the White Tower, the finest and rarest delicacies are brought to Sargon. Greasy potato pancakes, some as large as the great leader himself, are covered with applesauce, chocolate syrup, and iron filings, for the pirate king's pleasure.

The sound of chewing, gurgling, and swallowing fills the crater as each pirate works his way through the endless mountain of junk food. The feast has not yet ended. The first burp has not been heard, when Sargon rises. He lifts his hands. The pirates, seeing the leader about to speak, stop their feeding. Hunks of interstellar fried chicken are swallowed unchewed. Mouths are wiped on polyacrylic sleeves. There is silence in the great crater.

Sargon looks out over the millions of loyal followers. He speaks, "Feh! I don't like this food."

Feh! Sargon has said Feh! The space pirates look at one another in terror and wonder. Nothing like this has ever happened before. A deep silence hangs over the crater.

Sargon is idly toying with a hunk of potato pancake from the planet Fred in the galaxy of Betelmoose. "This can't be all there is," says Sargon the Mighty, Sargon the Malevolent,

Sargon the Munchmaster. "For all of time we have plundered every planet of its junk food. But, all of a sudden, it all tastes alike. The best potato pancake tastes pretty much like the worst. Can it be that life is without meaning? Is it all stale, flat, and unprofitable?"

Sargon is unhappy. His sadness instantly affects the ten million space pirates. Floods of salty tears turn the dusty floor of Wimpy to mud. Fat men rend their leisure suits, and beat upon the ground with fists the size of hams. A hideous and horrible moan rises from the tubby multitude.

Fat pirate captains try to tempt Sargon with jelly bean burritos, chicken fat popcorn balls, and hot dogs made of meat, fish, fowl, and lizard. Nothing interests him.

Nothing this horrible has ever happened in the long history of Spiegel. Sargon, and his father before him, and their fathers before them have never turned down any sort of food. What can be the matter? Is this the end of Spiegel? Are the fat space pirates doomed?

Sargon has been sitting, legs stretched in front, on the flat surface of the White Tower. Suddenly, he springs to his feet. "Aha!" Sargon shouts.

Aha? The great pirate leader has said Aha? Maybe there is hope. Ten million miserable fat space pirates wipe their eyes, blow their noses, and listen.

Sargon speaks, "My men, we have been resting on our past glories. We have become thin and lazy. Now that we are a great interstellar power, it is right that we should seek new and even grander conquests. You may ask, 'What more is there for us? Already the universe is ours—at least, everything we want in the universe is ours.' It is true, we have riches beyond measure. We are feared and powerful. Already we have enough junk food to last us until the end of time. What is left to add to our glory?"

The fat pirates look at one another, and scratch their heads, and fiddle with their horn-rimmed glasses. What, indeed, could be left? They don't know. "We don't know," they say.

"Knowledge!" shouts Sargon. "Knowledge! Knowledge is power! Now that we have achieved our material goals, we can devote ourselves to finding out the really important secrets of the universe. No wonder those potato pancakes tasted bad—we've lost all the excitement in our lives. Now, I charge you all to travel the reaches of space—not to pillage and plunder as we used to do—but to study and learn.

"In a year's time, let us all meet here again. Each ship's crew will report on what it has learned of the really important things in creation—namely, where the greasiest, heaviest, and most fattening cooking is to be found. Our wisest men will judge these reports, and determine the three most serious cooks of junk food in the universe. Then we will bring these three cooks here to Spiegel, and have a grand intergalactic cook-off. Each cook will have to cook for all ten million of us. Then we will vote to decide which cooking is really the most gross, greasy, sugary, and generally excessive. When we have done this, we will know, once and for all, which is the greatest junk food in all the universe. Now, my brave men, go at once—we meet in one year's time."

The ten million Fat Men dash for their spaceburgers. One by one, the great pirate ships take off, and circle the White Tower, where Sargon the Intelligent, Sargon the Inquisitive, salutes them.

Then, each spaceburger begins its journey into the uncharted vastness of space. The twelve green moons of Grabowsky dwindle into nothingness, as the spaceburgers speed away.

When the last spaceburger has vanished into the darkness of space; Sargon the Generous, Sargon the Gigantic, Sargon the Gross, takes the controls of his own spaceburger, and rockets off into the great unknown, in search of the perfect eatable.

Part 2

ABDUCTION

FROM
THE JOURNAL
OF NORMAN BLEISTIFT

July 15

I AM NORMAN BLEISTIFT, AND THIS IS MY
journal. A journal is like a diary, only a journal
is classier. Steve Nickelson suggested that I
keep a journal. I had found this neat book on
top of a garbage can. It doesn't have anything
printed in it—otherwise it looks like an ordinary book. Someone had written a poem, or
part of a poem on the first page. It was a lousy
poem. I tore the page out. I showed the book
to Steve Nickelson, and he said I ought to use
it for a journal, so that is what I'm going to do.

July 16

The only thing about keeping a journal is
this—there's not that much to write. Since it's
summer, I'm working full time at my job. My
job is helping Steve Nickelson at the Magic

Moscow. The Magic Moscow is a sort of ice-cream stand and health-food restaurant. It's the single most interesting place in Hoboken. There isn't a kid in Hoboken who wouldn't like to have my job. They can't have it, though. My boss—that's Steve—has promised that I can have the job until I'm sixty-five.

July 17

The reason the Magic Moscow is an interesting place is that everybody in Hoboken comes in there at least once a week. There are some very weird people in Hoboken. In fact, most of the people in Hoboken are weird in some way or other. For example, today someone finally ordered a Day of Wrath. Steve has been waiting for this for six months. The Day of Wrath is a special sundae.

Some of Steve's other specials include the Moron's Delight and the Nuclear Meltdown. To give an idea of what they're like, the Moron's Delight is served in a shoebox lined with plastic. The Nuclear Meltdown is served in one of those cardboard buckets, the kind you get chicken from the colonel in. The Day of Wrath is served in a knapsack.

This guy came in and ordered one. Steve has had signs up all over the place advertising the

Day of Wrath for months. Nobody has shown any interest. Even our Moron's Delight and Nuclear Meltdown customers have shown no interest in it. It costs fourteen ninety-five.

The guy was nothing special—just a regular middle-class guy in a leisure suit, overweight like a lot of our customers. He walked in, read the signs taped to the walls, and ordered a Day of Wrath, the same way anyone would ask for an ice-cream cone.

Steve went right to work, making up the Day of Wrath. It has a whole eggplant, two slabs of whole wheat pizza dough, all sixteen flavors of ice cream, fresh figs, pistachio nuts, a lobster, and assorted fresh garden vegetables and fruit. The whole thing goes into a freshly laundered regulation army knapsack, and Steve shoves it into the microwave oven. Two minutes later, out it comes, piping hot. Steve put on a certain record of music by Franz Liszt, and served it to the customer.

"This is for a real gourmet," Steve said.

July 18

Steve is depressed. Now that he's served a Day of Wrath, he says there's nothing left for him to look forward to. Also, he probably felt let down because the guy who ordered the Day of

Wrath didn't say anything. He just ate the whole thing, burped politely, asked if he could keep the knapsack, folded it up, paid his fourteen ninety-five, and walked out.

Of course, watching someone eat a whole Day of Wrath was fairly exciting. We get to see some impressive feats of gluttony at the Magic Moscow, but this was beyond anything we'd seen for some time.

Steve kept his hand on the telephone, ready to call the Hoboken Volunteer Ambulance Squad the whole time the man was eating.

There was no problem, though. The guy looked as though he could eat another one if he wanted to.

Steve said it was an anticlimax.

July 19

Just another ordinary day. We sold a lot of ice cream, hamburgers, bean sprout salads, deep-fried pumpkin rinds, two Moron's Delights and a Nuclear Meltdown.

Steve is still depressed. At one point, he went out in the alley behind the Magic Moscow, and sat on a box. I ran everything by myself for a couple of hours.

July 20

That guy was back, the one who ate the Day

of Wrath. He had four friends with him. They all looked more or less the same—fat guys in leisure suits with glasses. They ordered a Day of Wrath apiece, ate them, paid their seventy-four dollars and seventy-five cents, and walked out. Not one of them said a word. This was the most unusual event in the history of the Magic Moscow. It was stranger than the mad onion-ring-eater. That's a guy who eats ten or twelve orders of onion rings at a time—and he throws each onion ring in the air, and catches it on his nose before he eats it! This quintuple Day of Wrath eating beat the mad onion-ring-eater by a mile.

"The guy must have liked it," Steve said. "After all, he came back, and he brought his friends. The Day of Wrath may get to be a popular special yet."

July 21

When I got to work this morning, the Magic Moscow was gone! I mean it was entirely gone. The building was gone. The giant cow's head statue was gone. There was nothing at all in the place where the Magic Moscow had been but a neat rectangular hole in the ground.

And there was no sign of Steve!

STEVE NICKELSON'S REPORT
TO THE FLYING SAUCER CLUB
OF HUDSON COUNTY,
NEW JERSEY

ON JULY TWENTY-FIRST, I WOKE UP AT the usual hour, washed, dressed, and had breakfast consisting of some leftover pizza and a cup of hot chocolate, some sardines, and a bermuda onion. I then let my dog, Edward, out onto the roof, where he likes to stay in nice weather, and left the house. I live with my parents, but they weren't awake yet. I go to work very early in the morning.

On my way to work, I stopped in at Moe's candy store and newsstand, had a cup of coffee and a corn muffin, and bought a copy of the Times of Hoboken, *my favorite newspaper.*

I arrived at my place of business, the Magic Moscow, a gourmet restaurant I operate in the city of Hoboken. Upon arriving I found a large crowd of customers waiting to get in. Usually, business is not very brisk before five in the morning, but on this particular morning there were about twenty-five people waiting for me to open up. I assumed there was some sort of convention in town, a fat people's convention, since all of the people waiting for me to open were very fat. A few of them I had seen before—they had come to my restaurant and eaten my new special, the Day of Wrath. The rest of the fat people I did not recognize.

As soon as I unlocked the door, all twenty-five fat people rushed inside the Magic Moscow, and began waving what looked like bright blue bunches of garlic around. I started to ask what they were doing, but one of the fat people waved a bunch of bright blue garlic at me, and I found that I was suddenly unable to move or speak.

The blue garlic was obviously some kind of powerful drug. It was also powerful garlic. It smelled great. Even though I was hypnotized, or paralyzed, or drugged, or whatever, I couldn't help thinking that if I could get some of that blue garlic, I could create a special even better than my masterpiece, the Day of Wrath.

The twenty-five fat terrorists obviously had a truck or something parked in the alley. They ran out and came back with rolls of aluminum foil. They wrapped everything in the Magic Moscow with aluminum foil. They wrapped the tables and chairs, the kitchen equipment, the stores of food—everything. They even wrapped me in aluminum foil!

All this time, I was unable to move or speak. I could think, and that was all. I even noticed that I wasn't breathing, and my heart wasn't beating—but I wasn't dead. The fat terrorists had somehow put me in a state of suspended animation with that blue garlic. What a pizza I could make with that stuff! I thought that if I came out of the experience alive, I'd make a terrific effort to get some.

Once I was wrapped in aluminum foil, I was less able to tell what was going on. At this point I could only guess at what was happening. This is what I think happened next— the fat people caused me and the Magic Moscow and everything in it to shrink in size. The reason I think this is what happened is that someone—or something—picked me up and carried me! Being stunned by the bright blue garlic, and wrapped in aluminum foil, and shrunken to a tiny size, I can't tell for sure just how I was picked up. It felt as though a giant hand had picked me up, like a foil-

wrapped baked potato — a cold, foil-wrapped baked potato. It was at this point that I began to suspect that the fat people were not from this planet.

Later, I discovered that I was right. I was carried in my shrunken state to a giant space-burger, and, along with the Magic Moscow and everything in it, I was taken to the planet Spiegel.

I have promised not to reveal anything that happened once I was on the planet Spiegel, and I will keep my word. However, since no mention was made of keeping secret any of the events leading up to my landing on Spiegel, I offer this report in the hope of advancing scientific knowledge. As far as I know, I am one of the only Earth persons to have visited another planet under these circumstances, and therefore my report should be of singular value to the Flying Saucer Club of Hudson County, New Jersey.

Respectfully submitted,
Steven Ludwig Nickelson

REPORT OF THE MEMBERSHIP COMMITTEE OF THE FLYING SAUCER CLUB OF HUDSON COUNTY, NEW JERSEY

WE HAVE REVIEWED THE REPORT OF MR. Steve Nickelson about his supposed abduction by extraterrestrials. While highly interesting, this report does not impress us as being in any way authentic.

First of all, everyone knows that extraterrestrials are little green men with big heads, or shapeless pink things with eyes on stalks. There has never been any report in the history of flying saucer watching to suggest that beings from another planet are "fat people," as Mr. Nickelson describes them.

Many of our members have been abducted by beings from space, and none of them has reported being wrapped in aluminum foil and reduced to a tiny size.

Our club has always maintained the highest scientific standards. We must be careful not to discredit the valuable research we have done by endorsing the statements of cranks, loonies, prevai:~ators, or practical jokers.

No one has ever heard of a planet called Spiegel.

While Mr. Nickelson is well liked and respected, and his restaurant is regarded as the best in Hoboken, we feel that we must reject his statement absolutely.

One cannot help but wonder if his claim of being abducted by "fat people" is not just a publicity stunt to promote the bright blue pizza he has been featuring at the Magic Moscow.

Mr. Nickelson's application for membership in the Flying Saucer Club of Hudson County, New Jersey, is rejected.

The Committee

NORMAN BLEISTIFT SPEAKS

RIGHT AWAY, AS SOON AS I'D GOTTEN OVER the shock, I ran to the police station.

"The Magic Moscow has disappeared!" I shouted.

"Hello, Norman," said Sergeant Feeny, who was sitting behind the big desk. "How's your mother and father?"

"The Magic Moscow has disappeared!" I shouted again. I was pretty excited.

"What do you mean, disappeared?" Sergeant Feeny said. "You mean it's closed down?"

"I mean it's gone!"

"It burned down?"

"It's gone! There isn't a trace of it. There's nothing there but a hole in the ground!"

"Sounds like it may have exploded," Sergeant Feeny said. "I just came on duty. I'll check the blotter, and see if the Magic Moscow blew up during the night."

Sergeant Feeny read over the reports of things that had happened the previous night. "There doesn't seem to be anything about an explosion. I'll send Officer Mooney over to have a look. Officer Mooney! Will you go over to the Magic Moscow with Norman here? He thinks it may have blown up, and no one told us about it."

Officer Mooney and I walked over to where the Magic Moscow had been. It was still missing—there was nothing there but the neat, rectangular hole in the ground.

"It's gone, all right," Officer Mooney said, making a note in his little book, "but it doesn't look as though it blew up, Norman. You see, explosions are usually sort of messy. This area is actually very tidy. There isn't even a lot of dust around. I don't think it blew up. Of course, that's just my private opinion. It may have been an unusually neat explosion. I'll ask the fire department to have a look. They know about explosions."

Officer Mooney pushed the button on his two-way radio. It squawked and crackled. "This is Patrolman Mooney," he said. "Can we have the fire department at the intersection of Third and Bloomsbury—a possible explosion."

Two minutes later the whole fire department roared up, lights flashing, and sirens howling.

Chief Clone of the fire department inspected the square crater.

"This was no explosion," he said. "Explosions are messy."

"That's what I was telling young Norman," Officer Mooney said, "but I thought we'd better have an expert opinion."

"You did the right thing, of course," Chief Clone said, "but this is not the site of an explosion. The building that was here was obviously deliberately demolished by a professional wrecking company—an unusually neat professional wrecking company. I'd suggest that this matter be taken up with the buildings department of the city of Hoboken. They're the ones who issue permits for this sort of thing."

"Then it's not a police matter," Officer Mooney said, "so I'll be going."

Officer Mooney walked back toward the police station, and the fire department equipment rolled off in the direction of the firehouse.

I headed for the city hall and the buildings department.

In the buildings department, I talked to Commissioner Vasolini, the head of the department.

"You say that someone has demolished the Magic Moscow?" Commissioner Vasolini said. "Well, we don't have any record of it. I'll send a man over later in the week. If this is true, and if we find out who did it, that person will be in big trouble. You have to have a permit to demolish a building, and somebody owes the city of Hoboken three dollars."

I couldn't think of anybody else official to report the missing Magic Moscow to. I spent the rest of the day looking for Steve. I had a feeling I wasn't going to find him—and I didn't. He wasn't at home, and he wasn't in any of the usual places he liked to hang out in. The Magic Moscow was gone, and Steve was gone—and I didn't know where.

I was pretty depressed.

All day long, I kept going back to look at the hole in the ground where the Magic Moscow had been. People would stop, and look at the hole, and say, "Looks like they tore down the Magic Moscow."

Nobody seemed to really care.

AN UNNAMED THIRD PERSON WHO KNOWS EVERYTHING THAT HAPPENS IN THIS STORY SPEAKS

WHEN NORMAN BLEISTIFT WENT TO BED that night, after searching all day for his friend, Steve Nickelson, and not finding him, he had a hard time falling asleep. However, even though he was very worried, he was also very tired, and he finally did fall asleep.

While he was sleeping, fifteen Fat Men, in plaid sport jackets, climbed through his bedroom window, wrapped him in aluminum foil, and carried him away.

BUILDING INSPECTOR
GRIBNITZ'S REPORT
TO COMMISSIONER VASOLINI

WENT TO 301 BLOOMSBURY STREET.
Building ain't there. Nobody knows who done
it. Nobody got a permit. Somebody owes the
city of Hoboken three dollars.
  Further remarks:
  They done a very neat job.

                    Respectfully submitted,
                    Kevin Arthur Gribnitz

ON BOARD
THE SPACE CRUISER
CHOLESTEROL

*IT IS THE ETERNAL MIDNIGHT OF IN-
tergalactic space. The great spaceburger, Cholesterol, largest and mightiest
of the Spiegelian star fleet, is cruising
at maximum speed. The course is set
for Spiegel, and the crew has nothing
to do except idly monitor the instruments. Some of the space pirates are
playing a game of Twinkie checkers;
others are sleeping; still others are
carving replicas of the great ship out of
hard Neptunian salami. The ship is
homeward bound, leaving behind the
galaxy containing Earth. Throughout
the spaceburger there is an atmosphere of greasy contentment, and the
smell of frying blintzes in the gallery.*

The Cholesterol *is the flagship of the
pirate fleet, and deep within the great
machine are the quarters of Sargon the*

*Stupendous, leader of the fat pirates
of Spiegel, and master of everything
edible in the universe. Sargon reclines
upon cushions, casually munching
sandwiches made of Earth bagels,
and goose lard from the planet Mel in
the galaxy of Dildup. Accompanying
Sargon on his homeward voyage are
his chief lieutenants: Ted, Ned, Ed,
and Fred—the Fearsome Foursome,
the premier gluttons of the cosmos, the
burger-pest quartet, the imperial lard-
guard.*

SARGON: The time hangs greasy on my fingers.
Pirate captains, stir yourselves, and
provide me some amusement. What
games and sports have you planned to
divert me on this journey?

FRED: Master, if it should please you, Captain
Ted is prepared to do single combat
with the giant terrestrial shrimp of Nof-
tis, and having vanquished the beast,
we can roll it in breaded bean sprouts,
deep fry it, and eat it with vinegar and
garlic.

SARGON: We did that last night. What new sports
have you devised, my captains?

ED: Superior one, if you desire it, I can sing
a song in which I extoll the virtues of

all one hundred and six varieties of heartburn.

SARGON: That song again! Are you trying to make me mad? I warn you—don't get me mad!

TED, NED, ED, FRED: Master of everything. Please, please don't get mad! We beg you, spare us that disgusting spectacle!

SARGON: All right. I'm under control for the moment—but you'd better come up with something pretty amusing, and quick!

TED: Oh, great one! This is great! Oh, hee hee, I can hardly refrain from laughing just thinking about this fantastic stunt. Now listen to this—all four of us pirate captains will push raisins around on the floor—with our noses! Wouldn't you enjoy seeing such a preposterous sight?

SARGON: That does it! You will all die. Steward! Prepare the deep fryer for these witless buffoons.

NED: Oh, great Sargon, spare us. Forgive our stupidity. If we fail you in some way, you have only to instruct us. Do not punish us—although we are not worthy to live—only show us what sort of entertainment you prefer.

SARGON: Do I have to do everything myself? Very

well—I will permit you to continue your
miserable lives.

TED, NED, ED, FRED: Oh, Master! We love you.

SARGON: Naturally. Now, to devise some pleasant
entertainment. Let's see—we can play
bagel toss, or we can throw half-melted
ice-cream bars against the wall, or we
can have a whipped cream fight, or . . .
I have it! We can defrost the prisoner!
Let's get our captive, and thaw him out,
restore him to normal size, and have
fun asking him questions.

*A small foil-wrapped package is
brought in and placed on top of the
nuclear bun warmer. Soon, the rigid
object becomes limp, and it is un-
wrapped to reveal a one-tenth size
Steve Nickelson. The seemingly lifeless
form is sprayed with Spiegelian
seltzer, and it grows to full size, and
animation—it is Steve Nickelson as he
is known and loved by the citizens of
Hoboken.*

STEVE: You're the guy who ate the Day of
Wrath.

NED: Silence, dog! This is Sargon, known as
the merciless, the malevolent, the

mean. Speak when you're spoken to, or you'll feel my leatherlike vinyl two-tone oxford.

SARGON: Let the Earth creature speak, my men. Perhaps he will say something amusing.

STEVE: Did you like the Day of Wrath, or what?

SARGON: It was an amusing snack. Hardly filling, but fairly tasty. I was . . . favorably impressed.

STEVE: That's all? Favorably impressed? That's all you have to say about a culinary masterpiece?

FRED: Slime! Talk fresh to our master, will you? I'll have you drowned in imitation nondairy creamer. When Sargon the Magnificent says he was favorably impressed, the only decent response is to die of happiness on the spot. You want praise from the emperor of the universe? You want the pirate king to jump up and down and clap his hands, maybe? Mighty one! Give me permission to deal with this piece of worthlessness.

SARGON: Calm yourself, Captain Fred. Remember, this is an artist—one of the three

great sloppy chefs of all creation. We
must treat him kindly.

STEVE: One of the three great sloppy chefs?

SARGON: Yes. I may as well tell you that after I
sampled your little confection, I called
in a panel of supreme experts from the
planet Spiegel. They agreed with my
judgment that you are worthy of being
included in our three-way interplanetary cooking contest. We are hurrying to
Spiegel now to begin the cooking—and
eating. You will have the chance to
prove yourself against the other two
greatest greaseball cooks in all the universe.

STEVE: Really?

SARGON: Really.

STEVE: Oh, I wish my assistant, Norman
Bleistift, could be here to hear this.

SARGON: You have an assistant?

STEVE: Yes, Norman Bleistift.

SARGON: And he normally helps you cook?

STEVE: Sure.

SARGON: Pigs! Dogs! Monkeys! Lizards! Why wasn't I informed of this? The boy in the restaurant! That must be the assistant. Is that right, Nickelson?

STEVE: Sure. I told you. Norman Bleistift.

SARGON: Under the rules, every cook is entitled to have an assistant. Engine room! Full speed astern! We have to go back to Earth to get the assistant, because these dratted pirate captains didn't bother to find out that there was one. Now shrink this Earth being and put him back in the freezer. I don't want him to see the horrible things I'm going to do to you!

Part 3

SLAVES OF SPIEGEL

THE GREAT FAIR AT BLINTZNI SPAMGOROD

ONLY ONE SETTLEMENT EXISTS ON ALL the planet Spiegel. This is an insignificant trading village called Porky. In ancient times it was known as Blintzni Spamgorod, and it was a mighty city. In those days, a great fair was held in the city every year. Those were the days before the inhabitants of Spiegel turned to piracy. In those times, Spiegel was a planet of humble but bad-tempered garlic farmers, and the fair at Blintzni Spamgorod was originally a festival celebrating the garlic harvest. One year, in the distant past, following a sensationally good garlic harvest, the Spiegelian peasants went mad from an overdose of bright blue garlic. Led by a tribal chief known as Istvan the Impossible, the garlic farmers stole every morsel of food from the guests at the fair. This marked the beginning of the Spiegelian pirate traffic, and it was the end of the great fair.

Until now.

For almost a year, news has been circulating throughout the traveled parts of creation, of the challenge of Sargon, leader of the blimpish plunderers known as the pirates of Spiegel. News has spread of his edict that his men search for the most greasy, heavy, addictive, and calorific foods. Also, for almost a year, no fat pirates have raided any planet. For the first time in memory, every planet has been able to enjoy the full benefits of its harvest of sugar, goose fat, herring, and other products. As a result of this bounty, interplanetary trade has flourished. People are rich, as are androids, gleptoids, intelligent robots, werewolves, insubstantial thought-forms, mineral-creatures, astral jellyfish, giant Manx cats, and the clown-men of Noffo.

There is peace and prosperity everywhere. Happy with their wealth, and wealthy enough to devote some time to pleasure, the inhabitants of everywhere are all in the mood to have a good time.

So it is, that when the citizens of Porky on the pirate world, Spiegel, invite all interplanetary travelers to a great fair, and promise safe-conduct to everybody, everybody wants to go. The fair is planned to coincide with the return of the pirate fleet. In this way, all the visitors will be present for the great contest which Sargon has planned, to find the supreme grease monkey of all time and all space.

The fair is to begin on the Night of the Crumbling Moons, a month before the day set by Sargon for the return of the last of the space pirates.

On the Night of the Crumbling Moons, when the twelve green moons of Grabowsky appear to collide, and produce the illusion of smashing one another to bits, Sargon's great-grandfather, Irving the Whale, too old to go raiding, but still feared and respected, makes a long boring speech, and declares the fair open.

Beings from every world have come to Spiegel in spacecraft of every imaginable sort. Thousands of merchants have come with stores of strange merchandise to sell. Traders have come to trade. Buyers have come to buy. There are musicians and actors, jugglers and acrobats, fortune-tellers and wise men, dancers and swindlers. There are space-doctors tending to the ills of creatures from every world. There are barbers who charge according to how many hairs the customer has, and others who charge

according to how many heads. Tents and prefabricated buildings are erected. Of course,
knowing that this is the planet of the Fat Men;
many, many restaurants, sausage stands, pizza
parlors, soda fountains, bakeries, candy shops,
deep-fried chopped liver wagons, mayonnaise
carts, and bagel factories are brought to Spiegel for the fair.

The main street of Porky, renamed Blintzni
Spamgorod in honor of its former glory, has
turned into an endless colorful midway. Mer-
rymakers walk, crawl, hop, slither, fly, and float
back and forth all day and all night, enjoying
the many pleasant spectacles. There are roast
goose jugglers, meteor swallowers, monsters
able to turn themselves inside out, many-
mouthed musicians who can play fifteen horns
at once, pseudo-octopusian fandango dancers,
and whistlers from Glintnil. There are mixed
beast races, wrestling matches against giant
slothoids from Neptune, six-dimensional chess
games, screaming contests, and knocking
down three milk bottles with a baseball.

The atmosphere is filled with the smell of
good things to eat. As one walks along the
midway, one can hear a thousand kinds of
music. Everywhere are the happy sounds of

laughter, talking, snorting, growing, hooting, squeaking, and bellowing.

As the days of the fair go by, more and more of the fat pirates of Spiegel return. Usually never seen, this time they have brought with them their sweethearts and wives. Everyone is impressed at the sight of these beautiful women, almost as big as the pirates. Wearing stretch pants in every pastel color, with bright yellow hair piled high on their heads, they walk proudly beside their pirate lovers, smoking filter tip cigarettes.

The fair has been an unbelievable success. Spilling far beyond the boundaries of the renamed Blintzni Spamgorod, the colorful tents and stalls extend into the countryside for miles. Every day, more beings have arrived, and no one has left. Millions and millions of people and others have been enjoying the endless entertainment for almost a month.

Soon the last of the pirates will have returned.

Where is Sargon?

As the appointed night approaches, one year from the occasion of Sargon's great challenge, there is tension everywhere. It is rumored that already two of the three contestants in the great cooking contest have been found, and that Sargon himself is bringing the third.

Then, as the twelve moons of Grabowsky wax almost full, a single voice cries out in the midst of the revels of the great fair.

"Sargon comes!"

Soon the cry is taken up by a thousand voices—and then ten thousand—and then a million.

"Sargon comes!"

Every eye, sensor, antenna, and heat-seeking organ is directed to the sky. In the almost infinite distance, almost invisible, a tiny green speck can be perceived. It looms larger, catching the glow of the twelve green moons. It is the majestic flagship, the *Cholesterol.*

Sargon has returned to Spiegel.

SARGON'S TRIUMPH

SILVER BELLS TINKLE. HORNS AND FLUTES are sounded. Children laugh and shout. Women faint. Strong men cry. It is the triumphal procession of the great Sargon, returned to Spiegel after a year of travel to the far reaches of space.

Down the long midway of the great fair at Blintzni Spamgorod, vivid with flowers and colorful flags and ribbons, the mighty Sargon and his pirate crew march with measured step.

First in the long parade to honor Sargon come the gleptillian musicians, glepts, pseudo-glepts, and gleptiles from the galaxy of Twilbstein. Each gleptoid is capable of producing the sound of a full ninety-piece symphony orchestra from within his own body. A phalanx of a hundred such musicians, wearing gleptizoidal helmets, sound the fanfare welcoming

Sargon to the great city of Porky, and the great fair.

Next come rank upon rank of Freddians, known for their sweetness. These adorable inhabitants of the planet Fred distribute bouquets of space orchids, onions, and zitzkisberries to the insanely happy crowd, and put everybody in an even better mood—if that is possible.

Giant ducks from a planet of unknown name are led through the street, each duck held by a stout chain in the hands of a powerful Spiegelian pirate. The crowd cheers. The ducks snarl and hiss. The pirate duck handlers control the fearsome beasts.

A succession of strange and amusing animals is led before the crowd. Fluorescent lizards, singing walruses, lighter-than-air bears, wombats, both wild and domesticated, these and many other rare zoological specimens are presented to the enthralled spectators.

Next come famous people: foreign dignitaries, ambassadors from other worlds, heroes, celebrities, newscasters, athletes, and interplanetary rock stars.

Here is Rolzup, the Martian High Commissioner, a great favorite of the crowd. Here is the Ugly Bug Band, a famous rock group of which all the members are ugly bugs. Here is Dr. Kissinger, the reincarnated Attila the Hun, the three stooges, and the ghostly form of Alexander the Great. One after another, great personages walk or ride or are carried in the great procession. The crowd cheers.

Now comes plunder—for Sargon has broken his own rule, and done the tiniest bit of piracy, just to break the monotony on the way home. Carts laden with the prized potato pancakes are wheeled through the street, each propelled by fifteen sweating pirate captains. Next come carts drawn by immense Nafsulian horses, and piled high with Hershey bars, Milky Ways, Milk Duds, frog pralines, crystallized cabbage leaves, and copper sulphate jawbreakers. Atop each of the candy carts sit Sargon's lieutenants who toss handfuls of the sweets to the populace.

Now come the captives. In this case there are only two—but they are more interesting than the usual gangs of slaves, for these represent Sargon's entry in the great cooking contest. The captives consist of a slightly chubby, bearded man in white clothing, and a young Earth boy in pajamas. They walk before the chariot of Sargon himself, each with an immense rope around his neck.

Now Sargon himself is in view. The crowd

gasps at the splendor of his polyacrylic finery. His belt and shoes are of the whitest plastic, and his shirt and necktie are of matching paisley design. Sargon is the handsomest and heaviest of men.

NORMAN BLEISTIFT'S
SPACE JOURNAL

I'M WRITING THIS ON SOME URANIAN HAM-
burger wrappers. Later, when I get back to
Earth, I'll copy everything over in my journal.
Sargon says we can go back to Earth after the
cooking contest is over. Sargon is the boss
around here, so if he says we can go back, then
we can go back—if he means it. Sargon can do
anything he wants. If he should change his
mind and keep us here on the planet Spiegel
for ninety-nine years, there wouldn't be a thing
anybody could do about it.

It's an uncomfortable situation.

Steve doesn't seem to be all that uncomfortable. He's mostly preoccupied with the contest.
He really wants to win. Ever since he found out
that whoever wins the contest will be regarded
as the greatest sloppy chef in the entire universe, he can't think of anything else. I told

him that just being selected as one of the three finalists is a big honor—but Steve wants to win.

I didn't write the date at the top because I don't understand the Spiegelian calendar. All I know is that it's the year of the Jelly Doughnut. I don't know what day it is.

They're having a sort of world's fair on Spiegel. It's pretty nice, and I saw a lot of very unusual things. Steve says it's really lucky for a kid of my age to get to visit another planet at all, let alone one on which there is a big fair and a cooking contest.

I didn't get to see as much of the fair as I would have liked to because Steve and I are captives. We don't get to just walk around and do whatever we like. I think that's unfair. I mean, where could we escape to?

Steve and I are living in the Magic Moscow, which the space pirates have restored to its original size, and set up in this big crater. Outside, all around the Magic Moscow, there's a sort of fence made of cloth. It's like a big tent without a roof. There are space pirates standing guard outside the roofless tent. We're not supposed to go outside. I did peek under the edge of the thing once, and saw that there were two other roofless tents in the crater. I suppose the two other finalists are in those. I guess the pirates don't want the contestants to see each other yet.

Every now and then some fat Spiegelian pirate, or some weird space monster who has influence with the pirates, comes into our enclosure and has a look at us. In a way, it's a lot like being in Hoboken, except that the space monsters don't order anything to eat.

Steve is busy cleaning all his equipment, and getting everything ready for the contest. He's pretty nervous.

I wonder if the winner gets a prize. Steve says that he has something in mind that he wants to ask Sargon for—but first he intends to win the cook-off.

The Next Day:

Some pirates came in and asked if there was anything Steve needed for the contest. They said that we'd have to cook for at least ten million. Steve didn't blink an eye. He told them to come back in an hour and he'd give them a list of raw materials he'd need. Steve has this funny look in his eye. He's been smiling this grim smile all day. I'm getting scared. Can Steve have gone crazy?

I asked him. "Steve, have you gone nuts or what?"

"I'm not crazy, I'm inspired," Steve said.

"This space travel has given me a lot of ideas. What's more, when we were being led through the street the other day, I noticed a Spiegelian fruit and vegetable stand with some really interesting things on it. These space pirates obviously think I'm going to cook the Day of Wrath as my entry in the contest. No doubt I could win with it—but I'm not taking any chances. Right now I am in the process of creating a new special which surpasses everything. Next to this new special, the Day of Wrath will seem like a grilled cheese sandwich on white bread with a cup of instant tomato soup on the side."

"What will this new special be called?" I asked.

"I think I'll call it Sargon's Space Surprise," Steve said. "Now be quiet while I make out this list."

The space pirates came back to get Steve's list. He handed them six or seven sheets of paper, and they left.

In another hour, a spaceburger cargo ship appeared. It hovered over the enclosure containing the Magic Moscow, and dumped several mountains of strange Spiegelian vegetables, at least a hundred tons of bright blue garlic, eleven million large grocery bags (folded), and ten trash compactors from Sears & Roebuck's interplanetary division. Also, the spaceburger brought uncountable thousands of things in tubs, boxes, bottles, and jars, enough ice to make an iceberg, sacks of flour, and about a carload of fresh bean sprouts.

"Let's get to work sorting this stuff out," Steve said. "The contest is tomorrow, and we want to make sure we have everything."

FROM A RADIO BROADCAST

". . . THE PRESIDENT'S DOCTOR SAYS THAT the President's cold is much better. It is not as serious a cold as the one Lyndon Johnson had in 1966. The official first doctor says that the President will drink lots of liquids, take aspirin, and get as much rest as possible. Further bulletins will be broadcast on WXXO throughout the day and night.

"In the science news, it is believed that contact may have been made with intelligent life in space. For a number of years an enormous dish-shaped radio antenna, known as the 'big ear,' has been scanning space in hope of recording some sound—any sound—which might give evidence of life on other planets. Today, scientists at the Moskowitz Observatory, home of the 'big ear,' announced that they have been receiving some strange signals, which just might be evidence that we are not alone.

"WXXO interviewed Dr. Mildred Gurdjieff of the Moskowitz Observatory:

" 'For some time now, we've been listening to very remarkable signals on our highly sophisticated listening equipment. These signals do not appear to be any of the known forms of radio static or atmospheric interference which we ordinarily hear. In fact, we can't say exactly what these signals are. They consist of a series of gurgling, crunching, and slobbering sounds. One of my colleagues suggests that the signals resemble the sound one would hear if one listened to a very large group of sloppy eaters—say a thousand people eating spareribs and corn on the cob into a microphone. We will continue to record these sounds, and hope to someday decode and analyze these strange noises. Of course, we don't know if these are indeed signals from distant space, or just some new form of interstellar static, but we plan to continue to listen to these signals as long as we can receive them.'

"We have brought you a science note from WXXO news. Listen to the news headlines every seven minutes, in-depth news reports every half hour, and late-breaking headlines as they happen on WXXO. Now we return to our program of Rumanian music."

BEFORE THE CONTEST
Sargon Speaks

MY MIGHTY MEN, WE HAVE ALL SURVIVED and returned to Spiegel after a long year. Every pirate has carried out my orders and searched the great emptiness of space for outstanding greaseball cookery. Constantly in radio and telepathic communication, each pirate captain's discoveries have been considered by our finest gourmets and wisest men. I myself have traveled as far as the planet Earth in one direction, and as far as the planet Schwartz in the other.

Now our long quest is ended. We have found the three beings who are, without a doubt, the greatest culinary artists in all of creation.

Now, I greet you all, and also our many guests who have come to enjoy the great fair at Blintzni Spamgorod, our ancient capital.

The three supreme chefs are present, and

ready to prepare their single greatest dishes for our pleasure. When we have all sampled their skills, we will decide which is truly the greatest of all.

The three contestants are unknown to one another. Now, I, Sargon, your leader, will introduce them to one another, and to this distinguished gathering of connoisseurs.

First, from the planet Terraxstein, I introduce Evest Linkecsno. Linkecsno, as you can see, is a member of a race of giants. He will cook for us a 100-percent wool ragout, with béchamel sauce and anchovies, and a Plutonian chili side dish.

Next, I present Tesev Noskecnil, from the planet Horthy. Noskecnil is a humanoid slothoform, and he will cook a hot celery tonic soup, served with lead-dipped bagels and mammoth goose legs.

From Earth, comes our last contestant, Steve Nickelson, member of an unnamed species. Nickelson's offering is a brand-new recipe created just for our contest, called Sargon's Space Surprise. I caution the judges that just because Mr. Nickelson is the candidate I myself found, and just because he has had the good taste to name his new culinary masterpiece after me, is no reason to give him special favor in making a selection. I expect every pirate judge to vote his conscience in this matter. Afterward, those who disagree with me will be horribly punished as usual.

And now, let the contest begin!

BEFORE THE CONTEST
Norman Bleistift Speaks

SARGON SUMMONED EVERYONE ON THE planet to the big crater. Then he climbed up onto this tall vertical rock called the White Tower, and made a speech. Nobody paid any attention to me. I slipped out of the enclosure, still wearing the big white apron Steve had given me, and mingled with the crowd. I had to maneuver around quite a bit until I was able to find a space creature shorter than me, so I could get a decent view of what was going on. I finally took up a position behind a crab-man from Nildok. I could see fine—his antennae hardly got in the way.

As I was saying, Sargon made a speech about how great everything was, and then he introduced the contestants.

First was a giant named Evest Linkecsno. He appeared to be about eleven feet tall, sort of fat, dressed in white with glasses and a big bushy beard.

Next, Sargon introduced a humanoid slotho-form named Tesev Noskecnil. *He* was sort of fat, dressed in white, and had glasses and a big bushy beard.

Finally, Sargon introduced Steve, who, of course, is sort of fat, always dresses in white, and has glasses and a big bushy beard.

All three of the greatest sloppy joes in creation looked just about the same! What a remarkable coincidence.

I heard a fig-person from Witzbilb telling a lobster-man from Bongo about doppelgangers. The fig-person said that every being has more or less exact duplicates wandering around. The fig-person said that the three great slob chefs were doppelgangers, or in this case triplegangers. A gong was sounded. The contest was about to begin.

JUST BEFORE THE CONTEST
Norman Bleistift Speaks
Some More

THE TENTLIKE APPARATUS WAS REMOVED.
Steve hurried back from the top of the White
Tower, and rolled up his sleeves.

"Norman, this is just the same as lunch hour
in Hoboken," he said. "Don't be nervous. Just
pay attention—and whatever you do, don't get
between the space pirates and the food."

We had been up most of the night preparing.
The actual recipe was no problem. Steve had
that all worked out. The difficult thing was
keeping the Sargon's Space Surprises moving
at a constant rate. We had eleven million orders
to fill, and Steve didn't want any bottlenecks.
My back and arms were already sore from sorting all the ingredients and placing everything
needed to make a Sargon's Space Surprise in
each of eleven million large grocery bags.

"There won't be any time to stop once we get

started," Steve said. "No matter how tired you get—just keep moving. By the way, I'm paying you triple for last night and today's work."

That Steve is one considerate boss.

This was the order of construction Steve had worked out: Each large grocery bag contained most of the ingredients of a complete Sargon's Space Surprise. My job was to dump each bag into a Sears & Roebuck trash compactor, and push the button. There were ten compactors, so that as I dumped a bag into number ten, number one would be finished squashing everything. As each load of ingredients was flattened, I'd hand it to Steve. Steve would flip open the bag, add one gallon of peach ice cream, dust the whole thing with powdered coconut, add a handful of pickle slices and seedless grapes, and pop the whole thing into the microwave. He had a bank of six microwave ovens. Moving just right—fast, but not so fast that we were likely to start making mistakes— we could turn out a complete Sargon's Space Surprise every four or five seconds.

I did some figuring.

"Steve," I said, "averaging one serving every five seconds—even if we don't take a break— it will take us almost ninety-nine weeks to hand over eleven million servings. And I'm already tired from filling eleven million large-size grocery bags."

"I'm going to keep serving until I drop," Steve said. "You can take a rest if you want to. You don't win contests without working hard."

This is what each grocery bag contained: One Venusian cranshaw melon, a whole ham, three giant radishes (weighing six pounds) from Glintnil, five Bartlett pears, a kosher salami, one quart of Vermont maple syrup, two pounds of raw oats, and a Spanish olive.

"It's a sure winner," Steve said.

Part 4

MUNCHOMON

THE GREAT INTERPLANETARY COOKING (AND EATING) CONTEST
Sargon Thinks to Himself

NOW IS THE MOMENT OF MY GREATEST glory. This day surpasses that on which my great-great-grandfather surprised the Bleeeeghan worms and took away their chocolate-covered granola. This day will be greater in the history of my people than that on which the ancient, frozen Milky Way vault was found beneath the polar cap of the planet Bruce. For ten thousand years times ten, songs will be sung of the events of this day, of the great convocation of pirates and the cooking and sampling at the great fair at Blintzni Spamgorod.

And it is I, Sargon, who have done this thing.

Statues of Sargon in metal, marble, halvah, and tuna fish will be erected on planets great and small. Children will be told stories of my might. There will be fan clubs, and a television cartoon series. All beings will know and fear the name of Spiegel, and the name of Sargon.

See how my pirate captains trot from place to place, standing in line to sample the wonderful food. See how the contestants labor, hoping to be the honored ones of Spiegel. See the expressions of astonishment and admiration on the faces of our guests from other worlds.

The entire universe will never forget this day. I, Sargon, will form a company to manufacture Sargon dolls. Every man, woman, and thing in creation will buy one. With my riches, I will buy a Hershey bar as big as the moon. Greatness shall be mine, and all because of this day. And now, SARGON EATS!

THE GREAT INTERPLANETARY COOKING (AND EATING) CONTEST

Steve Nickelson
Thinks to Himself

Flip open the bag.
Flip.
Ice cream. Peach ice cream.
Shove it in. Shove it in.
Coconut. Put coconut. Put coconut.
Now pickles. Put pickles in.
Quick. Quick. Faster. Faster.
Oh no! Forgot the grapes!
Quick! Grab grapes. Put them in. Put them in.
The microwave. Open the microwave.
Take out the done one.
That one's done. Give it to the pirate.
Give. Give.
Put this one in the microwave.
Open the next microwave.
Give it to the pirate.
Flip open the bag. Flip. Flip.
Ice cream. Put in the ice cream.

Now the coconut.

That one's done. Open the microwave. Take. Take.
Give. Give. Give it to the pirate.

Next one. Now pickles. Put them in. Put them in.

Take.

Grab.

Put grapes.

Give.

Put.

Flip.

THE GREAT INTERPLANETARY COOKING (AND EATING) CONTEST
Described by Norman Bleistift

IT TURNED OUT THAT WE WERE ABLE TO move a lot faster in the atmosphere of Spiegel than we could on Earth. In fact, an Earth person on Spiegel can move exactly 693 times faster than on Earth. It makes sense if you think about it. Those Spiegelian pirates are really fat. You'd expect them to be slow—but on Spiegel, they scoot around like little bugs. It's the thin atmosphere (the only thing on the planet that's thin) and the reduced gravitational pull.

Plus, the microwave ovens on Spiegel are way faster cooking than the ones on Earth.

That was how we were able to fill eleven million grocery bags in a single night. We were too busy to think about it, but if we had, we would have realized that it was a major accomplishment.

So instead of taking ninety-nine weeks to make and serve eleven million Sargon's Space Surprises, it was possible for us to do it in a day—and we did.

I'm not saying that it wasn't hard work, but we were able to handle it. It *was* a little like the lunch rush in Hoboken, the way Steve said it would be. Of course, the space pirates and creatures were better looking and better dressed than our usual clientele, and we didn't have to take time to make change or ring things up on the cash register.

This was how the contest was set up. The pirates and assorted monsters formed an orderly line. They started at the location where Evest Linkecsno, the giant from Terraxstein, was handing out his wool ragout with béchamel sauce and anchovies and chili. The pirates and space things filed past Linkecsno's place, picked up the food, and kept going, still in line, eating as they walked.

The next place was where Tesev Noskecnil, the humanoid slothoform from the planet Horthy, was cooking. Noskecnil was supposedly serving something very plain. When Steve heard about it, he was sure that Noskecnil would be coming in third. What Tesev Noskecnil was supposed to cook was hot celery tonic soup, lead-dipped bagels and mammoth goose legs. It's the sort of thing you might expect to get in a school cafeteria on a lot of planets. I heard a banana man from Zalbar talking about it. What no one was prepared for was the unannounced side dish that Noskecnil was serving. It was Horthian Florff. Not only was it Horthian Florff, but it was from the most respected recipe, written in the sixth century on Saturn by the great Ben, a famous chef.

Now, serving something that wasn't announced had to be against the rules—let alone serving something from someone else's recipe, even the great Ben's. However, since Spiegel is a pirate planet, nobody really cared that Noskecnil was cheating. In fact, the pirates might have thought it was a good idea, if they were thinking about anything but food.

Horthian Florff is made as follows: It contains flounder, chopped chicken liver, vanilla ice cream, peanut butter, cashews, whipped cream, a cherry (one to a hundredweight), and pounds and pounds of paprika. It is whipped into a froth in a gigantic blender. Noskecnil served it in 48-ounce dixie cups with a wooden spoon.

During a break, I ran over and tasted some. It was sort of interesting.

Steve was really bugged about the Horthian Florff.

"Watch that slothoform guy get disqualified," Steve said. "If I had known cheating was allowed, I would have gotten hold of a couple million bottles of Fred's Bayou Hot Sauce, and really walked away with the prize."

Steve was worried. The pirates walking away from Tesev Noskecnil's place were licking their fingers.

THE GREAT INTERPLANETARY COOKING (AND EATING) CONTEST
Described by Captain Ned

Oooh!
Munch.
Mmmmm!!!
Gimme!
Slurp!
Yum!
Grab.
Chomp.
Ooooh!
Good!
Lick.
Gulp.
Bite.
Swallow.
Gurgle.
Slobber.

Burp!

Part 5

ESCAPE

THE DECISION OF THE JUDGES IS FINAL
Norman Bleistift Speaks

STEVE CAME IN SECOND.

The winner was Tesev Noskecnil, the humanoid slothoform from the planet Horthy. I could have predicted it.

I went back for seconds of the Horthian Florff myself.

At the end of the day, all the Spiegelian pirates voted on the three contestants. Sargon voted first. He voted for Noskecnil. Then the rest of the pirates voted.

It was unanimous.

The visitors from other planets didn't get to vote. Most of them were in the first-aid tents anyway. They all pulled through. Nobody died.

I was pretty tired at the end of the day. Steve was, too. While the pirates voted, Steve and I just sat on the floor of the Magic Moscow and stared into space.

After a while, Captain Ted, one of the pirates, came and told us that the voting was over, and Sargon was going to announce the winner. We followed Captain Ted to the White Tower. Evest Linkecsno and Tesev Noskecnil were already standing there.

Sargon made a speech about what a good contest it had been. He burped quite a bit while he was talking. Then Sargon announced that Tesev Noskecnil was the winner, Steve was the runner-up, and Evest Linkecsno was in third place. All the pirates cheered and belched.

Then Sargon announced the prizes.

TO THE NOSKECNIL BELONGS THE SPOILS
Sargon Speaks

PEOPLE OF SPIEGEL! OUR GREAT SEARCH is over! At last we have found the one greatest, the most superb, the ultimate slop-jockey in all the universe. Now Spiegel can rejoice. I, Sargon, of all the great pirate kings, have brought this wonder to pass. This is our finest hour!

A great monument will be made to commemorate this splendid day, with a five times life-size statue of myself, your brilliant leader, at the top.

Every year, on this date, we will hold a grand celebration, and the great fair at Blintzni Spamgorod will continue annually, ending with a great feast of Horthian Florff and other good things.

And now, we will reward the great chefs who have participated in the contest.

To Tesev Noskecnil we give the greatest honor any being in creation can receive. That is permanent citizenship on Spiegel. Yes, fortunate Noskecnil, you will be permitted to remain with us here on this magnificent planet for all time. Here you will prepare Horthian Florff and your other specialities day after day and year after year. But that is not all. You will also receive this set of plastic luggage, this beautiful color-coordinated living room set, this beautiful 1972 Chevrolet automobile, and a lifetime supply of aftershave lotion in the distinguished peanut-butter fragrance. Congratulations, contestant Noskecnil!

Now we reward the runners-up. To Steve Nickelson of Earth, we present six hundred pounds of finest Spiegelian blue garlic; and deluxe transportation for Steve, and his assistant, Norman Bleistift, back to Earth.

To Evest Linkecsno, the third runner-up, we give a color picture of me, Sargon, and twenty-four hours to get out of town.

And now, my mighty men, mighty women, and things of every description, follow me to the cooking place of our winner Tesev Noskecnil, where we will enjoy seconds, thirds, and fourths of his superlative Horthian Florff!

Noskecnil, begin cooking!

AWAY FROM THE PLANET
OF THE FAT MEN
From Norman Bleistift's
Space Journal

WE ARE TRAVELING ON A THIRD-CLASS Spiegelian cargo ship, a spaceburger used for transport. It's a local, stopping at planets and asteriods all along the way to Earth, where it will pick up a load of Pop Tarts.

We didn't get wrapped in aluminum foil or reduced in size this time. Instead, we get to sit in the galley, where there are lots of candy machines, ice-cream dispensers, and instant hot sandwich machines. The Magic Moscow, foil-wrapped and shrunken, is in the hold along with Steve's prize, the six hundred pounds of blue garlic.

The crew wanders in and out of the galley, dropping coins in the machines, and getting cellophane-wrapped salami and cheese sandwiches, ice-cream bars, and paper cups of hot chocolate. They are not first-class pirates. They just drive this big cargo spaceburger back and forth—loading and unloading. Their leisure suits are wrinkled, and their white plastic shoes are scuffed.

One of the pirates, Henry, explained to me, that due to some principle of space travel he didn't understand, we'd be getting back to Hoboken on the calendar date following the one on which we were kidnapped. That is if we get to Hoboken. Henry says that they may have to drop us off in Newark. If they do that, I don't know how we'll get the Magic Moscow back to Hoboken.

Steve says it hardly matters. He says after the workout the equipment got during the contest, we'll be closed down for a week making repairs.

Steve is not depressed about losing. Obviously, the first prize would not make most people deliriously happy. Tesev Noskecnil looked pretty depressed the last time I saw him.

Steve is happy with his prize of six hundred pounds of blue Spiegelian garlic. He says he has plans for it.

I'm going to stop writing now. Henry just looked in and told us we could come up to the control room. We're about to pass through an enormous flock of space chickens, and we want to see them.

END

The Snarkout Boys
and the Avocado of Death

I

I thought that going to high school was going to be a big improvement over what I was used to. It turned out to be just the opposite. For example, there's the biology notebook. The biology notebook is what we do in my biology class. Every page in every kid's notebook is exactly the same as every page in every other kid's notebook. We have to copy out these long, boring things the teacher writes on the blackboard. And we have to copy pictures from the textbook. One of the assignments is to copy the picture of a grasshopper and letter in all the labels showing what the different parts of the grasshopper are. The labels are in the textbook, too. When the notebook is all finished, we're supposed to put it in a folder and make a nice cover. We can put anything we like on the cover. If the cover is really nice and artistic, you'll get an A on the notebook— and for the course. If you copy everything you're supposed to and the cover is only so-so, you'll get a B. A kid with sloppy handwriting, one who can't draw, might get a C.

I would say that the biology notebook is typical of what goes on at Genghis Khan High School.

I've been going to that school for eight months, and I

still can't believe how utterly boring, nauseating, stupid, and generally crummy it is. I don't have a single class I like. I don't have a single teacher who's the least bit interesting. What's worse, most of the kids don't seem to care that the school stinks. They don't like it, but they aren't outraged about it. They just go through the motions—like robots, or zombies. The big thing for most of the kids is getting into various kinds of trouble outside of school. For my part, getting hold of beer and throwing up every weekend isn't any more interesting than the school.

I think I might have gone crazy in that miserable school if I hadn't gotten to be friends with Winston Bongo.

Winston Bongo is a very creative person. He's the inventor of Snarking Out. He also holds the world's record for number of Snark Outs successfully completed. Until he invented Snarking, no one on Earth had ever Snarked, as far as we knew. And until I became a Snarker, Winston was the only person to do it.

I have the second greatest number of Snarks to my credit, but I have no solo Snarks at all. So, I guess you could say that I was the co-inventor of team Snarking.

I met Winston Bongo on the first day of Mrs. Macmillan's English class. He came in late. He'd gotten delayed trying to borrow a Jewish star to wear to class. This is one of the few positive things that I've noticed at Genghis Khan High School. This Mrs. Macmillan has something against Jews. Years ago, she used to make speeches about Jews in her classroom. So this tradition got started: Every semester, kids who aren't Jewish, and Jewish kids who don't have them, borrow Jewish stars to wear around their necks in Mrs. Macmillan's class. It's fun to watch her panic when she realizes that she's facing another all-Jewish class. She believes that Jews creep around, plotting the end of civilization—and seeing all those Stars of David makes her crazy.

The first time I met Winston Bongo was in that class, on the first day. He walked in and tripped. He fell to the floor with more noise than I would have thought possible for one kid to make just falling down. It sounded like a chest of drawers falling down stairs.

I didn't know who he was at the time, but I noticed that he was sort of heavy and thick in his body. His black hair looked like it had been cropped with dog clippers. His nose was long and fat at the same time, and his eyes seemed to wander against his will.

"The poor kid is retarded," I thought. "I'll be nice to him."

Winston Bongo gathered up the books and pencils and sheets of paper he'd strewn everywhere when he fell. He sat down in the seat next to mine.

Later on, I would find out what Winston Bongo thought when he first saw me. "The poor kid is retarded," Winston thought. "I'll be nice to him." The fact is, I probably look as weird as Winston Bongo. I'm about the shortest kid in school. Also the fattest. People refer to me as No Neck. It's my nickname. I don't care for it. I happen to look like a penguin. Is that so bad?

The other thing that makes Winston Bongo appear to be not right in the head is this funny smile he's got. When he was taking that incredibly loud and clumsy fall, he was smiling, sort of to himself, no teeth showing.

It turns out that Winston Bongo is a fantastic wrestler.

He's taken private lessons at a professional gym, and he knows hundreds of falls and tumbles. His uncle is a professional wrestler. You can see him on television sometimes. His name is the Mighty Gorilla.

Of course, I didn't know any of this that day. I didn't know that Winston Bongo had taken the fall to amuse himself—on purpose. I just thought he was a big klutz.

After class, Winston Bongo looked at me. From the way he was looking, I thought he was going to make some remark—like calling me No Neck, or Fire Plug. I had this momentary feeling of anger and humiliation. Here I was about to be insulted by a kid who was obviously feeble-minded and had fallen over his own feet not a half hour before. But he didn't say anything insulting. "You ever do any wrestling? he asked. "You've got the build for it."

II

Winston Bongo lives in an apartment building about a block from the one I live in. His building is slightly more complicated to Snark Out of, because they have an elevator man. In my building the elevator is self-service. That makes Snarking Out less of a challenge.

Winston Bongo has to sneak down eleven flights of the service stairs and then slip past the little room where the elevator man sits watching the late movie on television. All I have to do is get dressed in the dark, get out of the apartment without waking my parents, take the self-service elevator to the basement garage, and go out a side exit so the night watchman in the lobby won't see me.

Then I meet Winston Bongo, and we take the Snark Street bus all the way downtown and get off across the street from the Snark Theater.

That's the main part—the technical part—of Snarking Out, except for the hats, of course. You have to wear a hat when Snarking Out. The idea is to keep anyone from guessing that you're underage when you ride the bus or buy your tickets at the Snark Theater. I question whether this works, or whether anybody cares that we're kids. We've each got a fake student activity card from Hun State University. Winston got them from his sister, who goes there. Mine has a girl's picture on it and is fixed up with ballpoint pen. It wouldn't fool anybody if they looked at it closely, but nobody ever does. And we get the student discount—fifty cents at all times—at the Snark.

Still, Winston invented Snarking Out, and he insists on hats. They have to have brims, so we can keep our faces in shadow. I have a cowboy hat, and Winston has a regular snap-brim his father used to wear years ago.

The Snark Theater has a different double bill every day, and it's open twenty-four hours around the clock. It shows movies I never heard of, and it shows them in strange combinations.

For example, a typical double bill might consist of a Yugoslavian film (with subtitles), *Vampires in a Deserted Seaside Hotel at the End of August*, and along with it, *In-*

vasion of the Bageloids, in which rock-hard, intelligent bagels from outer space attack Earth. Everybody gets bopped on the head until the scientists figure out a way to defeat the bageloids. I won't spoil the ending by telling what it is, but it has something to do with cream cheese.

I wouldn't say that every movie the Snark Theater shows is good, but they're all interesting in their way.

Another nifty thing about the Snark Theater is that there's a box in the lobby: You can write down the name of any film that was ever made and drop the slip of paper in the box, and the Snark Theater will get that film and show it. They send you a letter with a free ticket on the day they show the film you asked for. And if you tell them your birthday, they send you a free ticket on your birthday.

Winston Bongo found out about a movie from his uncle, the Mighty Gorilla. It was a film his uncle had seen once when he was wrestling in Germany. It was called *The Beethoven Story*—the life story of Ludwig van Beethoven. Winston requested it, and a couple of months later we Snarked Out and saw it. Winston saw it for free. We are always looking for obscure, unknown films to ask for. The difficult part is finding out about those films, unknown as they are.

Of course, we could go to the Snark Theater at ordinary times instead of slipping out of the house when our parents are sleeping—but that wouldn't be Snarking Out.

On a typical Snarking Out evening, I go home right after school and do my idiotic homework. While doing that, I like to listen to the radio. Lately, I've become something of a classical-music freak. There's this radio station,

WGNU, that plays all kinds of classical music. My favorite composer is this guy named Mozart.

My parents don't go in for much music at all. Once in a while they watch a singer on television, and that's about it.

In addition to doing my mindless homework and listening to some music, I feed my bird and clean up his cage. My bird is a parakeet. I bought him in the dime store. I also got him a king-sized cage, so he won't feel too crowded. When I'm home, I close the door to my room and let him fly around. His name is Nosferatu. He used to be called Pete. Pete Parakeet. I changed his name after I saw this old movie at the Snark. It's called *Nosferatu*, and it's the original Dracula story. It's ten times as scary as the version you see on television. The guy who plays the vampire is really bizarre. My parakeet is sort of bizarre, too. He's pale and skinny, if you can imagine a skinny parakeet. He looks like he's in bad health, but he's really all right. I've had him for about three years, and the whole time he's looked as if he might drop dead any minute, so I renamed him Nosferatu, after the skinny vampire in the movie.

My parents weren't too happy about my bringing home a pet. Also, my mother said that birds are bad luck.

You have to watch out for her. She makes up superstitions on the spur of the moment. For example, I actually believed it was bad luck to get a haircut on Thursdays until I was about eleven years old. I might have believed it longer, but I noticed that my mother had changed the unlucky day to Tuesday. She also told me that if you eat cherries and drink milk at the same time, you'll be dead within half an hour. I think one time someone she knew, maybe her boss where she worked, ate some cherry pie and a glass of milk and then happened to die a little while later. It's hard to track these things down, because if you question my mother directly, about anything, she gets cagey and denies everything. She says she's not superstitious.

III

On the evening I'm telling about now, my father called me to supper. "Walter! Come see what I've got."

What he had was an avocado. Whenever he brings one home, which is fairly often, he makes a big fuss about it.

"Looky, Walter, an avocado! What do you think of it?" My father is the only person I know who says "looky!" He also says "lookit!"

What I think of avocados is this: On principle, I do not eat green, slimy things. My mother doesn't eat them either. She says she doesn't like the taste of avocado. That's good enough for me. If there's any question at all about the taste, I'm leaving those suckers alone.

My father loves them. Every time he brings one home, he acts like it's a three-hundred-pound sailfish he's caught singlehanded, or an elk he brought down with a bow and arrow.

He's really enthusiastic about avocados. He skins them and digs out that oversized, stupid-looking pit, and then mashes up the slimy green part with a fork. Then he puts lemon juice and vinegar, salt and pepper, and powdered garlic and paprika on it. If you have to go to all that trouble to disguise the flavor, why bother, I say.

Then he makes a speech about it. "My goodness, this is one fine avocado," he says. "You have to know how to choose them. You have to look for the ones that are black and blasted looking. The pretty green ones aren't fit to eat. The funny thing is that they reduce the price of the really scrumptious ones just because they're ugly. I guess they want to sell them before they rot completely."

My father isn't a bad guy, in my opinion. There are just a few subjects, like avocados, on which he's irrational.

My mother had found another tuna-casserole recipe. This is something of a hobby with her. She's constantly finding these recipes in women's magazines. She tries another one at least once a week. They all taste like tuna fish. Usually they have things in them you wouldn't expect to eat with tuna fish—like grapes, hot-pickle slices, fried Chinese noodles.

"I hope you will appreciate this, kiddo," my mother says, "seeing that your mother took a healthy slice out of her finger whilst chopping up the ingredients." She usually manages to injure herself at least once while preparing a meal. She has a Band-Aid on her finger.

"Eat up, champ," she says. "It's American." My mother has an idea that tuna caught in Japanese waters is tainted with radioactivity, so she always shops for brands canned within the continental United States. Even Canadian brands are out. "They're too chummy with the Communists," she says. She calls Communists "Commonists."

If you were blind, or only knew my mother from talking with her on the telephone, you'd probably think she was about six feet tall . . . and maybe two hundred and fifty pounds in weight. It's her voice, and the way she talks. She sounds like she ought to be a big, slow-moving person, maybe a little sloppy. Actually, she's small and nervous, always well dressed, and a chain smoker. Once my father and I have started eating our meal, she brings a little ashtray to the table and puffs a cigarette between bites of food. This is far more disgusting than avocado eating. If I can possibly get out of it, I try not to have meals with my parents. I've complained to them about various nauseating things they do, but it doesn't do any good. "Everybody has a family," my mother says. I don't know what that means.

Our apartment is new. We are the first people ever to live in it. When we first moved into the building, it wasn't quite finished. The whole place smelled of paint, and there was brown paper on the floors in the elevator and the hallways. In those days, we had to take our shoes off outside the apartment door so we wouldn't track plaster dust onto the carpet.

Come to think of it, I've never walked on the carpet in our living room. There are these clear plastic runners my mother put down, making a kind of path through the living room to the dining alcove. The furniture has plastic covers, too. My mother says that when you decorate with light colors, you have to be careful. Nobody ever sits in the living room, except when my parents have company

—and then it has to be company wearing suits and ties, and fancy dresses. When they expect company like that, my father puts on a suit and tie, and my mother puts on a fancy dress and rolls up the plastic runners, and they all sit in the living room. I get called in to be introduced to the company. I always stand at the edge of the living-room carpet. The company says, "I understand you're a fine young man," or, "He looks like a football player. Are you a football player?" I'm at least a foot too short to be a foot-ball player. Besides which, I hate football.

"Yes," I say, "I'm a football player." This happens—having company in the living room—about twice a year. The rest of the time, nobody sits there.

When regular people—relatives and such—come over, everybody sits in the den. The den has a linoleum floor. Sometimes my father sits around in his undershirt. When he's feeling funny, he gets Nosferatu and gets him to sit on his head. Apparently, Nosferatu likes him. He'll sit on my father's head for an hour.

IV

The secret of Snarking Out on a school night is to get to bed extra early and then wake up in time to Snark—usually about 1:00 A.M. The problem is this: If you don't wake up in the time to Snark, your Snarking partner will be standing in the street at one in the morning, waiting for you. That would be poor form. However, if you set the alarm clock, it might wake up your parents.

This is how I solved the problem. I wrap my electric alarm clock in three or four undershirts and close it in a dresser drawer. When it goes off, the sound is muffled. You can't hear it outside my bedroom. I tried this out one day when my parents were out of the house.

Usually, I wake up just before the alarm clock is set to go off. I don't know why that is, but anytime I want to get up at a specific hour, I usually wake up at that hour. Those times I don't wake up, the tiny, muffled sound coming from my dresser wakes me. I stop the thing from sounding by pulling out the plug—otherwise, it would get louder as I open the drawer and unwrap it to get at the little button on the back. Also, I don't want it to go on buzzing too long, just in case one of my parents is sleeping lightly.

I take the unplugged alarm clock out of the dresser drawer and push the little button that stops it from sounding. Then, by the light coming from the streetlamps outside (we are only on the sixth floor—my mother won't live any higher because, she says, the fall from any higher is sure to be fatal) I reset the clock for the time I usually get up for school. I get dressed and put a pillow and a bunch of clothes and things in the bed to look like me in case anyone wakes up and peeks in. Then I sneak out.

On this particular occasion, I went to bed a little before nine o'clock. That's fairly early, I know, but it doesn't make my parents suspicious because they seldom stay up past eleven themselves. Also, I make a point of going to bed at all different times, to keep them off guard. When I get up at one in the morning, I already have had half a night's sleep. Then, if I can get back from Snarking between four and five, I can catch another three hours and wind up with a total of seven. I read in my hygiene book last year that you really need no less than eight, but I can get by with seven once in a while. Besides, at Genghis Khan High School, being half asleep helps kill the pain of spending a whole day with nothing worthwhile to do.

Actually, on this particular night I woke up at five minutes to one. I don't want to seem to be boasting, but my Snarking technique is so developed that I can be up, dressed, and out of the house in five minutes without making a sound.

It went without a hitch. I was in the street four minutes and forty-six seconds later, which equaled my best time previously. I have a stop watch right next to the bed, and the first thing I do when Snarking Out is punch the stop watch, and later slip it, still running, into my pocket.

Winston Bongo arrived a few seconds later, stop watch in hand. He pushed the button as he came up to the bus stop. "How long did it take you?" I asked.

"Seven minutes even." It takes him longer than me because he has to use the stairs and get past the elevator man. Still, seven minutes is very respectable, world-class Snarking time.

"The bus will be along at one-o-three," he said.

We had our hats on.

The bus was on time. We got on, paid our fares, and went to sit in the back. There was nobody else on board.

As the Snark Street bus got farther downtown, a few people got on and off. A lot of them were people we'd come to recognize from other rides on the Snark Street bus. There was an old black man with a chicken, for example. We've seen him lots of times.

"Do you know what's playing tonight?" I asked Winston Bongo. Usually I check the newspaper, but tonight I forgot.

"It's a Laurel and Hardy festival," he said.

"That's good." I like Laurel and Hardy. They have their movies on television sometimes, but they're always cut so they will fit in the half-hour kiddie-show format—and half of that is commercials for toys and breakfast cereals.

When we got to the Snark Theater, the place was packed. It was hard to find two seats together. Where did all these people come from at after one in the morning? Usually the Snark is a little less than half full at this hour.

And the audience was going crazy. They were laughing and hollering and carrying on. I'd never seen anything like it.

When we came in they were showing a movie—just ending—in which Laurel and Hardy are destroying this guy's house, and the guy is destroying their car. It's pretty funny, but not nearly funny enough to account for all the screaming and laughing. That was because we came in at the end. By the time the next movie came to the end we were screaming and hollering, too.

I've never had so much fun at the movies. As each new film started, and the audience heard the Laurel and Hardy theme song, everybody started cheering and clapping. We did it, too.

The thing about Laurel and Hardy movies that you can't get from the chopped-up versions on television is how beautiful they are. Things happen exactly at the moment they have to happen. They don't happen a second too soon or too late. You can even predict what's going to happen—and it does happen—and it surprises you anyway. It doesn't surprise you because it happened, but because it happened so perfectly. I laughed so hard that I cried.

Winston Bongo and I did something that night that we had never done before. There was even some question as to whether it was against the International Snarking Rules. What we did was leave the Snark Theater before the performance was over. Of course, there was a technicality involved—we didn't actually leave during the course of a film, but we left before all the films on the program had been shown.

The reason we did that was that we simply had enough. We didn't have the strength to laugh anymore. It was like eating five pieces of the best cake in the world—you just can't handle number six.

When we came out of the Snark Theater, we were staggering around, weak from all that laughing. Also, we felt sort of disappointed that we didn't have the strength to stay for the rest of the films. In the lobby, we noticed a sign we hadn't seen coming in. It said that anyone who had the time they went in stamped on their ticket stub could have his money back if he stayed through the whole program. So we weren't the only ones. That made us feel a little better.

Winston couldn't contain himself and did several very good falls while we were waiting for the bus.

Also, I love Laurel and Hardy because Hardy's fat, and I'm fat, and Winston Bongo isn't exactly a beanpole either.

V

It was only about two-thirty in the morning, a lot earlier than we usually got out of the Snark Theater. There was another hour and a half, at least, of Laurel and Hardy films that we weren't going to see. On the bus going home, we discussed whether to count this as a completed Snark Out or not. There was some talk about counting it as a half Snark, but that would always look sloppy on our records. Finally we decided, since we left the theater voluntarily, and had completed the sneaking out, and would, hopefully, complete the sneaking in, that this could count as a full Snark.

Then the bus broke down. There was a grinding noise, and it rolled to a stop. The driver fiddled around at the controls for a while and then spoke to the passengers. That was us, and the old black guy, the one with the chicken who had been on the bus with us coming the other way. This was a live chicken, by the way. The old guy is a familiar sight in the streets of Baconburg. Sometimes he makes the chicken perform for people.

"Look, folks," the bus driver said, "we seem to be stuck. If you like, I can give you a refund, or you can wait until the next bus comes in about twenty minutes, and I'll give you a transfer slip so you can ride it for free."

It was a nice night. "We're about halfway home," Winston Bongo said to me. "What do you say we walk the rest of the way? It's still early."

It was an unusually mild night for April. I agreed—we'd get a refund and walk home. The old guy with the chicken had decided to get off the bus, too. The bus driver gave us back our money, and we stepped off onto the sidewalk.

We were at the place where Snark Street takes a bend to the left. Across the street was Blueberry Park and the Blueberry Library. I'd ridden past this place lots of times, but I'd never been here on foot. It's an old part of town with lots of trees and old-fashioned little buildings, three or four stories tall, with steps going up from the sidewalk to the front doors.

Late as it was, there were quite a few people in the park. Some were sitting on benches, talking. There was a chess game going on under the streetlights, and a little crowd of people was standing around, listening to someone give a speech.

Blueberry Park and the library next to it were left to the city of Baconburg by James Blueberry, the toothpick millionaire. For a long time, the Blueberry Toothpick Works was the biggest industry in Baconburg. When Mr. Blueberry left the park to the city, he made certain conditions about the use of the place. In his will, it said that the city could have the park, as long as people were permitted to speak there. Anyone who wants to can make a speech there. He or she can say anything at all, and no one is allowed to stop the speech. They don't have to have a permit or anything like that. The other condition Mr. Blueberry made was that there was to be a wall around the park. The city got around that by building a little wall—only a foot high—all around the park. But anybody can make a speech there.

The tall old man in the raincoat—the one with the chicken—wandered across the street and joined the crowd listening to the speaker. Winston Bongo and I went over, too.

The guy giving the speech was a short guy in a raincoat. He had a thick black beard, and glasses.

"Cats and kitties," the guy was saying, "be hip to my lick. My wig may be uncool, but my jive is solid."

"What's he talking about?" I asked Winston Bongo.

"I don't know," Winston Bongo said.

"The Man is putting us little cats down," the guy in the raincoat was saying, "but us little cats are frantic, crazy, and gone. If we don't make the gig, then the gig is no-where!"

"Solid!" "Groovy!" people in the crowd called out.

"What does that mean?" Winston Bongo asked.

"I don't know," I said. "I didn't get a word of it."

"So if The Man says, 'Blow!' and us little cats don't dig the riff, all we have to say is 'Nowhere!' 'Later!' And that, cats and kitties, would be HEA-VY! So if we don't dig the flip, or the number, or the place his wig is at, we just take five until The Man cools it."

"Is he speaking English?" I asked Winston Bongo.

"The speaker is a hipster," someone said. It was the old black guy with the chicken. "He is also a trade unionist. He is discussing the possibility of a strike at the Wana-mopo Banjo Pick Factory. Many of these people are his fellow workers. What he has been saying, roughly, is this: Listen to what I have to say. My intellect may be limited, but my feelings are sincere. The employers are imposing on the workers, but the workers are very important. If we don't cooperate, then the factory can't produce anything. If the employers tell us to work, and we refuse, that will constitute a great disadvantage for the employers. So, if we don't approve of the tactics, or the ideas, or the attitude of management, we can go on strike until an agreeable offer is forthcoming."

"That's what he said?" Winston Bongo exclaimed.

"More or less," said the tall, old black guy with the chicken. "He's regarded as a very good speaker. I'm afraid I don't do his words justice."

"Well, thanks," we said, and moved through the crowd to the edge of the park. As we crossed the street we could hear the crowd clapping, and shouting, "Groovy! Groovee!"

About half a block up the street, we could see a puddle of very bright, very yellow light. As we got closer, we saw that it was a hot-dog stand with a sort of glass enclosure in front of it. There was a flickering blue neon sign in the window that said ED AND FRED'S RED HOTS.

We went inside the glass enclosure. There was a counter made of stainless steel and two windows through which you could be served a hot dog. "Two with everything," we said.

The guy behind the counter put together two hot dogs for us. They were somewhat fatter than the usual hot dog, and very red in color. Also, they had the greenest pickle relish on them I had ever seen, as well as mustard, chopped onions, and little bits of tomato. All the lights in the place were these yellow fluorescent lights—the kind that are supposed to keep bugs away—and there were a lot of them. This made the brightly colored hot dogs and relish look even stranger than they must have looked in broad daylight.

The hot dogs were sort of rubbery on the outside, and resisted when you bit into them. Then your teeth went through the skin with a sort of *snap*, and juice squirted everywhere. The relish had a chemical taste and caused a funny sensation at the back of my throat.

I can't say they were really delicious hot dogs, but they were certainly different. Winston agreed. As soon as we finished our hot dogs, we both felt like burping a lot. These were not like the hot dogs in the square plastic-coated packages our mothers brought home, or like the hot dogs in the cafeteria at Genghis Khan. They were not like the hot dogs at the ballpark or anywhere else. Like them or not, Ed and Fred's red hots were unique.

As I said, Snark Street takes a bend to the left a little past Ed and Fred's. Winston Bongo had the idea that we could take a shortcut by turning up a side street that appeared to cut diagonally to the left, at a sharper angle, before Snark Street made its bend.

We turned left. In two minutes we were lost.

We had wandered into the strangest neighborhood I had ever seen. None of the streets ran parallel. Some of them turned this way and that; some just stopped short. Once we found ourselves in someone's backyard, and once in a funny alley that looked like it could have been in Paris, with cobblestones, and posters on the lampposts.

Everything in that neighborhood was all mixed together. There were little apartment buildings like the ones near Blueberry Park, and there were little frame houses that looked like farmhouses. Also, there were buildings I can only describe as weird, with skylights and carving all over them, and pieces of tile and stone and broken glass set into the cement to make all sorts of designs. And even though it was pretty late—maybe after 3:00 A.M.—lots of lights were on, and we could hear music playing in some of the buildings we passed. Looking into the lighted apartment windows, we saw all sorts of strange things—odd-looking plants, and weird paintings, and plaster busts sitting on pianos and windowsills.

It was by far the niftiest neighborhood I'd ever seen. We weren't even bothered by being lost. We just wandered around, looking at all the strange buildings and enjoying the place, burping and tasting our red-and-green hot dogs.

Some of the buildings had statues on the outside. It all reminded me of movies I had seen at the Snark Theater. It looked like some place in Europe. It was all very old-fashioned. The streets were narrow, and the streetlamps gave a yellow light—not white. I liked the place.

VI

Then, suddenly, we were back on Snark Street, a few blocks from our own neighborhood. "I never knew that neighborhood, the one we were just in, existed," I said.

"Neither did I," said Winston Bongo.

"It's quite a place," I said.

"Yes, interesting," Winston said.

We said good-bye in the street and sneaked into our respective apartment buildings. All in all, it had been one of the most unusual Snark Outs in my experience.

I was in bed by four-thirty and up at eight. At nine I was in school, fresh as a daisy.

In addition to Mrs. Macmillan's English class—where we are reading *Silas Marner*, easily the most boring book ever written—Winston Bongo and I are also in the same biology class. This is where we work on the idiotic biology notebooks. The biology teacher is Miss Sweet. She's about seventy years old. Miss Sweet doesn't speak to the class at all. Instead, she talks to the specimens, plants, and animals in the classroom.

"Oh, dear," Miss Sweet says, "why do they keep sending all these children here? How am I going to take care of my plants and animals properly if they keep sending these children here?" (She's saying this to various growing and living things.) She especially likes to talk to her alligator. This alligator is about two feet long and lives in a glass aquarium. Everyone in the class lives in hope that the alligator will bite Miss Sweet someday. She takes the thing out of its tank and cuddles it and coos to it. The class hopes the thing will bite her, not because Miss Sweet is hateful in herself—after all, it's obvious that she's crazy and not responsible—but just because such an event would break the horrible monotony.

Miss Sweet writes out a passage on the blackboard for us to copy into our biology notebooks.

On dewy mornings the spores separate from the parent plants. In some plants spores are not produced, but in others they are a prominent method of reproduction. As-xual spores are produced by division of one or more cells in a sporangium. In the blue-green algae zygotes are produced by the fusion of two gametes in the gametangium. Among the bryophytes and most of the pteridophytes the as-xual spores are called simply spores. In heterosporous plants (some pteridophytes and all spermatophytes) there are two kinds of as-xual spores, megaspores and microspores. . . .

Needless to say, none of us understand a word of this. It is sort of amusing that Miss Sweet always writes the word *sex* "s-x," but that's not enough to keep our minds alive. We have to copy all this down—it runs to two pages—and it has to be included in our notebooks.

I don't know what a spore is. No one has ever explained it to me. What's more, I don't care what a spore is, and I never want to learn. When I think of spores, I think of Miss Sweet's classroom, the smell of decaying vegetable matter and not-very-clean alligator tank, and thirty kids scratching away, copying pages for their biology notebooks.

Every so often, Miss Sweet asks if there's a boy in the class who has a driver's license. There's always an older kid who is repeating biology—someone who thought he could get away with not turning in a notebook with the correct number of pages. She asks that kid if he would mind being excused from school early and going to the garage to get her car. Naturally, the kid is delighted to do it. She tells him to bring the car around to the back entrance of Genghis Khan and park it there. The word will spread throughout the school, and there will be a huge crowd waiting to see Miss Sweet drive her car after school. Miss Sweet's car is a hot rod. It's an early Chevy, with a very shiny coat of black paint and a special suspension and those big tires in the back. No one knows how she came to have a car like that. It's usually in the shop for bodywork, except when she sends a kid to get it and park it behind the school.

The crowd is waiting when Miss Sweet gets behind the wheel and sends the car crunching into the nearest tree. She does this every time. I, personally, have seen Miss Sweet smash the front of her car twice since coming to Genghis Khan. After she crashes it and is led out of the car, a bit dazed and shaken, she goes into the school and calls the garage to come and tow it away and fix it.

I don't understand why someone doesn't come and take Miss Sweet away. It's so obvious that she's out of her mind. I feel sort of sorry for her, but like everyone else I wish that alligator would bite her once. I wonder why I feel that way when I really should just pity the poor old woman. I think I want it to happen because I believe that I'm suffering worse than she is, and it isn't fair.

I assume that somewhere there's a school in which the biology class doesn't consist of a bunch of miserable kids locked in a room with a poor old lunatic every day, but that school isn't Genghis Khan.

On this particular day—the day after our unusual Snark Out in that strange neighborhood—Winston Bongo appeared to be more depressed than usual. Most days, we managed to at least wink or make faces at each other while we copied the pages about spores, or whatever. Today, Winston looked terrible. He clawed at his sheet of notebook paper, trying to copy the gibberish Miss Sweet had written on the blackboard, with an expression like that of some kind of ape. Later he told me he didn't feel so well.

Winston Bongo had come down with German measles. He called me up that night to tell me. The doctor had been called, and he said that Winston would have to stay in bed for at least a week, and wouldn't be back in school for maybe ten days.

Of course, Snarking Out was out of the question for Winston, but what about me? Winston said that this was a good opportunity for me to rack up a few solo Snarks. For some time we had been Snarking Out at least twice a week. Before I had teamed up with him, Winston had made eleven solo Snarks. He knew that I had none to my credit, and, decently, instead of complaining about his own illness, he encouraged me to improve my record.

I considered the possibility that I might come down with German measles, too, hanging around with Winston as much as I did. But on checking with my mother, I found out that I had already had German measles when I was much younger. You can't get it twice.

I confess I was a little afraid at the prospect of Snarking on my own. Winston had always been the leader of our expeditions into the night, not only because he had originated the sport, but because he had Snarked alone. By encouraging me to take a Snark by myself, he was inviting me to become his equal. I thought that was nice of him.

"Be sure to call me and tell me about your next Snark," he said over the telephone.

I had no choice. I had to go through with it. Thinking

about it, I decided that there was nothing to be nervous about. After all, hadn't I Snarked many a time with good old Winston? There was nothing wrong with my technique. I would do it. What was more, I would make a really good job of it, have something really excellent to report to my friend. I would do something creative, something to expand the horizons of the gentlemanly sport of Snarking. I thought of our adventure the night before. I could do something in that interesting part of town. Then it came to me. I would make a speech in Blueberry Park!

VII

That night at supper, I found out a good deal about the neighborhood we'd visited the night before. My father knows Baconburg well. Once he worked part-time as a cab driver, and he prides himself on knowing every street in town and every section of town.

"What do you call that old-fashioned area down near where Snark Street bends west?" I asked him.

"That's the Old Town," he said. "Lots of artists and bohemians and odd people live there."

"I was walking around there last . . . weekend," I said. "It's really strange, the buildings and all."

"Lookit," my father said, "it's like this, Walter. When a

city gets started, it's not a city. Maybe it's just a few farms near each other, and maybe a store, and later a post office —a little village. If the village is in a good location, near a river, or a railroad, or what have you, it may grow up to be a town and later a city. By the time it's a city, there are people laying out the streets, and putting consecutive nubers on houses, and all of that. But what happens to the little village? In some cities, it gets demolished, or it burns down, or it just rots away. But sometimes, it just stays there, a little town or village in the middle of the modern city—like the pit in an avocado."

It was clever of him to work in that reference to an avocado. I think my father would be the happiest man in the world if I'd once try an avocado to see if I liked it. There's no chance of that happening, much as I'd like to make him proud of me.

"So that's why the twisty, narrow streets, and the houses that look like farmhouses?"

"They are farmhouses," my father said," and nearby is Blueberry Park. Did you know that people make speeches in Blueberry Park?"

"You told me all about that," I said. That was how I knew about it.

"It used to be quite the thing, when I was a boy, to go down there and make a speech," he said. "You know, people talk about all sorts of things there, from serious political speeches to pure raving and nonsense. The thing is, the audiences can be pretty rough. If you can't hold their attention, they'll break in with all sorts of wise remarks, hoots, and hollers. If you aren't careful, you can get a tomato flung at you."

"Did you ever make a speech there?" I asked.

"Oh, I suppose I did once or twice," my father said.

"What did you talk about?"

"Well, as a matter of fact, I spoke about misunderstood and unpopular vegetables," he said. "It was just too much of a temptation for that crowd. It was the middle of summer, and people had a lot of fruit with them. They ruined a sport jacket of mine."

From the things my father was saying, it seemed to me that I just *had* to make a speech in Blueberry Park. After all, he'd done it. I decided to Snark Out and do it that very night.

It was an unusually mild April. The weather was almost like June. Of course, it wouldn't have surprised me to wake up one morning and find it snowing. Baconburg weather is like that. But right now it was balmy and pleasant, and the air was sort of good-smelling. As Winston and I had seen, lots of people were staying up late, enjoying the pleasant night.

I'd Snark that night, and go straight to Blueberry Park and make a speech. The next day would be Saturday, and I'd go over to Winston Bongo's house and tell him all about it. They'd let me visit because I'd had German measles already.

I got to bed early again, prepared to Snark for all I was worth.

I woke up with a funny taste in my mouth. I was excited and a little frightened. I hated to admit to myself that I was chicken, but there it was. I was scared to go Snarking alone. Of course, I could have just gone back to sleep and forgotten about it, but then I'd have to admit to Winston Bongo, as well as to myself, that I didn't have the nerve.

Besides, I thought about my father making a speech at Blueberry Park. Probably he didn't sneak out of the house to do it, but he had done it. That was something else I was scared of. I had never made any kind of speech under any circumstances. Here I was going to make a speech after one in the morning in a place where I might get pelted with tomatoes.

The more I thought about it, the more I didn't like the idea—and the more certain it was that I had to go through with it.

I got dressed, and slipped out of the house in my usual smooth way. I didn't forget to take my stop watch—five minutes until I hit the street.

Of course, there was no Winston when I got there. I felt a little strange at first. The bus came along, and I got on. I sat in the back. All of this was pretty familiar to me. It wasn't so bad. I started to feel more comfortable. The only thing bothering me was the speech. I was a little uneasy about standing up and talking in front of people. I could have just stayed on the bus, gone to the Snark Theater, and seen a movie. That would constitute a good Snark for the record book. I didn't have to go through with this speech bit.

But I did. I just wasn't willing to do an ordinary Snark as my very first solo. Winston Bongo had invented the activity and would be remembered in history for his great deed. I wanted to do something great, too. I wanted to contribute something to Snarking as a worldwide cultural activity. I was realizing that I wasn't content to be just a follower. I was out to do something to astound Winston Bongo—and generations of Snarkers who would come after us.

I got off the bus across the street from Blueberry Park.

I marched right up to the place where the speaker had been carrying on the night before. The crowd was standing around, listening to three different speakers. The three speakers were standing on top of the one-foot wall that surrounds the park. They were maybe fifteen feet apart and all going at once, full blast. At the back of the crowd, you could drift from one speaker to another by sort of moving along sideways.

Of course, the people in the crowd were answering the speakers, arguing with them and heckling them. Some of the hecklers, situated between two speakers, were able to answer back to two speakers, one after the other.

I wandered back and forth at the back of the crowd, picking up one speech and then another.

First speaker:	Brothers and sisters, God doesn't want us to eat meat! It is against nature's plan!
Shouts from the crowd:	Tell that to my dog!
	Didn't I see you at Burger King an hour ago?
	Listen to him! Listen to him! He's right, I tell you.
Second speaker:	Colonial rule must end! The British have broken too many promises for too long. I say get the British

out of Kenya, East Africa, today!

Shouts from the crowd:	Yaaay! Get those British out of Kenya!
	Idiot! The British have been out of Kenya for years!
	Don't eat meat! Don't eat meat!
Third speaker:	*Whoop! Huhn! Huhn! Huhn! Eeeeeeeek!* Wow! The devil. *Woooo!* The dev-vill! Dee dev-v-vil-l-l! *Eeeeek!* The devil gonna get us! *Whoooooo!*
Shouts from the crowd:	Right on, brother. Tell 'em! He's telling it like it is.
	It's all because of those British. They did it!
	Don't eat meat! Don't eat meat!
First speaker:	I never ate a hamburger in my life!
Shouts from the crowd:	It's the devil! He's right! It's the devil!

Second speaker:	They did it in Ireland! They did it in India!
Shouts from the crowd:	War! War with England. We beat them twice already—we can do it again!
Third speaker:	*Hooo! Hooo! Hooo! Humma, humma humma! Goo!*
Shouts from the crowd:	He eats meat! That's why he can't make sense! The devil made him eat a hamburger!
First speaker:	God says . . .
Second speaker:	Get the British . . .
Third speaker:	The devil's got me! *Ooooooh!*
First speaker:	Whole grains . . .
Second speaker:	Jomo Kenyatta . . .
Third speaker:	*Eeeeeek!*
First speaker:	. . . makes you sexually impotent . . .
Second speaker:	. . . agents after me . . .
Third speaker:	. . . devil after me . . .
First speaker:	. . . food companies after me . . .
Shouts from the crowd:	Right! Wrong! Shut up! Go! Stop! *Wheeee!*

VIII

The third speaker—the one talking about the devil—was the crowd's favorite. Mine, too. He wound up his speech by leaping into the air, waving his arms around, twisting, trembling, screaming, and kicking. He was really a good public speaker. He knew how to hold your attention, and he was obviously sincere. Even the don't-eat-meat guy and the free-Kenya-East-Africa guy stopped speaking and turned to watch and listen to the end of the devil's-gonna-get-you guy's speech.

At the very end, he threw himself high into the air and was caught, as he fell, by a number of people in the audience. They carried him away. I guess they were friends of his.

The other two speakers finished up, too—but nothing like the devil guy—and stepped off the wall to the cheers and boos of the crowd. Then two other speakers got started. One was a person who believed that animals should wear clothing. The other was a person who said that beings from other planets were putting stuff in our food to make us stupid. The crowd liked him. "It's working," someone shouted, "look at you!"

Gradually, I had edged my way up to the front of the crowd. I was having a good time. It was interesting to listen to the various speakers and observe their styles. They weren't all speakers, to be precise. One old lady played the harmonica, and another guy whistled. He didn't last very long.

I had sort of forgotten about my intention to make a speech myself. I was just enjoying myself, listening to the other speakers and the comments from the audience. If I had given it any thought, I might have told myself that I would just watch and listen tonight and see how it was done. Then I'd come back another night and make a speech myself.

Just being in Blueberry Park and listening to the others was enough to constitute a very respectable Snark, one I could report to Winston Bongo about. He'd be sure to be interested in the "devil" guy—I was planning to do a good imitation of him for my friend.

In other words, I was chickening out.

Then, right in front of me, the person giving a speech on how eating raw zucchini cures cancer came to the end. "Well, that's all I have to say," she said. "Who's next? You?" She was looking right at me.

The next thing I knew, the old zucchini lady had hopped down off the wall. I felt a sort of stirring in the little crowd of listeners behind me. Somehow I got up on the wall and faced them.

Only at that moment did I realize that I didn't have anything to talk about. I had been thinking about getting up the nerve to give a speech at all—I hadn't really pictured myself saying anything. For a second, I considered trying an imitation of the "devil" guy, but this crowd had just heard him, and I was pretty sure I couldn't bring it off in front of strangers.

I must have just stood there for a few seconds, because somebody shouted, "Well, let's hear it, pal!"

"I'm just a kid," I shouted back. I was going to say something about being just a kid, and would the people please let me off and not holler things at me. If I'd gotten all that out, I have no doubt they would have heckled me right out of the park. As it happened, I didn't get to finish my creepy cop-out beginning because someone shouted, "That's interesting." Another voice said, "I thought he was a streetcar!"

It wasn't really bad-natured, the heckling and shouts from the audience. In fact, those shouts sort of made me feel more comfortable.

"I'm just a high-school kid," I shouted back, "and that means I'm supposed to be getting educated."

"So?" a voice from the crowd asked.

"So I'm not, that's all," I said. "I'm not getting educated, and nobody else in my school is getting educated."

"That's because you're all lazy bums!" someone shouted.

"No, we're not!" I said. "If we lose interest, whose fault is it? I'm interested in the things people say here. How come I've never heard a word in Genghis Khan High School that made me want to stay awake for whatever comes next?"

"You kids are all on drugs!" shouted a voice. "You eat meat—that's what's wrong with you, sonny," shouted another.

"What's wrong with me," I said, "is that my school is part garbage can and part loony bin. My biology teacher is about a hundred years old and talks to things that can't answer back. My English teacher is a full-time professional

Jew-hater. My math teacher is always falling asleep in the classroom. My history teacher talks about nothing but his personal problems, and the gym teacher is some kind of homicidal maniac! That's what's wrong with me! I'm growing up ignorant, and I don't particularly want to!"

"Tell 'em, kid!" someone shouted. "That's good! That's good!" someone else said. "You poor kid, you're gonna grow up an idjit!" another member of the audience said. "Those meat-eating teachers! Those dirty meat eaters! I'll kill 'em!" someone was shrieking.

"Who allows those bozos to be teachers?" I shouted. "Look, maybe I'm a dope. Maybe I can't learn anything."

"You're no dope, kid!" I heard from the crowd. "Naw, he's real smart, I can tell," someone else said.

"Maybe I am a dope," I went on, "but how am I ever going to find out if I'm a dope or not? How can I find out if I can handle high school if nobody wants to teach me anything?"

"The kid's right!"

"It's a shame, those lousy bum teachers!"

"They're making stoopids out of our young kids!"

"Kill the meat eaters! Kill the meat eaters!"

I was a big success.

I didn't have a good ending for my speech, and I didn't have any actual suggestions about what could be done. Basically, my speech consisted of my saying "school stinks," and the audience more or less agreeing with me.

As soon as I was finished, I realized that, had I thought of it, I would have liked to end on a high note and jump off the wall to the loud cheers of my listeners. Instead, I just sort of petered out. "Well, that's all, I guess," I said and stepped down. There was some weak cheering, and one or two people patted me on the back, but most of the crowd was already listening to the next speaker.

"The government is ruining our feet!" he shouted.
"Tell 'em! Tell 'em!"
"Right on!"
"They ruined my brother's feet!"
"Eat meat and ruin your feet!"
"Whoopee!"

I made my way to the back of the crowd.

IX

I moved away from the park. I checked my watch: 2:10 A.M. My first solo Snark was a complete success, so far.

My next stop was Ed and Fred's Red Hots. I ordered one with everything and extra onions. There was someone else in the place, eating a hot dog under the yellow lights. It was a kid, a girl, a little taller than me, with a pointy rat nose and pimples. She had short blonde hair, tinged with green and sticking out in all directions. She was wearing a baggy red skirt that came below her knees and black, pointy shoes. She had skinny legs. She was also wearing a jacket about five sizes too big for her. It was orange and light blue. CUSTER, it said on the back in white letters.

"You go to Genghis Khan," Rat Face said.

I must have given her a look that said, "Do I know you?" or, "How do you know where I go to school?"

"I heard your speech," Rat Face said. "I go to George Armstrong Custer."

"Good school," I said.

"It's a toilet," Rat Face said. "You want a root beer?"

"Uh, sure, thanks," I said.

Rat Face went to the counter and got two small root beers. "What you said was good," she said.

"Thanks," I said. I wasn't too comfortable with this girl. She looked sort of sinister. I would have bet she had a knife on her.

"You ever go to the Snark?" she asked.

That took me by surprise. "Sure," I said. "Sometimes."

"You sneak out of the house when your parents are asleep?"

"That's right." This was really amazing. This was going to be a bigger part of my report than the speech I'd given. Winston Bongo was going to be as amazed as I was. It looked like I'd run into a natural Snarker.

"I would have gone there tonight," Rat Face said, "but they're showing two movies by this Italian guy, Visconti. *The Earth Trembles* and something else. I hate his stuff. I'm not about to pay half a dollar to watch some guys packing anchovies for two hours."

"Yeah," I said. I wondered how long this girl had been Snarking. She seemed to know a lot about movies.

"Now, next week there's the James Dean Festival. Aaah!"

"Yeah," I said.

"My name's Bentley Saunders Harrison Matthews," Rat Face said.

"I'm Walter Galt," I said.

"The kids call me Rat," she said.

"No kidding," I said.

"You can call me Rat."

"OK," I said. Bentley Saunders Harrison Matthews had an oversized comb sticking out of her pocket. A couple of times she ran the comb through her spiky blonde-green hair. The comb was bright pink.

"Uh, Rat, have you been Snarking . . . I mean, going to the Snark at night for very long?"

"Years, pal, years."

This was amazing. If this kid was telling the truth, she was possibly the world's champion Snarker. "Do any other kids from George Armstrong Custer do it?"

"Snark Out?" She used the same term! Incredible! "No, the kids at Custer are mostly insects, mentally. Some of the boys are not too bad—the ones I take automotive shop with, for instance—but they've been brainwashed to hate me. The girls are all subnerds. They fear me because I am a liberated woman. I ignore them. They get their kicks spreading rumors about me."

"Yeah, the kids at Genghis Khan are mostly subnerds, too." I liked that expression. It was the first time I'd heard it.

When Rat was telling me about the kids at George Armstrong Custer, she shoved her hands deep into the pockets of her too-large jacket and hunched her shoulders. She had a habit of bending her ankles so the soles of her shoes faced each other and standing on the sides of her feet. She was sort of cute, in a horrible way.

"Yeah . . . well," Rat said. "I'm not usually too friendly. I just wanted to say that I liked your speech."

"Yeah . . . well," I said.

"Yeah."

"Well."

"Yeah, well, maybe I'll see you at the Snark sometime," Rat said.

"Hey, yeah . . . well."

"Yeah, well, so long." Rat turned and hunched her shoulders a couple of times and walked out of the glassed-in, yellow-lighted enclosure in front of Ed and Fred's Red Hots.

X

The next day in school was mostly standard. There was only one event that I would have to report to Winston Bongo when I saw him that afternoon. Miss Sweet went around the classroom, passing out pairs of scissors, those lightweight, blunt-nosed things we used to get in first grade for doing paper cutouts. Then she came around with a big black can—like a paint can—and a pair of tongs. Reaching into the can with the tongs, she deposited a large, formaldehyde-soaked frog on the table in front of each kid.

"Cut them up, now! Cut them up!" she said to us.

I think it would be best to draw a curtain over what

then took place in the biology class. I will just say that I was not the only one to throw up.

Winston Bongo was delighted when I told him about the dissection lesson. I told him he might not have liked it so much if he had been there.

Then I went on to tell him about my triumph at Blueberry Park. He was impressed, as I knew he would be. He made me give my speech, as well as I could remember it, a couple of times. I also had to tell him what everybody else said. Winston said that for a first-ever solo Snark I had exhibited real genius. I was flattered. I knew that my friend did not pay compliments lightly.

I was saving Bentley Saunders Harrison Matthews, also known as Rat, for my big ending. When I described her and told Winston all about our conversation, he got so excited that I was scared I might have caused him to take a turn for the worse in his recovery.

"Do you realize what this means?" he sputtered. "We haven't been alone all this time! Who knows how many other Snarkers may exist! I never expected anything like this! We have to meet this Rat again and talk to her. Maybe she is in touch with other Snarkers. This could turn out to be a vast worldwide movement."

"I don't think she knows any other Snarkers," I said. "She's sort of antisocial."

"Just the same," Winston said, "She's a great genius. Look, she's invented Snarking Out all on her own. That makes her as great a creative being as . . . myself."

Winston Bongo was all for Snarking Out together that very night. I had a hard time convincing him that he was still sick, and had better stay in bed.

"Well, I'm going to get better in a hurry," he said. "I had planned to stay sick until the first day of Easter vacation, but this is too important."

Meanwhile, Winston made me promise to Snark Out as often as possible, and to look for Bentley Saunders Harrison Matthews in the Snark Theater, and, if possible, to bring her to see Winston.

I promised I would do that. I also promised to visit Winston every day, or call him on the telephone, and to bring him the pages of the biology notebook to copy. Also, I was to bring him the history notebook, which was pretty much the same as the biology notebook, and the social-studies notebook, which was different in that you had to find certain newspaper articles, cut them out, and paste them in. You didn't have to read them—just cut them out and paste them in, and hand in the notebook at the end of the year. All of Genghis Khan High School works on the notebook system. Our English notebook consisted of book reports, which were mostly written about movies we'd seen based on books. If we hadn't been regular moviegoers, we would have had to copy our book reports off the flaps of books like the other kids, but we liked our way better. Not that Mrs. Macmillan ever read the reports; she graded by weight, like the other teachers. The most any of the teachers would ever do would be to open a notebook at random and read part of a page. If this happened with, say, a history notebook, and the teacher found out that the page was your older sister's English homework from five years ago, it might go badly with you.

One of the tricks kids use in preparing nice, heavy notebooks is this: You take your actual, say, biology notes, maybe twenty-five pages' worth. Then you take twenty-five pages of just anything with writing, and shave a quarter of an inch off the outside edge of the page. You put a genuine page, then a shaved-down fake page, then a genuine page, and so on. This way you have a fifty-page notebook, a certain A. When the teacher flips the pages, the book will always open to a real biology assignment. When you've gotten your A, you can take apart the biology notebook and use some of the contents for your social-studies notebook.

Another thing you can do is obtain someone's last-year's notebook cover that got an A. You erase the grade and use it again. The theory is that if Miss Sweet liked the picture last year, she'll like it again this year. I know of a cover with a picture of Liberace on it with labels indicating eyes, teeth, nose, hair, etc., that has gotten five A's already, and, having paid three dollars for it, I have it in my drawer ready to get its sixth grade.

I could probably make my own cover and get an A with it, but it's more challenging to cheat. At least this way, we're actually learning some skills. And the teachers are cheating. The whole reason for the notebook system is so that if anyone accused them of never teaching anything, they could grab one of the notebooks and say, "Look, this kid knows all about sports and grasshoppers and all this stuff—how can you accuse me of never doing my job?"

I solo Snarked a couple of times during Winston Bongo's illness. I didn't go back to Blueberry Park. I wanted to polish up my speaking technique, but I thought it would be more fun to do that when Winston was along.

Instead, I went to the Snark Theater. I saw two good double features—*Alexander Nevsky*, an exciting Russian movie, and *Kiss Me Deadly*, a detective movie. Also I saw *Frankenstein* and Walt Disney's *Song of the South*.

I didn't see Bentley Saunders Harrison Matthews, *aka* Rat, although I looked for her. I was pretty sure she'd turn up at the James Dean Festival, since she'd mentioned it, and I planned to be there, looking for her.

XI

Winston got better. To celebrate, we Snarked Out and saw *The Mask of Fu Manchu* and *Mutiny on the Bounty* (the original version, with Charles Laughton and Clark Gable). We kept a sharp eye out for Bentley Saunders Harrison Matthews, but we didn't see her.

Easter vacation started, and with it the James Dean Festival. Every night the Snark Theater was showing a James Dean film, along with something else. The first night they had *Rebel Without a Cause* and *Attack of the Mayan Mummy*.

As we were watching the James Dean movie, I felt a sharp poke in the ribs. I looked over to my left and there was a skinny, angular figure. It was Rat, also known as Bentley Saunders Harrison Matthews.

"Hiya, Walter," Rat said. "Great stuff, huh?"

Rat was obviously a great fan of James Dean. She was all excited by his appearance on the screen and continually nudged me, pointed at the screen, and whistled, panted, moaned, sobbed, and made comments about James Dean's looks. At times, various members of the audience tried to hush Rat, but she would not be quiet.

"Leave me alone," she said. "Just because you can't appreciate a great actor is no reason I can't have a good time."

The James Dean movie ended—Rat cheered loudly—and *The Attack of the Mayan Mummy* came on. Almost at once, people began fidgeting, talking, and leaving. As the movie progressed, those people still in the theater were almost all engaged in conversation in normal tones of voice. People lit up cigarettes, friends called to each other, and someone behind me was humming and drumming on the top of the empty seat in front of him. Nobody complained. It wasn't the sort of movie you'd want to pay close attention to.

Rat had come up with a chrome cigarette holder about two feet long, and was smoking a black cigarette with a gold tip on it. There's no smoking in the Snark Theater, but people smoke anyway. If the usher has nothing to do, he'll tell you to quit smoking, but since he's usually got a cigarette in his mouth, nobody pays too much attention to him.

"This your friend?" Rat asked, pointing at Winston with the hot cigarette end.

I introduced the two Snarkers. It was a historic moment —two great pioneers in the same field meeting for the first time.

"Walter has told me a lot about you," Winston said. "I understand you've done a lot of Snarking Out."

"If you mean coming to the movies late at night, I've been doing that for a couple of years," Rat said.

"Would you say that you've averaged a Snark a week, or what?" Winston wanted to know.

"I come here on the average three times a week," Rat said. "Some weeks, when I'm bored, or when they've got movies I particularly want to see, I'll come here every night."

"Wow!" Winston Bongo said. "That means you've got the greatest Snarking record of anybody probably."

"Record, schmecord," Rat said. "I've got bigger fish to fry than counting how many times I go to the movies. Besides, if you're interested in records, you'll be interested in meeting my Uncle Flipping."

"Your Uncle Flipping?" I asked.

"Yes, my uncle, Flipping Hades Terwilliger," Rat said. "He's been coming here every night for fifteen or twenty years. He's probably here now. I'll call him."

Rat made a trumpet of her hands and bellowed out, "Hey, Uncle Flipping! You here?" Nobody objected. *The Attack of the Mayan Mummy* unreeled on the screen with nobody watching. In the row in front of us, two guys were unwrapping an elaborate picnic and arranging all sorts of food on a tablecloth they'd spread across their knees.

"That you, niece?" a voice called from way down in the first row.

"Uncle Flipping!" Rat shouted.

"Keep calling, I'll find you by your voice," Uncle Flipping called out. In a short while, we were joined by a man in a suit with all the buttons buttoned, a tight white collar and tie, and one of those straw hats you hardly see anymore.

Rat introduced us to her uncle. Uncle Flipping also appeared to know the guys with the picnic. They offered him a pickle, which he accepted and munched while he talked to us, half sitting, half leaning on a seat back in the row in front of us.

"These guys are interested in how many times you've come to this movie house in the middle of the night," Rat said.

"Let's see," Uncle Flipping said. "Every night for seventeen years—that's um, six thousand two hundred and five as of a couple of months ago. Add sixty—no, fifty-eight—that's six thousand two hundred sixty-three times. Six thousand two hundred sixty-three, that's it."

"Holy God," Winston Bongo said.

I knew what Winston Bongo was feeling. He was like some guy in the mountains of California, or some other primitive place, who invents the steam engine all by himself—spends years doing it. Then, when he's got it perfected, he comes down out of the mountains and finds out that it was already invented in 1543 by Blasco De Garay. Here was Winston, who had just gotten used to the idea that maybe Rat had done more Snarking than we had, and suddenly he meets Rat's uncle, who has come to the Snark Theater more than six thousand times. Of course, Winston was probably thinking, it isn't the same for an adult who doesn't have to sneak out of the house without waking anybody up.

"You understand," Uncle Flipping was saying, "that since I live with my brother-in-law, Saunders II—Bentley's father—and his family, I always have to sneak out to come here. Otherwise, I'd be waking up the whole house every night."

Winston Bongo was a broken man. It meant more to him than it did to me. I must say, I always Snarked more for the sport of it than to build up a world record, but Winston, as the inventor (he thought) of Snarking, was very concerned with how history would regard him. Now he realized that it wouldn't even mention him.

"Say, Rat Face," Uncle Flipping said. "Why don't you invite your friends home for breakfast? I believe it's the spring vacation, is it not?"

"Sure," Rat said. "You guys want to have breakfast at my house?"

"We'll have to go home and leave notes for our parents, indicating that we've gotten up extra early to go over to see a friend," I said. It occurred to me that this would be a new Snarking wrinkle—sneaking out in the middle of the night, then sneaking back in the wee hours of the morning to leave a note representing us as having snuck out some hours later, and then sneaking out again. It was very sophisticated. I was going to mention this new departure to Winston, but I thought it might depress him just then.

"I'll go along with you guys and wait outside while you write the notes," Rat said.

"I'm going to stay here and watch the James Dean movie again," Uncle Flipping said. "I'll see you all at breakfast."

XII

Rat waited in the street while Winston and I sneaked into our respective apartments. Once inside, I removed the pillows and things from the bed and arranged it as though I had been sleeping in it. Then I wrote a note:

> Dear Mom and Dad,
> I forgot to tell you last night. I have
> to get up extra, extra early to meet
> Winston Bongo. We're going to have
> breakfast at a friend's house. See
> you later.
>
> Love,
Walter

I taped the note to my bedroom door. I didn't expect it to arouse any curiosity. I had my parents trained to accept my irregular hours. Even when I didn't plan any Snarking adventures, I made a point of going to bed and getting up at all sorts of different times. Sometimes, when I had come home from a late Snark, I wouldn't go to bed at all—I'd just pretend that I'd been up since dawn and give my parents a cheerful good morning when they woke up. I don't have any trouble staying up all night. I just get to bed early the next night and catch up on sleep.

I met Rat and Winston in the street, "We can walk to my house." Rat said. "We've got plenty of time before breakfast. It isn't even dawn yet."

We began to walk. Winston appeared to have pulled himself together. It was obvious that he was going to have to give up his idea of being known as the Father of Snarking. I assumed he would just have to find another career. I must say, he was being a good sport about it.

Rat had a lot to say as we walked. It turned out that in addition to movies she had any number of interests. One of the things she talked about was poisonous snakes, which interested her. She knew a lot about them. Her favorite was something called the Gaboon viper. She said that the bite it could give was a doozy. She also said that she wanted to go out West and participate in a rattlesnake roundup. Apparently in some places out West, people go to areas where rattlesnakes are known to hang out in great numbers, and they catch scads of them. Then they have a big hoop-de-do and give prizes for the biggest snake caught, the most snakes caught, and the rarest snake caught. They also fry up a lot of rattlesnakes and eat them. It all sounded horrible.

"You don't have any snakes at home?" I asked Rat. Since I was going to her house, I wanted to know if I ought to be prepared for anything.

"Not at present," Rat said. That was all I wanted to know. I can live without snakes—and I plan to.

Rat was pretty outspoken. She had a lot of things to say

about James Dean and the things she would have been willing to do with him, and with no one else, if only he had not died. Winston and I got the impression that Rat knew a lot more about sex than we did, so we kept off the subject in order not to appear ignorant.

Another enthusiasm of Rat's was cars. She told us the make and year of various parked cars we passed. After a while, I wished she'd get back onto sex. For an antisocial kid, Rat certainly tended to chatter on once she got going.

And Rat told us about how it was at George Armstrong Custer High School. It seems that Custer High works on the notebook system, like Genghis Khan. Rat told us about some of the teachers there, and we told her about ours. Rat admitted that our Miss Sweet was, by far, crazier than any of the teachers at George Armstrong Custer. About the most distinguished teacher they had appeared to be this guy who weighed about four hundred and fifty pounds and wore a wig. That's picturesque, but it can't compete with an old lady who talks to plants.

We were walking in the direction of the Old Town. It seemed that was where Rat's house was. I was glad to have the opportunity to do some more exploring in that neighborhood. It was sufficiently late for almost all the lights in the houses to be out. The night was very mild. We talked quietly as we walked through the narrow, crooked streets.

We came to a stretch of pavement with an old iron fence running alongside of it. Heavy vines—creepers, I think they're called—had grown up and around the iron bars. Even though it was still too early in the spring for the vines to have leaves, they were so thick that it was impossible to see what was beyond the fence. I was reminded of haunted houses in movies. I imagined that there was a strange old mansion behind the overgrown fence.

We came to the gate. It had iron curlicues along the top. Attached to the gate was a little sign, flaking enamel on rusty metal, that said NO VISITORS.

"Here we are," Rat said. This was where she lived! I was only half surprised. She pushed the gate open. It squeaked, as I knew it would. It was just beginning to be light—not quite dawn, just a little before dawn. I could just make out the strange old house on the grounds behind the iron gate. It was just the sort of house I expected.

"Keep quiet," Rat said, "everybody's still asleep. We'll go to my soundproof room."

I admit to having been a little bit scared.

XIII

Rat unlocked the front door. Winston Bongo whispered to me, "I tell you, this house could be in a horror movie."

I agreed with him. The house had lots of towers and chimneys poking up out of it, and there were shutters hanging crookedly next to the windows.

The key Rat used to unlock the door was one of those big, old-fashioned ones about four inches long with fancy curlicues on the end. "Now, don't make any noise," she said. "Just follow me."

The inside of the house was just as weird as the outside. We were in some sort of entrance hall. There was a bunch of old-fashioned furniture, a worn-out carpet, and a big statue of what appeared to be a tall, skinny chicken. I could see what was in the hall, because there was a dim lamp making long, dark shadows everywhere.

We followed Rat to a door in the side of the staircase. She flipped a switch and a light came on, revealing some stairs going down. The stairs led to a basement. "Now *this* is my soundproof room," Rat said proudly, opening a door.

Rat's soundproof room was fairly large. It had thick carpeting on the floor and three or four thicknesses of carpet nailed to the inside of the door. There were heavy drapes on the walls, and squares of cork covered the ceiling. It was very quiet in there. I could hear myself breathe.

"You could shoot off a cannon in here and nobody upstairs would hear a thing," Rat said.

There were a few articles of overstuffed furniture in the room, and a huge wooden cabinet that looked like a stereo speaker, but it was much too big for that. On a table there was some powerful-looking, old-fashioned electronic stuff. I couldn't tell what it was.

"This is my hi-fi," Rat said. "I'll bet you guys have never seen anything like this. My Uncle Flipping put this together about thirty years ago. In those days, they really knew something about sound. My father helped me fix up this soundproof room when Uncle Flipping gave me all this equipment. Behind the drapes there's twelve inches of fiberglass batting, and the walls and floor are floating on rubber mountings. There's an electric fan that goes on with the lights to change the air, or it would get plenty stuffy in here."

"Is that the speaker?" I asked.

"That is the Klugwallah 850-ohm Sound Reproducing System," Rat said, "and this is a custom-built amplifier. Don't stand too near it when I turn it on; it can electrocute you at a distance of a foot on a humid night. This, here," Rat said, indicating another giant piece of wooden furniture, "is a free-standing Fluchtzbesser turntable. Inside that wooden cabinet is an eleven-hundred-pound piece of granite. Yes, sir, this is about the finest hi-fi ever assembled in the city of Baconburg."

"And it only has the one speaker?" Winston Bongo asked.

Rat gave Winston a sideways look. "Stereo is for sissies," she said.

Naturally we wanted to hear Rat's hi-fi. She flipped a bunch of switches on the amplifier. It was basically a big, black metal box, about the size of an air conditioner, with gigantic blackened tubes sticking out of the top. Various red lights came on when Rat flipped the switches, and there was a low buzzing, humming sound in the room.

"Just give the tubes a minute to warm up," Rat said. "You guys like Scallion?"

A pale blue aura of light appeared around the amplifier. Rat went to a shelf to get a Scallion album. Scallion is a rock group. They are famous for giving very creative performances. For example, they have a 35-foot-deep glass tank filled with water on stage with them. At one point in their concert, they all get into a diving bell, and it gets lowered into the tank. Then they play a number underwater. After that, the members of the band each come out an escape hatch and swim to the surface, playing and singing. Sometimes they take members of the audience captive and hold them for ransom. They won't give them back until they get a thousand dollars for each hostage.

They also wrestle a live gorilla onstage. Then they get run over by a United Parcel Service truck. For a finale, they set fire to an eighteen-foot-tall papier-maché mastodon. It's sort of their trademark.

Scallion all wear galvanized-iron suits. While they're somewhat more conservative than a lot of rock bands, musically they're considered OK. Besides that, they have a very good philosophy, which they express in their songs. For example, some of their popular songs include: "I'm Not Hurting Anybody, Why Don't You Leave Me Alone?"; "Everybody Is Against Me"; "Unhip People Are Jerks"; "I'm Neat"; "The System Stinks"; and "Human Beings All Gotta Be Like Me or I'll Kill Them." Their biggest hit is "Drool on Me."

I, personally, am not much in favor of rock music, being more of a Mozart fan, but many kids like Scallion a lot. Another feature of that band is that they don't actually sing. They sort of shout, scream, and gurgle, mumble, hum, and whistle.

Rat put a Scallion record on the Fluchtzbesser turntable and lowered the tone arm. What then followed was one of the strangest experiences I've ever had. The sound was so powerful, so intense, that I couldn't stay on my feet. My knees went rubbery, and I had to sort of crawl over to one of the overstuffed chairs. I noticed that Winston Bongo had a very strange expression and seemed to be gasping for breath. He looked like he was in pain. I know I was.

Once I got to the chair and managed to crawl into it, I felt my body being blasted into the cushions by the sound waves from the Klugwallah Sound Reproducing System. It felt as though I was facing into a strong wind—a hurricane, in fact—but it wasn't a wind, it was just wave after wave of vibrations blaring out of the speaker. I couldn't hear anything like music, even Scallion-style. I did hear various things popping and snapping inside my head. I was scared that my eardrums might be bursting.

Through all this, Rat was hopping around, snapping her fingers, and slapping her knees. At one point, she put her mouth close to my ear and shouted something. I couldn't make out what she was saying. I think it was something like "Great midrange tones, huh?"

Winston Bongo was making weak motions with his hands. He was trying to get Rat to turn the thing off. It took awhile, but finally Rat stopped cavorting around and noticed Winston's feeble motions. She switched off the deadly hi-fi.

Winston was sweating. "You little creep," he gasped, "how could you do such a thing? When I get my strength back, I'm going to kill you."

I was amazed at the silence in the room. I was also grateful that I was still alive and could hear. I hadn't gotten around to being mad at Rat for doing that to us, but I could see Winston's point. For a second, I considered punching Rat in the head.

"Oh, you don't like rock? Why didn't you say so? I just

keep that record around because it shows off the hi-fi. I think Scallion is sort of juvenile myself. Here, I'll put on some really good sounds for you." Rat got out a stack of records. When she put the first one on, Winston and I flinched, but she had turned down the volume to no more than an ear-splitting roar. Rat treated us to a concert of obscure rock groups, including Eevo, Weevo, Geevo, So-Silly Boodi, Ken and the Maniacs, and Thug.

It could have been worse. Rat could have been a disco fan, which, in combination with the Klugwallah-Fluchtzbesser, might have been fatal.

Rat switched off the custom monster amplifier. "It must be broad daylight by now," she said. "Let's go up and meet the family and have some breakfast."

XIV

We followed Rat upstairs. In the hall, I saw that what I had taken for a statue of a tall, skinny chicken was, in fact, just that. It was carved out of wood and still had some old gold paint sticking to it. Rat told us that the statue was a souvenir her grandfather had brought back from a trip. It seems that Rat's grandfather is a world traveler, always going to some weird place or other.

"As a matter of fact, we don't know exactly where my grandfather is right now," Rat said. "Last we heard of him he had boarded an Icelandic steamer, the *Pippicksdottir*, in Port Newark, New Jersey. He started the family business. Now he just travels. My father and Uncle Flipping run the business now."

"What business is that?" Winston Bongo asked.

"Our family owns Bullfrog Industries," Rat said. "Surely you're familiar with Bullfrog Root Beer? It used to be the most popular soft drink around here, more popular than Moxie, Killer Cola, and Doctor Feldman's Banana Tonic. It still sells quite a bit in certain parts of the country. Grandfather got the recipe from an old baba in the forests of Nepal."

"I've never heard of it," I said.

"Well, you'll have some with breakfast," Rat said. "We drink gallons of the stuff around here. Anyway, Bullfrog Industries does a lot more than make root beer now. The root beer was just the first product. Now our family company makes Bullfrog Glue, Bullfrog Yoghurt, Bullfrog Tennis Shoes and Sneakers, Bullfrog Rubber Bands and Office Supplies, and Bullfrog Space Technology Products. They all have the same secret ingredient that makes Bullfrog Root Beer the best."

"What's the secret ingredient?" Winston Bongo asked.

"I can't tell you. It's a secret," Rat said, "but I'll give you a hint: It hops, croaks, and eats flies."

Naturally, we thought she was kidding.

Through a large pair of glass doors we could see a bunch of people doing something in the garden. We sort of recognized Uncle Flipping; we had only seen him in the dark-

ness of the Snark. There were also some other people—
Rat's family, we supposed. They were being led in some
sort of exercises or calisthenics by a fellow in a long silk
robe with flowers and dragons embroidered on it.

"That's Heinz, our Chinese butler," Rat said. "He leads
the family exercises every morning before breakfast. I
usually don't do them."

The only thing that was Chinese about Heinz was his
robe. He had blue eyes, blond hair, a large, straight nose,
and a pink complexion. Heinz was going through some
strange slow-moving exercise that involved striking all
sorts of uncomfortable-looking poses, waving his arms and
standing on one foot. When he stood on one foot, we
could see that he was wearing high-topped basketball
shoes. The others, two men and two women, were wearing
bathrobes, pajamas, and nightgowns. They appeared to be
trying to imitate or follow the movements Heinz was making. None of them seemed to be able to do it. They were
all moving every which way, waving their arms, wobbling
on one foot, crouching, stretching, and jumping into the
air.

The family finished their exercises and filed into the
house. Rat introduced us to everybody. There was her father, Saunders Harrison Matthews II, her mother, Minna
Terwilliger Matthews, Uncle Flipping Hades Terwilliger,
whom we had already met, and Aunt Terwilliger. Aunt
Terwilliger was about six feet tall and skinny, and everybody called her Aunt Terwilliger.

Heinz, the butler, bowed low and said, "Please call me
F'ang Tao Sheh." Everybody called him Heinz.

After we had all been introduced, Saunders Harrison

Matthews II, Rat's father, said, "It's a pleasure to meet some of Rat's friends. Especially since you don't have hair dyed pink and strange clothing like some of the other people she's brought home."

We all went into the dining room. It was a nice room with lots of windows and a long table. Everybody sat down, and Heinz served breakfast. It was an unusual breakfast. We had Chinese gooseberries, which I had never seen before. They're fuzzy brown on the outside, and about the size of an egg. Inside they're green and taste somewhere between a banana and a lime. I liked them. We also had homemade crunchy granola with little tiny orange slices, corn-meal bagels, Uncle Flipping's special high-protein drink, which was like a gritty milk shake, and Bullfrog Root Beer, which was served hot in cups or in glasses with ice. The older people had theirs hot—Rat, Winston, and I had ours cold.

Everybody ate in silence until the Bullfrog Root Beer was served. Then the conversation at the table got started. Aunt Terwilliger began by making a sort of speech about grand opera. She was against it. Later, Rat told us that her aunt had just about every opera recording ever made. Her aunt spent hours in her bedroom every day listening to them, but all the rest of her time was spent arguing that people shouldn't listen to operas, and, above all, they shouldn't go to see them performed. Rat said that Aunt Terwilliger makes regular appearances in Blueberry Park, where she tries to convince people to live their lives opera-free. She feels that operas take up too much time. Also, she has an idea that people who like opera will become unrealistic, and not take their everyday lives seriously. Most of all, she believes that operas are habit-forming, and once a person starts listening to them, it's hard to stop, and one tends to listen to more and more operas until one's life is ruined.

Aunt Terwilliger has pamphlets printed up that she hands out. Her most popular one is called "Grand Opera, an Invention of the Devil."

I got the impression that Aunt Terwilliger made this same speech—the one about how terrible opera was for people, especially the working classes—every morning. The family listened to her politely and sipped their Bullfrog Root Beer.

Aunt Terwilliger was also against eating meat, which is why the Terwilliger-Matthews family never serves any.

When Aunt Terwilliger had finished about opera, Uncle Flipping Hades told us something about the work he did. He's in charge of Research and Development for Bullfrog Industries.

"Then you're a scientist," I said.

"Not just a scientist," Uncle Flipping said. "I am a mad scientist. Just ask my brother-in-law."

"Yes, that's true," Saunders Harrison Matthews II said. "Nobody down at the plant would deny that Flipping is crazy as a bedbug. Mad scientists—really mad ones—aren't that easy to come by. Plenty of companies haven't got one. We're lucky to have him."

"You are, indeed," Uncle Flipping said. "For years I was sane. All I had to think about was how to get bigger bubbles into the root beer and thereby save the company money—less root beer and more bubbles to each bottle, you know. Now that I'm mad, I can get into really interesting stuff. The firm lets me do research on anything I want. They feel that I might stumble on something really important any time. For example, I'm trying to develop an avocado that will grow in the coldest climates right now."

"My father is interested in avocados," I said.

"Then you're Theobald Galt's boy!" Uncle Flipping shouted. "I know your father well. He's a very talented amateur. He has very advanced ideas about avocados. The field of mad science lost a valuable mind when your father went into the synthetic-sausage business."

I had no idea that my father's liking for avocados went beyond the interest of an ordinary consumer. I didn't know whether to be proud of him or worried. Obviously, Rat's family was made up of people who were more or less insane. Uncle Flipping was even proud of it, and so was Rat's father.

Rat's mother, Minna Terwilliger Matthews, hadn't said anything so far to indicate that she was crazy, but I felt fairly certain that she would give us a sign before long. I liked Rat's family. The only crazy people I had met before this were on the order of Miss Sweet. This gang of loonies seemed to have a lot of fun. Besides, I loved my breakfast. Something about Uncle Flipping's high-protein drink was making me feel healthy and wide awake.

"I've got a picture of your father and the prize avocado of 1962," Uncle Flipping said. "I'll run upstairs and get it."

He never came down again.

XV

Uncle Flipping was gone from the table for a long time. While we waited for him to come back with a picture of my father and the prize avocado of 1962, Minna Terwilliger Matthews, Rat's mother, revealed just how crazy she was. I knew she wouldn't disappoint us.

"You know, I suppose," Rat's mother said, "that realtors are all actually beings from other planets. You see, they have to have some sort of disguise or cover so they can move among us Earthlings without drawing attention to themselves. What happened is that in the early 1950s they all came here in flying saucers. One by one, they replaced legitimate real estate brokers. Now all realtors are extraterrestrials."

I was deeply satisfied. Somehow I knew that when she got started, Minna Terwilliger Matthews would turn out to be perhaps the very best of the lot.

"Don't just take my word for it," she was saying. "You can find out for yourselves. They reveal themselves in little ways. Try telling one of them a joke. You'll see that they aren't like us."

Heinz, the non-Chinese Chinese butler, had gone upstairs to see what was keeping Uncle Flipping. When he came back down, he had a serious expression. "Mister Flipping is gone," he said.

Everybody looked solemn.

I was getting upset. He'd just been talking with us, so alive and enthusiastic. "Gone? Dead?" I said, involuntarily.

"No, no," Minna Terwilliger Matthews said, "not dead. Gone."

"Gone?"

"Mister Flipping has a tendency to vanish," Heinz said.

"How do you mean, vanish?" Winston Bongo asked. Of course, it was none of our business what happened in someone else's family, but we liked these loonies, and we were interested.

"Uncle Flipping vanishes fairly often," Rat said, "He disappears in a variety of ways. For example, once we heard a muffled shriek in the night, and he was gone. Another time, there were heavy footsteps in the library, after which he vanished."

"Yes," Saunders Harrison Matthews II added, "and there was the time he vanished, and we found an envelope containing five grapefruit pips under his pillow."

"My favorite was the time we found a stuffed monkey in his place," Aunt Terwilliger said.

"Very often there are ransom notes," Minna Terwilliger Matthews said.

"And, of course," Heinz said, "sometimes he's just gone. This is one of those times. One moment he's here, and then he's not. Gone."

"Let me get this straight," I said. "Uncle Flipping does this all the time?"

"Yes, that's right."

"He's here one moment, and gone the next?"

"Yes."

"And there are shrieks, heavy footsteps, sinister signs, and ransom notes?"

"Exactly."

"But he always comes back?"

"No, that's not quite right," Rat's father said. "He does come back sometimes, but generally we have to get him back."

"There have been times he came back by himself," Heinz said, "and there have been times the police called to say they had him, and would we come and get him. But usually we have to look for him."

"I'm having some trouble following all this," Winston Bongo said. "Is he being kidnapped, or just wandering off?"

"Kidnapped."

"Wanders off."

"A little of each."

It seemed that the family had differences about whether Uncle Flipping Hades' disappearances were voluntary or not.

"Well, what does he say about these disappearances after he gets back?" I asked.

He says different things," Minna Terwilliger Matthews said.

"He says he was kidnapped," Aunt Terwilliger said.

"He says he just went away to be by himself," Saunders Harrison Matthews II said.

"We all look for him," Rat said.

"Miss Rat has found him eight times, all by herself,"

Heinz said, smiling. "She's found him more times than anyone else."

"Except you, Heinz," Rat said. "You've found him more times than I have."

"Yes, but many of those times I had been called by the police to come and collect him," Heinz said. "Those times hardly count."

"I believe all this has some connection with the underworld," Saunders Harrison Matthews II said.

"Oh, Saunders Harrison, not the underworld!" Minna Terwilliger Matthews said.

"Yes, dear, the underworld. I'm sure of it."

"Well, I can't imagine what my brother would have to do with gangsters," Minna Terwilliger Matthews said.

"Not gangsters, dear, the underworld," Saunders Harrison Matthews II said.

"In any case," said Heinz, "shall we go about searching for Mister Flipping in the usual way?"

"Yes, Heinz," Rat's father said. "We'll all keep a sharp lookout for Flipping, especially at night."

"My uncle has never been found, or even turned up, except at night," Rat said to us. "We all more or less go about our business, but we also keep looking for him. There's no telling where he'll turn up. Of course, Heinz and I put a little special effort into looking for him—that's why we've found him more than anyone else."

"You and Heinz are perfect wizards at finding Uncle Flipping, dear," Minna Terwilliger Matthews said.

"Could we help you look for him?" I asked.

"Oh, no, no, there's no need for that," Aunt Terwilliger said, "but thanks all the same. It's a very kind offer."

"But we'd really like to help," Winston Bongo said. "It's our spring vacation, so we don't have anything to do. Besides, we've never looked for anyone missing before."

"Yes," I said, "we'd really like to help."

"Well, that's awfully nice of you both," Saunders Harrison Matthews II said. "Perhaps you'd like to help our little Rat look for her uncle. I could call your parents and let them know that you'll be spending a lot of time over here after dark. I know that Flipping's friend Theobald Galt will agree. He's looked for him once or twice himself. Presumably he can assure Mr. Bongo's parents that looking for Flipping is a wholesome and educational activity."

My father had searched for Flipping Hades Terwilliger? I was learning quite a lot about him this morning. He appeared to have a much more interesting life than I had thought.

"OK," Rat said. "Meet me in front of the Snark at midnight."

"The Snark? I thought we were going to look for your uncle?"

"We are," Rat said. "He's never missed a show. Even when he's missing, he gets in there somehow—in disguise, or crawling out of the sewers. I don't know how."

"He gets the kidnappers to take him there," Rat's mother said. "They're realtors, you know."

"If you know he's going to be at the Snark, it shouldn't be any trouble to find him there," I said.

"It's not that easy," Rat said. "I've only found him at the Snark once. It isn't easy to find disguised people in a dark movie house."

"The forces of the underworld change his outward appearance," Bentley Saunders Harrison Matthews' father said.

"I suggest you young people go home and get some rest. You'll have a long night of searching," Heinz said.

We said good-bye to Saunders Harrison Matthews II, Aunt Terwilliger, Minna Terwilliger Matthews, and Heinz, the Chinese butler who wasn't Chinese. Then we promised Rat that we'd all meet in front of the Snark at midnight and left for home.

XVI

Winston Bongo and I talked it over on the bus. Rat's Uncle Flipping was missing, and that was a usual occurrence. It seemed to both of us that Uncle Flipping, who was undoubtedly crazy like the rest of the family, just took it into his head to disappear from time to time. Winston thought that he'd probably turn up all by himself if nobody did anything about it. Still, the idea of a hunt for the missing loony sounded like fun. We would do our best to help.

I thought it would be a good idea if we took naps. We'd been up all night and would probably be up all night again, looking for Flipping. The only thing that still had to be settled was whether our parents would go along with the idea of our taking part in the search. I wondered if we should have said something to stop Rat's father, Saunders Harrison Matthews II, from making a call to my father to get permission. After all, it would have been just as easy to sneak out the way we always did.

When I got home, I found out right away that it was going to be all right. "Your old man called from the office," my mother said. "He says that you're going to go out looking for Flipping Hades Terwilliger, and that you'll be out till all hours. He says that it's great fun and that I should let you get some sleep during the day. He also asked me to call the mother of that friend of yours, Winston Bongo, and get her to let Winston go along with this nonsense."

"Did you call her?" I asked.

"Sure," my mother said. "Why not? If my son is going to get sick, lose his hair, and go insane from keeping irregular hours, why shouldn't his best friend?"

"Do you really think people lose their hair and go insane from staying up late?" I asked.

"You can look it up in any medical journal, pal," my mother said. "But if you want to be a baldheaded half-wit by the time you're twenty, that's your business. Just stay away from the Commonists. They're out in force after midnight, just looking for a softheaded kid such as yourself to indoctrinate."

I told my mother I would stay clear of any Commonists I might meet.

"Good boy," she said. "I don't much care if you grow up stupid, or even skinheaded, just so long as you are a decent American and make me proud of you."

My mother always equates stupid people and crazy people. There was no point in getting into an argument about this. If she sensed I was winning, she'd turn crafty and deny everything she'd said. As for me, I was aware that it is possible to be crazy as a coot and still be very bright. Just look at Rat's whole family.

I went off to get some sleep.

I slept until about six in the evening, right through lunch and the whole afternoon. What woke me up was the sound of my father tuning in the evening news on television.

I went into the family room where he was watching.

"I hear you're out to look for Flipping H. Terwilliger," he said. "That's great sport. I've been out looking for him myself."

"What's it like?" I asked.

"That would be telling," my father said. "Just have a good time, and remember that you're apt to find many things besides old Flipping. Here's some operating capital." He gave me five dollars.

"Did you go looking for him recently?" I asked.

"Everybody is entitled to have his own experience," my father said.

I couldn't get another word about the subject out of my father. He just settled down and watched the news. He's like that. He doesn't think it's a good idea to tell his kid too much about experiences and that sort of thing. Still, I wished he would have told me more about the time he went out looking for Uncle Flipping. It seemed I was always finding out interesting things about my father, but he never wanted to talk about them.

"I've got a surprise for you, champ," my mother said.

The surprise was tonight's recipe. It was called Tomato Surprise—tomatoes filled with tuna salad. I wasn't all that surprised. Someday my mother is going to receive an award for using more tuna fish (from American waters) than anyone in history.

I managed to get my supper down, and then, since I was sort of bored and didn't have anything else to do, I went over to Winston Bongo's house.

Winston was sort of restless, too. His parents had agreed that he could participate in the Uncle Flipping hunt. He had had his supper, which, coincidentally, was tuna fish, too. We had the whole evening to kill before meeting Rat in front of the Snark Theater.

"Look," I said, "why don't we go down there early and see the movies?"

"Not a bad idea," Winston said. "We have to be there at midnight anyway."

It was drizzling. We caught the Snark Street bus and headed downtown.

It felt strange to be taking that ride so early in the evening. The bus was fairly full of normal daytime people.

The double bill at the Snark was pretty entertaining. They had *Gidget Goes Hawaiian* and *Gaslight*. Strangely, the theater wasn't nearly as full as it usually is after midnight. We kept an eye out for Uncle Flipping, just in case, but we didn't see him.

When the movies were over, it was still short of midnight by a little more than a half-hour. We looked around for Rat, in case she had gotten there early. She wasn't in sight, so we decided to go across the street to the Hasty

Tasty Café for a snack. We had noticed the Hasty Tasty Café before, but it was always closed. They must shut down at midnight. From the windows of the Hasty Tasty we would be able to keep an eye on the front of the Snark. We'd see Rat if she showed up, or Uncle Flipping, if he arrived before Rat did.

We each got a chocolate-covered doughnut and a glass of milk. The doughnuts tasted like rubber, and the milk was warm. We got our doughnuts and milk at the counter and carried them over to a table near the window. The place was nearly empty. They were getting ready to close. A guy was mopping the floor, and there was a strong smell of ammonia.

Of the few customers in the Hasty Tasty, an abnormal percentage appeared to be weird or crazy. For example, there was a guy who looked like Sherlock Holmes as played in the movies by Basil Rathbone. He had that same big, bent nose, only this guy had his whole face covered with some kind of white make-up, and his hair was painted on—maybe with shoe polish. He had the same sideburns as Basil, but they were paint. The Sherlock Holmes with the painted-on hair was sitting with a short guy in a beat-up tweed jacket, who had a wig made out of a dust mop.

Neither of us was able to finish his rubber doughnut.

We saw Rat across the street. She saw us at the same time and waved to us. We crossed the street and met her under the marquee of the Snark.

XVII

"You guys been here long?" Rat asked. We told Rat that we'd been there since before eight.

"Any sign of Uncle Flipping?"

"Well, we didn't see him in the theater," Winston Bongo said, "and we kept a pretty careful watch on the Snark from across the street."

"Yes," I said, "except when we were distracted, looking at the guy who looks like Sherlock Holmes, with the painted-on hair."

"A guy who looks like Sherlock Holmes with painted-on hair!" Rat shouted. "Was there a fellow with him with a wig that looks like a mop?"

"Yes, there was...."

"Incredible!" Rat shouted. I'd never seen her so excited.

"Oh, this is serious," Rat said. "This is very serious. This is more serious than anything that's ever happened before. Every time Uncle Flipping disappears or wanders off or goes cuckoo, we worry that it may have something to do with those two, and now you've seen them. Are they still in the café?"

"They were when we left," I said, "just a couple of minutes ago.... But who..."

"In a minute," Rat said, and sprinted across the street toward the Hasty Tasty. As she ran, we could see that there were no customers at any of the tables. Rat shook the locked door. The lights in the Hasty Tasty Café went out. Apparently there was a back exit, because none of the workers in the café came out, even though we stood around for quite a while.

Rat crossed the street, dejected. "They're probably a block away by now," she said.

"Who are those guys?" we asked.

"Sit down here, and I'll tell you about them."

We sat down on the curb a little way down from the Snark Theater, and Rat told us about the odd-looking men Winston Bongo and I had seen in the Hasty Tasty.

"Years ago my Uncle Flipping took a trip to Iceland," Rat said. "I believe he mentioned to you this morning that he has been trying to cultivate a strain of avocado that will grow in cold climates. This project has been one of the great enthusiasms of his life. When he went to Iceland, he made a sort of safari into the interior. He had lots of scientific equipment with him, things for testing the volcanic soil, instruments to record temperature and humidity, all sorts of timekeeping devices, meteorological devices, cameras, tape recorders—in fact, everything any scientific expedition takes anywhere.

"His intention was to find out exactly what the growing conditions in Iceland were. Having done that, he wanted to duplicate those conditions, artificially, in Bullfrog Industries Laboratories and develop an avocado that could thrive under those conditions. Then, he planned to go back to Iceland and start an experimental avocado plantation.

"When Uncle Flipping came back from Iceland, his behavior was very strange. He stayed in his room for about a month. He wouldn't talk to anybody. He would only eat mandarin orange slices in cans—and the cans had to be opened in his presence. He kept hundreds of tennis balls around him at all times, in plastic lawn-and-leaf bags. Worst of all, Uncle Flipping developed an unreasonable fear of moths. The mere sight of a moth was enough to send him into screaming fits. After a while, the family began to wonder if maybe something had gone wrong with him mentally. My father sent for a famous specialist, Dr. Pierre Ramakrishna, who confirmed our worst fears. Uncle Flipping was suffering from brain fever.

"Dr. Ramakrishna took Uncle Flipping to his sanatorium in Switzerland, where he cured him with his special diet of deep-fried foods. It took months of eating nothing but onion rings, french-fried potatoes, shrimp tempura, hush puppies, and Dr. Ramakrishna's special hot dogs in batter, but Uncle Flipping finally got well and came home.

"It was a long time before Uncle Flipping could talk about his experiences in Iceland. I, personally, still don't know all that happened, but my father does. I do know that after coming back from Dr. Ramakrishna's sanatorium, someone sent my Uncle Flipping a stuffed Indian fruit bat on his birthday every year. When the stuffed fruit bat would arrive, Uncle Flipping would go into his room with a lot of tennis balls.

"Uncle Flipping told my father that an international master criminal was after him. Apparently, he had discovered something, or brought something back from that trip to Iceland that was very valuable. This international criminal of the most dangerous kind knew he had this thing, or had discovered this thing, whatever it is, and Uncle Flipping has lived in mortal fear of him ever since. The brain fever was brought on by my uncle's escape from him. The stuffed fruit bat every year was a signal—one that only Uncle Flipping would understand—that he was still after him."

"And that master criminal was one of the guys we saw in the Hasty Tasty, right?" Winston Bongo asked.

"Wrong," Rat said. "The master criminal is Wallace Nussbaum, the king of crime. The two men you saw were Osgood Sigerson, the greatest living detective, and his friend and companion Dr. Ormond Sacker. The reason they're important is that there can only be one reason for Osgood Sigerson to be in Baconburg, and that is that there is a really important criminal around here. Sigerson's archenemy is a monster by the name of . . . guess."

"Wallace Nussbaum," I guessed.

"That's it," Rat said. "If Sigerson and Sacker are here, it can only be that they're on the trail of Nussbaum, and Nussbaum is on the trail of . . ."

"Uncle Flipping!" I shouted.

"Who's missing and could already be in Nussbaum's clutches," Rat went on. "This is especially serious. Nussbaum is capable of unthinkable acts of cruelty. Not only is he a terrible person, he is the most capable criminal ever to live. He was a major in some South American army, but he was kicked out for terrifying chickens. He holds the world's boomerang record, and he may be the most advanced mathematician alive today. Wallace Nussbaum is no ordinary criminal."

"What would Nussbaum do to Uncle Flipping if he caught him?" Winston asked.

"All I know is that he would stop at nothing," Rat said. "My father told me that once he wanted to get information out of someone, and he kept him in a huge vat of egg foo yung for days until he talked."

"That's horrible," Winston Bongo said.

"This sounds much worse than I had thought," I said. "Don't you think we ought to tell the police?"

"The Terwilliger-Matthews family takes care of its own problems," Rat said. "Besides, Nussbaum has eluded the police all over the world for years. Even Osgood Sigerson hasn't been able to catch him. But you're right—it is worse then we thought, and dangerous. If you fellows want to drop out now, I'll understand."

"What are you going to do?" we asked.

"I'm going to look for my uncle," Rat said.

"Then we're going with you."

"Thanks," Rat said. "You're both good guys."

"Now, hadn't we better get started looking for him?" I asked.

"Yes, indeed," Rat said, "and we'll have to work fast if we want to find him before Nussbaum does. Fortunately, we have the advantage of knowing the city better than he does—at least I do. What's more, I know all the places Uncle Flipping tends to go when he's off on his own. Have either of you ever been to Lower North Aufzoo Street?"

Neither of us had.

"Well, we're going there right away," Rat said.

XVIII

Neither Winston nor I had ever heard of Lower North Aufzoo Street. However, when we got to Upper North Aufzoo Street, we recognized it immediately. It's that curving street that runs along the Baconburg River on the edge of the business district. It's sort of a thoroughfare; there aren't any stores or entrances to buildings along it. There's a sidewalk on either side, a sort of guardrail made of concrete on the river side, and that's all. The cars go whizzing along at about forty-five miles per hour.

What we'd never noticed before about Upper North Aufzoo Street was that there was a concrete staircase leading down from the sidewalk at one point. It looked as though it might be going down to a subway, but it wasn't.

We went down the staircase.

It was quite a contrast. Upper North Aufzoo Street, above us, was nearly deserted and quiet. Lower North Aufzoo Street was a jumble of activity. There were bright yellow fluorescent lights making the street-below-a-street as brilliant as day. Big trucks rumbled along. Some were parked, being loaded or unloaded. Truck drivers and guys who work loading and unloading stood around, chewing on cigars, talking, and joking. There were piles of garbage, broken cartons, and big barrels of wastepaper filling the sidewalk every so often. There was a lot of noise down there. Trucks grinding gears and honking horns and banging into the curb, guys hollering, things bumping and crashing, all amplified by an echo. It was almost too much to take in all at once.

"Welcome to the underworld," Rat said.

A blind guy with a big German shepherd dog was playing his saxophone. The guys from the trucks tossed coins into his cup. There was also a guy doing elaborate pictures on the sidewalk with colored chalk. Rat said he was a screever, the only one in Baconburg. The pictures were pretty good. Most of them were portraits of famous people—the President, TV actors, that sort of thing. There was also a portrait of James Dean. This got Rat started, talking about how the great tragedy of her life was that James Dean had died before she was born. She said she wanted to hitchhike to Hollywood someday and visit his grave.

"What is this place?" I asked.

"It's fairly obvious," Rat said. "This is the city beneath the city. There is where the guts are. It goes round the clock. I'm sort of surprised you didn't know it was here. You see, all the truck deliveries to the business district come through here. Also, this is where all the garbage gets picked up. Besides that, this is how you get into the network of steam pipes that heat all the big office buildings. Some of the guys you see coming and going are maintenance workers. Some work in the sewers or installing the underground phone lines; others just get to and from work through here—janitors, clean-up people, night watchmen, all of those. You can get in a service elevator here and go up into the big hotels and office buildings and stores. And then there are people who live by trading with the people who come through here, or beg from them, or rip them off. There's even music and art down here—the saxophone player and the screever. And there's food and drink. In fact, let's stop into Bignose's Cafeteria. There's a chance Uncle Flipping will be in there at this hour."

There were a few bars lining Lower North Aufzoo Street. Most of them had red neon signs that said 50¢ A DRINK. There was also a fairly large cafeteria, brightly lit inside, with big plate-glass windows. A sign made of blue neon tubing over the windows said BIGNOSE'S CAFE-TERIA. A big red neon sign that flashed on and off said EAT-EAT-EAT.

We went in.

"That's Bignose," Rat said.

We could have guessed. Bignose was about five foot nothing, with a truly enormous honker. He was little and skinny and insignificant except for his beak. He was like a nose with a man attached.

"Come over here, boys," Bignose said from behind the steam table. He had such a deep voice that it made the windows vibrate when he spoke and drowned out all the noise coming from outside. "I've got spaghetti and fried squid tonight."

"We'll just have a snack, Bignose," Rat said. "Has my uncle been in?"

"Three coffees and three Napoleons," Bignose said, filling three big mugs, which he held in one hand. "I think maybe I saw him; maybe it was last night. It was pretty busy awhile ago. I get confused. Here, gimmie. I'll punch your tickets."

Bignose pushed three Napoleons and three cups of coffee across the high glass counter at us and held out his hand. Rat had taken three tickets from a little machine near the door as we came in. She gave them to Bignose, who punched them with a conductor's punch and handed them back.

Rat gave us each a punched ticket and a Napoleon and a cup.

The way it works at Bignose's is this: You get your ticket punched with the amount of whatever you pick up at the counter. Then, when you're leaving, you present your ticket at the cash register, and that's how much you pay. I'd never seen that system before. I also had never seen a Napoleon before. It's a pastry. It's flaky and creamy, and it tastes great! The coffee had a lot of milk in it. It was pretty good, too.

I had two Napoleons, Winston had two, Rat had three.

While we were sitting in Bignose's, a green wagon done up like a sort of house, and drawn by a big white horse, rattled by.

"What's that?" I asked

"Gypsies," Rat said. "Gypsies hang out down here. See over there?"

If we leaned over, and looked out the window down Lower North Aufzoo Street, we could see a woman in a long skirt, chopping wood outside another one of those green house-type wagons. There was a stovepipe sticking out the top. It was smoking.

We took our tickets to the cash register and paid for our

coffees and Napoleons. The lady at the cash register was smoking a cigarette. She had carrot red hair, and a lot of lipstick.

We went outside into the noise and bustle of the street.

"What now?" Winston Bongo asked.

"Now we take a walk," Rat said. "That way."

Rat indicated the end of Lower North Aufzoo Street, past the gypsy wagons, where the bright yellow lights stopped and the street curved away into darkness. We started walking. Away from the noise and brightness, it smelled musty. Now and then we got a whiff of wood-smoke from the gypsies' stoves. Soon, the gypsies were behind us. The street seemed to be getting smaller. It was like walking into a tunnel.

XIX

I can't say I liked the part of Lower North Aufzoo Street we were now walking along as much as the area around Bignose's Cafeteria. It was damp and sour-smelling. Instead of the bright fluorescent lights, old-fashioned, dim, yellow-white streetlamps were fastened to the concrete wall every so often. Each lamp made a puddle of light around it. In between it was pretty dark.

Now and then a truck would rumble by, making a lot of noise. The ceiling was much lower than in the bright part of Lower North Aufzoo Street, and the rush of air and the roar of the engines as the trucks went by made us uncomfortable. It was even more uncomfortable after they passed, because it seemed much darker after the brightness of the headlights.

"This is a great place to get mugged," Winston Bongo said.

"I'll say," I said.

There were fragments of trash on the sidewalk, and every now and then I would feel something squishy beneath my feet.

"I'll bet there are rats down here," I said.

"My fellow rats," Rat said.

A lot of the time, we walked without saying anything. I was looking everywhere for rats and muggers in the shadows. We seemed to be going downhill.

I really didn't like it down there. I was reminded of a depressing Polish movie I had seen at the Snark once. It was all about people getting lost in the sewers underneath Warsaw in World War II. The air got fouler the farther we went. I wanted to turn around and go back. I wanted to go back to Bignose's. If Winston had said anything about going back, I would have agreed with him. I'm sure that if I had suggested going back, he would have agreed with me. He was humming tunelessly to himself, which he only does when he is very displeased with what is happening. But Winston didn't say anything, and neither did I. We just went along with Rat. The steel taps on Rat's shoes made an echo in the dark tunnel street.

Then we saw something! Something dark and rumpled and shapeless was blocking the pavement ahead of us, not far from a streetlamp!

I knew what it was at once, but I didn't want it to be what it was. I tried to think of something else it could be —something besides a human body.

It couldn't have been anything else. We slowed down, almost to a stop.

"Oh, God, suppose it's someone dead?" I said.

"Suppose it isn't," Winston said.

We could make out the figure now. Someone wrapped in something was sitting propped with its back against the wall. Long, skinny legs were stretched across the pavement. I could see skinny ankles and big, pointy shoes.

We had come to a full stop a few paces from the figure —far enough to turn and run like mad if it happened to be someone we should run from.

The figure didn't move. We didn't move.

"I think it is someone dead," I said. "I can't see him breathing."

"Come on, there's three of us," Rat said. "There's nothing to be scared of." Nobody moved.

Then we heard a sound. It was horrible. It was unearthly. It was something between moaning and cooing. A high-pitched sort of metallic voice was saying, "*Aaook, aaaaoook, oooook, koooo!*"

"Oh, no!" Winston said.

"What is that?" Rat said.

"Let's go," I said.

"*Ooook, oooook, puk-puk-puk,*" said the voice.

"That's a chicken!" Rat said.

The figure slumped against the wall stirred. The old black man rearranged the raincoat that was wrapped around him. When he shifted position, we could see the chicken in his upturned hat on the pavement beside him.

"It's that guy! The one with the performing chicken!" Winston said. "You see him everywhere!"

"Oh! People!" the old man said, getting to his feet. "This is upsetting. This is rather embarrassing. I was just resting —that is, the chicken and I. I'm quite nonplussed. I really don't know what to say. You see, I wouldn't want it known that I make a practice of taking naps on the pavement on Lower North Aufzoo Street. Really, I was just feeling tired, and so I sat down. I'm not a vagabond. I have a home to go to. Please promise me you won't mention this to anyone."

We promised we wouldn't.

"Thank you, young people," the old man said. "Adverse publicity can be a real nuisance. As an impresario, I just can't afford to be thought of as a person who takes naps in the street. Not that I mind for myself, but it might damage the chances of my protégé." He gestured toward the chicken. "This is Dharmawati, the greatest performing chicken of the age."

The chicken bowed.

We bowed to the chicken.

"And I am Captain Shep Nesterman," the old guy said. "May I know whom I have the pleasure of addressing?"

We introduced ourselves.

"I am delighted to make your acquaintance," Captain Shep Nesterman said. Dharmawati, the performing chicken, hopped onto his shoulder and then onto his head, and he placed his hat over her. "Are you walking?" the chicken trainer asked. "I would be pleased to accompany you."

"We were going that way," Rat said.

"Perfect!" said Captain Shep Nesterman. "I was planning to go that way myself. Now I'll have the pleasure of your company, if it would not be an imposition."

"Not at all," Winston said.

"No, no, it would be our pleasure," I said.

"We'd be delighted if you'd come along with us," Rat said.

Something about the way Captain Shep Nesterman talked made all of us behave in a super-polite manner.

We began to walk. Captain Shep Nesterman made polite conversation with us, and Dharmawati, the greatest performing chicken of the age, occasionally clucked under his hat.

The walk through the dark part of Lower North Aufzoo Street was much more pleasant now that Captain Shep Nesterman had joined us. There wasn't any reason to feel more secure—an old man like that wasn't likely to be any help if we were set upon by muggers—but somehow he gave us confidence. It was as if he belonged down there, or at least knew the place well enough to be unafraid to go to sleep there.

At one point we came to a puddle that stretched from one wall of the tunnel street to the other. It was too wide to jump over, so we had no choice but to walk through it. We got soaked to the ankles.

After the puddle, the street seemed to incline slightly upward. No doubt that had been the lowest point, and that was why the water had collected there.

Soon, the sour, damp, underground smell began to be mixed with whiffs of fresh air and the smell of rusty iron. The ceiling was getting higher.

Then the concrete walls gave way to a network of big

iron girders. Fresh air poured through. We could see the night sky, which seemed bright after the darkness of the tunnel. Actually, it was bright, lit up with the glow of the lights of Baconburg. But there weren't any lights near us. On the other side of the iron girders, there seemed to be just open space and the smell of earth and things growing.

The ceiling was high above us now, and I realized that we were walking under a sort of causeway. Above us was Upper North Aufzoo Street. Now and then, we could hear a car or truck rumble along the elevated roadway.

Then Upper North Aufzoo Street veered away to the right, and we were out under the sky. The old-fashioned streetlamps were farther apart now and mounted on iron lampposts. There were some beaten-up iron fences bordering the sidewalk, and behind them what seemed to be fields.

"We're out in the sticks!" Winston said.

"Haven't you ever been in Tintown before?" Rat asked.

Winston and I had never heard of Tintown, much less been there.

"Tintown gets its name," Captain Shep Nesterman said,

"from the improvised houses here. There used to be a lot of them. During hard times in the past, people sort of camped out here. They made shacks and shanties out of old packing crates, cardboard, and abandoned cars. Flattened tin cans were a popular roofing material—hence the name. The land belonged to the city of Baconburg. There was a plan to make a railroad yard here, but it never got built. Times got better, and the squatters—the people who had built the houses—went away, most of them. But some of them stayed. If you squat on land—build a house on it —and no one claims the land for a certain period of time, the land becomes yours, after a fashion. At least, no one can make you move off."

"My father told me that there used to be hundreds of slapped-together houses along this street, Scrap Ankle Road," Rat said.

"Yes, it was quite a place," Captain Shep Nesterman said. "It was like a little city unto itself. I was once mayor of Tintown."

"You were?"

"Oh, yes. We had a mayor, a police department, schools, places of entertainment. It was really a wonderful place. The city of Baconburg didn't provide any services because it regarded the whole settlement as illegal, so we made our own government. Of course, all that is gone now. Now there are just a handful of houses, and Beanbender's Beer Garden."

"Beanbender's Beer Garden?"

"Oh, a wonderful place! It's still going strong. Beanbender's was always *the* place to go in Tintown. You can just see the lights of Beanbender's now."

In the distance, way down Scrap Ankle Road, we could see some dim, flickering lights. They had a warmer color than electric lights, and as we got closer we could see that they were from kerosene lanterns. It turned out that there wasn't much, if any, electricity in Tintown.

Turning around, we could see the tall buildings of Baconburg, mostly dark against the night sky. Our walk underground, down Lower North Aufzoo Street, had taken us in a big, curving sweep below the business district, away from the river, and out into this place, which seemed to be on lower ground than the rest of the city. It was a big, flat, open plain that was swampy in spots, with clumps of tall swamp grasses and plants here and there. The flat place must have gone on for at least a couple of miles in all directions.

Beanbender's was a strange-looking structure. At first, it was hard to get any idea of its shape; it just seemed to be a collection of odd-looking dark lumps in the night. Then we could see that Beanbender's was made up of a number of dead trucks and a couple of railroad cars arranged in a circle, like covered wagons in the movies, made into a circle for protection against the Indians.

All the dead trucks and railroad cars were covered with wooden shingles and banked with earth and gravel above the wheels. A number of kerosene lanterns were fastened to the outside of the circle. There was a door, with a lantern on either side, lighting up a sign painted on a board. BEANBENDER'S, it said.

When we walked into Beanbender's we were smacked in the face by a whole lot of warmth, light, and good smells. There were lots of people in the open areas made by the trucks and railroad cars. They were sitting at tables made of old giant cable spools and old doors laid across sawhorses. The whole place was lighted by candles stuck in bottles and kerosene lamps, and together with the wood shingles that were tacked onto the trucks and railroad cars, the dozens of flames made a warm, reddish glow under the dark sky.

In the middle of the circle was a big iron thing—sort of a basket—and some logs were burning in it, making more friendly light, good smells, and crackling noises.

There was a guy playing a little accordion, and some people were singing along with him. People had big mugs of beer and big, crisp-looking sausages and baked potatoes in their hands. They held the sausages and the baked potatoes wrapped in a paper napkin and took bites of them between swigs of beer. Even though it was late at night, three or four little kids ran around among the tables.

It was the greatest place I had ever seen.

Winston Bongo thought so, too. Rat, of course, had been there before. "Have a beer?" she asked.

I had tasted beer before, and I hadn't liked it. It was sour and sort of soapy tasting. I never understood why anybody wanted to drink it. However, in Beanbender's it seemed that holding a mug of beer in one's hand was the thing to do, so I went up to the bar and got one along with Rat and Winston and Captain Shep Nesterman.

Beanbender's beer was nothing like the stuff in cans that my father drinks. It had a nutty taste, and it was cold and good. The guy at the bar was Ben Beanbender, the owner of the beer garden. He didn't ask us for identification or anything. He just filled mugs from a big barrel and handed them to us. I also got a baked potato. Ben Beanbender poked a hole in one end with his thumb, slapped in a hunk of butter, salted and peppered the potato, wrapped it in a napkin, and handed it to me. It was great! The potato was almost too hot to hold, and the salty butter dribbled onto my sleeve. It tasted just fantastic with the beer. The beer and the baked potato cost fifty cents. It's the best deal in Baconburg.

"Let's find a place to sit," Captain Shep Nesterman said, "and enjoy the passing parade."

I didn't understand exactly what Captain Nesterman meant at first, about enjoying the passing parade. I was too wrapped up with my first impressions of Beanbender's and the fabulous taste of my beer and baked potato to really take in what turned out to be the best thing about Ben Beanbender's Beer Garden in Tintown.

It's the greatest place to watch people in this world!

For sheer variety of types of human beings, bizarre characters, ugly men, beautiful women, odd costumes, shapes and sizes, and strange styles of speaking, singing, moving, and dancing, there simply can't possibly be any place better.

What's more, everybody talks to everybody else in Beanbender's. Just sitting there, you get involved in conversations, arguments, and philosophical disputes. People just sit down at your table and start talking.

XXI

Captain Shep Nesterman had turned his hat upside down on the table, and Dharmawati, the performing chicken, had settled down in it. Now and then, Captain Shep Nesterman would give Dharmawati a sip of his beer or a nibble of his baked potato. Apparently, Captain Shep Nesterman was well known at Beanbender's, because a lot of people said hello to him and asked if he and Dharmawati were going to perform that evening.

"We may perform later," Captain Shep Nesterman would say, "if our guitarist shows up."

A few faces in the crowd were familiar. I thought I recognized some of the people from Blueberry Park. I definitely recognized the devil's-gonna-get-you man. He was sitting quietly with two pretty girls, sipping his beer.

A fellow in a turban, with a bushy, black beard, sat down.

"Shim bwa la boo," the guy in the turban said.

"Bwa loo sha bim," Captain Shep Nesterman said.

"May your eyebrows be blessed, brother," said the guy in the turban.

"May angels sit upon your ear," said Captain Shep Nesterman.

"How do you think St. Louis will do in the National League next season?" the guy in the turban asked.

"Not as well as Pittsburgh, unless Mac Schwartz's shoulder gets better," Captain Shep Nesterman said.

"Yeah, he was having a good season until he got injured," the guy in the turban said.

"Best pitcher in the league," Captain Shep Nesterman said.

"Yeah . . . well, sha la boo shim," said the guy in the turban.

"Sha loo sha loo," said Captain Shep Nesterman.

The guy in the turban got up and left.

"Excuse me for not introducing you," Captain Shep Nesterman said. "He's the Grand Shapoo of the Church of the Holy Home Run, and with the least encouragement he'd sit here talking baseball and religion until we were all bored out of our minds."

The guy with the accordion was dancing on a table with a glass of beer on his head. He squatted down and kicked out with one leg and then the other, playing the little accordion all the time and not spilling a drop of beer. Everybody clapped in rhythm, and he kept it up for about five minutes. At the end of his dance, the accordion player shouted, "Fooey on the Czar!" and poured the glass of beer over his own head. Everybody clapped and threw money. We threw some dimes. The accordion player waved his hand over his head and picked up the money.

Captain Shep Nesterman applauded politely. "An energetic fellow," he said, "but he is very limited in his repertoire. I don't mean to put him down, but I've seen that same table-dancing routine a hundred times. You'll see a really creative performance later, if Paco shows up."

A skinny, nervous fellow sat down. "Hello, hello, hello," he said, shaking hands with each of us. "Captain

Nesterman," the skinny, nervous fellow said, "I have done it! As you know, I started out by painting a picture of my bedroom, with all its contents. That was wrong. It didn't say what I wanted to say. I thought about it, and threw out my bedroom chair. Then I painted a picture of my bedroom without the chair. That was a little better, but it still did not convey my innermost thoughts. So then I threw out my chest of drawers and painted the bedroom without the chair and chest of drawers. By this time, I knew I was on the right track. I threw out my bed, my bedside table, my alarm clock, the picture of the Grand Shapoo of the Church of the Holy Home Run that used to hang on my wall. Then I painted my bedroom with absolutely nothing in it. I really thought I was all the way there, but somehow it didn't quite work. I was miserable. For weeks I lay on the floor, unable to sleep, thinking, thinking, thinking. I tell you, Captain Nesterman, I wasn't sure I would come out of this creative crisis as a sane person. I was at the end of my rope, when it came upon me in a burst of inspiration! All this time, I had been trying to paint my bedroom! Get it? I had been trying to *paint my bedroom*! But I had not had the actual pure experience of painting my bedroom! I was excited, I can tell you! I went out and got paint, white paint, pure white. I painted the walls of my bedroom. I painted the ceiling. I painted the floor. I painted the window, both the frame and the glass. I painted the door and the doorknob. In short, I painted every single part of my bedroom pure white, including the lightbulb in the ceiling. Then I went and got my canvas and brushes, and I painted a picture of my bedroom. It came out perfectly!"

"Has anyone seen the painting?" Captain Shep Nesterman asked.

"Seen it?" the excited, skinny painter shouted. "The Museum of Modern Art in New York has bought it for fifty thousand dollars! Which reminds me, here's the three dollars I owe you. I have to go now—I'm painting my bathroom." The skinny painter shook hands all round again and hurried off.

"I knew he'd be a success," Captain Shep Nesterman said. "What a talented fellow."

A woman with a rag around her head and lots of jingly gold jewelry was the next person to sit down with us. Her name was Madame Zabonga. She offered to tell our fortunes by examing the beer and butter stains on our sleeves. It cost a quarter. I had her tell mine. She looked at the places where the butter from my baked potato had dripped and told me a whole lot of things about myself. She said that I was a nice boy, and that I would grow up to be a nice man, and that I didn't like school, and that I liked to eat and sleep. None of this seemed to be worth a quarter. Then she said that I would share in a secret and experience danger. I was embarrassed to ask for my money back, so I didn't, but I thought the whole experience was a load of horseradish. I was sorry I had wasted my money. I could have bought another beer or a baked potato with that quarter.

Paco arrived. Paco was the guitar player who accompanied Captain Shep Nesterman and Dharmawati, the performing chicken, at least when they performed at Ben Beanbender's Beer Garden in Tintown. Paco had black hair, parted in the middle and slicked down with grease.

He also had a thick black moustache that curled up at the ends.

Paco greeted us gravely and asked Captain Shep Nesterman if he and Dharmawati wished to perform that evening.

"In fact, Dharmawati is in excellent voice, and feeling limber, and so am I," Captain Shep Nesterman said.

Paco, who was always serious, unsnapped his guitar case and took out the instrument. Then he carried a chair to the middle of the room, not far from the fireplace. When the people saw Paco, they all began to clap and shout. They got up and dragged tables and chairs away, so there was an open space in the middle of the beer garden, with Paco sitting to one side of it. Someone brought Paco a little footstool, and he put one foot on it. Then, with the guitar balanced on his raised knee, he spent a long time tuning it, with his head bent down, listening to sounds so soft nobody in the place could hear them.

When Paco was satisfied that the guitar was in tune, he strummed a single loud chord and nodded to Captain Shep Nesterman. Captain Shep Nesterman arose and, carrying Dharmawati on his wrist, wings flapping, he walked into the firelight.

The crowd went wild. There was a lot of applause and cheering.

Captain Shep Nesterman nodded to Paco. Paco nodded to Captain Shep Nesterman. The crowd was silent.

Then Captain Shep Nesterman put Dharmawati on the floor. He stood up very straight, put his arms in a certain position—one in front of him and one in back—and stamped his foot very loudly.

Paco strummed a few chords.

Captain Shep Nesterman stamped his feet a lot of times in rapid succession. He kept his back very straight and did subtle things with his arms. He looked good.

Captain Shep Nesterman was getting into some tricky steps. As his movements got more complicated, Paco's playing got fancier. It was getting pretty good. Captain Nesterman was really stamping around pretty well. Up to this point, Dharmawati had just stood there next to Paco. Then she began to sing! It was a wild sound; a sort of high-pitched moaning and crowing and crooning. It sounded wild, and sort of sad. Paco watched Captain Shep Nesterman, and what he played depended on what Captain Shep Nesterman did in his foot-stamping dance. Sometimes Dharmawati would sing to Captain Shep Nesterman's dancing, and sometimes Captain Shep Nesterman would dance to Dharmawati's singing. Sometimes Paco would sing along with Dharmawati, and sometimes Paco would take a solo. Then Captain Shep Nesterman would wait, and Dharmawati would wait, until he was through. It was really great! Each of them was making up what he or she was doing as they went along, and the whole thing blended together. The audience was really going crazy. They were great performers—all of them—including the chicken.

XXII

Captain Shep Nesterman finished up his act by taking two sets of castanets out of his pocket and adding their clicking to the stamping, strumming, and singing. The last bit of the act—the part with the castanets—was particularly wild and active, and Dharmawati got off some of her best sounds. The crowd went wild when it was over. They would have shouted the roof down if there had been a roof. There was a shower of money. People were throwing coins, and coins wrapped in dollar bills, and fives and tens. Captain Shep Nesterman and Paco shoveled up the money while Dharmawati took the bows.

It really was a great performance. I never thought I would be wildly applauding a singing chicken, but I was. It wasn't just the novelty of a singing chicken either—she was really good! After hearing her sing, I had a lot more respect for Dharmawati than I'd had previously.

We were so wrapped up in the performance of Captain Shep Nesterman and his ensemble that we failed to notice that someone had joined us at our table during the singing, dancing, guitar playing, and castanet clicking. As Captain Shep Nesterman, Paco, and Dharmawati made their way back to our table, we became aware that a very fat man in a white suit was seated with us, his chair pushed back a little way so that he would have been out of our field of vision when we were watching the entertainment.

"Ah! Mr. Gutzman!" Captain Shep Nesterman said as he approached the table.

"I'd like to buy that bird," the fat man said in a voice that seemed to rumble from deep within his suit.

"So you've told me a hundred times at least," Captain Shep Nesterman said, "but Dharmawati and Paco and I are a team. The chicken is not for sale."

"I like you, Captain Nesterman," Mr. Gutzman said. "You're a man who likes a chicken, a rare quality in these evil times."

Captain Shep Nesterman introduced us to Mr. Gutzman. He said that Mr. Gutzman was an old friend of his and only appeared to be a shady character. In reality, he said, Mr. Gutzman was only a sort of part-time crook.

Mr. Gutzman chuckled. "Oh, ho, ho, you're a caution, Captain Nesterman. A real caution. But as much as I enjoy sitting here and exchanging witticisms with you, I must get to business. I bring a message. It is this: A certain party would like to see the three young people in private."

"And that certain party is?" Captain Shep Nesterman asked.

Mr. Gutzman leaned forward. He made a trumpet of his hand and whispered, "The man with the secret information, the same one who sent you to the underground street tonight."

"In that case," Captain Shep Nesterman said, "you three had better go with Mr. Gutzman here and see whoever he's talking about. For my part, I have no idea who or what he means."

"Oh, ho, ho, you're a real pleasure to deal with, Captain," Mr. Gutzman said. "Upon my word, you are. Well, young people, kindly follow me."

Mr. Gutzman got to his feet with considerable effort and made his way through the crowded beer garden. We exchanged looks and followed him.

As we moved away from the table, Paco arrived with three mugs of beer for Captain Shep Nesterman, Dharmawati, and himself.

"We'll be right here, kids!" Captain Shep Nesterman called after us.

Mr. Gutzman led us to a dark corner of Beanbender's Beer Garden. In the side of one of the shingled-over railroad cars, there was a door. Mr. Gutzman knocked four times, and then twice. The door opened. A very large, muscular man was inside. He kept his face turned away from us and stayed in the shadows.

"It's me—Gutzman," Mr. Gutzman said. "Tell a certain party that the three kids are here."

The big, muscular figure disappeared into the dark interior of the railroad car. This was a little scary. I wondered why we were letting this fat, sinister character take us inside a dark railroad car. For all we knew, he was planning to kill us, or hold us for ransom.

Mr. Gutzman must have sensed the thoughts I was having—and the thoughts of Rat and Winston Bongo, too. "I assure you, there is nothing to fear," he said. "A certain party wishes to speak to you, that is all."

"Then why doesn't he just come out here and speak to us?" Winston Bongo asked.

"That is none of my business," Mr. Gutzman said. "I was simply told to bring you to a certain party, just as Captain Nesterman was told to make sure that you turned up at Beanbender's."

That was something that hadn't occurred to me. We hadn't met Captain Shep Nesterman by accident; he had been waiting for us in the underground street!

The heavyweight guy came back to the door. "He says to send them in," he said. "You go and have a beer with Captain Nesterman, Gutzman. You won't be needed again tonight."

We stepped through the door in the side of the railroad car. It was fairly dark inside and hung with heavy curtains, which made a sort of passageway. "Go that way," the big guy said, "and knock on the door at the end." We never saw his face.

I was more or less terrified as we walked along the corridor made of curtains. There was a dim green lightbulb that gave just enough light to see by. The drapes seemed to be a sort of purplish color.

We arrived at the door, which was a big steel one, and knocked.

"Enter!" said a muffled voice on the other side.

We pushed the door open. We entered a room too dimly lit to really see anything in, but it had the feeling of being well furnished. Sitting at a desk, next to a green lamp that hardly gave any light, was a figure wearing a hooded robe. It was like a monk's robe. He had his hood up, and his face was entirely hidden in shadow. I felt like running away.

"Thank you for coming," said the hooded figure. There was something familiar about the muffled voice coming from within the hood. I couldn't place it; I thought maybe he sounded like some movie actor, but I couldn't think which one.

"I regret there are no chairs for you," the hooded person said. "I will try to keep this interview as brief as possible."

It can't be too brief for me, I thought.

XXIII

"Also, please excuse me for not introducing myself," the hood said. "There are reasons why it is best that you should not know my identity. Now, I will ask you to give an account of your activities this evening. Before you begin, I will tell you that I know that you are looking for a certain party—a certain Flipping Hades Terwilliger. Now, tell me what you did from, say, midnight on."

We looked at each other. It was confusing. Who was this guy in the hood? He could easily have been in cahoots with Wallace Nussbaum. In fact, he could have been Wallace Nussbaum himself. I decided I'd better be careful of what I'd say. Winston and Rat had made the same decision.

"We just . . . uh . . . sort of fooled around," Winston said.

"That's right," Rat said, "while looking for my Uncle

Flipping, of course. . . . We fooled around and sort of vaguely looked for my uncle."

"Yes," I said. "You know, we ate some stuff in an all-night cafeteria, and we sort of walked around and told jokes and just sort of . . . uh . . . fooled around."

"And this Uncle Flipping? Why are you looking for him?" the man in the hood asked.

"Well, they're worried about him at home," Rat said. "Our butler, Heinz, isn't feeling well, and they might have to call the doctor, and they're worried that Uncle Flipping doesn't know that . . . uh . . . Heinz isn't feeling well," Rat said.

"And is that why you're looking for Flipping Hades Terwilliger?" the man in the hood asked.

"Yes, well, you see, he didn't say where he was going," Winston Bongo said.

"And he didn't say when he'd be back," I said.

"And you know nothing about a man named Wallace Nussbaum?" the hooded man asked.

"Who?"

"You know nothing of a man named Wallace Nussbaum?"

"Who's that?"

"And have you ever heard of Osgood Sigerson?"

"Osgood who? We've never heard of him. We don't know what you're talking about."

"I think you know very well what I'm talking about. I think you know who Osgood Sigerson is, and I want to know if you've seen him tonight."

"Mister, we came here with Captain Shep Nesterman, had a beer and a baked potato, sat around for a while, and that's all. We don't know anything about any Nussbaum or Sigerson. We don't know what you're talking about."

"What would you say if I told you that something very unpleasant might happen to you unless you told the truth? You know, no one knows you are here, and I can get very nasty if I want to."

"We're telling you the truth," Winston Bongo said. "Besides, it's not a good idea to threaten us. We're plenty strong—Miss Matthews is armed—and I know quite a lot about self-defense. I'm the nephew of the Mighty Gorilla, and he's taught me lots of tricks."

"I'm sure he has, Winston Bongo," said Osgood Sigerson, laughing and throwing back his hood. "As a matter of fact, it was your uncle, the Mighty Gorilla, who was so careful to keep his back turned when you came in. I have hired him as a bodyguard and general man-of-all-work during my present . . . activity. I do apologize to you all for the little dramatic display. It was essential that I find out how well you can keep a secret, even under adverse conditions. I never doubted you, but we're playing a dangerous game, and I had to be sure that you were people I could count on."

Osgood Sigerson was as weird-looking as ever with his painted-on sideburns. While he was talking, he took out a pipe and began smoking some tobacco, which smelled even fouler than the rotten cigarettes that Rat smoked.

"Mr. Sigerson," Rat said, "do you know where my uncle is? Does Nussbaum have him?"

"I'll tell you everything," Osgood Sigerson said, "but first, let's have some lights on. Let me get out of this nasty hot robe, and we'll have a slice of avocado pie. Then we'll have a talk about the events of this night."

XXIV

The heavyweight guy came back. This time we could see his face.

"Hello, nephew," the fireplug said.

"Hello, Uncle Gorilla," Winston Bongo said. He introduced Rat and me to his uncle. We shook hands. It was the first time I had ever met a celebrity.

"Now for the avocado pie!" Osgood Sigerson said. On a side table there was a pie covered with a sheet of plastic wrap, some paper plates, and a knife. "I'm sorry we don't have any utensils," Osgood Sigerson said, "but fingers were made before forks, you know."

It was when Osgood Sigerson mentioned the avocado pie that I first remembered something I hadn't thought of for a couple of hours. What with all the excitement and possibility of danger, the fascinating atmosphere of Beanbender's Beer Garden, and being afraid of the mysterious man in the hood, I had neglected the obvious fact that I was dealing with crazy people here. Now, it has to be understood that I liked Rat very much, and her family, too, but there wasn't any question that they were stark, raving mad. And Captain Shep Nesterman was not your normal type of person either. I mean, who in his right mind dances with a chicken? Of course, Osgood Sigerson, the world's

431

greatest detective according to Rat, with his white clown make-up and painted-on sideburns, had to be regarded as at least extremely eccentric. All this had temporarily escaped me, but when he mentioned the avocado pie, it all came back.

By the way, the pie tasted just as horrible as I thought it would.

"Avocados are also called alligator pears. Did you know that?" Osgood Sigerson asked as he took a second helping. "In answer to the question someone asked a little while ago," Osgood Sigerson said, munching his avocado pie, "the answer is yes."

"Yes?"

"Yes."

"Yes what?" Winston, Rat, and I were thoroughly confused.

"Yes, I believe he has him."

"He? Has who?"

"Didn't someone ask me whether I thought that Mr. Flipping Hades Terwilliger was in the hands of that fiend Wallace Nussbaum?"

"You think Nussbaum has my uncle?" Rat asked.

"I believe it may be so. Right now, my friend and associate Dr. Sacker is out checking on a few details for me. When he comes back and makes his report, based on the information he brings me, I will be able to deduce whether or not Nussbaum holds your uncle captive. I do everything by deduction, you know. You give me an insignificant fact or two, and I can figure out just about anything. Dr. Sacker is first-rate at accumulating insignificant facts. He's a prince of a fellow. Oh, my! I should have saved him a slice of avocado pie, and I've eaten the last one. Mr. Gorilla, would you be kind enough to dash down to the All-Night Zen Bakery to pick up another avocado pie? Also, see if they have any avocado eclairs, avocado-chip cookies, anything at all as long as it has avocado in it. There's a good fellow. You'll have lots of time to chat with your nephew later."

The Mighty Gorilla left. I sank into a chair. Osgood Sigerson licked the tip of his finger and ran it around the inside of the pie plate, picking up avocado crumbs. Rat and Winston looked at one another without expression. I knew what they were thinking. My own father is an avocado addict, and I know how depressing it can be to deal with one.

Sure enough, Osgood Sigerson launched immediately into a long discussion of avocado pastries around the world. I felt right at home, but I could tell that Rat and Winston were suffering intensely.

Rat made an attempt to change the subject. "Mr. Sigerson, you say that you believe Wallace Nussbaum has kidnapped my uncle."

"Yes, yes," Osgood Sigerson said. "As soon as Dr. Sacker returns with the information I asked him to gather, I'll explain everything in detail. Now, where was I? Oh, yes. In Bombay, India, I once was privileged to sample some avocado fritters at the home of Chief Inspector Mookerjee of the Bombay Metropolitan Constabulary. They were deep-fried and folded into a triangular shape. Good? I tell you, they were absolutely marvelous. They were not unlike a banana-and-avocado fritter I enjoyed in Dar es Salaam. . . ."

He went on like that. Sigerson seemed never to run out

434

of avocado stories. Many of them I recognized from my father's store of information about the disgusting things. Apparently these were stories well known among avocado slaves the world over. I knew all about the banana-and-avocado fritters in Dar es Salaam, and have always hoped and prayed that I would be able to live my life without having to eat one.

It was a big relief when the Mighty Gorilla came back with an armload of avocado pastries. A minute or two later, Dr. Ormond Sacker arrived.

We were introduced to the great detective's friend and associate. Osgood Sigerson handed around cheese-and-avocado Danishes, and we all settled down to listen to Ormond Sacker's report.

XXV

Dr. Ormond Sacker was dressed in a suit made of a fuzzy plaid material. He wore a bowler hat of dark green, under which he wore his wig, which looked like a dust mop. Out of his plaid waistcoat he dug a rumpled sheet of paper, and, holding a cheese-and-avocado Danish in one hand and the sheet of paper in the other, he began to speak.

"I've made some notes, Sigerson, of the matters you re-

435

quested me to observe. First of all, I went to the Baconburg hay-and-feed dealer, as you requested. There I
learned that a number of bales of straw had been sold to a
man with blue-tinted eyeglasses and a heavy foreign accent. The dealer did not deliver them. They were picked
up in a taxicab by the man who had made the purchase. I
then went to the center of town and made enquiries of the
proprietor of the out-of-town-newspaper stand. Only one
copy of the *Times of Iceland* was sold today—to a man
with blue-tinted eyeglasses. The proprietor, a Mr. Fat
Schneiderman, was unable to tell me if the purchaser of
the newspaper had a foreign accent or not.

"Also, as per your instructions, I visited the Baconburg
Museum. In the stuffed-bird exhibit hall everything was
normal and in place, except for the rare-birds-of-the-
North-Atlantic exhibit. The stuffed giant puffin was missing. I questioned the guard about this—a Mr. Anolis—and
it turned out that the bird had not yet been missed. It was
evidently stolen. Mr. Anolis was of the opinion that it was
a prank or practical joke, the bird being of no value except
for purposes of study.

"I then consulted the Baconburg telephone directory, as
you asked me to do, and discovered that there are exactly
one hundred and fifty-two storage warehouses in the city.
Of these, only twenty-five have areas in which the temperature can be thermostatically controlled; only eleven have
proper cold-storage rooms; only three have twenty-four-
hour access for customers; and only one, Roosman Brothers Storage Warehouse, has cold storage *and* round-the-
clock access.

"I next contacted animal trainers around the city, and as

you predicted, there is an orangutan missing. It is a fifteen-year-old Sumatran male, the property of Shandar Eucalyptus, a circus performer. Mr. Eucalyptus was very upset about the missing orangutan and has offered a reward."

"Very interesting," said Osgood Sigerson. "And when did the animal disappear?"

"Yesterday," Ormond Sacker went on. "Mr. Eucalyptus informed me that the orangutan, named Howard, is a very obliging beast and will obey anyone.

"As to the other things you wanted me to check on: The coldest temperature in the nation yesterday was in Palmyra, New York, where it was an unseasonable twenty-six degrees Fahrenheit; no cargo planes have been chartered in the past three days; there are no rumors of major scandals in any European governments; the international currency market is normal; none of my underworld informants have seen a Panamanian dwarf with red hair; the films scheduled at the Snark Theater for tomorrow are both science-fiction ones, *Attack of the Pit People* and *Guacamole Monster* —they are both directed by the Mexican director Manuel Traneing—and your shirts will be back from the laundry on Thursday."

"Excellent, Sacker, excellent!" Osgood Sigerson said. "These are the pieces that complete the puzzle." All the time that Dr. Ormond Sacker had been talking, the world's greatest detective had been filling the room with clouds of dense, sickening pipe smoke. I wasn't sure, but I thought it might have been scented with avocado. To make matters worse, Rat had gotten out her cigarette holder and black cigarettes and was adding to the stink. I sat there helplessly. None of what Ormond Sacker was reporting made the least sense to me. I just took it all in and tried to keep from being sick; it was the avocado pie and Danish as much as the pipe smoke that was getting to me. I noticed that not only did Osgood Sigerson have a lot of pure white make-up on his face, not only were most of his hair and all of his sideburns painted on, but his nose was probably a fake.

"Young Miss Bentley Saunders Harrison Matthews, what do you know about the giant Indian fruit bat?" Osgood Sigerson asked, pointing his pipe at Rat.

"Well, they're the largest variety of bat," Rat said. "They eat fruit. They can have a wingspan of as much as six feet. And someone sends a stuffed one to my Uncle Flipping on his birthday every year."

"Aha!" Osgood Sigerson shouted. "It's one of the trademarks of that monster Nussbaum, as is the orangutan, by the way. That villain has left a trail of misery all over the world, marked by stuffed Indian fruit bats and stolen orangutans. We're up against the archfiend himself, Sacker, there's no doubt of it."

"Mr. Sigerson, what about my uncle?" Rat asked.

"Your uncle," Osgood Sigerson said sternly, "is in the greatest possible danger. There are no limits to what that devil Nussbaum will do. I could tell you a story about egg foo yung, but it's too horrible."

"My father told me that Nussbaum once kept a person in a vat of egg foo yung," Rat said.

"I was that person," Osgood Sigerson said. "After three days, I was able to make my escape. The egg foo yung is just one example of the cruelty of which Nussbaum is capable. We are up against no ordinary criminal. No decent person—not even I, who was his prisoner—has seen his face. He has a veritable empire of crime under his control. He can make things happen halfway around the world, just by whispering a single word. If I were capable of fear, I would be afraid of Nussbaum."

"Are we going to catch him?" Winston's uncle, the Mighty Gorilla asked. The Mighty Gorilla hadn't said very much all the time we had been in Osgood Sigerson's room, or hideout, or whatever it was. I hoped we'd get a chance to talk to him later. Maybe I would be able to get his autograph.

"Catch him?" Osgood Sigerson said. "I hope so. But the first thing to do is rescue Flipping Hades Terwilliger."

"Do you know where he is?" Dr. Ormond Sacker asked.

"I know exactly where he is," Osgood Sigerson said. "Mr. Gorilla, kindly bring the car around. There's no time to lose."

The Mighty Gorilla left. "Let's take some of these avocado eclairs with us," Osgood Sigerson said. "We may be on the hunt for a long time."

XXVI

Osgood Sigerson hurried us out a side door. We found ourselves outside Beanbender's Beer Garden. A shiny black car pulled up with the Mighty Gorilla at the wheel. Rat identified the car as a

1962 Studebaker Lark. The Mighty Gorilla was wearing a chauffeur's cap.

"Get in," said Osgood Sigerson. "We must make speed!"

We piled in. Rat and Dr. Ormond Sacker sat in the front with the Mighty Gorilla. Sigerson, Winston Bongo, and I sat in the back seat.

"Tell him where to go," Sigerson said to Dr. Sacker.

"Tell him?"

"Yes, tell him."

"I don't know where to tell him to go," Dr. Sacker said.

"Give Mr. Gorilla the address of Roosman Brothers Storage Warehouse," Sigerson snapped. "We're wasting valuable time here!"

Dr. Sacker gave the Mighty Gorilla an address. The Mighty Gorilla stepped on the gas. The powerful car surged forward. We blasted around a corner on two wheels, and the Mighty Gorilla pointed the glistening nose of the Lark toward the lights of Baconburg.

"Sacker, I should tell you that we may be going into some considerable danger," Osgood Sigerson said. "Have you got your lacrosse racquet with you?"

Dr. Ormond Sacker indicated a lacrosse racquet lying on the floor of the car and smiled a grim smile at Sigerson. To the rest of us, Sigerson said, "The doctor is the most dangerous man in America with a lacrosse stick."

"Mr. Sigerson," I asked, "will you tell us where we're going, and what you expect to find there?"

"I will explain as much as I can a bit later," Osgood Sigerson said. "For now, I suggest it would be best if we kept our minds clear for the dangerous action we will soon embark upon. If you like, I will enhance your education by giving a short talk on the history and manufacture of tennis balls."

Osgood Sigerson launched into a flood of facts about tennis balls. He evidently knew all there was to know about them and had a very good time relating all this knowledge to us.

Out of basic human decency, I will not relate what Sigerson said, or comment on it further, except to say that he kept it up all the way to Roosman Brothers Storage Warehouse.

The warehouse was located on a dark and deserted street on the south side of Baconburg. A single lightbulb burned over the door. The Mighty Gorilla brought the luxurious Studebaker to a stop directly in front of the door. There wasn't another car on the street. It was starting to rain.

We went inside. Near the door was a small desk where a night watchman or attendant should have been. There was no one in sight.

Then we heard a low moan. Sigerson spryly hopped over the desk and vanished behind it. In a moment we had all crowded around. Lying on the floor, bound hand and foot with what must have been a thousand feet of Scotch tape, was a man.

"Doctor, have a look at this poor fellow and tell us what you think," Sigerson said.

Doctor Sacker knelt over the figure. "He's not in too bad a condition," Sacker said. "He seems to have been struck with some force by a large, heavy object, something dense but not too hard, and with an irregular surface."

"Such as a pineapple?" Sigerson asked.

"Yes," Doctor Sacker said, "a pineapple would fit the

description. But why do you think this poor chap was hit with a pineapple?"

"Because here it is!" said Sigerson, holding up a somewhat bruised pineapple. "You will notice that there are various scraps of fruit here and there all over the office," Sigerson went on. "This was obviously the work of Howard, the orangutan kidnapped by Nussbaum. It will not have been the first innocent anthropoid set on a course of evil and criminality by Wallace Nussbaum. But you say that the watchman will recover?"

"Completely," said Doctor Sacker.

"Then let's go," Sigerson said. "I have no doubt that Nussbaum has long since fled, but we may find Flipping Hades Terwilliger, or some trace of him."

"Aren't we going to untie this poor fellow?" I asked.

"That's just what Nussbaum wants us to do," Sigerson said. "We'd be hours picking at the Scotch tape with our fingernails. No, we'll leave him as he is, resting comfortably. His coworkers will be along in a very few hours to help him."

Sigerson pushed a button and ushered us all into the service elevator. "Just taking a wild guess," he said, "I would say that the cold-storage rooms are on the top floor, close to the refrigeration equipment on the roof." He pushed the button for the top floor. Next to the button was a white card that said COLD-STORAGE ROOMS—TOP FLOOR.

"All of you wait here in the corridor," Sigerson said. "I'm going to reconnoiter."

Osgood Sigerson made his way down the corridor, sometimes crouching, sometimes almost crawling, sometimes flattening himself against the wall and listening intently. He disappeared around a corner. There wasn't a sound for a while. Then he was back.

"I've found it. You may all come with me," he said.

We followed the world's greatest detective down the hallway to an open door. "It's in here," Sigerson said. "There's no danger."

We entered a room that was intensely cold. It was a maze of electrical wires of every color, which hung in loops from the cooling pipes, snaked along the floor, and coiled up and down the walls. The wires were connected to various pieces of complicated-looking equipment, black boxes with switches and dials, digital readouts, TV screens, and blinking lights. In the middle of the room there was a large pile of straw surrounded by a crude wooden railing. On the pile of straw, about the size of the average kitchen stove, was something egg-shaped, dark green, and glistening. At various points, wires were plugged into the surface of the thing. A single shaded light fixture hung above the strange object, casting a strong illumination on it. The light fixture seemed to be swaying slightly, causing the shadow cast by the object to shift and move. It made the enormous avocadolike thing appear to be pulsating, breathing, alive.

"Gentlemen," Osgood Sigerson said, "the Alligatron! The only mature *Persea gigantica* in captivity!"

XXVII

"What *is* that thing?" Rat asked.

"You mean it isn't obvious?" Osgood Sigerson replied. "This is a sort of quasi-kinetic-bionic-cybernetic device. In short, you might call it a vegputer."

"Oh," Rat said, "of course. Why didn't I know that right away? A vegputer! How simple! I have only one minor question: What on Earth is a vegputer, or, for that matter, a quasi-kinetic-bionic-cybernetic device?"

"Ah, I see how it is," said Osgood Sigerson. "Your scientific educations have been neglected. This has been one of the best-kept secrets of all time up until now, but I simply assumed that any high-school boy or girl would be able to figure out what this object is just by looking at the equipment surrounding it. I'll take a few moments to explain it to you."

Osgood Sigerson removed a number of pieces of wood from his pocket. Each one was a little bigger than a large lead pencil. The world's greatest detective screwed the bits of wood together end to end, making a long, thin stick, which he used as a pointer, indicating various parts of the Alligatron as he spoke.

"The Alligatron is, to put it as simply as possible, a gigantic avocado. All living things produce various exotic emanations—radio waves, electrical pulses, mysterious vibrations. In the case of members of the vegetable kingdom these emanations are quite weak and have generally been regarded as having no importance. The common or garden-variety alligator pear or avocado is well known to be the source of a surprising number of such emanations, for its size.

"Even so, the combined radiation, pulsation, and so forth of the average avocado do not amount to much and are barely measurable. In the case of this, the *Persea gigantica*, or giant avocado, the signals are much stronger. In fact, some years ago, working with an earlier hybrid much smaller than this one, the leading—and only—avocado researcher in the world, Mr. Flipping Hades Terwilliger, was able to cause a low-wattage lightbulb to flicker, powered by the electrical current present in the avocado.

"It was only when a very large avocado had been developed and more sophisticated monitoring techniques had been found that some really amazing discoveries were made.

"This enormous avocado is a living, thinking, feeling thing. By the way, it also makes a beautiful salad. The various items of equipment that I am now indicating with my pointer serve the purpose of monitoring and recording the, shall I say, thought processes of the vegetable part of the Alligatron. Other devices you see here are, in effect, amplifiers of certain electrical emanations of the avocado. Still others are controls, which stimulate certain functions of the giant fruit. And there are points of connection for still other devices that will help to project, or broadcast, the processes of this remarkable specimen.

"Obviously, strict temperature control is called for to keep the whole apparatus at peak operating efficiency—hence the refrigerated room. Once the avocado gets ripe and mushy, there's nothing to do but eat it. Yummy."

At this point, Osgood Sigerson stopped speaking and looked at the giant avocado as though he wanted to eat the whole thing then and there.

"Uh . . . Mr. Sigerson," I said.

"Yes, young Mr. Walter Galt," the world's greatest detective said.

"I just wanted to know . . . uh . . . why?"

"Why?"

"Yes, why make this complicated computer thing out of a giant avocado, assuming that it's even possible."

"Oh, it's more than possible," Osgood Sigerson said, dabbing his finger at the place where his false nose was coming loose. "It's a reality. As to why, I can give you a full explanation. An ordinary computer, while capable of elaborate operations, cannot produce actual thought waves. The Alligatron can not only produce thought waves of a very particular kind, but it can be made to project them.

"An Alligatron of this size has the thought power equal to that of seven hundred and fifty thousand licensed real-estate brokers—an apt comparison as there are now almost exactly seven hundred and fifty thousand licensed real-estate brokers in the continental United States."

"My mother thinks real-estate brokers are extraterrestrials," Rat said.

"She's perfectly correct," Osgood Sigerson said. "All licensed real-estate brokers are extraterrestrials—that is, they've all been taken over by extraterrestrial thought forms. And that, gentlemen and lady, is the purpose of the

Alligatron. Flipping Hades Terwilliger, working in secret, has evolved a way to repel these space invaders by counter-emanations of pure thought generated by the Alligatron. The natural frequency on which an avocado resonates is ideal for making contact with the thought forms that have taken control of our realtors."

"And Nussbaum?" Doctor Ormond Sacker asked.

"Obviously, Nussbaum is working on behalf of the invaders from space," Osgood Sigerson went on. "This place is Flipping Hades Terwilliger's secret laboratory. For some time, Mr. Terwilliger has been in the habit of suddenly disappearing for days at a time. It has been to this place that he has come on such occasions. He created an elaborate story of madness and pursuit by a master criminal to discourage inquiry. Of course, elements of his story were true—Wallace Nussbaum has been after him the whole time. However, through international contacts, such as Osgood Sigerson—that is, myself—Mr. Terwilliger was able to keep watch on Nussbaum's movements. While it isn't easy to catch Nussbaum, the police of four continents were able to keep sufficient pressure on the evil mastermind to prevent his coming to Baconburg for a time.

"Now, with Flipping Hades Terwilliger's research about to bear fruit, Nussbaum has made his move—a desperate break from cover—to try to wreck the Alligatron before it can be put to use to rid the world of the space realtors.

"Some months ago, Nussbaum dropped out of sight in the obscure Alpine village of Rackenbach. His trail remained cold until the American papers began to report a strange rash of orangutan thefts. Anyone versed in the history of crime could draw only one conclusion: Nussbaum was active in America.

"The trick was to find Mr. Terwilliger's secret laboratory before Nussbaum could. By the looks of it, we were only minutes too late. Still, there is hope. Nussbaum seems to have made off with Terwilliger, but has left the Alligatron intact. Possibly, he wants to keep it for himself in order to have power over the space realtors when the invasion is complete. This also argues well for the survival of Flipping Hades Terwilliger. Nussbaum will want to keep him alive and well to get the secret of the Alligatron from him."

"So the thing to do now . . ." said Doctor Ormond Sacker.

"The thing to do now is to find Nussbaum and get Flipping Hades Terwilliger back from him before any further damage is done," said Osgood Sigerson.

"Where do you think Nussbaum is?" Rat asked Osgood Sigerson, "and where do you think he has my uncle?"

"Yes," Doctor Ormond Sacker put in. "Hadn't we better go after them at once?"

"It's rather late," Osgood Sigerson said. "My suggestion is that we all repair to our various beds and have some rest. Tomorrow will be soon enough to go after that villain, Wallace Nussbaum."

"But you said that Nussbaum is dangerous," Winston Bongo said. "Shouldn't we try to get him before he does some harm to Flipping Hades Terwilliger?"

"It is just because Wallace Nussbaum is dangerous that we must take careful steps," Osgood Sigerson said. "Crime fighters need their rest to do their best work. Although I cannot but think that Mr. Terwilliger is having an unpleasant time of it, we must wait until tomorrow night. Then I hope to have the pleasure of bringing Wallace Nussbaum, that terrible malefactor, to justice at last."

It was arranged that the Mighty Gorilla would drive Rat, Winston Bongo, and me home. Osgood Sigerson and Dr. Ormond Sacker had a little bit of last-minute sleuthing to do before they returned to their temporary secret headquarters. The following night, at eight, we were to meet Osgood Sigerson in what he called "an amusing little restaurant." He pronounced the word *restaurant* with a sort of French accent. The place was the Hasty Tasty, where Winston and I had had a rubber doughnut at a time that seemed long ago but had been, in reality, at the beginning of this long night.

XXVIII

In the car going home we finally got a chance to talk with the Mighty Gorilla. This was what I had been waiting for all night. Of course, meeting the world's greatest detective and seeing the amazing Alligatron had been very interesting, but the Mighty Gorilla was famous. He had wrestled all the strongest men in the world. Besides, he was Winston's uncle.

"Yes, nephew," the Mighty Gorilla said, "I've worked for Mr. Sigerson a number of times—between athletic contests, of course. The first time I worked for him was in London. I was there, having just defeated the Horrible Fly. This Horrible Fly is a very popular European wrestler. He can walk up walls just like a fly, and his most effective hold consists of his actually dropping on you from the ceiling. He wears this helmet with big goggles over his eyes. It looks like he has flies' eyes. He's a very nice gentleman outside the ring. Well, I managed to pin the Horrible Fly, and then I met Mr. Sigerson. He needed a part-time bodyguard and driver while he worked on a case involving a giant Equadorian strangler.

"Another interesting wrestler I met was the Irish Bull. He was seven feet tall and weighed four hundred and sixty-seven pounds. I beat him, too, but it wasn't easy."

It was really interesting to listen to the Mighty Gorilla's stories. Before I got out of the car, I got him to autograph the greasy napkin from Beanbender's I had been carrying around in my pocket all night long.

It was just dawn when I got back to the apartment. My father was already awake, sitting in the breakfast nook, having a cup of tea. I had never known that he was such an early riser, although he was usually awake before I was.

"Hello, Walter," my father said. "Did you have fun looking for Flipping Hades Terwilliger?"

No one had actually said anything about keeping the events of the night secret from our own parents, but I had the general sense that I wasn't supposed to talk. I just said, "Yes, it was sort of interesting."

"Did you find him?" my father asked.

"Not yet," I said. "We're going to keep looking, starting again tonight."

"That's right," my father said. "You never find him in the daytime."

I felt like asking my father some questions about his own experiences in looking for Flipping Hades Terwilliger, but I suddenly realized that I was very tired. I was used to staying up most of the night, but sitting in the Snark Theater is very different from tramping all over town and racing around to secret laboratories with the world's greatest detective.

I wished my father a good night. He wished me a good morning, and I dragged myself off to bed.

XXIX

It was around two in the afternoon when my mother woke me up. "It's your no-good friend, Winston Bongo, on the telephone," she said. She always called him my no-good friend, except when she talked to him. Then she called me his no-good friend. "You might as well make plans for supper," my mother said. "Your father has to go to a meeting of the Association of Synthetic Sausage Manufacturers tonight, and I'm going to the Baconburg Ladies' Anti-Commonist Bridge League. If you and that other bum would like to fix yourselves something here, there's fresh tuna salad in the refrigerator."

I made my way to the telephone. "Hey, Winston," I said. "You want to eat out with me tonight? I thought we could go to Bignose's before we meet the others."

"Good idea," Winston said. "I think my mother is making krupnik or something again tonight." Winston's mother is a really awful cook. She's so bad that Winston tries to get invited to eat at my house whenever he can. To make matters worse, Mrs. Bongo is always taking cooking courses at the Baconburg Adult Education Center. Currently, she was taking a course in Polish cooking, but it wouldn't have mattered what nationality of cooking it was —she was sure to ruin whatever she made.

"Let's ask Rat if she wants to join us," I said.

"Fine. I'll call her and say it's your idea," Winston said. "I wouldn't want to give the impression that I'm asking for a date."

"I'll ring your bell at about six," I said.

"Okay," Winston Bongo said.

I hung up. My mother was polishing the plastic carpet runner. "I just want you to know that I don't approve of any of this all-night-long foolishness," she said. "For some unexplained reason, your father seems to think it's good for you to stay up to all sorts of hours, looking for that loony tune, Flipping Hades Terwilliger. He's always been crazy, you know. See that you don't get too near him."

My mother thinks craziness is catching, like a cold. Ordinarily, I might have given her an argument—and lost— but this time I was more interested in something else she'd said.

"Do you know Flipping Hades Terwilliger?" I asked.

"Sure, I know him," my mother said. "He's batty. He and your father were the only two members of the Avocado Club in high school—but it was all Flipping's idea. Your father is no bugbrain. He's completely sane, responsible, and *compos mentis*, take it from me. He could probably have been a senator or something if he didn't associate with muffinheads like Terwilliger. It looks as though you're going to turn out just the same, running around as you do with that Bolshevik, Winston Bongo."

"Winston's no Bolshevik," I said.

"Of course he's not going to admit it," my mother said, "but I'm keeping my eye on him just the same. If he ever gives you any literature, pamphlets or anything, you bring them straight to me, you hear?"

"Aw, Mom, Winston never gave me any pamphlets," I said.

"He's waiting for the opportune moment," my mother said. "There's no point in your trying to protect him. Just promise me that if he ever starts talking politics with you, you'll call the nearest FBI."

My mother went back to work on the plastic carpet runner, and I wandered back to my room to try to clear my head after the conversation with my mother. The phone rang again. I went to answer it. By this time, my mother was vacuuming the ceiling, and I could hardly hear whoever was on the other end.

It turned out to be Winston Bongo. He was calling to say that Rat wouldn't be joining us at Bignose's. It seemed that there was some kind of commotion or emergency at her house, and she would meet us at eight at the Hasty Tasty with the others. However, Winston said, he'd heard from his uncle, the Mighty Gorilla. The Mighty Gorilla had planned to eat at Winston's house before going to the Hasty Tasty, about which he apparently knew, but when he'd found out that his sister was going to try out a new recipe, he had lost his nerve and had decided to eat with us at Bignose's.

What was more, the Mighty Gorilla was going to pick us up in the powerful Studebaker Lark limousine, and we'd ride to Lower North Aufzoo Street in style.

The whole evening promised to be pretty exciting. I felt really grown-up and special. Here I was going to eat supper with an important celebrity and be driven there in a fancy car besides. Then I'd go to a meeting with the world's greatest detective and maybe get to help in the capture of a criminal mastermind.

I decided I'd better get spruced up. I went to take a shower, after which I was going to put on my special shirt that my father brought back from Hawaii when he was in the army.

We got the royal treatment at Bignose's. Bignose recognized the Mighty Gorilla at once and made a big fuss over him. The Mighty Gorilla had to promise Bignose six or seven times that he would be sure to

mail him an autographed picture. Bignose said he would
frame the picture and hang it up behind the cash register.

We didn't have to slide our trays along the shelf made
of chrome tubing and pick out what we wanted to eat.
That was too bad, because I actually like that part. Instead,
Bignose put on a clean apron and waited on us at one of
the tables. It certainly is different when you go places with
somebody famous.

The food was incredible. It was more than incredible. It
was beyond the power of words. It was . . . well, let me put
it this way, it changed my life. Winston Bongo's, too. This
is what Bignose served us: some kind of a salad made with
dandelion greens, a sort of baked lamb with lots of herbs
and garlic and a kind of cheese sprinkled on top, and roast
potatoes. There was also a freshly baked whole-wheat
bread with a crunchy crust and sesame seeds on it. For dessert there were Napoleons and cups of rich coffee with lots
of cream.

It was good cooking. That's what changed my life, and
Winston's. Both of us had been victims of bad cooking
since we were babies. Gradually, we realized that the food
at home was horrible. We got clues from things like being
the only kids in school who liked the school-cafeteria food
better than what we got at home. We both had experienced
food outside our homes at various times, and it had always
tasted better. Of course, our mothers were well-meaning
—just very untalented—and what we got at home contained all the recommended vitamins, minerals, calories,
and all that, and we were able to eat it, which not everyone could do. Our mothers certainly meant us no harm;
they just couldn't cook. Now, of course both Winston and

I had found plenty to eat outside our homes, and there were all sorts of things we liked, but most of it was on the order of snacks and junk. What Winston and I experienced that night at Bignose's in the company of the famous Mighty Gorilla was *good cooking*, and it was the first time either of us had ever had it.

Needless to say, the wonderful food put us into a very good mood, and we had a superior time, sitting around and listening to the stories of the Mighty Gorilla, and feeling important and grown-up. Bignose asked if he could sit with us and listen to the Mighty Gorilla's stories for a while. Everybody else in the cafeteria wished they could be sitting with us, too. You could tell from the way they watched us the whole time we were there.

I neglected to mention that the Mighty Gorilla is a very stylish person. He had on a suit with red-and-black checks about two inches square. Also, he has flaming red hair that stands straight up, and an interesting red nose. He wears a monocle, and he carries a cane—it's actually more of a club. Of course, Winston's uncle has been to Europe and everyhere, so he knows how to dress.

With Bignose sitting with us, it was impossible to discuss the case we were working on with Osgood Sigerson, so we kept the conversation sort of general. Mostly we talked about wrestling. All of us had questions about wrestlers we had seen on television, and the Mighty Gorilla knew all of them. He also told us about wrestlers in Japan and Australia and other places he had been. As we sat there with the Mighty Gorilla and Bignose, neither Winston nor I could have decided which was more glorious—to be a wrestler or to be a cook.

By the time we set out in the luxurious Lark limousine for our meeting with Osgood Sigerson, Dr. Ormond Sacker, and Rat at the Hasty Tasty, we were all feeling pretty good. It was because of the wonderful meal at Bignose's.

"I hope this Nussbaum guy puts up a fight," Winston Bongo said. "I'd like to show Uncle Gorilla how strong I am."

"Personally, I hope there isn't any violence," the Mighty Gorilla said, "but if there's a need for any strong-arm stuff, I'll let you handle it, nephew."

"Good," Winston said. "I feel as though I could wrestle an elephant."

"If it should happen that you have to wrestle an orangutan, which is more likely, be sure it doesn't get a hold on your feet," the Mighty Gorilla said. "Orangs are natural geniuses at wrestling, and if one gets hold of your feet, it's all over."

It was wonderful how much the Mighty Gorilla knew about wrestling. You could learn a lot just hanging around with him.

"The best orangutans for wrestling purposes come from the island of Maggasang in the Java Sea," the Mighty Gorilla said. "If one of those babies gets you by the foot, look out!"

The great car silently came to a stop outside the Hasty Tasty. We went inside. Osgood Sigerson was sitting alone at one of the tables.

"Good evening gentlemen," said the world's greatest detective. "You are just on time. I expect Miss Bentley Saunders Harrison Matthews, the female you affectionately call

Rat, to arrive at any moment. My colleague Dr. Sacker may be a bit late. Meanwhile, I invite you to enjoy the offerings of this excellent establishment. The specialty of the house is raisin toast. Karl, the chef, is famous for it. I am just starting on my third helping. I recommend it."

I had my misgivings about eating anything in the Hasty Tasty, remembering the rubber doughnut. To be polite, I ordered some raisin toast and a cup of coffee. Winston and the Mighty Gorilla did the same.

To nobody's surprise, the raisin toast was horrible and the coffee was undrinkable.

"Aren't you going to eat that?" Osgood Sigerson asked, snatching the intact-except-for-one-bite stack of raisin toast from my plate. "There's no sense letting it go to waste. I'll eat it."

As a general rule, I don't eat raisin toast. I don't know anybody who does, except my father. Maybe it's a taste that goes with liking avocados.

Rat showed up. She looked excited, as though she had something remarkable to tell us. Before she could speak, Osgood Sigerson held up a finger for silence.

"Good evening, young Miss Matthews," he said. "Correct me if I am wrong, but were you not about to tell us that Heinz, the Chinese butler at your family's home, has disappeared without a trace?"

"Yes!" said Rat, amazed. "But how did you know that?"

"Tut! It is elementary," said Osgood Sigerson, "but I will not take time to tell you how I know about his disappearance just now. Instead, I will tell you something equally surprising. My esteemed friend and companion, Dr.

Ormond Sacker, has also vanished. He's gone without a trace, a thing he has never been known to do before."

"That's terrible," I said.

"It is also significant," said the world's greatest detective. "A well-trusted family retainer vanishes, and my well-trusted friend and companion vanishes. There's bound to be a connection between these two strange events, but we'll get back to that later. At the moment, I want to tell you all how I spent my day."

XXXI

Osgood Sigerson got out one of his horrible pipes and began to speak. "As all of you know, the main commerical street of the Old Town is Nork Avenue. This street intersects Budhi Street at the very center of the bohemian and artistic district. Here, all sorts of unconventional persons congregate. There are painters and writers, scholars and actors, as well as many others who exist on the fringe of well-regulated society.

"The absolute center—the navel, so to speak—of this busy community is the Nor-Bu Drug Company, located on the northeast corner of the intersection I have mentioned. It is to the Nor-Bu Drug Company that the residents of the artists' quarter repair, not only to have their prescriptions filled, acquire baby oil, cigars, note paper, magazines, ear plugs, boxes of cheap candy for their loved ones, water wings, household solvents, paperback books, toothbrushes, postcards, and souvenirs of Baconburg, but to partake of the food and drink, and society, at the famous Nor-Bu Drug Company soda fountain. It is here, at the long marble counter, that the artistic and intellectual lights of the city sit all day, drinking cola and reading the New York papers. It is the best place in Baconburg to engage in conversation—and to gather information.

"I should say that in addition to the various practitioners of the arts who frequent the soda fountain at the Nor-Bu Drug Company, many stool pigeons, card sharpers, bunco steerers, dacoits, cutpurses, granny bashers, yobs, and unlicensed librarians also congregate there. These representatives of the criminal class favor the strawberry malteds for which the Nor-Bu is justly famous.

"So it was that I, disguised as a gentleman thug, spent the day in pleasant conversation with the artistic and criminal fringe of society. My object, of course, was to find out what I could about our friend Mr. Nussbaum. In the course of chatting with my fellow devotees of the strawberry malted, I also got wind of a major bank robbery that is being planned, and I was invited to join a ring of bus thieves. All this will be reported to the authorities when I have a free moment."

"But what about Nussbaum?" the Mighty Gorilla broke in. "Did you find anything out about him?"

"And what about my uncle, Flipping Hades?" Rat asked.

"And what about Dr. Sacker?" I asked.

"In a word," Osgood Sigerson continued, "my interviews with the colorful clients of the Nor-Bu Drug Company were rewarding. By the way, did you know that there's a talented painter in this city who has done a picture of his bedroom with every object that is moveable removed and every stationary object painted white? It's quite a concept. And people say there's no good art in the provinces! Now, where was I? Oh, yes! Nussbaum has Flipping Hades as his captive. That's certain. And I very nearly know where. As to Dr. Sacker, I can't think what's become of him. He was in and out of the Nor-Bu all day, disguised as a disqualified Mexican bullfighter. The last I saw of him, he was in the act of shadowing a suspicious man in a beret. Sacker thought he had the build of an orangutan. I didn't agree. The fellow came in to buy cough drops and had the look of a Ceylonese orchestra leader. I'm seldom wrong in judging a person's occupation and place of origin, but Sacker insisted and followed the fellow when he left."

"Did you happen to notice what flavor of cough drops the man in the beret bought?" the Mighty Gorilla asked.

"Certainly. Tangerine Eucalyptus," Osgood Sigerson said.

"It could have been an orangutan," the Mighty Gorilla said, "that's the flavor they like. They're the devil if they get you by the feet."

"Of course, I could have been mistaken," Osgood Sigerson said. "There's a first time for everything. Still, I hardly think I'd be likely to make such an elementary mistake."

At that moment, Dr. Sacker rushed in. He was out of

breath and appeared to be very excited. "Sigerson!" he gasped, dropping heavily into a chair, "it *was* an orangutan! I have definite proof!"

"Possibly," Osgood Sigerson said, "but what proof could you have? Remember, there are many people who have a funny way of walking."

"Here's the proof!" Dr. Ormond Sacker said, and triumphantly handed Osgood Sigerson a newspaper clipping.

I read the clipping over Osgood Sigerson's shoulder. It had a picture of an orangutan and was all about the disappearance of Adolph, an orangutan who had previously lived in the zoo in Colombo, Sri Lanka, the country that used to be called Ceylon. The article said that Adolph was a genius among orangutans, and that he had great musical talent. In fact, on a number of occasions, the ape had conducted the Sri Lanka National Orchestra. He specialized in the work of German Romantic composers.

"This clipping proves that *I* was right!" Osgood Sigerson said.

"What do you mean?" Dr. Ormond Sacker asked. "I said that it was an orangutan, and you said it wasn't."

"I said it was a Ceylonese orchestra conductor," Osgood Sigerson said, "and if this clipping is correct, so was I. I do admit that you were partly right in that you noticed that the suspect in question was an orangutan, but that is a minor point. The outstanding thing about him is that he *was* the conductor of a Ceylonese orchestra."

"The outstanding thing about him is that he led me to the place where Nussbaum is hiding!" Dr. Ormond Sacker shouted triumphantly.

"He did?" Rat, Winston Bongo, the Mighty Gorilla, and I all asked excitedly.

"Of course he did," Osgood Sigerson said coolly. "You must forgive me, Sacker, my dear fellow, but I have this irresistible urge for dramatics and indirection. I'm afraid I played on your little weaknesses of personality once again. Of course, I saw that it was an orangutan right away. Anybody could have seen that. The reason I argued with you was in order to prompt you to follow the creature, thinking it was your own idea. I mean no offense, old man, but you have a perfectly terrible shadowing technique—except when you are angry and trying to prove a point. Then you're just like a bloodhound. I insisted that the creature wasn't an orangutan just to make you mad enough to stick to his heels like grim death."

"You mean you knew it was really an orangutan all the time?" Dr. Ormond Sacker asked, crestfallen.

"The Sri Lankan government consulted me about that case weeks ago," Osgood Sigerson said. "Now cheer up, old fellow, nobody could have followed him as well as you did."

"Oh, really, Sigerson," Dr. Ormond Sacker said, blushing, "you're too kind. Anybody could have done it."

"You're lucky he didn't grab you by the foot," the Mighty Gorilla said. "There's no getting out of it when one of those orangs gets you by the foot."

XXXII

"Dr. Sacker, you said that the orangutan led you to the place where Wallace Nussbaum is hiding," Winston Bongo said.

"Yes, that's right," Dr. Ormond Sacker said. "At least, I am fairly sure he did. I didn't see Nussbaum—not that I know what he looks like—but it stands to reason. This was the progression of my logical deductive thought: One, here is an orangutan that disappeared some time ago under mysterious circumstances—an orangutan, I might add, with no reason to leave his previous situation, a celebrity, a famous orchestra conductor. Two, who is it that has a strange, mysterious, mystical power over orangutans? Wallace Nussbaum! Three, Nussbuam is known by my distinguished colleague Sigerson to be in this city—only recently an orangutan has been abducted right here in Baconburg. Four, now an orangutan that disappeared in a city in Asia appears here in Baconburg. I submit that the beast is working for Nussbaum, and that it will lead us to him, if it has not already done so. It stands to reason, does it not?"

"Good work, Sacker," Osgood Sigerson said. "I'll make a detective of you yet. You worked that out almost exactly as I had already done."

"You mean you had already figured all this out?" Dr. Ormond Sacker asked the world's greatest detective.

"Elementary," said Osgood Sigerson. "Would I be the world's greatest detective if I hadn't?"

"Sigerson, you're a genius!" Dr. Ormond Sacker said.

"That is true," Osgood Sigerson said.

"Mr. Sigerson, do you think that the disappearance of our butler, Heinz, is connected with all of this?" Rat asked.

"I am certain of it," said Osgood Sigerson, "and now let us waste no more time in idle theorizing. I give to my dear friend Dr. Sacker the honor of telling you where the orangutan led him, a fact already known to me."

"Sigerson, there's no one like you!" Doctor Ormond Sacker exclaimed warmly, "and thank you for the honor of being the one to tell. The orangutan led me to the Sausage Center Building."

"That's where my father works!" I shouted. The Sausage Center Building is the largest building in Baconburg. It looks like a giant castle or fort. In it are the offices of a whole lot of sausage manufacturers, the National Sausage Council, the editorial offices of Sausage magazine, and downstairs on the ground level is The Smiling Sausage, which is a restaurant. Nobody actually makes sausages in the Sausage Center Building, but every office in the building has something to do with sausages. My father has his own company, Galt's Synthetic Sausages. He is one of the few sausage manufacturers whose product contains no meat at all. In fact, they are made entirely in the laboratory. My father sells them mostly to restaurants, especially those places along the toll roads.

"The Sausage Center Building is exactly right!" Osgood Sigerson said. "Now, would you like to tell our friends exactly where in the Sausage Center Building the orangutan led you?"

"Certainly, old friend," Doctor Ormond Sacker said. "In the Sausage Center Building there is a movie theater, which is no longer in use. I saw the orangutan enter the theater through a side door. I followed him no farther, but hurried back here to make my report, although, of course, you already knew all of this, Sigerson."

"Enough talk!" Osgood Sigerson said. "The time has come for action! Into the car, everybody! The game's afoot!"

"Those orangutans get a hold on our feet, we'll all be in trouble," the Mighty Gorilla said.

The powerful car sped along silently. We all sat in grim silence. Finally, Osgood Sigerson spoke. "This is it. I can feel it. The archfiend Wallace Nussbaum is almost in my grasp."

The Sausage Center Building loomed in the darkness before us. I could hardly hear anyone breathing. My mouth felt dry. The Mighty Gorilla cracked his knuckles. Osgood Sigerson adjusted his false nose. I remember wondering at that tense moment how he came to lose his actual nose. It must have been in a desperate struggle with some fiendish criminal, unless, of course, the false nose was merely a disguise to confuse his enemies.

"We'll go through a window," Osgood Sigerson said. "Sacker, do you know where the disused movie theater is located?"

"I think it is over at that end of the building, on the

ground floor," Dr. Ormond Sacker said, indicating the place with his lacrosse racquet.

"Bring the car to a stop over there, Mr. Gorilla," Osgood Sigerson said, "and I warn you all, not a sound!"

We followed Osgood Sigerson in single file without making a noise. The world's greatest detective sprang like a cat to a window ledge, took something out of his pocket, and with a tiny clicking noise picked the lock and slid the window open. He then motioned for us to stay below in the street and vanished inside.

In a few minutes, he reappeared and motioned for us to follow. One by one we scrambled up to the ledge, and Osgood Sigerson helped each of us inside. Soon we had all assembled in a small, dark room.

"This is perfect," Osgood Sigerson whispered. "We are in a storeroom at the back of the theater. Through that door is the projection booth, and through that one, the auditorium. There is a short flight of steps going up to the projection room and a step or two down into the auditorium. From this vantage point, we will be able to observe, or at least hear, all that goes on. At present, the theater seems to be empty. Now, I suggest that we all take positions behind these boxes and packing crates and wait in utter silence. I caution all of you not to make a move without my signal. And not a sound! This may be the greatest danger any of us has experienced. Now, quickly, all find hiding places!"

I squeezed into a space between a sort of locker or broom closet and a corner. Rat and Winston crouched behind a large box. The Mighty Gorilla knelt down behind a thing like a canvas laundry hamper on wheels. Dr. Ormond Sacker disappeared behind a file cabinet, and Osgood Sigerson silently slid a bookcase a few inches away from the wall and slipped behind it.

A very dim glow from a distant streetlamp kept the room from being totally dark. Still, even after I'd had plenty of time to get used to the darkness, all I could make out were indistinct dark shapes.

We waited in silence for what seemed forever. My knee was getting stiff, and I itched in places I couldn't reach. Even though the room was cold, sweat trickled down my back. I tried to practice silent breathing. Apparently everybody else was doing that, too, because there wasn't a sound in the room.

I could hear the ticking of my watch. It sounded as loud as a drum. I slipped it off and put it in my pocket. My nose itched; I prayed that I wouldn't sneeze. An hour must have gone by, maybe two. My feet were numb.

Then I suddenly felt ice cold all over. Something was moving outside the room. Something was making a noise. It was a rasping, shuffling, sliding sound. It was getting closer. Whatever was making that noise, I knew I didn't want to see it.

Then I saw it. The door to the auditorium opened and, framed in the dim light from the empty theater, I saw a hideous shape. It was the size of a big man, as big as the Mighty Gorilla, but shorter, with short, bowed legs. The head of the thing was large and ragged looking and topped by a sort of smooth, rounded shape. I smelled a faint, sweetish odor. Bananas. I realized that I was looking at an orangutan wearing a raincoat and a beret. The creature was much larger than I had imagined. It hesitated, closed the door behind itself, and shuffled to the other door, the one leading to the projection room. It went through the door and shut it.

I was pretty shaken up after my first look at the orang-utan. I never got a chance to get hold of myself, because the next thing to happen was a really bloodcurdling fiendish laugh that came from the auditorium.

"So, my dear Mr. Flipping Hades Terwilliger, you still don't want to talk, is that so?" said someone in the auditorium. The voice was evil-sounding, cruel, and also somehow familiar. I couldn't place it. "You won't talk?" the voice continued. "How would you like to see *Das Dreimaederlhaus* for the sixth time?"

"The monster!" I heard Osgood Sigerson whisper. "He's forcing him to watch German movies!"

"Shall I have Adolph roll the film?" the fiendish voice asked, "or are you ready to talk? After this comes seventy-two hours of German comedies."

"This is too inhuman," Sigerson said under his breath. "We have to rush those vile torturers before that poor man has to watch another foot of film. Sacker! You and the young people will burst into the auditorium and neutralize Nussbaum with the lacrosse racquet. Mr. Gorilla and I will go into the projection booth and deal with Adolph."

"Let's see," the evil-sounding voice went on. "This one is called *Funny Jokes in Dusseldorf*. Here's another called *Laughs and Stunts on the Riviera*, and this one sounds good, *Hilarious Clowns on the Farm*. You'll have to watch all of these, Mr. Flipping Hades Terwilliger. Don't you want to talk and spare yourself a lot of horrible pain?"

"You don't realize who you're dealing with, you criminal," we heard Flipping Hades Terwilliger say. "I'll never reveal the secret of the Alligatron!"

"Adolph!" Nussbaum shouted. "Roll the film!"

"Rush the doors!" Osgood Sigerson whispered. "*Now!*"

XXXIII

It all happened so fast. There was no time to think. I've heard people say about battles in war and accidents and things like that that there was no time to be scared. I was scared plenty, but I moved forward with the others on Osgood Sigerson's signal.

Sigerson and the Mighty Gorilla bounded through the door into the projection room, where Adolph, the orangutan orchestra conductor from Ceylon who had been abducted by Wallace Nussbaum and turned to crime, stood. Dr. Ormond Sacker, brandishing his lacrosse racquet, burst through the door into the auditorium with Rat, Winston Bongo, and myself crowding after him.

It turned out to be perfect timing. At the very moment we entered the theater, the lights went out and the screen became illuminated with the first frames of the German movie with which Wallace Nussbaum intended to torture Flipping Hades Terwilliger.

Coming into the movie house through a door in the corner at the end farthest from the screen, we got a perfect view of everything. There was someone sitting in the very first row, right in the middle. That would be Flipping Hades. Standing to one side, his back to the screen and his face horribly distorted by the light from the projector, was Nussbaum. I didn't have time to study him. Dr. Sacker didn't hesitate for a moment. He thundered down the aisle, waving the lacrosse stick and bellowing, "Spread out! Cover the exits! Don't let him get away! Shoot to kill!"

Nobody had anything to shoot with, as far as I knew, but we did spread out, Winston sprinting across the theater through a row of seats. Rat followed him about halfway, and I ran along behind Dr. Sacker.

"Surrender, you scoundrel!" Dr. Sacker shouted. "Get the tear gas and the nets ready, men! Don't release the dogs until I give the order! Arf! Arf! Woof! Grrrr!"

Then Dr. Sacker began blowing on a police whistle. There was a lot of shouting going on. Everybody was shouting and screaming. I was doing it, too, I discovered.

"Don't eat meat! Don't eat meat!" I screamed at the top of my lungs.

All this happened in a few seconds. Nussbaum, blinded by the light of the projector and confused by all the shouting and whistling, hesitated for a moment. His face was alternately brown, green, red, and blue as it picked up colors from the German movie, the soundtrack of which was blaring, adding to the confusion.

There were shouts and noises coming from above, too. In the projection room, a horrible battle was taking place. I felt my heart sink when I heard the Mighty Gorilla's voice cry out, "Oh, Lordy, he's got me by the foot."

We were almost upon him when Nussbaum got his bearings. He put his head down and ran like a football player, first to the right, toward Dr. Sacker and me, then, suddenly changing direction, he vaulted over a row or two of seats, shifted to the left, and began to sprint up the other aisle toward Winston Bongo.

Dr. Sacker, Rat, and I began to cross the theater, going as fast as we could sideways, down three separate rows of seats. Before any of us could get across, Nussbaum, now visible only as a fiendish silhouette, encountered Winston Bongo.

Winston was in a wrestling stance, arms and legs spread wide apart, head lowered, knees bent, blocking Nussbaum's progress up the aisle. Nussbaum hesitated, and then reached inside his coat. He pulled out an object—I couldn't tell exactly what it was, but I later learned that it was a stuffed Indian fruit bat—which he raised above his head, making ready to bash Winston.

"Oh no! He's going to brain him!" I shouted.

Winston made a deft, understated movement, a sort of half turn, crouch, and feint with his right hand.

Nussbaum left the floor and described a half circle in the air, landing on his back. In the next instant we were all upon him. Dr. Sacker sat heavily on Nussbaum's chest, holding the lacrosse stick across his neck and growling, "Arf! Arf! Woof!" Winston dropped to his knees and busied himself tying Nussbaum's feet together with his belt. Rat and I each grabbed one of the master criminal's hands.

The house lights went on, and Osgood Sigerson appeared, sauntering down the aisle as though he were out for a morning stroll. Following him was the Mighty Gorilla, whose red-and-black-checked suit was badly rumpled and torn in places.

"That went very well, did it not?" the world's greatest detective said. He picked up Nussbaum's discarded Indian fruit bat. "I will keep the miscreant covered with this," Sigerson said, "while one of you boys unties Mr. Terwilliger. He must be very uncomfortable, trussed up like that."

XXXIV

"Mildred," my father shouted, "I can't find my gold-plated collar button anywhere." He was on his hands and knees, looking under furniture in the bedroom. My father is possibly the last man on earth who uses collar buttons. He has these shirts made without collars. At the front and the back there are these little buttonholes. The collar is separate, and you button it on. I think this kind of shirt started to go out of style about a hundred years ago. My father gets them somewhere, and he keeps his collar buttons, which look sort of like tacks with a little ball where the point should be, in an old nose-putty can.

I could hear him hollering for help while searching for the gold-plated collar button as I sat in my room, labeling a picture of an earthworm for the biology notebook.

Everything was back to normal.

That night, I planned to Snark Out with Winston and Rat. We still Snarked pretty often, but we no longer kept score. Tonight's films were *The Hound of the Baskervilles* and *Sherlock Holmes Faces Death*, two first-raters.

It was hard to believe that not very long before I had been present on that night of excitement, terror, and violence when we captured Wallace Nussbaum, the international archfiend and king of crime.

The most exciting thing to happen since that night was that my father, without my knowledge, had slipped a slice of avocado into a bologna sandwich he made me, and I had eaten it, and I liked it. This made him very happy. Still, I am not a fanatic like him. For example, I am not going with him to the annual American Avocado Fancier's convention, unless it's definite that Osgood Sigerson is going to be there. My father thinks that Sigerson won't come. Apparently, they've never met. Sigerson seems to make it to the convention only every other year, and somehow those years my father doesn't go. He goes to the Sausage Maker's Association convention instead, which takes place the same week.

My mind went back to that night in the deserted movie theater in the Sausage Center Building. I could see it all as clearly as if it were happening right before my eyes.

"Let's unmask him," Osgood Sigerson had said.

"Unmask him? What do you mean?"

"Nussbaum! He's evidently disguised," said the world's greatest detective. "Doctor, just give that beard a tug and peel off those eyebrows, and we'll see what we have."

Dr. Ormond Sacker pulled gingerly at Nussbaum's beard. It came right off. So did the eyebrows, revealing—

"Heinz!" Rat shouted.

"Swine!" Wallace Nussbaum hissed at Osgood Sigerson. "You haven't done with me yet!"

"That remains to be seen," said Osgood Sigerson. "At the present moment, trussed up as you are with my good friend Sacker's extra-strong shoelaces, I'd say that I've very nearly done with you—at least I will have when the police arrive to arrest you."

"Arrest me? On what charge?" the archfiend asked, sneering.

"Orangutan rustling will do for the moment," Osgood Sigerson said. "The poor beast tied up with electric cord in the projection room should be evidence enough to have you sent away for a number of years. People in this part of the world don't look kindly on orangutan rustling, Nussbaum."

"I thought I was finished when that brute got me by the foot," the Mighty Gorilla said. "How did you ever subdue him, Mr. Sigerson?"

"Some years ago," the detective said, "I took some lessons in baritsu, or the Japanese system of wrestling. As I recall, I answered an advertisement on the back of a magazine. That instruction stood me in good stead this night. I will write a letter to the baritsu master of Piscataway, New Jersey, offering my thanks and endorsing his method. That should result in his becoming a very rich man."

All this time, Rat and Flipping Hades Terwilliger were standing amazed, speechless. Finally, Rat spoke. "Heinz! Heinz is Nussbaum? I can't believe it!"

"Yes, it was the butler," Osgood Sigerson said. "I knew it all along."

"Nussbaum, you monster," Dr. Ormond Sacker said. "You'll do no more damage now."

"We'll see about that," said the master criminal.

"And how are you feeling?" Osgood Sigerson asked Flipping Hades Terwilliger.

"I never felt better in my life," said Rat's uncle. "I could have held out for weeks. What this poor fool didn't know is that I *like* German movies. I had already seen *Das Dreimaederlhaus* ten or fifteen times voluntarily. It's almost my favorite movie, after *Maedchen in Uniform.*"

Sigerson shuddered involuntarily. "You're a man of peculiar tastes, Terwilliger," he said.

"My only worry," Flipping Hades Terwilliger said, "was that Nussbaum, frustrated because I would not reveal to him the secret of operating the Alligatron, might destroy it. Tell me, is my masterpiece all right? It would take ten years at least to grow another avocado of sufficient power."

"The Alligatron is perfectly safe," Osgood Sigerson said. "We saw it only last night, and it appears to be intact."

At this point, Wallace Nussbaum collapsed in a fit of hysterical laughter. "Fools! Fools! You are undone!" he shrieked. "Oh, this gives me so much pleasure! You have forgotten Howard, my other orangutan, my newest helper! Howard has been given instructions to utterly destroy your accursed machine, Terwilliger! By this time he is certain to have completely wrecked the thing and has probably eaten half of it." Nussbaum's face was contorted in an expression of evil glee. "Go! Have him arrested. He won't put up much of a fight, stuffed to the gills with avocado as he is. So, you see, I have the last laugh! Terwilliger, your Alligatron is no more!"

"Sigerson! Can this be true?" Dr. Ormond Sacker asked.

"Of course it can!" Osgood Sigerson snapped. "Why didn't you remind me about Howard? Do I have to think of everything myself? This was almost a perfect case, except for your bungling, you nitwit!"

"Sigerson, please forgive me," Dr. Sacker said.

"Of course, old fellow," the world's greatest detective said. "I keep forgetting that no one is as intelligent as I am. The fault is mine."

"Oh, Sigerson, you're too good," Ormond Sacker said.

"Yes, I am," said Sigerson.

"But," I said, "if the Alligatron is destroyed, that means there is no way to repel the extraterrestrial thought forms that have invaded Earth by taking over the bodies of every licensed realtor in the United States."

"I'm afraid that's right," Flipping Hades Terwilliger said.

"But that means every licensed realtor in America is a creature from outer space!" I shouted. "What are we going to do about it?"

"Well," said Osgood Sigerson, the world's greatest detective, "I suppose we'll just have to live with it."

The Last Guru

Chapter 1

Uncle Roy's room was over the garage, behind the house on Pearl Street, where Harold Blatz lived with his mother and father. Uncle Roy bet on horse races. He also bet on ball games, and spent a lot of time in a place called Mike's Bar and Grill. Uncle Roy liked to wear his hat in the house, and he used to hold a toothpick and a cigarette in his mouth at the same time. He was Harold's best friend.

Uncle Roy sold shoes—not in a regular shoe store. He had sent in a coupon from the back of a magazine, and the Ojibwa Shoe Company of Roselle, Illinois, had sent him a sample shoe, cut in half lengthwise, so you could see the patented cushion toe, a cardboard foot measurer, and a book of snappy styles for men and women. Uncle Roy would measure the feet of the people who came to Mike's Bar and Grill, and take orders for shoes. Sometimes he would get into his old

Studebaker Lark, and drive around to people's houses, selling shoes. He didn't earn much money, but he didn't pay any rent either, and he ate most of his meals with Harold and his parents, so he didn't need much.

Harold stopped in to visit Uncle Roy after school almost every day. Harold would drink ginger ale, and Uncle Roy would tell stories, or play his guitar, or report to Harold on the shoes he had sold, or the bets he had made that day. Uncle Roy had been a cowboy, a soldier, and a merchant seaman. He had lived in a lot of different places, and he liked to tell stories about them. Harold loved these stories. Uncle Roy had a way of telling about things that made them seem real. They were true stories from Uncle Roy's life, like the time he had an apartment in Cincinnati, right next to the zoo. In the summertime, Uncle Roy could hear rhino fights through his open window. He would buy White Castle hamburgers, and bring them to his apartment in a paper bag, and sit by the open window, eating hamburgers and listening to the rhinos fighting, late in the summer night. When Uncle Roy told stories like that, it was as if he could see them happening—and Harold could see them too.

Uncle Roy was a good listener. He was interested in whatever Harold had done, or planned to do. Uncle Roy would sit on his bed, plunking his guitar, while Harold talked about the things he was interested in. These included school, sports —at which Harold was not very good, but he kept trying—and model ships. Harold had built a number of model sailing ships. The best one he had built so far was the whaler, *Charles W. Morgan,* which he made from a kit. He had loaned it to Uncle Roy, and it stood on the dresser in his room.

Another good thing about Uncle Roy was that he could keep a secret. He and Harold had a number of secrets, one of which got to be more than three years old. That was the secret about the bet. Both Harold and Uncle Roy knew that Harold's parents didn't like Uncle Roy's habit of betting on horse races. They didn't want Harold to grow up with the idea that it was a good thing to do. Even Uncle Roy had explained to Harold that people who got in the habit of betting always wound up losing money. Uncle Roy said he just bet for fun. He knew that he would lose most of the time. Of course, Harold wanted more than anything to bet on a horse race. He was always trying to get Uncle Roy to place a bet for him—kids were not allowed at the race track. He talked about it so much that Uncle Roy offered to make a deal with him—and established their three-year secret. The deal was this: If Harold stopped talking about having Uncle Roy place a bet for him, and never mentioned it again, Uncle Roy would place one bet for him—just one—when he was twelve years old.

Harold was nine when this deal was made. It had to be a secret because of Harold's mother and father. They liked Uncle Roy, but it made them nervous to bring up their son with him around. They might not understand about the bet.

Uncle Roy thought that Harold would probably forget about their secret deal. Of course, he might remember, but then Uncle Roy would place the bet for him, Harold would lose his money, and it would be a good lesson for him—like the time Harold had wanted to smoke, and Uncle Roy had cured him by giving him a six-cent cigar.

When Harold was nine years old his allowance was two dollars per week. Out of this, Harold managed to save an average of eighty-eight cents per week. When he was ten years old, his allowance was raised to two dollars and seventy-five cents. He saved one dollar and forty-three cents per week. When he was eleven, he got three-fifty, and saved a dollar ninety-six. Also Harold mowed lawns, shoveled snow, raked leaves, delivered papers, and baby-sat. In three years he earned four hundred and sixteen dollars. Together with his saved allowance, Harold had six hundred thirty-eight dollars and four cents by the time he was twelve years old.

Harold told Uncle Roy that he wanted to bet it all. He wanted to bet the whole six hundred thirty-eight dollars and four cents on a horse. Uncle Roy made Harold bring his bankbook, and show him that he had actually saved all that money. It wasn't that Uncle Roy didn't believe Harold, he just wanted to see it with his own eyes.

After Harold showed him the bankbook, Uncle Roy did his best to talk him out of betting. Harold insisted. The deal was that Uncle Roy would place a bet for him. The deal didn't say how much the bet was to be. Uncle Roy tried hard to persuade Harold, but the best he could do was to get Harold to round off the amount to an even six hundred.

Uncle Roy thought it over. Clearly, Harold's ideas about betting were all out of proportion. Maybe he needed a big lesson—something he'd never forget. If Harold lost the six hundred dollars he had worked and saved for three years to get—on a single bet—maybe he'd lose his taste for betting in a hurry. The more Uncle Roy thought about it, the more he liked the idea. Also he had never bet more than five dollars in his life—he wanted to know how it would feel to walk up to the betting window and buy six one-hundred-dollar tickets. Uncle Roy made up his mind. It was the only way to teach Harold a lesson. He'd help him pick a horse that was sure to lose.

Uncle Roy didn't have to help Harold. Harold picked a horse that was sure to lose, all by himself. Kanthaka, a horse nobody had ever heard of, was the name Harold picked from the racing form. Kanthaka was entered in a race against a bunch of fast horses with good records. Uncle Roy smiled to himself. It was almost too sad to go through with. For a moment he considered betting Harold's money on the favorite, who paid two-to-one —but this was a lesson.

Uncle Roy left for the track with Harold's six hundred dollars pinned to his undershirt. Kanthaka was paying ninety-to-one. That meant, if he should win, anyone who bet on him would win ninety dollars for every dollar he bet. Of course, it also meant that the chances he would not win were ninety times greater than the chance of his winning.

Uncle Roy bet the money before he looked at the horses. Then he went to have a look at them. Kanthaka was the biggest horse Uncle Roy had ever seen. He was milk white, and had red eyes and a silver mane and tail. All the other horses looked scared of him. Kanthaka won the race and paid Harold fifty-four thousand dollars. Uncle Roy came home with a splitting headache, a frozen expression, and the fifty-four thousand dollars. He felt numb all over.

Harold wasn't even surprised that Kanthaka had won. He had already figured out how much his winnings would be, and wanted to tell Uncle Roy what he planned to do with the money. Uncle Roy didn't want to discuss anything just then. He wanted to lie down with a cold towel on his forehead. He asked Harold to tell his mother and father that Uncle Roy would not be having dinner with them that evening.

Harold told Uncle Roy that he would stop by after school to discuss his plans for the money, and tiptoed out while Uncle Roy rummaged in his dresser drawers for a bottle of aspirin.

Chapter 2

Uncle Roy had not slept very well. He had gotten up, turned on the light, and looked at the check for fifty-four thousand dollars six times during the night. In the morning he didn't feel like getting out of bed. He was still wearing his pajamas when Harold came in after school. Harold had brought a popsicle for Uncle Roy and one for himself—they both liked lime. Harold pulled up a chair, and sucking on his popsicle, started talking about maybe doing a lot of training during the summer, and going out for the track team in the fall. Uncle Roy started to scream—did Harold realize that he had won fifty-four thousand dollars the day before? How could he sit there calmly sucking on a lime-flavored popsicle and talking about the school track team? Didn't he realize he was rich?

Harold said he didn't want to bring up the subject of the money right away, because it seemed to have upset Uncle Roy the day before. However, he did have some plans he wanted to discuss, if Uncle Roy didn't mind. Uncle Roy had crawled back into bed, and was biting chunks off his popsicle with the sheet pulled over his head. No, he didn't mind—in fact, he was very curious about what Harold planned to do with all that money. Harold said he planned to invest it. That seemed sensible to Uncle Roy. He was afraid that Harold wanted to bet it on another horse. No, Harold wanted to invest it—but he couldn't really manage it by himself. He felt he ought to have an adult take care of his investments for him. Would Uncle Roy help him manage his money? Uncle Roy had uncovered his head. Part of his popsicle had fallen off, and landed in his pajama pocket. He was busy fishing it out. Uncle Roy said he really didn't know very much about investing. Wouldn't it be better if Harold got a stockbroker? Harold said that he would get a stockbroker, but it would be better if Uncle Roy acted as if he were the investor, and it was his money. People would think it was strange for a kid of twelve to be buying stocks. Uncle Roy thought about that—it made sense. Harold said he wanted Uncle Roy to take half the money, but Uncle Roy wouldn't hear of it. He said he would be happy to take care of it for Harold, but he didn't want any of it for himself. Uncle Roy was a little afraid of any amount of money over sixty dollars.

Uncle Roy thought they should look for a stock-broker who could tell them what companies were good investments, but Harold did not agree. He wanted to pick the companies himself. He also wanted Uncle Roy to find a stockbroker who did not seem to be too busy. Uncle Roy thought that the better a stockbroker was, the busier he would be, but Harold insisted—after all, it was his money. The next day Uncle Roy made some telephone calls from Mike's Bar and Grill. He picked a stockbroker named Armand Vermin, who also sold personalized greeting cards, and washed cars on the side. When he told Harold about him, Harold said he sounded fine.

Harold had been reading the financial pages in the newspaper, and had found a stock he liked— MacTavish's, a chain of roadside drive-in sandwich shops. MacTavish's stock had appeared a year before at ten dollars a share, but the company was not doing well. For one thing, nobody liked their product—meatless hamburgers. Their specialty was the Zenburger, a charcoal-broiled pickle patty served on a bun with Russian dressing. They also served french fried turnips, and carrot, celery, and pumpkin flavored milkshakes. Hamish MacTavish, the president of the company, had spent millions of dollars on the restaurants, which had beautiful plastic furniture and lots of electric signs. Hamish MacTavish believed in health food, and was sure the American people were ready for snacks that were good for them. So far, there was no evidence that he had been right, and MacTavish's stock was selling for forty-six cents a share. Harold told Uncle Roy, and Uncle Roy told Armand Vermin to buy as many shares of MacTavish's as he could get hold of. By the end of the next day Uncle Roy was the official owner, and Harold the real owner, of one hundred and fifteen thousand shares in MacTavish's Incorporated.

Even though MacTavish's pickleburger stands were not doing very well, Hamish MacTavish was far from broke. He also owned the Croco-Cola Company—the most famous soft drink in the world, that comes in bottles with little bumps on them like a crocodile's skin. Hamish MacTavish felt terribly guilty about getting rich selling Croco-Cola because he knew it was full of sugar, and terrible for people's teeth. The pickleburgers were his way of trying to make up for giving everybody on earth cavities. He was going to spare no expense to make MacTavish's Incorporated a success. He hired the best advertising agency in the world, and told them to start thinking of a way to make everybody want MacTavish's pickleburgers.

Every day Uncle Roy and Harold looked in the papers, and every day the price quoted for Mac-Tavish's was forty-six cents. Armand Vermin sold Uncle Roy some Christmas cards with his name embossed in red on the inside, and Harold started work on a model of the clipper, *Sea Witch.*

The advertising agency called Hamish MacTavish almost every week to tell him their ideas for making pickleburgers popular. Hamish MacTavish didn't like any of the ideas. He rejected free balloons, slogans, billboards, contests—every idea the advertising agency came up with, Hamish MacTavish didn't like. The people who worked in MacTavish's pickleburger stands spent whole weeks without seeing a customer, and the stock was listed every day at forty-six cents a share.

At last the advertising agency came up with an idea that Hamish MacTavish liked—a clown. The clown was named Hodie MacBodhi. He had big feet and a red nose, and he was dressed like a Japanese monk, with a shaven head and a black robe. Hodie MacBodhi rode a unicycle and recited little poems with a Japanese accent. The poems were all about Zenburgers, french fried turnips, and celery milkshakes. The advertising agency made filmed commercials with Hodie MacBodhi, and Hamish MacTavish bought time on every television station in America. They also made radio commercials, rented over a million billboards, and got stories into all the newspapers about Hodie MacBodhi. Hodie MacBodhi appeared as guest on television game shows, and late-night talk shows. He also made personal appearances at shopping centers, and MacTavish's stands. Everybody loved Hodie MacBodhi—especially kids. On Saturday mornings there was a Hodie MacBodhi commercial every five minutes on the stations that ran children's programs. People started to eat pickleburgers. MacTavish's introduced a new sandwich called Big Zen—two pickle patties with goat cheese and an onion—and started another advertising campaign about that. Big Zens were an instant success. Everybody ate them. The President of the United States was driving from the White House to a golf course, and he stopped the official limousine and sent a Secret Service man into a MacTavish's to get him a Big Zen and a celery shake. The story got into the papers.

Six months after Harold had bought MacTavish's stock, it was estimated that every man, woman, and child in the United States, Canada, and Mexico ate at least one pickleburger every day of their lives. The stock was up to three hundred and ninety dollars a share, and had split twice. Harold's stock was worth one hundred seventy-nine million, four hundred thousand dollars. Armand Vermin had dropped the greeting cards and car washing, and was concentrating on watching Harold's investments. He still thought they were Uncle Roy's.

Harold decided to sell some of his MacTavish's stock and buy a company called General Integral Tensile Structures, or G.I.T.S., for short. This company made paper and cardboard buildings.

The cardboard was coated with wax, so it wouldn't get soggy in the rain, and a whole house could be delivered on a truck and put together in a few hours. Even though G.I.T.S. had proof that their prefabricated houses were just as good as plastic or plywood ones, nobody liked the idea of living in a paper house, and the company was doing badly. Just about the time Harold bought stock in G.I.T.S., Hamish MacTavish was offering MacTavish's franchises for sale. Anybody with seventy-five thousand dollars could open his own MacTavish's stand, if he would agree to buy all his pickles and other supplies from Zen Pickles Incorporated, which Hamish MacTavish owned, in partnership with Harold, who had bought half the stock through Uncle Roy. A number of companies bid on the contract to build the new MacTavish's stands, and G.I.T.S. got the job, and made millions. Of course their stock went up. It was about this time that Harold and Uncle Roy lost track of how much money they had made. Armand Vermin had a new Rolls Royce, and was building the biggest house in town, but Harold continued to go to school and build ship models, and try to get the other kids to let him play basketball with them. And Uncle Roy continued to sell shoes for the Ojibwa Shoe Company (which Harold owned now) and to hang out in Mike's Bar and Grill, and bet on horses. Uncle Roy didn't even call Armand Vermin on the telephone very often. He and Harold had gotten bored with the financial pages, and just told Armand Vermin to buy any stocks or companies that were for sale cheap. Some of them increased in price a little, some increased a lot— all of them made money. Armand Vermin started some companies for Uncle Roy too. He started Stilletto's Pizza, which was a chain like MacTavish's, and Precisko, a model ship kit manufacturer —Harold's idea. Both companies made more than fourteen million dollars in the first six months.

Harold was not yet thirteen years old. He didn't know it, but he was the owner of the fifth largest private fortune on earth. Harold was the real owner, but Uncle Roy was the one who officially owned everything. It didn't make any difference to them. It had never occurred to them to use the money for anything except making more money. If Harold had wanted five dollars of his money to spend on a model ship kit, he wouldn't have known how to go about getting his hands on it. Making money had been fun for a while, and then the numbers got so big that neither Harold nor Uncle Roy had any idea of what it all meant. They just sort of left it to Armand Vermin, who was enjoying himself with it.

It could have gone on like that. Harold and Uncle Roy never even mentioned it much any more, except that every now and then Uncle Roy would remind Harold to try and get good grades, because he could afford to go to a good college later, and he didn't want his grades to keep him out. It could have gone on, but someone got curious—someone who was a reporter for the *Wall Street Journal.* The reporter found out who Uncle Roy was, and wrote a story about him. Then a whole lot of reporters turned up one morning, and asked him a lot of questions, and snapped pictures of him. Uncle Roy finally had to lock himself in his room. The reporters didn't go away. They hung around the house and made nuisances of themselves until late at night. Harold's parents were very puzzled. They wanted to know what it was all about. Harold told them that Uncle Roy had made a lot of money in the stock market. They were still puzzled. The reporters were back the next day. There were always crowds of them hanging around. They asked questions about Uncle Roy in Mike's Bar and Grill, and in the street. Nobody knew what they were talking about. Then Uncle Roy's picture was on the cover of *Time* magazine and *Newsweek,* both at once. There were long stories about him—how he was the fifth richest man in the world. Everybody in town read them. Then the crowds were outside the house all day and all night. Everybody in town was there, not just reporters. The police had to come and keep people from climbing in through the windows.

Uncle Roy had not been out of his room for

three weeks. Harold's mother took him a tray three times a day—and four policemen had to go with her to keep the reporters and neighbors from stopping her with questions, requests for money, inventions, and paintings, and other things they wanted to sell. Harold had managed to get to school the first couple of days, but then he was spotted too, and people started to follow him, so Harold was locked inside the house with his parents.

Harold's father couldn't go to work at the hardware store, and the groceries were brought in by policemen. The most horrible part of it all for Harold's parents was that they couldn't understand it. They knew that Uncle Roy never wanted to be rich, never had any way of getting rich, and was never going to be rich. They knew he never invested in anything but horses that lost. The whole family was miserable, but the most miserable of all was Uncle Roy. He wanted to go to Mike's Bar and Grill and talk with his friends. He wanted to go to the race track. He wanted to be left alone. He had not gotten dressed for almost three weeks, and mostly stayed in bed, staring at the ceiling.

Finally, he couldn't take it any more. He loved Harold, and he had never betrayed a confidence before, but this time he had to do it. He got dressed, went downstairs, and told the whole story to the first reporter that grabbed him. He told everything—from the deal, and the six-hundred-dollar bet, to Armand Vermin and the stock market. He told them it was all Harold's—the whole works. It had always been Harold's. Harold had made every decision. Harold owned all the money. It was a hard story to believe—a crowd of reporters had gathered with tape recorders and notebooks and cameras—it was a hard story to believe that a twelve-year-old boy had made this great fortune in less than a year. But, looking at Uncle Roy, it was equally hard to believe that he had done it. After he finished talking to the reporters, Uncle Roy walked into the house, and told Harold what he had done.

Chapter 3

"Gadzooks!" Harold's father said. "Roy, do you mean to tell me that you let this child bet on a horse race?"

Uncle Roy looked very embarrassed. "Fred, it was going to teach him a lesson. He was supposed to lose, and learn what betting was all about."

"He learned a lesson, all right," Harold's father said. "How's my son going to grow up properly, and pay attention in school, and make something of himself, when he's got umpteen million dollars on his mind?"

Harold was miserable. He knew his father was going to be upset when he found out about the bet.

"It isn't right to let a little boy bet on horse races," Harold's father said, "and owning all those companies! Last week the hardware chain I work for was sold to an outfit called Precisko—no doubt, Harold owns a piece of that."

"All of it," Harold said very quietly.

"All of it!" Harold's father was jumping up and down. "My twelve-year-old son is my boss! It isn't normal!" Harold's father rushed out of the room. Uncle Roy rushed after him, trying to explain that he had never intended for things to work out this way. The last thing Harold heard him say was, "Look at it this way—at least you'll never get fired."

Outside the Blatz house, the crowd was getting larger. There were quite a few policemen guarding the house, and it had been a number of hours since anyone had gotten close enough to try to crawl through a window. The police had set up yellow wooden sawhorses with POLICE DEPARTMENT stenciled on them, and the crowd just stood there, looking. Harold's mother was very unhappy about what the crowd had done to her flower garden. At the moment, there was a large policeman standing in what had been her pansy patch. She didn't understand any of this. "I don't see what good it does them to just stand there and look at us," she kept saying.

Harold's father and Uncle Roy came back into the living room. They were still arguing about the bet. Harold asked Uncle Roy to call Armand Vermin, and ask him to come over right away. Harold thought that maybe Armand Vermin would have some suggestions. Neither Harold nor Uncle Roy had ever seen Armand Vermin. Uncle Roy had always conducted their business over the telephone at Mike's Bar and Grill. Uncle Roy dialed the number. Harold's mother opened the front door, just a crack—there was a cheer from the people standing outside—and asked the policeman standing there to be on the lookout for a man named Armand Vermin, and to let him in when he arrived. Then she went into the kitchen to make coffee. Harold and his father and Uncle Roy sat down to wait for Armand Vermin. Every now and then, Harold's father would mutter something about a twelve-year-old boy betting on horse races. Harold and Uncle Roy didn't say anything.

Armand Vermin arrived. He drove right up onto the lawn in his shiny silver-gray Rolls Royce. There was a tap on the door, and the policeman opened it to let Armand Vermin in. Armand Vermin was the most splendid figure that Harold, or Uncle Roy, or Harold's mother had ever seen. He had silvery hair, and a neat silver moustache. He had a sort of golden, healthy complexion that looked as though he spent a lot of time outdoors, doing fun things, like sailing and playing golf. He was wearing a beautiful silvery suit. Armand Vermin was only about five feet tall, but he seemed to be taller than anyone else in the room. Armand Vermin had small, neat hands and feet. He had highly polished shoes, and on his little finger he wore a ring with a huge diamond that flashed and sparkled, and reflected tiny points of light that danced on the walls and ceiling. Under his arm, Armand Vermin had a briefcase of some rich-looking leather with a shiny silver lock. The family stared at Armand Vermin. Nobody said anything. Armand Vermin stood just inside the door. "Where Roy?" Armand Vermin said.

"I beg your pardon?" Harold's father said.

"Where Roy? Roy? Roy is name—yes? Roy call Armand Vermin; say come. I come. Where Roy?"

"I'm Roy," Uncle Roy said.

"Oh. Roy. Hello, Roy. What want?" Armand Vermin said.

The long story was told again. Armand Vermin listened while Harold and Uncle Roy started with the bet, and went on to everything else that had happened. Harold's mother served coffee and cookies. The only thing Armand Vermin said was, "More coffee, lady."

Harold and Uncle Roy finished their story. "O.K.," Armand Vermin said. "Now listen. Can't be fifth richest man—whole world—live in regular house, regular street. Silly. Armand Vermin only twenty-sixth richest man—whole world—has moat with sharks. See?"

"Sharks?" Harold said.

"Sure, sharks," said Armand Vermin, "and sometimes wise guy gets in anyhow—tries to sell Armand Vermin something, borrow money, like that. Not easy be real rich. Now. Word get around, not Roy fifth richest man—whole world

—instead, little kid fifth richest man. Everybody go crazy. Tourists. Charities. All the time people. Everybody go nuts. Too bad."

Harold was hatching an idea. "What if I give away all the money?" Harold asked. "What if I give it all to charities, and things? I don't really want it. If I got rid of it everything would get back to normal. The crowds of people would go away; Uncle Roy could go back to Mike's Bar and Grill; I could go back to school; my father could go back to work; my mother could start a new flower garden."

"Too late," Armand Vermin said. "Everybody know you rich. Nobody believe you give it all away. You give that much away, they think you got more. Make you more crazy. Also, you give money away—screw up economy. Too much money turn loose all at once. No good give it away. Instead better you run."

"RUN?" the whole family shouted at once.

"Sure, run. You got to run. Can't stay locked up in house. You run. Armand Vermin arranges." Armand Vermin picked up the telephone. "Go pack. You leaving soon." Then he dialed a number.

While Armand Vermin was talking on the telephone, the family had a little conference. "Maybe we ought to take his advice," Harold's father said, "at least until things quiet down a bit."

"I do think we ought to go away for a little

while," Harold's mother said, "at least until we can talk things over quietly, and decide what to do."

"I'm not going anywhere," Uncle Roy said. "I'm going to stay here and look after things, and start growing a beard. Once the rest of you leave, it should start to quiet down. I'll be able to go out after dark once my beard grows in." Uncle Roy wanted to get back to hanging out in Mike's Bar and Grill, and selling shoes. He had traveled a lot when he was younger, and now he didn't like anything to change his routine. Harold's father and mother agreed that it might be a good thing if Uncle Roy stayed behind and took care of the house.

"Hurry up. Pack," Armand Vermin said. "Helicopter come in five minutes."

"I can't be packed in five minutes!" Harold's mother said.

"Don't take much. Buy what you need. Armand Vermin brought money just in case." Armand Vermin clicked open the briefcase. "Two million," he said. "Didn't know what was all about, so didn't bring much." He handed the briefcase to Harold's father, who started to faint, and then got hold of himself. "I pay myself back out of kid's money," Armand Vermin said.

"Look!" Harold said. "There's a helicopter landing in the back yard!" It was a very large helicopter, painted red and white, with the Croco-

Cola emblem painted on the side.

"Hurry up. Go before crowd gets ugly," Armand Vermin said.

The family ran for the helicopter. The crowd was shouting. They were calling Harold's name. The news that it was Harold, and not Uncle Roy who owned the world's fifth largest fortune had already gotten around. People were waving newspapers with headlines that read: TWELVE-YEAR-OLD BILLIONAIRE!!!!

The inside of the helicopter was fixed up like an elegant living room. There were comfortable chairs, bookcases, a television set, and a telephone. In the middle of the cabin was a big red-and-white Croco-Cola cooler. It was the private helicopter of Hamish MacTavish. He had loaned it to the Blatz family at Armand Vermin's request. There was a stewardess with a big smile. She was wearing a uniform that looked something like a Croco-Cola label. The stewardess got Harold and his mother and father fastened into armchairs, with seatbelts attached, and the helicopter took off. Harold looked out the window as the house, the crowds of people, the neighborhood, and all of Rochester, New York, dropped away.

Harold's mother was crying. She was still upset about the people trampling all over her flower beds. Harold's father looked as though he still hadn't figured out everything that had happened. Harold was worried. He wondered if Uncle Roy was going to be able to take care of himself.

The telephone rang. It was Hamish MacTavish. He wanted to talk to Harold. "My boy!" Hamish MacTavish said. "Of course I knew all along that it was you and not your uncle who made all those brilliant investments. I feel as if I know you already, you fine young man. I was a boy genius, too, you know. We'll have a lot to talk about when you get to the castle."

"Castle?" Harold asked.

"My goodness, I forgot to tell you," Hamish MacTavish said. "I'm having you flown to Kennedy Airport in New York City, where you will board a special plane—passports and all that sort of thing are taken care of—and then you'll fly to my castle, Schloss Krokenstein, in the Bavarian Alps. You'll be able to rest up, and make plans there."

"That sounds very nice," Harold said. "I'll tell my parents." Harold said goodbye to Hamish MacTavish. "We're going to Europe," he told his parents. "We're going to a castle in the Bavarian Alps, called Schloss Krokenstein."

"My poor flowers," Harold's mother said.

"Imagine, letting a twelve-year-old kid bet on a horse race," Harold's father said.

Chapter 4

The airplane that took Harold and his parents to Germany was even fancier than the helicopter. It was a private Croco-Cola Company jet. At the airport in Munich people in smart red-and-white uniforms conducted the family to a small airplane, also red and white. It had been eight hours since Harold and his mother and father had left the house in Rochester, New York. Harold's mother had cheered up a bit, and was curious about where they were going. Harold's father was still mumbling now and then about Uncle Roy being a bad influence on Harold, but he was in a better mood too. The food on the airplane was very good, and they all had lots of Croco-Cola. Harold was very excited. He had never been in an airplane of any kind, and now he had been in a helicopter and a big jet. Best of all was the little airplane that took the family from Munich to the little airfield near Schloss Krokenstein. The Alps

were beautiful. Harold had never seen anything
he liked so much. And the ride was exciting—the
little airplane dipped and soared on the currents
of air above the mountains. Every now and then
Harold's mother would say, "Eeeep!" when the
plane took a dip. Harold's father was turning a
beautiful sea green. He kept his lips tight shut and
stared at his knees.

The little plane landed with three bumps on the
airfield at Schloss Krokenstein. They were apparently three bumps too many, because Harold's
mother and father both made horrible moaning
noises with each bump.

A red-and-white Land-Rover, painted to resemble the Croco-Cola label, drove out to meet the
airplane. A tall man with silver hair and a moustache stepped out. He had the same healthy complexion as Armand Vermin. Harold was sure it
was Hamish MacTavish.

"Welcome to Schloss Krokenstein," said Hamish MacTavish. "I hope you had a pleasant trip."
Hamish MacTavish shook hands with Harold and
his parents.

"Excuse me, Mr. MacTavish," Harold's father
said. "I've been trying to figure something out for
a whole day."

"And what might that be?" Hamish MacTavish
asked.

"I'd like to know," Harold's father said, "just
why we have had to flee our home with nothing

but the clothes on our backs and two million dollars in cash; why we have flown halfway around the world in Croco-Cola airplanes; why we are here, why you are here, and what this is all about."

"I am here because this is one of my homes," Hamish MacTavish said, "and you are here because it is my honor to have you as my guests. As to the rest, I suggest we drive up to the castle, and have a nice hot Croco-Cola, while we talk it over."

The castle of Schloss Krokenstein was at the very top of the Krokenberg, a very high mountain. The airfield was cut into the mountain about three-quarters of the way to the top. The ride in the Land-Rover was almost as exciting as the flight over the mountains. Harold's mother said, "Eeeep!" a couple of times. Hamish MacTavish was a very good driver. Sometimes it seemed as though the Land-Rover was going straight up. "There's a footpath to the castle that's much easier," Hamish MacTavish said. "I purposely had this road made as difficult as possible to discourage tourists. After things have blown over a bit, you'll be able to walk down to the village of Krokenbach at the foot of the mountain."

"What do you mean 'blown over'?" Harold's father asked. "I still can't seem to grasp exactly what's going on."

"We're almost to the castle," Hamish MacTavish said. "Let's wait until we're comfortable to have our talk."

The road to Schloss Krokenstein was rocky from the start, but now it was even rockier. The trees had gotten smaller and scrubbier, and then they stopped altogether. For the first time the Blatz family was able to see the castle. It was made of dark stone—almost black. Fat round towers with tiny slit windows rose up from the rocky peak of the Krokenberg. The wind was very cold. "Schloss Krokenstein was built in the eleventh century by a local prince," Hamish MacTavish said. "I've had the inside completely modernized, of course. You'll be very comfortable here, for as long as you have to stay."

"Mr. MacTavish, we're very grateful that you want us, of course," Harold's mother said, "but we really don't understand why we are here—I mean, obviously we couldn't stay in our house with all those crowds of people standing outside day and night; but I expected we'd just spend a night or two at a motel, until we could figure out what to do. It seems like an awful lot of trouble for you—bringing us here, and all."

"It is no trouble at all, dear lady," Hamish Mac-Tavish said, "and I will answer all of your questions directly—Ah! There's old Souchong."

A very old man, so old that he walked doubled over, had opened the tiny iron door that was apparently the main entrance to the castle. Harold wondered why such a big castle would have such a little door. The old man, Souchong, looked as though he might be Chinese, or something close to Chinese. It turned out later that he was from Tibet.

"Souchong is a wonderful butler," Hamish MacTavish said. "He may be old, but he's agile as a mountain goat. You see, it's next to impossible to get servants from the village. This castle is situated eleven thousand feet above sea level, and even the mountain people in these parts have a hard time doing a good day's work at this altitude. Some years ago, I had the happy idea of importing all my servants from the Himalayas. Old Souchong is like a fish in water at eleven thousand feet. By the way, you may find the air a bit thin at first. I wouldn't do anything too strenuous until you get used to it." Hamish MacTavish chatted merrily as he and old Souchong ushered their guests into the castle.

The inside of the castle was quite a shock. Bright fluorescent lights, and bright plastic furniture—the kind they had in MacTavish's restaurants—made a surprising contrast to the nine-hundred-year-old exterior of the castle. There was a life-size statue of Hodie MacBodhi, made out of plastic with an electric light in his nose; and the high-gloss vinyl linoleum was patterned with pictures of Zenburgers and pumpkin milkshakes.

"Oh, Mr. MacTavish," Harold's mother said, "you have a lovely house."

"Thank you," said Hamish MacTavish. "I had

the devil of a time with the Bavarian Historical Landmarks people before they'd let me do it the way I wanted. As it is, they wouldn't let me put an electric sign on the outside. Backward people, these—it's easy to see why they never invented the pickleburger."

Souchong showed the Blatz family to their rooms, which were all exact replicas of MacTavish's restaurants in different cities in the United States, complete even to the deep fryers and plastic garbage cans in the shape of Hodie MacBodhi, holding a sign which read, "Feed Me." Harold's room was a replica of the MacTavish's in Hoboken, New Jersey. Hamish MacTavish had promised that after everyone had a hot bath and a change of clothes (fresh clothes, with Croco-Cola labels as part of the design, had been provided) they would all meet for a hot Croco-Cola and a nice long chat.

Chapter 5

"This Croco-Cola is from my private stock," Hamish MacTavish said. "It doesn't have a grain of sugar in it. When the research boys came up with it, I thought I had solved the problem of my life—sugar in soft drinks. Strange to say, when we test-marketed the stuff, nobody liked it. Too good for them, if you ask me. We made it just like this, with Yugoslavian wildflower honey."

Harold and his parents didn't like the special private-stock Croco-Cola very much either. It had a very strong taste of honey, and the drink was of about the consistency of maple syrup. Also, it was served steaming hot in big metal mugs with Hodie MacBodhi's face stamped on them.

Hamish MacTavish sniffed the clouds of steam coming from his cup of Croco-Cola. He smiled. He was evidently enjoying it. The group was seated in a room about twice the size of the gym in Harold's school. Huge banners hung from the walls; they all had Croco-Cola or MacTavish's emblems. There were metal statues of Hodie Mac-Bodhi, and a great table, made of realistic wood-grain plastic, at which the Blatz family and Hamish MacTavish sat.

"I'm sure you have waited long enough for an explanation," Hamish MacTavish said. "If you will be patient, I will tell you why I decided to bring you here, and what you can expect in the immediate future." Hamish MacTavish brought out a huge pipe carved to resemble a Zenburger. He lit it, and exhaled a cloud of blue smoke that had a subtle fragrance, like shredded carrots. "You have no idea what a stir has been caused by the news that Harold, here, is the fifth richest man in the whole world. People get carried away by stories of that kind, and, since nothing interesting has been happening in the world for the past few months—just the usual wars, crime in high places, revolutions, pollution, ordinary run-of-the-mill events—because the news has been so dull, the whole world has been ready for some great enthusiasm, some kind of fad or fear or personality to get all excited about. Now it so happens that I was just waiting for such a period to introduce a new line of vegetable ice cream—cucumber, potato, summer squash, with all the vitamins left in—but Harold's story broke all by itself, and that has become the biggest news in the world. Everybody is talking about it—there are Harold Blatz T-shirts and dolls being rushed into production. Two unauthorized biographies of Harold will be on the newsstands tomorrow morning. A major film studio is planning to do a film based on Harold's life, with the Beatles playing Harold at different ages, and Walter Cronkite playing himself. I have all this information from Armand Vermin, who has been doing a few little jobs for me lately. By the way, Mr. Vermin is taking care of your interests—the movie studio is paying two million dollars for the rights to the life story, and the publishers of the unauthorized biographies will be sued for every cent they've got. Anyway, the whole world is going Harold Blatz crazy, and it will get a whole lot worse before it gets better."

"Mr. MacTavish," Harold's mother said, "I don't understand why everyone is so excited about this. It's true that Harold is a very nice boy, but aside from making a whole lot of money in the stock market, he isn't very different from a lot of boys."

"I agree with you utterly," Hamish MacTavish said. "I have always been rich, and it doesn't make me any better than anyone else—only more powerful. I don't know why people get all worked up about matters that are basically none of their business, but they do. They also like quiz shows and Salisbury steak and a lot of other things I don't understand. You just have to accept it as a fact—people all over the world have nothing better to do than think about Harold, watch Harold, make up stories about Harold, and practically break their necks trying to get close to Harold. The thing to decide now is what are we going to do about it? You can see that you couldn't have stayed in your house. Those crowds would never have gone away. Of course, you are welcome to stay here as long as you like, but I'm afraid that it won't be very long before you are discovered, and then this place will become very much like a prison."

Harold's mother and father looked at one another nervously. It was starting to dawn on them —Harold was a celebrity, and they were too. It wasn't nice. They had never had a lot of friends. They didn't like to go where there were big crowds of people. They liked being left alone.

"Of course, you will be safe as long as you stay in the castle—I have an electric security system and the dogs—but it is only a matter of time until the whole world comes to Krokenbach looking for you. I expect you'll want to work out something a bit more permanent." Hamish MacTavish's pipe made a gurgling noise as he smoked it.

Harold spoke. "Mr. MacTavish, couldn't we just walk around like ordinary people? At first, it might be kind of annoying, dealing with all the people who are curious about us, but after a while they'd see how ordinary we were, and just get bored with the whole thing and leave us alone."

"Harold, my boy," Hamish MacTavish said, "there is a certain lady—the widow of a popular president—whose picture has been on the cover of at least four gossip magazines every month for eleven years. And she isn't as interesting as you are. Do you think you could stand all that attention for eleven years?"

"I suppose not," Harold said. "What do you suggest?"

"I suggest we all think it over," Hamish Mac-Tavish said. "I'm certainly glad that I'm only the ninth richest man in the world, and that it didn't come on suddenly. We have a few days anyway to make our plans. The word won't leak out that you're here—not for a while."

Hamish MacTavish told the Blatzes to amuse themselves in the castle and the grounds. He said that he was going to be in touch with Armand Vermin and other smart men, and receive some suggestions about how the Blatzes could avoid unpleasant publicity. He told them that Souchong would get them anything they wanted.

Hamish MacTavish left the room. The Blatzes didn't see him again for four days. They spent their time wandering from room to room in the great castle, and taking walks in the little park outside. There was an excellent view in every direction, and Harold's mother said it was very restful. Harold didn't like it much. There wasn't really anything to do. Harold could have asked Souchong if he could get him a model ship kit—but he didn't feel like it. He didn't know how long they would be there, and he hated to leave a model unfinished. Also there was something about all the plastic furniture that was getting on Harold's nerves. He was bored. His father didn't say anything, but Harold had the impression that he was bored too.

On the fifth day, Hamish MacTavish appeared, just as the family was sitting down to their Zenburgers at lunch. "I'm sorry to have neglected you so long," he said. "I haven't forgotten your problem. I've been working on it, and I've been keeping in touch with Armand Vermin. He says that everything is comparatively quiet at home, and Roy is able to go out without causing a riot. That takes care of the good news. By the way, have you had a chance to walk down to the village of Krokenbach yet?"

Harold and his parents said they had not. "That's too bad," Hamish MacTavish said. "I just learned that the first busloads of magazine reporters have arrived. Too bad you didn't get to see it —it's a lovely village. I'm afraid you won't be able to stay here much longer. *Gawk* magazine has bought a neighboring mountain, and will probably be installing their telescopes and long-range listening equipment in the next few days. We'll have to act soon. Have you decided what you are going to do?"

"Mr. MacTavish," Harold's father said, "we have no idea what to do. We don't have any experience with this sort of thing. We were hoping that you would have some suggestions."

"Well, I'll certainly try to help you," Hamish MacTavish said, "but it isn't going to be as easy as I thought. Harold is more famous than Mickey Mouse already. A number of primitive tribes in New Zealand and New Guinea, and places like that, have stopped paying taxes and are saving money to buy him as their king. Ninety-nine percent of the babies born since the story broke in the news magazines have been named Harold or Haroldine. The only country where they don't know who Harold is, is Iceland—and we certainly can't send you there. I wouldn't send my worst enemy there. I must confess, I haven't been able to think of a place to send you where you will be able to live a normal life. I don't suppose you'd like to spend a few years on a yacht?"

Mr. Blatz explained that he had been in the navy, and was seasick the whole time.

Hamish MacTavish seemed genuinely upset. He really wanted to help the Blatz family, and he couldn't think of a way to do it. He tried to make helpful suggestions—but none of them were acceptable for one reason or another. Plastic surgery for the whole family was ruled out. Staging a fake accident and pretending to be dead was voted down, and hiring actors to pose as the

Blatzes and draw attention away from the real family seemed too complicated. Finally, everyone fell silent, and sat staring at their mugs of pumpkin milkshake.

A strange thing about the butler, Souchong, was that he had not spoken a word the whole time that the Blatz family had been visiting Schloss Krokenstein. Harold wondered if he could speak. He could obviously understand English. Souchong had been standing, with his hands tucked into his sleeves during the conversation that had just taken place. Now Souchong spoke, for the first time. "So! This is a problem? Fooey! Where I come from, any six-year-old could figure out what you should do. Dopes." Souchong was silent again, staring at the opposite wall.

Hamish MacTavish seemed annoyed. "Five years since you opened your mouth last, and all you do is criticize!" he shouted. Hamish MacTavish glared at Souchong. Souchong continued to stare at the wall. "Well, if you have a suggestion, let's hear it," Hamish MacTavish said at last. Souchong didn't move. He continued to stare at the wall. Slowly a faint smile appeared on his old wrinkled face.

"If you want my advice," Souchong said, "you won't try to hide. Rich people should be able to do whatever they like. What's the good of being rich if you have to stay in your house all the time? You should go where you don't have to hide. Go where it won't seem strange to anybody that you are richer than they are. Go to a place where extremes of wealth and poverty exist side by side. Go to my part of the world, dopes."

"He's right, of course!" Hamish MacTavish shouted. "He's always right. He doesn't talk much, but when he does he always gets right to the point. It's the perfect solution." Souchong had gone back to staring. It was clear that he had nothing more to say.

"I don't quite understand," Harold's father said. "I was under the impression that Souchong came from Tibet. Is he saying that we should go there?"

"Of course, Tibet itself is out of the question," Hamish MacTavish said. "It was never the easiest thing in the world to get into Tibet, and now the Chinese Communists have made it even more difficult to get in—let alone to live there—but some place in India, or the Indo-Tibetan border country, would be perfect. You see, for hundreds and hundreds of years Indian peasants have been among the poorest people in the world, and Indian princes have been among the richest. They're used to it. If someone owns white elephants with gold trappings, and goes around covered with jewels, the neighbors don't get excited. It's always been like that. How would you like to live somewhere in India for a while? I can arrange it."

Harold's mother said that she had always wanted to go to India—ever since she saw a movie about India with Lauren Bacall. Harold's father said he would like to see the Himalayas. Harold said it was all right with him, too.

Hamish MacTavish hurried off to make some telephone calls. He was back in fifteen minutes. "It's all set," he said. "The Croco-Cola distributor for one of the northern provinces is a maharajah I know very well. He says he will be very happy to have you as the guests of his state. He is preparing accommodation for you in a little village high in the mountains. He says it's very beautiful. Also it is very hard to get to, so you won't have to worry about reporters and people like that, and the maharajah's private army will be instructed to keep people who don't belong there away from the whole area. You can leave whenever you like."

Chapter 6

It was only a matter of hours until the first camera-bearing helicopter swooped over Schloss Krokenstein. Early the next morning, the Blatzes could see the sun glinting on the huge terrestrial telescope that *Gawk* magazine was installing on the nearest peak. Harold's mother said it made her nervous to have people looking at her all the time, especially through telescopes. It was obviously time to leave.

"Mr. MacTavish," Harold's mother said, "we're so sorry to have been the cause of all this trouble. Will the photographers and reporters and helicopters go away after we leave?"

"Not for some time, dear lady," Hamish MacTavish said, "but I don't mind. I plan to convert my castle to the first European Mega-MacTavish's. I don't see how the Bavarian Landmarks Commission can object that I'm despoiling the natural and historical environment with all these machines flying over every two minutes, and that huge telescope on the next mountain. No doubt *Gawk* will convert their installation to some sort of a tourist attraction rather than cart that monster telescope down again—you know, SEE THE ALPS—that sort of thing. You really did me a favor by coming here. I've got the electric sign in the dungeon—it will be installed by the end of the week. At last I can bring the pickleburger to the simple Bavarian peasants."

There was a siren, and Hamish MacTavish hurried off to see what had happened. It turned out that two Italian newspaper reporters, in rubber suits, had climbed over the electric fence, and were being held at bay by the huge mastiff dogs that patrolled the grounds of Schloss Krokenstein.

When Hamish MacTavish got back from having the Italian newspaper reporters kicked out, he said, "I don't wish to seem to be hurrying you on your way, but it really would be best if you left on your journey to India now. I expect things to get very busy here in the next day or two."

Hamish MacTavish drove the family down to the little airfield, and said goodbye to them. The airplane was waiting on the runway. Dozens of photographers were partially concealed in the bushes around the airfield, and they rushed the plane just as the Blatzes were boarding. The plane got away just in time to avoid being mobbed by the photographers.

Back to the airport in Munich, onto a Croco-Cola Company jet, the Blatz family repeated their trip to Schloss Krokenstein in reverse—only this time their destination was India.

The Maharajah of Mahamurghi met Harold and his parents at the airport in Delhi. He was a nice little man, with a big moustache. He was very polite. He had the Blatz family transfer to his private Croco-Cola Company airplane, and take off for his private landing field near Dankar Gömpa. From there, the family traveled by Rolls Royce station wagon to the Maharajah's palace at Mahamurghi. The Maharajah told Harold that Mahamurghi means "Great Chicken." There was an old legend about it in his family.

Everything was very comfortable in the Maharajah's palace—there were beautiful things to look at, nice smells, and music, and things to eat. There were lots of servants, who brought things to the Blatzes on little silver trays. Harold's mother liked it a lot. She said it was just like the movies.

The Maharajah had a couple of very old elephants named Alice and Roger. They had belonged to his grandfather. He told Harold he could ride them whenever he wanted, but not too far, because they got tired easily. Harold liked the elephants. He took rides on them every morning. Usually he would ride Alice, and Roger would just come along for the walk.

There was a lake in the palace grounds, and sometimes Harold, Alice, and Roger would go swimming together.

The Blatz family stayed with the Maharajah for two weeks. During that time the Maharajah was busy making arrangements for his guests to go to the village of Dorje-Zetz, high in the mountains. He said that nobody there would bother them, and they could come and go as they pleased. The Maharajah had his own army, and tough-looking soldiers and a lot of mules turned up, and waited on the edge of the palace grounds. There were pens for the mules, and tents for the soldiers. They were going to take Harold and his family to Dorje-Zetz.

Of course reporters and photographers turned up, but the Maharajah simply had them clapped in jail. Mrs. Blatz was worried about this, and told the Maharajah that she felt sorry for the reporters and photographers, who were only doing their job. The Maharajah told her that his jail was nicer than the nicest hotel in Europe, and that he would let all the reporters and photographers go after the Blatzes had left. He also said that the reporters and photographers had gained an average of twenty pounds each, and were having the time of their lives.

The Maharajah's jail was filling up, and all the preparations had been made. It was time for the family to start on their way.

It took almost a week to get to Dorje-Zetz by mule train. Harold liked every minute of the trip. He enjoyed riding his mule, Alfred. He liked the cold fresh air. He liked the panoramic mountain views. Often the trail was steep and rocky, and the mules picked their way along ledges thousands of feet high. Harold's parents were not all that comfortable, but they both said they liked the mule ride better than flying in an airplane. Every evening the soldiers prepared camp, and cooked a delicious meal. Little tents woven of yak hair were set up, and everyone slept very well. Because of the cold winds the Blatzes wrapped up in heavy woolen overcoats, even heavier than blankets. They were given heavy felt boots to wear, and thick, pointed woolen caps.

By the second or third day of the trip, Harold felt as though he had been riding mules his whole life. He felt as though he had been born riding a mule. He sat effortlessly, wrapped against the wind in his warm coat, boots and cap, and watched the mountain landscape move past him and beneath him, as the caravan wound upward toward Dorje-Zetz.

Harold smelled Dorje-Zetz before he saw it. There was a faint smell of spices in the air—and something else, a sweet smell, as though someone were burning pencil shavings. For a whole day before they had gotten to the valley in which Dorje-Zetz was located, the mule caravan had passed little piles of stones, and little fluttering flags on bamboo wands, stuck into the piles of stones. The piles of stones, and the flags got more numerous as they got closer to the village, and then the smell started, faint at first, and not all the time, then stronger and more often. It was incense. The villagers were burning it in honor of their guests. When the mule train got to the beginning of the valley, they found coils of incense, that looked like rope, smoldering by the piles of stones. Harold noticed that the soldiers often picked up a stone and added it to the piles that marked the way, and sometimes, he did it too.

Dorje-Zetz was halfway up the opposite wall of a very steep valley. The bottom of the valley was green. It was the farmland where the peasants of Dorje-Zetz grew their crops. The houses were higher up, where the soil was rocky and uneven. Every day the villagers would go down to the valley floor to tend the crops, and every night they would climb home. The houses were small and neat, made of square stones, and covered with a light mud-colored stucco. The roofs were made of squares of wood, and on each square was a large round stone, to keep the wooden part of the roof from blowing away in case of a high wind.

Some of the people from the village came out to meet the caravan. They were short, muscular people, with nice smiles. Harold and his parents liked them. They were quiet. Harold liked that.

He liked quiet people. The villagers helped the soldiers carry the boxes of household provisions, clothing, and furniture to the house that had been prepared for the Blatz family.

It was a perfect house. Harold's mother said so. It was just about the size of the house they had lived in, in Rochester, New York. The rooms were small and clean, and there was a little garden outside. The walls were painted white, the floor was made of smooth dark wood, and there were wooden shutters on the windows. It was a quiet house, like the rest of the houses in the village. The Blatzes knew at once that they would be happy living there.

The soldiers and the mules left the next day, and the Blatzes went about settling into their new home. The population of Dorje-Zetz was friendly, but they did not all crowd in to say hello to the new family. They were careful not to do anything to make the Blatz family uncomfortable. They were very polite people, and yet they didn't seem cold or distant. The Blatzes felt very much at home with them, even though they couldn't understand a word they said. Nobody in Dorje-Zetz spoke a word of English.

Something remarkable happened to Harold and his family—they got to feel as though they had always lived in Dorje-Zetz, almost overnight. All the strange smells of the place, and the mountain views, and the fresh cold air became familiar to them at once. It only took a day to put away their belongings and set up the things they had brought with them—and no sooner had this been done than it felt to them as though the things had always been in the little house. Harold's mother was busy preparing their first meal in their new home, and it seemed totally familiar, more familiar than all the meals she had prepared in their old home. In two or three days, it became difficult to remember things about Rochester, and the days of flying around in Croco-Cola Company helicopters and airplanes. Nothing seemed as real as Dorje-Zetz and the present.

Harold and his father began to take long walks in the mountainous countryside. His mother had bought a simple loom from one of the neighbor ladies, and was taking lessons in weaving. All the Blatzes were picking up the local language. Harold decided to start attending the village school, and his father sent to Delhi for mountain-climbing boots, and rope, and other gear. He was getting serious about climbing, and spent part of every day dragging himself up rock faces with some of the village men, who didn't bother with ropes or special boots. Harold's mother had the beginnings of a very nice garden. It was hard for them to believe they had ever lived anywhere else. It was equally hard for them to believe they had lived in Dorje-Zetz for more than two months already.

Chapter 7

The only time the Blatzes remembered their old life was when they got a letter from Uncle Roy. This happened every two or three weeks, when a special messenger from the Maharajah of Mahamurghi would come by. Nobody knew exactly where they were but the Maharajah. Even Hamish MacTavish had only a general idea of where they were. People wrote to the Blatzes in care of the Maharajah.

When a letter came from Uncle Roy, Harold and his mother and father would remember that they missed him. They wrote to him, asking him to come and stay with them in their mountain village, but Roy was not interested in travel. Things had gotten quiet enough for him to hang out with his old friends again, and he was satisfied. Uncle Roy would always forward a letter from Armand Vermin, telling the Blatzes about Harold's fortune. It continued to increase.

Harold and his father had a conversation about all of Harold's money, and the village of Dorje-Zetz. They thought they ought to use some of Harold's money to do something for the village. At first Harold's father thought maybe they should build a hospital, but Harold reminded him that nobody in Dorje-Zetz ever seemed to get sick. The village had a good enough school for the few kids who were of school age. Everybody had a good enough house to live in. Harold and his father couldn't think of anything the village needed. They decided to ask the people who seemed to run the village. This wasn't an official group—just five or six of the oldest people, who were given a lot of respect, and looked as though they would be the ones to make the decisions, if any decisions were ever made.

The village elders talked it over for three days and nights. Then they went to see Harold and his father. They said they couldn't think of anything they needed, but they were very grateful that Harold and his father wanted to give the village a gift. They said that anything at all would be fine with them. It was just the answer that Harold and his father had come to expect. They finally settled on a six-lane bowling alley, which they ordered from England. The bowling alley came prefabricated with its own building, a juice bar, and a supply of balls and shoes and score sheets. It was an instant success with the villagers. They turned out to have some very good bowlers among them, once they got the hang of it.

Life went on in the little mountain village. Harold was doing well in school. His father was climbing some pretty difficult mountains, and had quit using ropes. His mother was doing nicely with her weaving, and was now spinning her own yarn. Her garden was doing well. The quiet people of Dorje-Zetz were the nicest neighbors the Blatzes had ever had, and some of them were slowly becoming friends. The Blatzes never gave it a thought, but they were happier than they had ever been in their lives.

One day a bunch of strangers appeared in the village. Except for the caravans which brought mail and supplies from the outside, no stranger ever appeared in Dorje-Zetz. These strangers were tall, dirty, rough-looking men. They all looked a little like Anthony Quinn. They needed shaves. They were dressed in coarsely woven red woolen blankets. Their feet were wrapped in rags. Some of them were carrying greasy burlap bags. They came out of nowhere. Nobody saw them coming. They were just there—all of a sudden— like that.

The strangers went straight to the bowling alley, where Harold was having a game with some of his friends from school. A crowd of citizens followed them. One of the strangers, the tallest and dirtiest, and toughest-looking, tapped Harold on the shoulder. "Excuse me, kid," he said, "my friends and I would like to talk to you for a few minutes."

Harold was surprised to hear anyone speak English. No one in Dorje-Zetz but Harold, his mother, and father spoke English. This tall, dirty, unshaven, tough-looking guy spoke English out of the side of his mouth, in a kind of hoarse whisper. "My name is Dupdup Drng'pa," the stranger said. "These other men you will meet later—all very nice men, but not important for the moment. Right now we are interested in asking you some questions." Harold said he would be happy to answer Dupdup Drng'pa's questions if he could.

Dupdup Drng'pa took a greasy burlap bag from one of the other men. "Take your time," he said. "Does this look familiar to you?" Dupdup Drng'pa had removed an old teapot from the bag. It was made of dirty-looking white china, and it was cracked in a dozen places; the handle was missing. Harold took the teapot and turned it over in his hands.

"This does look sort of familiar," Harold said, "but I can't remember where I've seen it before. It feels like something that used to be around the house when I was little, but I know it was never in our house. It makes me feel sort of weird."

"O.K.," said Dupdup Drng'pa. "Now have a look at this." He reached into the bag, and came out with a funny-looking brass thing, long and cylindrical with a bulge on one end. It had a greasy silk cord with a tassel attached to it. "Tell me what this is, and if you've ever seen it before," Dupdup Drng'pa said.

"This is an old-fashioned pen case, with a place to carry ink in the end—that's what the bulge is for," Harold said. "Nobody uses them any more, and the last person who used to carry one was old Blabab Hoopdup, a Sanskrit scholar who left this earth in the year 1873. In fact this was his personal pen case." Harold felt very strange as he said this, because he had never heard of anyone called Blabab Hoopdup, and he had no way of knowing what the pen case was, or who it might have belonged to. "I wonder how I knew all that," Harold said.

"Never mind," Dupdup Drng'pa said. "Just have a look at this." He reached into the bag and produced a shiny silver cup.

"I've never seen this before in my life," Harold said, "which is no wonder, because it is practically brand-new. It is yours, Dupdup Drng'pa. You sent away to Sears and Mookerjee in Madras for it with the money you received from your uncle on your last birthday." Harold was amazed to hear himself saying these things. He knew he wasn't lying to the stranger; he knew that his answers were the truth. But he had no way of knowing these things. Nothing like this had ever happened to him before.

"Just one more," Dupdup Drng'pa said, and showed Harold a little ivory elephant with scratches and toothmarks all over it.

"That's mine!" Harold shouted. "Where did you get that? I had it when I was a baby!"

"Kid, we would like to go and see your mother and father now," Dupdup Drng'pa said. He and all the other strangers seemed excited.

The villagers of Dorje-Zetz seemed excited too. They had been paying close attention to the conversation between Harold and Dupdup Drng'pa. Every time Dupdup Drng'pa handed Harold an article to examine a hush would fall over the watching crowd; and when the article was handed back, they would all talk excitedly. As Harold left, to take Dupdup Drng'pa to his parents, he noticed that the villagers were attaching garlands of flowers to the bowling alley, and painting things on it in Sanskrit, and burning incense in front of it, as though it were a shrine.

Chapter 8

"Mr. Blatz, I am Dupdup Drng'pa, and these other men are all monks. We come from the monastery of the Golden Alligator, which is in Tibet. It is the central and largest monastery of the Silly Hat sect, to which we belong." Dupdup Drng'pa and the other men were all crowded into the tiny living room of the Blatz house.

"Our monastery," Dupdup Drng'pa went on, "is also the last surviving monastery of the Silly Hat sect anywhere on earth. It is located in such a remote corner of Tibet that no one has been able to find it, on purpose or by accident, for the past seven hundred years. Likewise, we very seldom leave the monastery of the Golden Alligator, and only learned on our way here that Tibet has been occupied by China, and the Dalai Lama has fled the country. These things are news to us, but we are not upset because the Silly Hat Order has existed in Tibet for thousands of years, long before the coming of Buddhism. We have survived through any number of political upheavals—nobody ever bothers us. I wonder if we could have something to drink."

Mrs. Blatz brought all the monks Croco-Cola, six thousand bottles of which had been packed in by mule train—a gift from the Maharajah of Mahamurghi. Dupdup Drng'pa continued. "The leader of our order is Rabdab Blooblah. He is about one hundred and fifty years old. In spite of his comparative youth, he is a very wise man, and we are very attached to him. Ordinarily, people in our part of Tibet live to be three or four hundred years old. When the head lama of our order dies, we have to find out where his soul has gone. Usually, after an interval, we find a child who recognizes certain objects that belonged to our leader in his last life. We take that child to the monastery of the Golden Alligator, and educate him to be the leader of our spiritual order. Since we believe that when you die, your soul leaves your body, and goes into the body of someone who is being born at that moment, we know the exact age of the child we are looking for. It is just a matter of finding the one into whom our departed leader's soul has gone."

"I don't understand any of this," Harold's father said.

"It doesn't matter," Dupdup Drng'pa said.

"This is the important part: This time our leader isn't dead. Rabdab Blooblah is only about one hundred and fifty years old, as I said, and is not apt to die for two hundred years at least. This time, our leader has sent us out in search of a boy in a bowling alley—which confused us, since none of us had any idea what a bowling alley was. He told us to take with us certain objects to show the boy, to see if he recognized them. But they were not possesions of Rabdab Blooblah, our present leader. They were things which had belonged to Dimdap Kram'ba, the founder of the Silly Hat sect thousands of years ago. His last reincarnation was in the year 1341. There has not been a sign of him since—until now. In addition to recognizing certain of the objects we brought with us, our leader Rabdab Blooblah told us that the boy we were looking for would be very lucky in matters of money. Is your son Harold lucky in that way?"

"I'd say he is the luckiest boy on earth," Harold's father said.

"Then there is no question!" Dupdup Drng'pa said. "The soul of the venerable Dimdap Kram'ba resides in the body of the boy you know as your son Harold! He must return to Tibet with us."

Harold's mother began to cry. "Oh, Fred, our boy is going to Tibet, and we'll never see him again."

"Please don't alarm yourself," Dupdup

Drng'pa said. "Our leader only wants Harold to visit him. There is no need for him to remain in Tibet permanently."

"This is the silliest thing I ever heard of," Harold's father said.

"You should see the hats we wear when we're at home," Dupdup Drng'pa said. "Are you going to allow Harold to come back with us to visit Rabdab Blooblah?"

Ordinarily, Harold's mother and father would never have even considered such an idea. They would have said that twelve-year-old boys don't go on expeditions to Tibet without their parents, let alone going on a visit to someone named Rabdab Blooblah, who was one hundred and fifty years old, and the leader of something called the Silly Hat sect. But things had changed quite a bit since the Blatz family had come to live in Dorje-Zetz. Things had changed in ways that the Blatzes never realized. They felt calm about most things, ever since they had come to live in the high mountains. When Harold's father went for his climbs in the high mountains, he found himself thinking about things he could never have even imagined in Rochester, New York. When Harold's mother worked at her loom, she sometimes made up songs that were so beautiful and strange that she lost all track of time, and weaving, and everything else. They had long since stopped wondering how it was that their son, Harold, had won so much money on a horse race, and made so many millions of dollars in the stock market. They had stopped wondering about why Hamish MacTavish and the Maharajah of Mahamurghi had gone out of their way to be so nice to them. Harold's father had long since ceased to be amazed by the amazing thoughts that came to him when he was high in the mountains. Harold's mother had long since ceased to marvel at the beautiful songs that came to her when she worked at her loom.

"Harold, would you like to go to Tibet with these men?" Harold's father asked.

"Well, I would like to see what kind of hats they wear," Harold said.

"Harold will stay with us for two years," Dupdup Drng'pa said. "Exactly two years from today, he will return to Rochester, New York. You have the word of the Silly Hat sect for this. Also, we will see that his education is not neglected. As the incarnation of Dimdap Kram'ba, Harold will be entitled to learn our most closely guarded secrets. When he returns to Rochester, New York, he will know more about the mystic East than any person in the West has ever known."

"Well, that will certainly be nice for him," Harold's mother said. She kissed Harold. "We'll wait for you in Rochester, dear."

"There's no sense in standing around," Dupdup Drng'pa said. "We have a long way to go."

Harold and the Silly Hat monks walked out of Dorje-Zetz. They were over the first mountain, and out of sight within ten minutes—ordinarily a two-day walk. Harold's mother and father walked over to the bowling alley to watch the villagers burning incense and chanting and singing.

Chapter 9

In the months following the return of Harold's mother and father to Rochester, New York, three letters were received from Harold. In one of the letters, Harold asked that a kit to build the ship *Flying Cloud* be sent to him in care of General Delivery, Kalimpong, West Bengal. In another letter he asked that a Stilletto's Pizza franchise be granted to a man in Dorje-Zetz. In the third letter, he asked his parents to have a large cave excavated under the house for Harold to use when he returned. In all the letters Harold said that he was having a nice time with the monks, and sent Dupdup Drng'pa's regards to his family. Also in each letter he suggested the name of a horse for Uncle Roy to bet on. Uncle Roy played the horses Harold suggested, and won every time.

Harold's father did not go back to his job in the hardware store; instead, he went to work helping Armand Vermin take care of Harold's fortune,

which was now the world's third largest. Uncle
Roy continued to sell shoes. He had shaved off his
beard, but kept a rakish moustache, which he
thought made him look younger.

Without Harold around, the hysteria and
crowds that had made life unbearable in the
house on Pearl Street subsided, and it was
unusual for Uncle Roy, or Harold's father, to be
stopped in the street, by someone who was curious about Harold's wealth, more than once or
twice a week.

Harold's mother missed him, of course. She
kept a calendar in the kitchen, and marked off the
days leading up to the day—exactly two years
from the time Harold had gone off with the Silly
Hat monks—when Harold would come home.

The day scheduled for Harold's return got
closer and closer, and yet there was no word from
Harold. It got to be just a couple of days before
the day of his promised return, and still his parents had heard nothing.

At Kennedy Airport, in New York City, an Air-
India jetliner had just landed. It was the midnight
flight from Bombay, India. Waiting in the airport
were thousands of young people, dressed in
white, and carrying bunches and garlands of
flowers. Lined up on the runway were more than
a dozen shiny black Rolls Royce, and Cadillac,
and Mercedes-Benz limousines. The airplane tax-
ied to a stop. The movable staircase was wheeled

up to the airplane, and the door opened. Standing in the doorway was a tiny old man, dressed in white, with a flowing white beard, and a white turban. Hundreds of the young people, dressed in white, gave a cheer, and rushed out onto the field, singing and throwing flowers. The old man in the white turban was carried by the young people to one of the waiting limousines, and driven away. The young people ran after, singing and throwing flowers.

Another figure appeared in the doorway of the airplane. It was another tiny man dressed in white, with a flowing white beard, and a white turban. Some hundreds of the young people, dressed in white, who were left, gave a cheer and rushed out onto the field, singing and throwing flowers. The old man in the white turban was carried by the young people to one of the remaining limousines, and driven away. The young people ran after, singing and throwing flowers.

Yet another figure appeared in the doorway of the airplane. It was again another tiny man dressed in white, with whiskers and turban. He, too, was carried to a limousine, and driven off, pelted with flowers, a crowd of young people running after the limousine, singing and chanting.

It went on for some time; the midnight flight from Bombay gave up guru after guru, and the crowd of devoted followers gradually diminished.

Unnoticed by anyone, a group of men stood in

line, awaiting the call to board the just-after-midnight flight *to* Bombay. These men had expensive trench coats on, over their white clothing, and had their white beards tucked inside the collars of the trench coats. They all wore expensive Italian slouch hats, and sunglasses. Each one was carrying a stereo set, or an electric all-purpose kitchen utensil, or a set of Wilson golf clubs.

The line of swamis incognito stood, holding their boarding cards and electric appliances, inside the terminal building. The last of the limousines had gone, its red tail lights twinkling at the far end of the field, where the special VIP gate led to the highway. The last of the kids in white clothing had gone. The field was almost deserted—just a few maintainance mechanics, and a few crushed flowers. The movable stairway had been removed from the open door.

Then, from somewhere, a *very* large snow-white elephant appeared. It was painted here and there with brilliant colors, and was wearing a headpiece of huge rubies and diamonds. It was led up to the plane by fifty men wearing dirty red blankets. They were unshaven and tough-looking. They all looked a little like Anthony Quinn. The swamis incognito were going through customs, and didn't notice. The ground-crew mechanics were busy trying to fix something in the engine of the airplane with muffler tape, and didn't notice.

The elephant's back was covered by a rich brocade cloth, topped by a little house made out of solid gold. Out of the open door of the airplane stepped Harold, into the golden howdah. He was wearing a dirty red woolen blanket, and a shapeless woolen hat. Nobody said anything. The elephant moved away from the airplane, the fifty monks, from a cave near New Paltz, New York, walking along with their hands resting on the elephant.

Chapter 10

At 11:00 A.M. the monks, the elephant, and Harold arrived at the house on Pearl Street. Harold's mother was overjoyed to see him; and his father took the day off, and came home from Armand Vermin's office, where he worked, when he got the news by telephone that Harold was back. Harold had brought gifts from Tibet, little statues made of gold, and he gave one each to his father and mother and Uncle Roy. The statues were all alike, little figures of a man wearing a silly hat. They were supposed to represent Dimdap Kram'ba, whose reincarnation was Harold.

Harold's mother made him his favorite meal, salami and eggs. She also cooked salami and eggs for the fifty monks. The elephant was tethered in the back yard. The family sent out for sixty Stilletto's pizzas for him.

That night, Harold slept in his own bed. The fifty monks spent the night in the cave under the house, and departed at dawn, with the elephant, who was burping.

Harold spent the morning with his family, telling stories about his visit with Rabdab Blooblah, and the monks of the Silly Hat Order. His father and mother were very proud of the way he'd grown. Living in the high mountains had made him tough. He had a good set of muscles. Uncle Roy was glad to see Harold again. He was happy that Harold hadn't changed, and they were still good friends.

The family sat around the breakfast table, laughing and telling stories, until it was time for lunch. After lunch, they sat around the table laughing and talking some more. At about two o'clock the family got tired of laughing and talking. Harold's father wandered into the living room to watch television. Uncle Roy had an appointment to deliver a pair of shoes; and Harold's mother wanted to start clearing up the mess that cooking fifty-four orders of salami and eggs had made, plus snacks, breakfast, and lunch. Harold felt like walking around and having a look at the old neighborhood.

The first stop Harold had in mind was the candy store. Harold had always bought his comic books there, and wanted to catch up on what was happening to some of his favorite heroes. It had been hard to get up-to-date comics in Tibet. Rabdab Blooblah had a few, but they were years out of date. In some of them Superman had knit cuffs on his uniform. Harold headed for the candy store. He was still wearing his red woolen blanket —his old clothes were all too small for him now.

The candy store was gone. In its place was a store with a handcarved wooden sign, like they had in Tibet, only much nicer. The sign said, AQUAMARINE SELF-DISCOVERY CENTER. There was another sign painted on the store window, MYSTERIES OF THE EAST; BOOKS ON ASTROLOGY, MEDITATION, ESP, FOOT REFLEXOLOGY, TAROT; PSYCHIC READINGS; HEALTH FOOD; PHRENOLOGY. Harold went in. Sitting at a desk was a tall skinny young man. He was sitting with his eyes closed, humming to himself. "Excuse me," Harold said. "Do you still sell comic books?"

"Nope," the young man said. "Nobody sells comic books anymore."

"What? Nobody?" Harold asked. He was really astonished.

"Nobody I know of," the young man said. "I don't know, maybe you'd find some if you went into a neighborhood where there were a lot of poor people. Nobody around here reads them anymore."

"That's really amazing," Harold said. "What do they read?"

"They read *Six Easy Steps to Nirvana,* by Dr. Weary, or *Hum Your Way to Enlightenment* by Alan W. Plotz, or *Your Feet Are Your Head* by Brother

Jimmy, or *What God Said to Me* by Sister Profit, or *Yoga for Six-Year-Olds* by Swami Rabinowitz, or . . ."

"Why do people read stuff like that?" Harold asked.

"Why?" The young man looked surprised. "Why? What a question! Don't you know what's happened in the past couple of years? Where have you been?"

"I've been living in a little village high in the mountains," Harold said. "Then I went to stay in a place even farther away."

"Well," said the young man, "that explains it. You don't know about the important stuff that has been going on for the past couple of years. You see, America is in the middle of a spiritual rebirth. People are turning on to the teachings of the masters."

"Oh, that's good," Harold said.

"Good? It's wonderful," the young man said. "Now you can have your feet massaged, so your personal problems clear up, and your sinuses get better in any city, town, or village in the U.S.A. Kids are learning to meditate in the second grade, and everybody eats nothing but natural organic vegetarian food." Harold looked around the shelves at the cans of beansprouts in molasses, and chocolate-covered dukhi beans.

"You mentioned the teachings of the masters," Harold said. "What does that mean?"

"Well, ever since the spiritual rebirth movement started, all these wonderful teachers have appeared," the young man told him. "Lots of them come from India, like Swami Mookermooker, and Swami Jeejee, and Swami Chapati; but there are a lot of Americans who have studied with qualified mystical masters in India and other places, like Buttered Rum Crass, and Dr. Weary. They're heavy too."

"I'll bet they are," Harold said. "How did all this get started?"

"I don't know for sure," the young man said. "I mean two years is a long time to remember anything, but I sort of think it started with this Japanese guy, Hodie MacBodhi. He's a great spiritual teacher, one of the biggest. Here's his book." The young man showed Harold a book. The title was *You Are a Pickle!* The publisher was MacTavish Books Incorporated.

"I'll take this one," Harold said, "and all those other books you mentioned; and you'd better give me anything else you think is good."

Harold went home with two big shopping bags full of books. He put them in the cave under the house, into which he had moved most of his bedroom stuff. That night he stayed up late reading.

For most of the next two weeks, Harold stayed in his cave, reading. He came up for meals with the family, and made a couple of trips to the AQUA-MARINE SELF-DISCOVERY CENTER. Finally he got tired of lugging the shopping bags full of books home, and had Armand Vermin simply buy the place, and send the contents over in a truck. Harold read an average of sixteen books per day. He made notes in Sanskrit with a turkey bone dipped in ink.

At the end of two weeks, Harold made a telephone call to Armand Vermin. He told him to get in touch with the Rolls Royce works and order a car made entirely of twenty-four carat gold. He also told him to buy ten thousand diamonds, perfect ones, of between one and three carats. He also told him to book Yankee Stadium, the Houston Astrodome, and the Civic Center in San Francisco, all for the same week. Armand Vermin wanted to know what was up. "I'm going into the guru business," Harold told him.

Chapter 11

This is what happened while Harold was away in Tibet:

Hodie MacBodhi, the clown that Hamish MacTavish had hired, the one who was dressed up as a Japanese monk and rode a unicycle, was more popular than anyone could have imagined. Even Hamish MacTavish didn't expect Hodie MacBodhi to remain popular for more than a few weeks, or at most, months. But people loved Hodie MacBodhi, and took him seriously. He was interviewed on television and written about in newspapers and magazines. People wanted to know his opinions about everything—not just Zenburgers. Anything that Hodie MacBodhi said was reported on the television news. He was the most popular person in America until the news about Harold being the fifth richest man in the world got out. Then, for a while, everyone forgot about Hodie MacBodhi, and the news was full of

Harold Blatz. But Harold disappeared too soon. When Harold went to live in Dorje-Zetz, and nobody could find him, the newspapers were full of "WHERE'S HAROLD?" stories for a while—but when it became obvious that Harold was really well hidden, and not likely to be found, people got bored with him, and went back to their former enthusiasm for Hodie MacBodhi. But there was a difference this time—Hamish MacTavish had been thinking about Hodie MacBodhi, and how well he was going over. The sensation over Harold had given him time to make some plans about Hodie MacBodhi.

Obviously, Hodie MacBodhi could do more than just sell pickleburgers for MacTavish's. He was a real celebrity. With him, Hamish MacTavish could do some really big things. Even as Harold and his parents were leaving Schloss Krokenstein on their way to India, Hodie MacBodhi was on a Croco-Cola Company jet, flying to a meeting with Hamish MacTavish. They had never met in person, and Hamish MacTavish wanted to see what sort of a fellow Hodie MacBodhi was.

It turned out that Hodie MacBodhi really was a Japanese monk, and very sincere. He belonged to a very old Japanese sect known as Blong Buddhism. It was older than Zen, and very hard to understand. The best that Hamish MacTavish could make of Hodie MacBodhi's explanation of Blong Buddhism was that if you spent twenty-four hours a day meditating, you aren't apt to get in very much trouble.

Hamish MacTavish couldn't understand much of what Hodie MacBodhi said to him, but he was sure that Hodie MacBodhi was a good man. Hodie MacBodhi explained that he had been sent to the United States by his spiritual master, Blong Kong Feng, to spread the message of Blong Buddhism. Hamish MacTavish decided to help him. They made a long-playing record called *Blong! You Are a Pickle!* and offered it for sale in MacTavish's pickleburger stands. It was a record of instructions in Blong meditation, the first exercise of which was to make believe that you are a pickle. The record sold fifty-three million copies in a week. Hamish MacTavish contributed all of the profits to the Blong Pickle Foundation. Of course the sale of his pickleburgers doubled with all the attention Hodie MacBodhi and pickles were getting.

America went Blong Pickle crazy. There were Blong meditation groups in schools and offices everywhere. The record went through edition after edition, and was always selling out. Hamish MacTavish was satisfied that he had finally done something good for mankind.

There were other styles and schools of meditation and mystical enlightenment besides Blong. Some of them had been operating for a long time. The Mushroom Thought Society, of Palo Alto,

California, for example, had been in existence for a good many years; and the Hairy Cricket Brotherhood of San Anselmo, California, and the Unifriction Church, and the Great Orange Brotherhood; Chu Dup Froggie Institute, Buttered Rum Crass Society, and many others all taught and practiced different forms of meditation and chanting and incense burning and seeking after mystical truth. They all lost a lot of members when Blong got popular—but that state of affairs didn't last.

Soon, when the whole country was meditation-conscious, people began to leave Blong, which was really very difficult to understand, and try other things. Soon the Chu Dup Froggie Institute, which practiced a sort of Tibetan-style meditation and bell ringing, and gong crashing, and incense burning, had to expand its headquarters and open eleven branch offices in different parts of the country. The Buttered Rum Crass Society began to publish its own books and records, and the Hairy Cricket people and the Unifriction Church were buying up restaurants, and hotels and movie theatres as fast as they could. *Time* and *Newsweek* magazines said that there was a nationwide movement toward new mystical cults.

Certain gurus and swamis and yogis and spiritual masters in India and other places read *Time* and *Newsweek* and bought airplane tickets for the United States. They arrived and started cults and sects and meditation groups. All of them were instantly successful. Harlan Flensburg, a famous poet who believed in meditation, and bell ringing, and gong crashing, and incense burning, said that America was going to save the world because of its new spirituality.

Hamish MacTavish and Armand Vermin were busier than they had ever been, starting companies to import incense and gurus. They were manufacturing meditation cushions, and white meditation robes, and special shoes to help your feet meditate when you walk, and little electric biofeedback machines to help you know when you are meditating correctly. There were guru bureaus which arranged speaking tours for new swamis who had just arrived, and there was a Gurus' Union, to which most of the important spiritual leaders belonged. Regular churches and synagogues and places of worship could not hope to function unless the priest or minister or rabbi had some sort of Eastern guru to help him with his services and sort of back him up.

By the time Harold arrived back from Tibet, *Time* and *Newsweek* estimated that nearly every man, woman, and child in the United States, Canada, and Mexico spent at least four hours a day in meditation, bell ringing, gong crashing, or incense burning. Most people had belonged to at least five mystical sects in the past fifteen months,

and belonged to at least two at the time the statis-
tics were being compiled.

On the other hand, nobody was going to
school. Production of goods and services had
dropped by half. Undertakings such as health care
and sanitation had become very inefficient—
health care, because people went to herb doctors
and shamans as much as regular doctors; sanitation, because the people who took care of that
sort of thing were meditating at least four hours
a day. There was danger of nationwide protein
starvation because most people had been told by
their gurus to become vegetarians, and although
industrial pollution had been cut in half, many
people were suffering from asthma and other
complaints because of the great clouds of incense
that hung over most of the nation's cities.

To make matters worse, the balance of international trade was in poorer condition than usual,
because all of the gurus and swamis and yogis
were taking their money back to their home countries, in most cases India. It was estimated by *Time*
and *Newsweek* magazines, before the Unifriction
Church bought them both, that the average per
capita income of an Eastern mystical teacher was
1.5 million dollars—home-grown American mystical teachers made slightly less.

And yet, nobody was any happier than before
the great spiritual movement. Harlan Flensburg

said he couldn't understand why people were so miserable, now that there were so many opportunities for everyone to meditate, ring bells, crash gongs, and burn incense.

Less than half of 1 percent of the families in the United States did not meditate, bell ring, gong crash, or incense burn. Harold's mother and father and Uncle Roy were in that less than one-half of 1 percent.

Chapter 12

Harold started with an advertising campaign. He created something called a "media blitz." In a media blitz, every sort of communication—television, radio, newspapers, magazines, billboards, posters, pamphlets, cars with loudspeakers, men carrying sandwich boards, skywriters, bumper stickers, letters in the mail, every means possible —is used to get a message to the public, all at once. Harold started by having Armand Vermin buy the fifteen largest advertising agencies in America, and getting them to drop all their other work, and just work on Harold's campaign. The campaign consisted of one message that was repeated over and over, everywhere. An average person going to work or school, in an average town or city, would see and hear the message an average of two hundred times a day. They would see it in newspapers and magazines, they would hear it on the radio, and from loudspeakers on cars that patrolled the streets; they would see it on leaflets that were dropped from airplanes, they would see it on posters on lampposts and telephone poles. One of the things that Harold was very specific about when he gave instructions to Armand Vermin, for the fifteen advertising agencies, was that he wanted a poster on every single lamppost and telephone pole in the United States. There were also posters on every fence and exterior wall in the United States. The posters were in full color. They were plastic-coated, so the rain wouldn't damage them, and they glowed in the dark.

The posters, and the billboards, and the skywriters, and the bumper stickers, and the advertisements in the newspapers and magazines all said the same thing:

HAROLD BLATZ, FOURTEEN-YEAR-OLD
TOTALLY, UTTERLY, COMPLETELY
PERFECT
SPIRITUAL MASTER
AND THIRD RICHEST SINGLE PERSON
IN THE ENTIRE WORLD—EVER—IS
COMING TO CHANGE YOUR WHOLE LIFE
SOON!

The posters were red, white, and blue, and had a color picture of Harold wearing a beautiful cloth-of-gold suit. He had borrowed the idea from Reverend Goon, who had enjoyed some success in the early days of the spiritual rebirth movement. Everyone thought the posters were beautifully designed, and didn't even mind that they were put up with a new space-age miracle adhesive, and could only be removed with an industrial-size electric sander or a blowtorch.

After a week of the media blitz, Harold started another one, even bigger. This media blitz was divided into three parts: eastern, western, and southern. In the eastern half of the country, notices were posted everywhere announcing that Harold would appear at Yankee Stadium in New York. In the western half of the country, notices were posted that Harold would appear in the Civic Center in San Francisco. In the South, notices announced that Harold would appear in the Houston Astrodome. All of the appearances were announced for the same day, and within two hours of each other!

Special free buses and trains were chartered to take people from every part of the country to New York, Houston, and San Francisco. For those people who didn't want to go, giant television screens were set up in movie theatres, public buildings, and open places. Giant television screens, the size of drive-in movies, were set up outside the Astrodome, Civic Center, and Yankee Stadium, as well, to handle the huge overflow crowds that were expected. And Harold bought time on every television and radio station in the country to broadcast the events at the three huge gatherings.

As the day of Harold's three appearances approached, no one in the United States could talk of anything else. Harold had bought a supersonic jet fighter from the USSR and arranged for it to take him from one city to another. At each airport, a helicopter would be waiting to take Harold to the auditorium. He would start in San Francisco, make his appearance, and two hours later, he would walk onto the stage of the Houston Astrodome. Two hours after that, Harold would appear at Yankee Stadium. He would be home in Rochester, New York, in time to watch the whole thing reported on the late news.

To entertain the crowds while they were waiting for Harold to appear, three of the most famous rock bands had been hired. The Rats, The Swine, and Gingivitis were the names of the famous rock bands. Any one of them could fill the Astrodome, the Civic Center, or Yankee Stadium. There were loudspeakers set up outside the auditoriums, so the crowds that couldn't get in would be able to hear them. Harold had ordered a lot of big pictures of himself, several stories high, to be hung up inside the auditoriums, and on some buildings outside. He also directed that elaborate light shows be put on when the bands

were playing, and arranged for the three biggest
fireworks displays in the history of the world to be
set off as he was leaving.

Of course, all the publicity reawakened interest
in Harold, and circumstances resembled the time
when the news about Harold's millions had gotten out. This time the Blatz family was ready for
the onslaught of reporters, cameramen, and curious people. The fifty monks from the cave near
New Paltz, New York, were called upon to serve
as a sort of private police force and bodyguard for
Harold and his family. The monks patrolled the
neighborhood, carrying great big clubs, the kind
that cavemen are always shown carrying in cartoons. The monks looked so tough, and had such
serious scowls, that nobody tried to get too close
to the Blatz house. In fact, the neighborhood was
never quieter.

The newspapers ran all the old stories about
Harold Blatz's fortune, and went on to say that he
was now the third richest person in the world.
Nobody knew what to make of the statement that
he was a totally, utterly, completely perfect
spiritual master, but most people were inclined to
believe it. After all, being very rich seemed to go
with being spiritually enlightened. Reverend
Goon owned most of New York State, and the
Chu Dup Froggie Institute was the largest single
property owner in California. Most of the better
spiritual teachers were millionaires. If Harold was

totally, utterly, completely perfect, it made sense that he ought to be extra rich too.

Harold's parents were puzzled by all this activity, to say the least. They were surprised to learn that Harold was a totally, utterly, completely perfect spiritual master—especially since he hadn't changed a bit, since before he got rich, and went to Tibet. During the media blitz, the totally, utterly, completely perfect spiritual master was busy building a model of the U.S.S. *Constitution*.

Chapter 13

The day for Harold's appearances came. Everything went off better than anyone could have expected. The crowds were enormous. People, especially young people, started to gather at the places where Harold was to appear, two and three days early. The tickets were free, and it was first come, first served. There was some fear that fistfights would break out, and that some people with free tickets would try to sell them at high prices to people who hadn't been able to get them. Nothing of that sort happened in any of the three cities where Harold was scheduled to appear—partially because of the atmosphere of peace and harmony that prevailed in all three places, partially because of the numbers of monks, all of them over two hundred and fifty pounds, who patrolled the areas around the auditoriums with huge clubs and stony faces.

Gingivitis gave a four-hour concert in the Civic

Center in San Francisco. The crowd was the largest ever seen in that city. As the concert came to an end, the giant pictures of Harold were unfurled, and the light show started. Giant spotlights swept all around the inside and outside of the auditorium. On the giant television screens the people saw a flag-draped podium, with the spotlights sweeping over it. It seemed as though the inside was outside, and the outside was inside. The movements of the spotlights in the hall and outside were synchronized to seem like one continuous flow. Gingivitis was playing "God Bless America." Thousands of white doves were released. Police sirens and red lights screamed and flashed. A huge silver helicopter was overhead suddenly—all the spotlights were focused on it, making it gleam like the sun. The helicopter slowly settled. Then it was out of sight for a minute. Then Harold appeared on the stage, and on the giant television screens outside, and on the giant television screens in movie theatres and public places all over the country, and on every home television screen in America. Every spotlight was on Harold now, and his gold suit shone more brilliantly than the helicopter—more brilliantly than the sun; it made a sort of burned-out white spot on the television screens.

The crowd went insane. The screaming and shouting drowned out the band and the sirens. The noise of the crowd turned into one throbbing deafening roar. It sounded like the ocean, only much, much louder. Later, it turned out that people fifty miles away from San Francisco could hear the crowd when Harold appeared.

Harold didn't say anything. He just stood there wearing the gold suit, and smiling. Then he put his hands up—the way Richard Nixon used to do. The crowd cheered even louder. Harold gave a signal, and a monk brought him a large leather bag. It was full of diamonds. Harold threw these to the audience, as he was carried out of the auditorium on the shoulders of fifty monks.

The cheering in San Francisco had still not died down when Harold appeared at the Houston Astrodome. The event at the Astrodome was the same as the one at the Civic Center, and the event at Yankee Stadium was the same. In all three cities the fireworks went on all night. Practically nobody in America went to sleep that night—except the Blatz family, of Rochester, New York, who all went to bed right after the late news.

Chapter 14

Harold's appearances were an overnight, total success. Everyone who had previously believed in Blong Buddhism, or any of the other major mystical cults instantly switched to Harold Blatzism. Everybody in the United States who followed one or another of the popular gurus (that is, 99.5 percent of the people) switched to Harold, and regarded him as their mystical teacher. Similar figures were reported from the rest of North, South, and Central America, and there were strong indications that much of Europe and Asia was going Blatz. On the morning following Harold's three appearances, the President of the United States had one of Harold's red-white-and-blue, plastic-coated posters framed and hung in the Oval Office. Several towns and cities commissioned sculptors to make statues of Harold out of bronze, to be placed in front of city halls, and in town squares. Special issues of magazines were rushed into print carrying whatever pictures and stories about Harold they could find.

The fifty monks who guarded the Blatz house had their work cut out for them, but somehow they managed to keep Harold's new disciples out of the neighborhood.

Of course, Harold had not said one word yet. All he had done was appear, look nice, and throw a few thousand diamonds to the crowds. But somehow, that seemed to do the trick. There was no doubt that Harold was indeed the totally, utterly, completely perfect spiritual master, as advertised. Harold had taken over the entire mystical enlightenment field in a single night. Now the nation and the world waited for Harold to speak. They waited for days. Harold kept to himself, building a model sloop in a bottle, and spoke to no one outside his family. Finally he sent a message to Armand Vermin, to be transmitted to the world through the fifteen advertising agencies. Harold planned to appear at Soldier Field in Chicago, in six weeks' time. There he would give a little talk. The country went crazy when the news got out. People set up their tents outside Soldier Field, the big stadium in Chicago, on the very day it was announced that Harold would appear there six weeks later. This time there was no media blitz. Harold's fifteen advertising agencies just sent typed notices to the newspapers and television and radio stations. The news got around well enough without any big posters or paid advertisements. Everybody was interested in what Harold was going to say, and the various radio and television networks planned to broadcast the event without being paid. This was a good thing, because even Harold Blatz, the third richest person in the world, could not have afforded another advertising campaign like the first two—not to mention the cost of the extravagant shows at the three big auditoriums, the cost of the bands, the fireworks, the radio and television coverage, the transportation. In fact, Harold was now far from being the third richest person in the world.

After Harold made his announcement about speaking at Soldier Field in Chicago, he was silent, and the country waited. Harold finished his ship-in-a-bottle project, and started on something a little bit different—a model of the atomic freighter *Savannah.*

Harold's mother and father, and Uncle Roy, didn't know what to make of all this. They had some discussions with Harold about his future. They wanted to know how long he intended to go on being a boy guru, and what sort of a career was that, and didn't Harold think that he ought to consider learning some sort of a trade? Harold said that he was considering that very thing, but that he would like to continue being a boy guru for just a little while longer, and then he wanted to discuss his plans for the future with his family.

Harold's mother and father and Uncle Roy said that sounded perfectly reasonable, and they were happy that Harold was a level-headed boy.

Meanwhile there were great changes taking place in the spiritual rebirth movement. The other gurus and swamis and mystical teachers had not been able to get even one disciple back from Harold Blatz. Dr. Weary, who had been the spiritual leader of tens of thousands, had gotten a job as a caseworker for the welfare department in New York City. Reverend Goon, who had been paying a mortgage on most of upstate New York, had defaulted on everything, and gotten a job as a credit manager in a discount department store in North Carolina. The market was flooded with used Rolls Royces, and Mercedes-Benzes, and Cadillacs which had belonged to mystical masters. Hamish MacTavish was stuck with eleven million pairs of meditation shoes, and millions of meditation cushions, and meditation robes. Harlan Flensburg, the famous mystical poet, was interviewed on television, and he said he simply didn't know what to do. It seemed to him that it might be a mistake to meditate, or ring bells, or crash gongs, or burn incense until everyone had heard from Harold Blatz—after all, it might be that everyone was doing it wrong. At the same time, Harlan Flensburg was worried that the world, or at least the country, might come to an end if nobody meditated, rang bells, crashed gongs, or burned incense for a whole six weeks. Another thing that bothered Harlan Flensburg was that nobody seemed sufficiently unhappy during this six-week period in which there was virtually no meditation, bell ringing, gong crashing, or incense burning going on. It seemed to him that things should be worse, not better. The only answer he could think of was that actually Harold was meditating, bell ringing, gong crashing, and incense burning "for all of us"—and that "we were about to receive a great and wonderful message" when Harold spoke at Soldier Field.

Harold finished the nuclear freighter *Savannah*, and began work on a very large model of the *Bon Homme Richard*. He also hoped to finish a model of the *Pinta* before his talk in Chicago, and the *Niña* and *Santa María* afterwards.

Harlan Flensburg was not the only person who had noticed how much better things were since everyone had quit their gurus and become followers of Harold Blatz. Things had never been so peaceful and tranquil, and a lot of people noticed an improvement in their asthma.

Chapter 15

The day of Harold's appearance at Soldier Field in Chicago arrived at last. The city of Chicago was filled to overflowing. Every hotel room within a hundred miles was taken, and people were sleeping in the parks. They had been there for weeks. The mayor of Chicago had banned all automobiles from the area around Soldier Field to the Loop, the center of town, and the streets were packed with people on foot. National Guard troops from Illinois, Indiana, and Wisconsin were on duty to keep order. No one could guess at how many people had come to hear Harold Blatz speak, but the crowd was certainly over ten million. It was impossible to approach the stadium where Harold was to appear, or even to make one's way through the streets. Police cars were parked at every corner with loudspeakers on top, to relay the radio broadcast of Harold's talk. People had brought transistor radios and portable television sets. This time there were no special giant television screens, courtesy of Harold Blatz. There was no rock band, and there would be no fireworks.

The mayor and the police department were terrified at the thought of such a large crowd. What if something happened? Something was sure to happen. There would be lost children, and people getting sick, and not enough food, and not enough toilets. What if there was a fire? What if there was a stampede? With ten million people—some said it was twelve or thirteen million—standing shoulder to shoulder in the streets of Chicago, there wasn't anything the mayor or the police department or the National Guard could do if something terrible happened. In fact, nothing of the sort happened. People were in a very good mood, and as little emergencies came up, they were handled on the spot, by whomever happened to be closest. The day was mild, and there wasn't a chance of rain. People passed around sandwiches, and there was a general holiday feeling.

A great cheer began, and spread from street to street, as Harold's helicopter came into view. The gold Rolls Royce, and the fifty Silly Hat monks were already waiting at Soldier Field, having come in by helicopter early that morning. The stadium had been packed since the night before. The vast parking lot, empty of cars, was standing room only, as was most of Chicago from the Near South Side to just beyond the Loop. There were also thousands of pleasure boats in Lake Michigan, to the east of Soldier Field, their radio and TV antennas bristling, waiting for Harold to speak.

Harold stepped out of the helicopter into the waiting gold Rolls Royce. Then he began a slow circuit of the field. Walking behind the Rolls Royce were the fifty monks. For the first time, they were wearing their silly hats in public. The crowd was stunned. The hats were the silliest things anyone had ever seen. They were more silly than anyone could imagine. They were too silly to be described. Every one was different. The crowd in the stadium was undecided whether to giggle, or be impressed by the Silly Hat monks. One thing that everyone was sure of was—this was the real thing. This was it! This was not going to be surpassed tomorrow, or next week by something else. Something was going to happen in a little while that had never happened before, and would never happen again.

The crowd was not as wild or excited as the crowds had been at Harold's first three appearances. The cheering was enthusiastic, but it didn't go on and on for hours like before. People knew that Harold intended to talk to them, and everyone was anxious to hear what Harold had to say.

The gold Rolls Royce completed the circuit of the field, and drove up to the stage that had been erected in the middle. Harold got out. He was wearing his silly hat. It was sillier than any of the other silly hats. It was the silliest thing ever seen on earth. It was so silly that it left the people speechless. There was no cheering. Harold walked slowly up the stairs to the stage. Everyone stared at his silly hat. In the press booth, radio announcers whispered, describing what Harold was doing—they didn't even try to say what his silly hat was like. Television cameras followed Harold's every move, and outside the stadium, in the streets, people pressed portable radios to their ears, and peered into the screens of portable television sets. In houses and apartments, in Chicago and all over the country, people sat in front of their televisions. Satellites picked up the signal and beamed it to Europe and Asia. The broadcast went out over AM, FM, short-wave, long-wave, and medium-wave radio. It was piped down to loudspeakers in coal mines, by telephone lines.

Harold stood on the stage, not speaking, and not moving. He stood for a long time. The fifty Silly Hat monks stood in line, facing out, around the four sides of the stage. After a while, the white elephant, from New Paltz, New York, ambled out of the shadows, all by itself—it was wearing the rich brocade cloth, and the gold howdah. It stood a little distance from the stage, quietly rocking from foot to foot. Still, Harold did not speak. The crowd was totally silent. Nobody talked. Nobody coughed. Nobody scratched. The audience sensed that Harold was composing himself, making himself quiet, and they did the same.

Harold stood still. The monks did the same. The crowd in the stadium did the same. The elephant rocked from foot to foot. Outside the stadium, the millions of people waited quietly. All over the world, people sat beside their televisions and radios, quietly. Even dogs and cats and pet parakeets, and farm animals, and zoo animals were quiet. Millions of people listened to their own breathing, and the ticking of their wristwatches. People could have hardly spoken if they wanted to. Nobody got tired. Nobody felt the need to sneeze, or scratch, or go to the bathroom. Everyone was being quiet with Harold, waiting for Harold to begin to say what he had come to say.

It went on like that for fifteen minutes, then for an hour, then for two hours. People who had paid out thousands of dollars to mystical masters to learn to meditate, and had never been quiet for five whole minutes, found it was no strain to be quiet with Harold for two whole hours. The wind blew through trees—quietly. Birds flew from branch to branch—quietly. Rivers flowed. Flowers turned to follow the movement of the sun. Seeds grew in the earth. In some places, a quiet rain fell—in other places the sun shone, quietly.

Then Harold cleared his throat, and began to speak.

Chapter 16

"A little while ago, I came back from Tibet. While I was there I visited a lamasery called Golden Alligator. It is the central place belonging to the Silly Hat sect of Tibet. All of these monks belong to the Silly Hat sect. The reason I was a visitor there is that the monks believe that I am the reincarnation of Dimdap Kram'ba, the founder of the Silly Hat order. While I was there, I was able to learn all the principal secrets of the order.

"Now, it might be useful to explain that the dumbest, most ignorant, laziest, most foolish, half-witted, thick-headed Silly Hat monk who ever lived knows more about the secrets of mystical meditation than Dr. Weary, Reverend Goon, Buttered Rum Crass, Alan W. Plotz, and all the swamis in India put together on the best day of their lives. Therefore, while it might be a slight exaggeration to say that I am the totally, utterly, completely perfect spiritual master, it is true to say that I am a *more* totally, utterly, completely perfect spiritual master than any you have run across before this.

"This is what the Silly Hats believe: People are just about standard—more or less the same. Everything worthwhile about people comes from one place, and everything worthless about people comes from not paying attention to what that place is. If somebody wants to worship God, or the Great Life Force by meditating, or ringing bells, or crashing gongs, or burning incense, or chanting—that is O.K. with the Silly Hats. The Silly Hats themselves practice in a spiritual way by wearing the silliest hats possible. The more spiritually advanced a person is, the sillier the hat he wears. This prevents other people from getting the idea that he is anyone to take seriously. You see, we think the hats are funny. Don't you think the hats are funny?"

At this point some people in the stadium started to giggle. Then they started to laugh. Then others started to laugh. The fifty monks began to point at one another's hat, and laugh, and roll on the ground. People who were watching the events on television began to laugh, and the television cameramen zoomed in for close-ups of the silly hats. People who were listening to the radio heard the announcers cracking up, and started to smile. Soon they were laughing hard. In the stadium, people were falling out of their seats.

Tears streamed down their faces. They pounded one another on the back, and hung with their arms around one another's shoulders, unable to stand from laughing so hard.

Harold was laughing too. He was staggering around among the microphones, doubled over, clutching his stomach. Every now and then, he would approach the microphones, and try to say something, but he was laughing so hard that it just came out sort of screaming and giggling, and all he was able to do was look up at the audience through his tears, and point to his own silly hat. This would send the audience into new gales of laughter, and Harold would retire from the microphones, helplessly screaming with laughter.

This went on for some considerable time. Finally the laughter subsided to a constant low level of tittering and groaning, with an occasional guffaw breaking out here and there. Harold tried to speak again, and this time was able to choke out a few words, wiping his eyes, and still holding his stomach. "I'm going to go in a few minutes," Harold said. "There's really only one more thing of any importance that I wanted to say. Tomorrow morning I am mailing to every man, woman, and child on earth an official parchment certificate signed by me, and by Rabdah Blooblah, the leader of the Silly Hat Order. This certificate will state that the bearer is a fully enlightened person, and Grand Exalted High Lama of the Silly Hat

Order, than which there is no higher spiritual designation on Earth. As Grand Exalted High Lamas, you will be free to wear the silliest hats you can find or think up, or not, as you choose. By virtue of having received the certificate, you will actually become a totally, completely, utterly perfect spiritual master—the real thing. Don't be surprised if you don't feel any different—you may have been closer to it than you thought." Harold waved goodbye. The crowd cheered and screamed, and waved wildly to Harold, as he and the monks, who had pulled themselves together, moved toward the helicopter at the far end of the field.

Chapter 17

The cost of preparing and mailing the certificates which made every man, woman, and child on earth a fully enlightened person, and Grand Exalted High Lama of the Silly Hat Order, was enormous. In order to pay for the stamps alone, Harold had to have Armand Vermin sell all his MacTavish's stock, and a lot of other stuff. The printing and envelopes had been expensive, and finding out the address of every single person on earth had made it necessary for the fifteen advertising agencies to hire a lot of extra people. Then there was the problem of people such as the Ituri Rain Forest Pygmies, who live in a jungle, and move from place to place all the time; the only thing the advertising agencies could do was send a big bundle of certificates to the Pygmies, and hope there would be enough to go around. It was a complicated job, and nearly impossible to do without any mistakes. Still, the fifteen advertising agencies handled the assignment as well as they could, and by the end of a week, a certificate had been mailed to every man, woman, and child in the civilized world, and Iceland.

Harold waited for news about the effect the certificates were having. He also waited for the rest of the bills connected with renting Soldier Field, and the biggest mailing ever undertaken in history. By the end of the second day after Harold had made his announcement, the first certificates began to arrive. Everybody had the same reaction to them—they were wonderful. The certificates were richly printed on genuine simulated parchment. They had little decorative flourishes on them, and words written in Sanskrit. There was a place for the person who received the certificate to fill in his or her name. The certificates were so obviously official—with Harold's actual facsimile signature, and Rabdab Blooblah's, and all the nice printing, and the Sanskrit words—that it was impossible for anyone receiving one to believe anything other than that he or she was in fact a real enlightened person, and a Grand Exalted High Lama of the Silly Hat sect.

People began to turn up everywhere with silly hats. Also the meditating and bell ringing and gong crashing, and incense burning started up again with a vengeance—but it didn't last. Everyone wanted to lead the meditation or bell ringing or gong crashing or incense burning as befitted their rank. Since everybody had the same rank, everybody wound up meditating or bell ringing or gong crashing or incense burning by themselves. People would receive their certificates, and sit around home, with the rest of the mail unopened, admiring the certificate and watching themselves, to see if they looked or felt any different. Most people did. In a survey taken by one of the big newspapers, most people reported that they did feel something—more enlightened, and sort of grand, and exalted, and high. After sitting around and admiring the certificate and feeling suddenly in touch with the ancient wisdom which 99.5 percent of the people in America had sought for so long, most people went out in search of someone to show off to. This was fine for the first couple of days, when not everybody had received their certificates—this was the period when many people got hold of silly hats—but by the end of the week, when everybody had gotten their certificates, or three or four (Harold had told the fifteen advertising agencies it was better to be safe than sorry), it was impossible to find anyone to impress with newly attained enlightenment or certificates, or silly hats. Things got boring, and meditation, bell ringing, and the rest of the mystical arts dropped off to almost nothing.

Some of the mystical masters of meditation tried to make a comeback, but it was hopeless. The best credential any of the gurus had was their

certificate from Harold, and Rabdab Blooblah—
and just anybody had that. The swamis were permanently out of business. Even Harold was no
more and no less than a Grand Exalted High
Lama—he had said himself that there was no
higher spiritual designation possible. So people
began to lose interest in Harold, too.

Now that Hodie MacBodhi didn't have any
more influence than the rest of the Grand Exalted
High Lamas on earth, people began to notice that
MacTavish's pickleburgers tasted terrible. Sales
began to drop again.

The one-half of 1 percent of the population
who had never been interested in the spiritual
rebirth went on exactly as before, except that now
they were fully enlightened like everybody else.
Lots of people went back to worshiping in
churches, or temples, or mosques in the old familiar ways, or loosely organized themselves into
groups which worshiped together. Some people
even went on with meditating and bell ringing,
and gong crashing and incense burning, but they
had to do it without any gurus. The gurus were all
out of business.

Harold was out of business too. When he had
paid his last bill, the only thing the Blatz family
had left was their house and the gold Rolls Royce.
They had a family meeting, and discussed what to
do, now that Harold was no longer a millionaire,
or a boy guru.

After talking it over for a couple of evenings, the family decided they would sell the house and the gold Rolls Royce, and move to Florida. With the money from the sale of the car, Harold's father bought a small motel. Harold's mother liked Florida because she could have a garden all year around. Uncle Roy liked Florida because Blatz's Motel was not far from a famous racetrack, and just across the road was a place called Stan's Bar and Grill, which Uncle Roy said was just like home.

Harold arranged to go to summer school, and to take an exam for early entrance to the University of Florida. Living in the Himalayas, and especially in Tibet, had made Harold much stronger than he had been, and he felt sure that he would be able to make the track team in college. He planned to major in Physical Education.

om mani padme hum

Young Adult Novel

1

Kevin's new social worker was Mr. Justin Jarvis, and Kevin didn't like him one bit. He was constantly smiling, and he spoke in a smooth, soft, voice that made Kevin nervous.

Most annoying was the knowledge that Kevin depended on Mr. Jarvis completely. Kevin's mother was in the madhouse. Mr. Jarvis called it a psychiatric facility—but it was a madhouse, nothing else—and Kevin's mother was mad. She had gone mad the day Kevin's father had been in the accident at the methane works —the day he had been deprived of speech, sight, and hearing, and the use of his legs. Dad was in the veteran's hospital now, little better than a vegetable.

When Kevin was taken to visit his father, all he could do was sit and stare at the broken form in the wheelchair. His father horrified him, and made him feel angry. "How could you leave me like this?" Kevin thought.

What was Scott Shapiro, Kevin's father, thinking about in the wheelchair? Was he remembering the day he had been blown into darkness and silence forever by the exploding methane tank? Was he remembering that last morning, before the accident, before his wife, Cynthia, had gone mad? Was he remembering the news that had come that morning, that Kevin's sister, Isobel, had been arrested for prostitution?

As far as Kevin knew, Isobel was still downtown, working the bars across the street from the bus station. He wished he could talk to her. Isobel had always been the only one in the Shapiro family who understood Kevin.

Maybe some day Isobel would be brought in to the alcoholism treatment center where Kevin was staying. There was always a chance of that. Kevin had done his earliest drinking with Isobel.

If the vice squad ever caught her, they might bring her to the alcoholism treatment center. She wouldn't be sent to regular jail—after all, she was only fifteen—just two years older than Kevin.

Kevin felt the wad of money in his sock. He had earned sixty-five dollars that morning, selling pills to the other kids in the treatment center. In addition, he had twenty dollars he had stolen from Mr. Jarvis.

So here was Kevin, a thirteen-year-old alcoholic,

pusher, and thief. His mother would probably never get well, his father certainly wouldn't, and sister Isobel was turning tricks on State Street. It seemed to Kevin that there wasn't a chance in the world that he would ever get his life straightened out.

And he was right. So we hit him over the head and fed him to the pigs.

2

This is Charles the Cat speaking. The sad story of Kevin the messed-up thirteen-year-old is one of the pastimes of the Wild Dada Ducks. It is a story entitled, *Kevin Shapiro, Boy Orphan*. The Wild Dada Ducks tell this story to one another. Each Wild Dada Duck makes up as much of the story as he likes, and the story is always changing. Sometimes Kevin is an orphan, sometimes a juvenile delinquent, a druggie, a lonely child of feuding parents, a social misfit, a homosexual, a weakling who wants to play sports, and any number of other kinds of hard-luck characters.

Kevin Shapiro, Boy Orphan is different from the novels in the Himmler High School library in that he never solves his problems. Instead, we usually kill him from time to time. Kevin is indestructible. You can kill him as often as you like. He can be brought back to life in the next chapter, which usually gets told the following day during lunch.

In addition to myself, Charles the Cat, the other Wild Dada Ducks are the Honorable Venustiano Carranza (President of Mexico), Captain Colossal, Igor, and the Indiana Zephyr. Those are not our real names—they are our Dada names. We don't use our real names anymore.

There is also the Duckettes, the Wild Dada Ducks ladies' auxiliary, which has no member at all at present. Should suitable females present themselves for membership in the Duckettes, we will consider them, but there have been no applicants as yet. Dada is generally a misunderstood art movement.

It was the Honorable Venustiano Carranza (President of Mexico) who first told us about Dada. In those days El Presidente was known as Pecos Bill. When we heard about Dada, we all agreed to devote our lives to it, took new names, and began our historically important work of reshaping culture, righting the wrongs of the past, and producing new works of Dada Art. Starting with Himmler High School, we intend to bring about a world Dada Renaissance. We have already written a Wild Dada Duck Manifesto.

THE WILD DADA DUCK MANIFESTO
On this, the natal day of Marcel Duchamp (the first Tuesday of every month at 4:00 PM), the

Board of Medical Advisors of the Empire of Japan declares that the institution formerly known as Margaret Himmler High School will henceforth become the Municipal Vacuum Cleaner. Teachers will report for re-processing as diesel railroad locomotives, and students will adopt the appearance and function of electro-computerized kitchen appliances. Those who choose not to comply with the ruling of the Imperial Medical Board will be required to present a paper cup not filled with cherry pits or gravel at the office of the ex-administrator of unexpected nasal events. All others will be required to present paper cups *not* filled with cherry pits or gravel at the nose of the official administrator of ex-events. By this simple measure, world peace, brotherhood, and unlimited happiness has been secured for all mechano-humanoids.

Fellow machines! Dis-unite! This call to arms, torsos, and feet will not be repeated except by request.

One hundred thousand copies of the Wild Dada Duck Manifesto, printed on black paper with black ink were not made, and were not distributed to the students and faculty of Himmler High. This was the first important action of the Wild Dada Ducks, and it was met, as we hoped it would be, with wild indifference.

By the way, it turns out that the Honorable Venustiano Carranza (President of Mexico) had not made

Dada up in his own head. It is a real movement, and Marcel Duchamp was a real person. I found that out only after being a Dadaist myself for months.

3

At this point, I would like to describe the members of the Wild Dada Ducks. The Honorable Venustiano Carranza (President of Mexico) is tall and thin. The Indiana Zephyr is tall and thin. I, Charles the Cat, am not tall, and thin. Captain Colossal is tall and not thin. Igor is not tall and not thin. Because Dada is a serious movement, we try to remain dignified in expression and dress. We laugh as little as possible, at least in the presence of others, and we always wear neckties. My favorite necktie is black with a red plastic fish about five inches long attached to it with miracle glue. The Honorable Venustiano Carranza (President of Mexico) has a wheel from a baby carriage which he wears on a chain around his neck, over his tie. Igor has a banana on a string which he wears around his neck. He talks with the banana, whose name is Freddie, and also uses it as a mock microphone and make-believe pistol. Captain Colossal and the Indiana Zephyr are also stylish, but they do not have one favorite kind of attire—they alter their appearance from day to day.

This brings me to the response to the presence of the Wild Dada Ducks on the part of the other students at Himmler High. I am sorry to say that a great many of them are hostile to our Dadaistic expression of our innermost feelings. I am even sorrier to say that many more of the Himmler students are not hostile. They are totally indifferent. As far as I know, the Wild Dada Ducks have no active supporters in the school—not even any sympathizers. In a nutshell, they don't care about us, or they hate us. This includes teachers.

Of course, being resourceful Dadaists, we have decided to capitalize on the situation as it exists. Our every move as Wild Dada Ducks is calculated to make people ignore or detest us all the more. In this way, the population of Himmler High is doing what we want it to, without knowing it.

Of course we don't take any of the indifference or abuse personally. It is not as individuals that we are hated and ignored, but as Dadaists. What is more, we recognize our responsibility to educate and enlighten the people at Himmler.

And so, we are very busy Wild Dada Ducks. Some examples: In the main hall of Himmler High there is a large glass display case. It has electric lights in it, and was formerly used to display trophies won by the school's teams. Some time ago vandals opened the case and stole the trophies. There was a big uproar about it. As Wild Dada Ducks, we approved of this, feeling that the vandals might be groping their way toward Dadaism—and wrote a letter to the school paper saying so. The letter was never printed. The Wild Dada Ducks discussed this, and decided that the school was unable to deal with our clear-sighted philosophical analysis of the theft because it was grieving over the loss of the trophies. As a humanitarian gesture, we decided to give the school a new trophy, a better one than all the ones that had been stolen.

It was easily done. First we went to a junk-yard and bought a fine used toilet—just the bowl, without the tank or seat. This we lovingly cleaned and polished until it was very beautiful, and looked much better than new. The only difficult part was getting access to the empty display case—but since there was nothing in it, it wasn't particularly closely watched. With a giant pair of pliers, Igor smashed the dinky cheap lock on the case. We then placed the shining, lovely, toilet in the case. (We had smuggled the art object, wrapped in brown paper into the school the day before.) We turned on the electric lights. Then we replaced the dinky cheap lock with a new, beautiful one, made of brass, and very shiny. To prevent future vandals from getting into the case, we left the keys for the lock inside, next to the beautiful toilet. We had polished them too.

The total effect was wonderful! The toilet bowl

gleamed in the warm electric light, and made all the Wild Dada Ducks very proud and happy. Now all the people at Himmler would be able to take pride again. Now there was a trophy even finer and more significant in place of the cheap ordinary ones that had been stolen. What was more, now all the people at Himmler would have a chance to think about what a beautiful object a toilet is! We had done a heroic thing.

And was it appreciated? Of course not! There were only two opinions expressed by all who saw our work of art. Some thought it was terrible, and some thought it was funny. However, everybody came to see it, and nothing else was talked about for the two days the toilet remained in the case, shining like a beacon of truth in the main hall of Himmler High.

The principal had our magnificently polished lock removed with a hacksaw, and the art work was removed and discarded—it would wind up on the same dump we had gotten it from.

Everybody suspected that we were the artists, but we remained silent. After all, we did not do what we did for credit, but for the benefit of mankind.

And now a word about Dada music. The Wild Dada Ducks are happy to note that there's a lot of very acceptable Dada music being performed these days. This is the only area in which the kids at Himmler show any signs of culture. Some of the groups approved by the Wild Dada Ducks are the Slugs, The Yeggs, The Noggs, and The Yobs.

4

Kevin Shapiro, Boy Orphan, Chapter One Thousand
Fifteen:

Kevin didn't want anyone to see him thinking about
Aunt Lucille, because whenever he thought about her
there was a good chance he might cry. It made Kevin
feel all soft and weepy when he remembered sitting in
front of the huge stone fireplace at Red Oaks, Aunt
Lucille's great house in the Kentucky Blue Grass country. There, Kevin had had his own little room up in the
attic, and his own Thoroughbred horse to train and
ride. Winky was the name of Kevin's horse, and he had
fed him and cared for him from the time he was a little
colt. It had looked as though Winky had a great future

as a racer, and Kevin was going to ride him in the Kentucky Derby.

All that changed the day Kevin was sent to Lexington with Simms, the handyman. They had driven over in Aunt Lucille's Rolls Royce to get a new silver snaffle for Winky. How could Kevin have known that something would go horribly wrong at the nuclear reactor in Cogginsville, just two miles away from Red Oaks? How could Kevin have known that Aunt Lucille and Winky, and all the other horses, and Red Oaks itself would light up with a strange blue glow, and that the entire place would be put off limits, and quarantined forever by the Atomic Energy Commission? Kevin would never see Winky and Aunt Lucille again—and how was he to know? Still, Kevin felt that somehow it was all his fault.

Another artistic project of the Wild Dada Ducks was our play, *Chickens From Uranus,* a science-fiction thriller. We made wonderful posters to announce our play. They had pictures of heavy machinery and really nice angular lettering that Igor does. It's almost illegible.

We put the play on in the lunchroom. Here it is:

CHICKENS FROM URANUS

Adapted from *MacBeth* by William Shakespeare

Dramatis Personae

TICK AND TOCK, *two Roman Emperors*
LORD BUDDHA, *a rock star*
HENRY FORD, *a teen-age starlet*
THE DEVIL, *the devil*

(All the characters appear wearing paper bags over their heads. The bags are decorated with cutouts of pictures of bulldozers, tractors, military tanks, automobiles, and chickens.)

TICK: Moo! Moo! Moo! Moo!

TOCK: Arf! Arf! Arf! Arf!

BUDDHA: Woo! Woo! Woo! Woo!

H. FORD: Meow! Meow! Meow! Meow!

THE DEVIL: (Whistles like a bird)

ALL: (Leafing through a deck of cards) Three of clubs. Jack of diamonds. Two of clubs. Ace of diamonds. Five of hearts. Queen of spades. Two of spades. King of clubs . . . (and so on until all the cards have been read).

ALL: (Hum) Mmmmmmmmmmmmm. Mmmmmmmmmmmm. Mmmmmmmmmmmm.

Finis

It isn't much of a script in terms of length, but the actual performance took a good twenty minutes, because we spoke extremely slowly, and moved very slowly, like robots. It was a great performance, and to prove it, nobody paid any attention to it. The best actor was Captain Colossal, who had the part of Henry Ford. It took him almost half a minute just to say "meow."

Amazingly, we were summoned by the Lord High

Executioner (that's Mr. Gerstenblut, the vice-principal), as a result of our performance. He said that Himmler High School did not approve of our activities. He said that we had disrupted the lunch period by putting on an unauthorized play. Naturally, we thanked him for praising us, at which point he got angry. He shouted at us. He also told us that we were in violation of the Himmler High School Dress Code by wearing fish and baby-carriage wheels around our necks. And lobsters. On this particular day, the Indiana Zephyr was wearing a very large red plastic lobster which we all admired.

Mr. Gerstenblut told us that if we didn't shape up we'd be in trouble.

Even though the Wild Dada Ducks are pacific, peaceful, non-violent, and even ultra-non-violent, we will not run from a fight if there is no other way. It was clear to us that Mr. Gerstenblut was making an ultimatum which could lead to only one response. War.

Kevin Shapiro, Boy Orphan, Chapter Six Thousand Four Hundred and One.

Kevin's head was swimming. Could it be? Was it possible, after only doing it once? Of course, he'd heard of it happening to other kids, but somehow he had never considered it as something that could happen to him. After all, Brenda knew what she was doing —she had told him so. She had said not to worry. Kevin had believed her. He had trusted her. He knew Brenda wouldn't lie, but now, here he was, looking at the doctor's face, which loomed as large as a face on a movie screen. The doctor had a kindly expression, but it all seemed like some kind of horrible nightmare. "Yes, there's no doubt about it," the doctor was saying to Kevin, "you are two months pregnant."

5

The most aggravating thing the Lord High Executioner said to us was that since the Wild Dada Ducks was not an officially sanctioned Himmler High School student activity, as far as he was concerned, the Wild Dada Ducks did not exist.

We held a council of war. It was decided that we could not overlook this insult. Venustiano Carranza (President of Mexico) made a stirring speech. Igor and the Indiana Zephyr wanted to engage in prolonged terrorism, but Captain Colossal reminded them that any action we might take should be in keeping with our Dadaist principles.

There was some discussion of flooding the library

and holding war canoe races there as a gesture of indifference to Mr. Gerstenblut's ill-mannered remark. While everyone agreed that the idea had merit, and it would be worth looking into for some future activity, it was generally felt that our response to Mr. Gerstenblut's insolence should be expressed more directly, even though that would not be the most Dada approach.

Finally, it was decided that, since the Lord High Executioner had questioned our existence, that the appropriate response would be to bring his existence into question.

It was agreed that we would issue a public statement of Mr. Gerstenblut's lack of reality, failure to be, and non-presence, in the world as we know it.

Captain Colossal printed up several hundred cards in the print shop. To make it classier, we printed them in French.

> Horace Gerstenblut
> n'existe pas.

Since less than 3% of the kids at Himmler take French, there was considerable interest in the cards. People didn't know what they said. Also, we distributed them in an interesting way. We put stacks of them in the bathrooms of both sexes. People picked them up when they went to the bathroom, and handed them around.

Not only did we have revenge on Mr. Gerstenblut, it was also the most successful work of Art so far undertaken by the Wild Dada Ducks. That is, it was the first thing we had done in which people had taken such an active interest. We were a little sorry we hadn't printed something about Dada on the card.

We knew the cards were a big success because Igor takes French, and dozens of people asked him to translate the *Horace Gerstenblut n'existe pas* cards they were carrying around with them.

We didn't know how much of a success the cards were until the last period of the day, during which we were called out of our respective classes and assembled in the office of the Lord High Executioner.

Mr. Gerstenblut had fifteen or twenty cards on his desk. "What do you fellows know about this?" he asked, handing cards to each of us.

"It's in French," Captain Colossal said.

"It has your name on it," I said.

"It says that you don't exist," Igor said.

"And what do you weirdos have to do with these?" Mr. Gerstenblut asked.

"I'm afraid we can't tell you," Venustiano Carranza (President of Mexico) said.

"And why not?"

"Because you don't exist."

610

Kevin Shapiro, Boy Orphan, Chapter Eleven Thousand
Six Hundred.

So that was why it had been the easiest fight Kevin
had ever been in. No wonder the new kid hadn't been
able to land a single punch. "That's right, you miserable skunk," Mr. Jarvis said, "you beat up a blind boy."
Kevin felt the hot tears well up in his eyes—his eyes
that could see. Mr. Jarvis was right—he was a miserable skunk. How could he have been so stupid? What
made it worse, Kevin sort of liked the new kid. He
hadn't wanted to fight him. Something had caused
Kevin to lose all control when the kid made that remark
about homosexuals. Kevin wondered what had made
him so mad. And he really liked the kid.

Mr. Gerstenblut told us that he was going to let us
off because he didn't have any proof—but he was
going to watch us. He said that we were nihilists, and
he wasn't going to stand for any of that at Himmler.

We looked up nihilist in the library. We were tickled.
Of course we weren't nihilists—Dadaists are construc-
tive artists—but we all agreed, if we couldn't have been
Dadaists, nihilism would have been a fairly decent second choice.

6

Imagine our surprise when we found out that there was a kid actually named Kevin Shapiro in the school! The Indiana Zephyr was the one to first discover this item of historically important information. The Wild Dada Ducks were all excited to think that there was an actual person bearing the name of the hero of our communal creation, *Kevin Shapiro, Boy Orphan.*

"Who is this kid?" Igor asked. "What does he look like?"

"We will adopt him," the Honorable Venustiano Carranza (President of Mexico) said. "Kevin Shapiro will be an orphan no more!"

"Yes," I said, "we should adopt this flesh-and-blood

Kevin Shapiro in honor of the hero of our Dada young-adult novel."

"But let's keep our interest in the fortunate young man a secret!" the Indiana Zephyr said.

"A dark secret," said Igor.

"Good! Good!" said the Honorable Venustiano Carranza (President of Mexico). "We will become the secret helpers of this Kevin Shapiro."

"We will help him to lead a full, rich, Dadaistic life!" I shouted.

"And he will never know who is helping him!" Captain Colossal said.

We were all getting very excited about the existence of a real-life Kevin Shapiro.

To tell the truth, we had all been getting fairly fed up with the Kevin Shapiro story we took turns telling, and I, for one, had the feeling that it might be time to kill him off once and for all. Now, the news that there was a real Kevin, and that he was going to be unknowingly adopted by the Wild Dada Ducks, breathed new life into our little artistic circle.

The only Wild Dada Duck who knew what the real Kevin Shapiro looked like was the Indiana Zephyr. We got up from the table where we had been discussing this remarkable development, and went for a little stroll around the lunchroom, so the Indiana Zephyr could point out our new adoptee.

It never fails to strike me, when the Wild Dada Ducks go anywhere, what a dignified and impressive picture we must make. Dressed in the finest Dada taste, serious, and intelligent looking, the Wild Dada Ducks are as fine a body of young men as anyone could hope to see.

We made our little promenade around the lunchroom, the Indiana Zephyr looking for our darling child, Kevin Shapiro. At last he pointed him out. "That's him over there," the Indiana Zephyr whispered.

Kevin Shapiro was better than any of us could have hoped. He was perfect. In fact, he was wonderful. He was magnificent. He was short, maybe five-two, and skinny. His hair was pale blond, and he wore it in a style known as a flattop. This is a crew cut with the hair standing up straight. The hair at the sides of the head is longer then the hair at the top of the head. The total effect is that of making one's head appear flat. It's a 1950s style that has come back into fashion because of some pre-Dada rock groups. Kevin Shapiro also had glasses, big cumbersome-looking plastic ones. His skin was very pale, and he had a little nose. We fell in love with him instantly.

Kevin Shapiro, never dreaming of his good fortune, was hunched over a box of Grape-Nuts, which he had opened by pulling apart the flaps on the side of the box, along the dotted lines. Into the waxed paper lining of the box, Kevin Shapiro had poured the contents of a carton of milk. The milk was dribbling out the corners of the box as he ate the cereal with a plastic spoon.

"This is auspicious," the Honorable Venustiano Carranza (President of Mexico) said to the rest of the Wild Dada Ducks. "Grape-Nuts is a Dada food, especially when you eat it out of the carton like that."

"Munch on, little Kevin Shapiro," Captain Colossal said, under his breath. "The Wild Dada Ducks will watch over you from this day forward."

7

"The first thing we ought to do," said the Honorable Venustiano Carranza (President of Mexico), "before we start helping Kevin Shapiro, is to find out all we can about the adorable little fellow."

This is the reason that the Honorable Venustiano Carranza (President of Mexico) is the undisputed leader of the Wild Dada Ducks. His foresight and methodical thinking is equalled only by his great artistic talent and Dadaistic style. It was agreed then and there, in the lunchroom, while Kevin Shapiro was finishing up his Grape-Nuts, that we would do exhaustive research about our little adopted boy.

Each of us, without being obvious or calling attention

to himself, would endeavor to find out all there was to find out about Kevin. In this way, the Honorable Venustiano Carranza (President of Mexico) pointed out, we would be able to see if there were any areas of deficiency in the life of our little adoptling. We would begin by supplying whatever Kevin lacked. Later we would help him to become a great culture hero— all without ever revealing ourselves, of course.

It was agreed that the following day, after school, we would meet at the Balkan Falcon Drug Company across the street from Himmler High, and discuss the information we had gathered.

The Balkan Falcon Drug Company is our favorite meeting place. It is generally shunned by other Himmler High students because of the foul temper of the fat old lady behind the counter, and the poor quality of the soda fountain—warm soda, filthy spoons, inedible hamburgers, and the like. However, the Wild Dada Ducks like the place, because it has booths, it's never crowded, and raisin toast costs only twenty cents an order.

So it was that the Wild Dada Ducks gathered at the Balkan Falcon Drug Company after school the following afternoon. Having been insulted by the fat old lady behind the counter, and having provided ourselves with raisin toast and hot chocolate in grimy cups, we proceeded to report to one another on what we had learned about our dear little Kevin Shapiro.

As each Wild Dada Duck spoke, I took notes. When everyone had made his report, I read back to the others all I had written:

Kevin Shapiro is a freshman. He is an average student, and likes Biology best of all his classes. His least favorite class is Physical Education, in which class his performance is perfectly miserable. He is nearsighted, and wears his glasses all the time. He lives in an apartment in one of the new buildings near Mesmer Park with his parents. He has no brothers or sisters. Kevin's family has a late-model Japanese sedan, a color television, and an old cocker spaniel, named Henry, who is overweight. Kevin walks Henry twice a day, before he leaves for school, and when he returns in the afternoon. In the evening Kevin's father walks Henry. Kevin has few friends. Those people he does know are mostly involved in comic book collecting. None of them go to Himmler. Kevin has a fairly large collection of old comic books, and almost every Saturday he goes around the city, looking for comics in various used-book stores. Every year, Kevin attends the comic collector's convention, where he buys, sells, and trades. His favorite comics are science-fiction ones. He also likes science-fiction movies.

All of this information had been assembled without any of the Wild Dada Ducks questioning Kevin directly, or drawing any special attention to themselves. We had found all this out by following Kevin, and by engaging various people in casual conversation—working in our questions about Kevin in such a subtle way that nobody ever suspected that we were interested in gathering information about him. Naturally, we were very proud of ourselves. We had gathered quite a lot of highly significant information about our beloved little friend, entirely in secret, and in the space of a little more than twenty-four hours.

"Now," said the Honorable Venustiano Carranza (President of Mexico), "let's discuss what all this data tells us about the lucky lad we have decided to guide and help without his knowledge."

"He leads the most boring life I ever heard of," Igor said.

"There isn't a trace of Dada consciousness in anything he does," Captain Colossal said.

"Except the fat cocker spaniel," I put in.

"Yes," said the Indiana Zephyr, "the fat cocker spaniel has some style, but it isn't really enough to make a Dadaist out of little Kevin, our adopted child."

"I agree," said the Honorable Venustiano Carranza (President of Mexico). "It's hard to tell where to begin helping Kevin Shapiro. The sad truth is, he's evidently a nerd."

"But there's hope," Igor said. "We might be able to rehabilitate him."

"Exactly!" said the Indiana Zephyr. "We have to do something to shake Kevin out of his dull, normal, un-Dada life-style."

"That will cost you forty cents," said the Honorable Venustiano Carranza (President of Mexico). "Pay each Wild Dada Duck ten cents for saying 'life-style.'"

There are fines for using certain words—such as life-style. If a Wild Dada Duck should say, "Have a nice day," it can cost him five dollars.

The Indiana Zephyr fished out four dimes, and

handed them around. "Well, you know what I mean," he said.

"Look out! Here comes you-know-who!" Igor said.

Kevin Shapiro had just entered the Balkan Falcon Drug Company. He walked toward the booth where we were sitting. We hadn't seen Kevin Shapiro walking before this. He had a fascinating walk. He sort of bobbed up and down, and worked his shoulders as he walked, as though he was listening to music—with a bad beat.

Kevin Shapiro came right up to our booth. He stopped walking, but continued to hunch his shoulders.

"Quit asking questions about me!" he said.

There was an uncomfortable moment of silence. Finally the Honorable Venustiano Carranza (President of Mexico) spoke. "You want us to quit doing what?" El Presidente asked, looking puzzled.

"Just quit!" Kevin Shapiro said.

"I assure you, old fellow," Captain Colossal said, "we have no idea what you're talking about."

"I'll punch out your face, see?" Kevin Shapiro said. He shook a pale skinny fist under the nose of Captain Colossal. "Just quit, that's all."

Kevin Shapiro turned, hunched his shoulders, and bobbed out of the Balkan Falcon Drug Company.

8

"He's a genius!" the Indiana Zephyr said.

"Definitely," Igor said.

"I think he's more than a genius," Captain Colossal said.

"I think he may be God," the Honorable Venustiano Carranza (President of Mexico) said.

"Definitely," I said.

It was clear to the Wild Dada Ducks that Kevin Shapiro had plenty of style, insolence, and punkishness —the raw materials of personal greatness. We loved and admired our adopted boy more than ever.

"We have to do something really wonderful for Kevin Shapiro," the Indiana Zephyr said.

"Yes," said the honorable Venustiano Carranza (President of Mexico), "nothing is too good for little Kevin. He will inspire our Dada masterpiece."

"But what are we going to do?" I asked.

"How about printing up cards again?" Captain Colossal asked. "They could say Kevin Shapiro is the greatest."

"That's not nearly big enough," said the Indiana Zephyr. "I don't mean to suggest that there's anything wrong with the idea of issuing a Dada card—the Horace Gerstenblut card was a great work of Art—but this is for Kevin. It has to be special."

We all agreed. The Wild Dada Ducks fell silent, chewing the crusts of our raisin toast, all of us trying to think up something magnificent enough to do for Kevin Shapiro.

"We want to call everybody's attention to the fact that Kevin Shapiro is a great person, isn't that right?" I asked.

"Yes," said Igor, "so what's your idea?"

"I don't have an idea yet," I said, "I just wanted to make sure I understood what we're after."

"A person as great as Kevin Shapiro ought to be world famous," El Presidente said.

"That's right!" Captain Colossal said.

"It would be wrong for only us Wild Dada Ducks to know about Kevin Shapiro," Igor said.

"We ought to let the whole world know what a splendid person Kevin Shapiro is," I said.

"Aren't there special guys who work for famous people—movie stars, and politicians, and people like that?" the Indiana Zephyr asked. "You know, they get their names in the paper, and they make sure everybody knows how great they are."

"That's right," I said, "publicity agents, they're called."

"That's it!" the Honorable Venustiano Carranza (President of Mexico) said. "That's what we have to do for little Kevin Shapiro! We have to make him famous and loved by everybody!"

"We'll be his publicity agents!"

"We'll get everybody to appreciate him!"

"We'll make him famous!"

"This is a chance to do something not only for our beloved Kevin Shapiro, but for the whole world!"

"This is a great day for world Dada Culture!"

"So what do we do first?"

"How about printing up a lot of cards?"

"Captain Colossal, can't you think of anything but printing up cards?" the Honorable Venustiano Carranza (President of Mexico) asked.

"Maybe we could print up posters," I said.

"That's it!" everybody said. "A really great poster of Kevin Shapiro—in color."

"We'll print thousands!"

"Everybody will want them!"

"It's perfect!"

"Wait a second!" Igor said. "That will cost a lot of money—probably hundreds. Do we have that much?"

The fact was, the Wild Dada Ducks didn't have any money to speak of. Between us we hardly had hundreds of cents, let alone dollars.

"Isn't that always the way?" the Honorable Venustiano Carranza (President of Mexico) said. "Lack of money once again thwarts a great Artistic enterprise. We'll have to keep thinking."

We kept thinking.

The more we thought, the more the idea of printing up something in the school print shop seemed to have merit. First of all, it didn't cost anything. Captain Colossal could run off the cards almost any day after school, and as long as we were willing to use whatever scrap paper the print shop had lying around, the whole production would be free.

The Honorable Venustiano Carranza (President of Mexico) grumbled quite a bit about printing cards again. He wanted to do something we had never done before. However, since no one including El Presidente could come up with anything that was both good and possible, we finally fell back on Captain Colossal and the printing press. The Honorable Venustiano Carranza (President of Mexico) insisted that we at least make these cards a bit larger than the last batch, and try our best to give them a decent Dada quality. We spent the next hour working on the text for the card. When we finished, and everybody had expressed approval, we gave the final copy to Captain Colossal, with instructions to do his utmost to give the thing an appearance we could all be proud of.

Two days later, in the Balkan Falcon Drug Company, Captain Colossal presented an edition of two thousand cards. They were excellent. Not only was the printing job superior, but the Captain had managed to get some very handsome green cardboard, and some printer's cuts showing pictures of this and that which he had artistically arranged to make the cards even more impressive. The whole effect was very fine, and we were all pleased.

9

It is funny how fate takes its cut. That is one of the
favorite sayings of the Wild Dada Ducks. It means that
however carefully you plan things, however much
you're sure how things are supposed to turn out—
something you never thought of can change everything. Fate will take its cut.

When the Wild Dada Ducks planned and executed
the handsome works of Art in honor of Kevin Shapiro,
events were already moving in a direction none of us
could have guessed. But that is always the way things
work. That is why Dada is the greatest Art movement.
The Dadaist assumes things are going to go wrong—or
at least in an unpredictable direction—so he isn't sur-

prised when it happens. He is surprised when it doesn't.

We distributed the Kevin Shapiro cards in the same manner as the Horace Gerstenblut cards. That is, we left stacks of them in all the bathrooms. Once again we had cause to wish there were some girls in the Duckettes, as darting in and out of the girls' bathrooms was dangerous and scary. However, we got the cards distributed without anyone seeing us, and without meeting anyone apt to get upset.

Because the Wild Dada Ducks are constantly preoccupied with Dada Art and Philosophy, we frequently neglect the events of day-to-day life at Himmler High School. Ask any of us who won the big basketball game last night—and we will ask who was playing. It isn't that we necessarily disapprove of such activities—it's just that you can't lead the way in an Artistic revolution and keep track of every little detail.

So it happened that none of us had the slightest idea that the day we distributed our sincere tribute to Kevin Shapiro was also the day of the Himmler High School Student Council election.

Just as they had done with the Horace Gerstenblut cards, our fellow students picked up the new Kevin Shapiro edition, talked about it, passed cards around to their friends, and tried to guess who Kevin Shapiro might be, and what the cards meant. Of course, that is not the proper way to appreciate the cards. They are works of Art to be enjoyed, and experienced—not analyzed. However, that is not our concern. As Dada Artists, we provide the Art, the public can do what it likes with it. Besides, the message of the cards was perfectly obvious. The cards were intended to notify the world in general, and Himmler High in particular, that Kevin Shapiro was an exceptionally great human being.

In fact, that part of our message did appear to have been picked up by a great many people, because, after having a look at the cards, discussing them, and swapping them around, ninety-seven percent of the students at Himmler High went and voted for Kevin Shapiro.

They voted for him for Student Council President, and for all the positions on the student council. All told, Kevin Shapiro received about 28,000 votes from approximately 4,000 students.

We didn't know anything about this, because the voting was by secret ballot. The results of the election would be announced in an assembly of the whole school the next day.

The day of the Student Council election was like any other day in the lives of the Wild Dada Ducks. We had executed our Artwork, we went to our classes, we picked up ballots for the student council election, and each voted for Kevin Shapiro for all seven places, including Student Council President.

At the assembly the following day, the official candidates for office were all lined up, sitting in a row on folding chairs on the auditorium stage. They were wearing suits and dresses. They had sat in the same order, wearing the same outfits, the week before when each candidate had made a campaign speech.

Mr. Gerstenblut, the vice-principal, and Mr. Winter,

the principal, were both on stage too. Mr. Winter made a short speech about how we were lucky to live in a democracy and be able to vote in elections, and the usual stuff they tell you at school elections. The Wild Dada Ducks have nothing against democracy, except that it doesn't go nearly far enough—but the thing about being elected to a school office that we find boring is that you wouldn't get to pass any real laws, even if you got elected.

Miss Steele, the chairman of the election committee, came out to read the results of the tabulation of all the votes.

"We have a very remarkable situation here," Miss Steele said. "It seems there have been a great many write-in votes for a candidate who hadn't even announced that he was in the race. Now ordinarily, the election committee would insist on the rule that states that if a candidate for Student Council President is not one of those duly nominated, votes for that person will be discounted. The rule further states that if the person with the winning number of votes is not one of those duly nominated, the duly nominated person with the next largest number of votes will be elected. However, in this election, one extremely popular young man has gotten practically all of the votes, for all the offices on the Student Council—and, as you may have guessed, he is not one of those duly nominated."

"The committee feels that it will be best if we declare the election as having miscarried," Miss Steele went on to considerable booing. "We are going to hold another election, by show of hands, here this morning—but in the interest of fairness, we would like to invite the young man who got so many votes to come up on the stage and say a few words. You've already heard from the other fine candidates. Now, will the young man who has already demonstrated that he has the confidence of his fellow students, please approach the stage? Will Kevin Shapiro please come up and say a few words?"

There was a thunderous outburst of applause. There was also a good deal of neck-craning and looking around, since almost nobody in the school knew who Kevin Shapiro was.

From the very last row in the auditorium a small thin figure shuffled and bobbed down the aisle, and then bounded up the steps to the stage. It was our boy. It was Kevin Shapiro. The Wild Dada Ducks started a cheer that was wildly taken up by everyone else in the school. Kevin Shapiro, cool as you please, stood on the stage, waiting for the cheering and clapping to die down. I noticed for the first time that Kevin had these really klutzy shoes. They looked like Frankenstein boots. I think he picked shoes with the thickest possible soles, in an attempt to get an extra inch of height. The shoes made Kevin Shapiro look incredibly Dada. He shifted from foot to foot and waited for the crowd to be quiet.

Finally the last whistle and foot-stomp and cheer had echoed through the auditorium and Kevin Shapiro spoke.

"Hey," he said, "I don't want to be any slob President of the Student Council. Don't vote for me, see?

Vote for these idiots here."

The applause was deafening. It went on for about ten minutes.

Kevin was re-elected by a landslide.

10

The Wild Dada Ducks were filled with pride and delight. In just one short day following our public expression of appreciation, Kevin Shapiro had been almost unanimously recognized as the finest example of humanity in the whole school. The crowd in the auditorium was going crazy. The cheering had consolidated into a continuous roar, as Kevin Shapiro, now elected for the second time—this time by acclamation—approached the microphone.

It took a long time for the audience to become quiet. Kevin Shapiro, who appeared to us to be a born public speaker and leader of men, patiently waited until the last expression of enthusiasm had been uttered. He held up both hands in a gesture for silence, which was at the same time friendly, endearing. Kevin Shapiro was the most beloved person in all of Himmler High School at that moment.

"Look," he began, "I thought I made myself clear. I do not want to be on your stupid Student Council. Just leave me alone. Anybody bothers me, I'll bash his face in, see?" Kevin shook a fist meaningfully, and returned to his seat.

There was another spontaneous demonstration of support for Kevin Shapiro, but no amount of cheering and chanting could induce him to leave his auditorium seat and speak to the students again. The crowd showed no sign of leaving peaceably, and finally Mr. Winter, who has an astonishingly loud voice, took over.

Mr. Winter declared the day's exercises over, and by executive order abolished all elections in the school until further notice.

This is why the Wild Dada Ducks—and apparently Kevin Shapiro—do not take school elections seriously. Mr. Winter has the last word.

The crowd left the auditorium in an ugly mood. Every teacher in Himmler High knew that the rest of the day was going to be grim. There was a lot of resentment expressed toward Mr. Winter for abolishing elections, and this resentment extended to all figures of authority, especially teachers.

Somehow, nobody seemed to be angry at little Kevin Shapiro. He had twice rejected the nearly unanimous vote of the entire student body—and in no uncertain terms. He had called them stupid, and made it plain that he couldn't be bothered to serve as Student Council president. And yet, no one appeared to have taken offense. The students of Himmler High School respected Kevin's wish, and mostly left him alone. It was really unheard-of behavior. I mean, the majority of the students are far from being philosophers, let alone Dadaists. To tell the truth, most of the kids are only human on a technicality. They take great mindless pride in their school—they go to all the games and scream bloody murder—about once every other year there is a mass fist-fight with the students from Kissinger High School, our great rival.

Now, Kevin Shapiro, a little, skinny, bespectacled kid, had openly rejected one of the institutions of Himmler High. In effect he had rejected the whole population of the school—and nobody tried to kill him! The only thing the Wild Dada Ducks could make of this remarkable behavior was that, like us, simply anybody who saw Kevin Shapiro could not help loving him. Captain Colossal said he had charisma. Igor said it was star quality. Whatever it was, Kevin definitely had it, and we were all very proud of him. We were ashamed to remember that up until the last minute, we were all going to vote for the Marquis de Sade.

11

Of course, school elections, and assemblies, and all of those things are dumb. Anyone would realize it, if it were given any thought—but generally, nobody thinks about those things. The Wild Dada Ducks do not approve of school elections, naturally, because we are for the abolishment of government as we know it. We want the machines to take over. That is, we want ordinary, loyal, everyday machines, like dishwashers and buses and pencil sharpeners, to take over the government—not computers and robots, which are probably really in charge already. The Wild Dada Ducks do not approve of school elections, but the ordinary unenlightened Himmler High School students just love them.

At least that's what we thought until the election of Kevin Shapiro (who refused to serve). To tell the truth, we weren't sure what was going through the minds of our fellow students. Mostly, we were proud of how popular our boy, Kevin Shapiro, had become because of the distribution of our Dada card. We didn't consider what might be the innermost thoughts of the other kids in the school.

Later we got an idea of what the whole school thought of Kevin Shapiro.

They worshipped him.

Kevin was the single biggest hero in the school. He was the only hero in the school. In a single moment, he had expressed the secret truth about school elections, the school, the world, being a kid—everything. Every kid in the auditorium that day realized the reality of his situation when Kevin Shapiro said that he didn't want to be on any stupid student council. Most kids wouldn't have said anything like that, even if they were thinking it—but Kevin did.

Like the Wild Dada Ducks, every kid in the school had realized that Kevin Shapiro had a style all his own. Just as we had predicted, he was a natural leader.

Kevin's wish that he be left alone only made everybody love and respect him more. All the girls were in love with him. All the boys were afraid of him. Simply anybody would have died of happiness if Kevin Shapiro had smiled at them, or winked, or spoken, or anything.

All this was true, but nobody actually realized it—or realized the extent or importance of it. When we filed out of the auditorium that day, nobody was conscious of the great event that had taken place—with the possible exception of Mr. Winter and Mr. Gerstenblut, both of whom looked worried. They had taken courses in being a principal, and they knew they had the makings of an uprising on their hands. They knew this, or they may have known it—but there was nothing they could do but wait.

The Wild Dada Ducks were not worried, even when Kevin Shapiro passed by us in the crush of people leaving the auditorium. He smiled a grim smile, and rubbed his belly, as if he was thinking about something good to eat. "I'll get you for this," he said.

We just attributed his remark and gesture to his natural charm, and were even a little flattered that he had spoken to us. We didn't understand that Kevin Shapiro was the king of the school—and we didn't understand the power a king has.

Everything appeared to go back to normal at once. As far as the Wild Dada Ducks were concerned, the election and the assembly in the auditorium were part of the Dada Work we had started with the cards—and it had been our most successful exercise so far. Now it was over, and we all felt good about it.

12

Nothing changed at first. The day after the student council elections, and the day after that, life at Himmler High School was normal, average. Students went from class to class, the Wild Dada Ducks met to discuss Art and Culture in the Balkan Falcon Drug Company, and Kevin Shapiro ate alone in the lunchroom. Mr. Winter and Mr. Gerstenblut appeared in the halls very often, looking alert and nervous, as though they expected to find something important going on— but nothing was going on.

That's what they thought.

That's what we thought.

That's what everyone thought.

It was on the third day after the election that the Fanatical Praetorians first appeared. We didn't know they were the Fanatical Praetorians at first. They were all the kids in Himmler High who were shorter than Kevin Shapiro, and they all had sailor hats.

These sailor hats were of the variety worn by Donald Duck in the early cartoons. They were soft and white, with a ribbon hanging down in the back. I don't know where they got them. There was a blue band around the bottom of the hats with the words *S.S. Popnick,* printed in white. They must have been Navy surplus, but from which country's navy, I don't know.

The short kids in sailor/duck hats all sat in the lunchroom, not too close to Kevin Shapiro, but surrounding him on all sides. They all ate Grape-Nuts from little cartons into which they had poured milk. Most of them had big Frankenstein shoes like Kevin Shapiro. All of them had sworn an oath to protect Kevin with their lives.

Kevin Shapiro had recruited the Fanatical Praetorians, and administered the oath. Not only had he organized a bodyguard, and, as we gradually learned—an illegal government within the school—Kevin Shapiro had also started an Art Movement.

It was called Heroic Realism.

We didn't find all these things out at once. At first, all we knew was that a bunch of little kids in sailor hats were trailing around, a respectful distance behind Kevin Shapiro, and if anyone approached him or tried to talk to him, they would make a wall of their bodies, and threaten the person who intended to approach.

Since Kevin Shapiro didn't like to talk to people, and mostly wanted to be left alone, there weren't many confrontations with the Fanatical Praetorians. It seemed a little weird, and that was all.

Then came Heroic Realism. As we had found out when we were doing research about him, Kevin Shapiro was a big comic book fan. It turned out that what he liked best about comic books was the artwork. The Wild Dada Ducks had declared comic books unartistic a long time ago. Not only did we find the stories predictable and boring, but the pictures seemed particularly awful to us. For the most part, they showed guys with too many muscles and heads too small for their bodies.

Kevin Shapiro loved comic books.

Heroic Realism declared that anything that wasn't a comic book was no good. Anybody who didn't like comic books was no good. Conversely, anybody who liked comic books was a great person. That, as far as we could make out, was all there was to Heroic Realism.

Every student in Himmler High was a Heroic Realist. Except us, of course. Also, every student in Himmler High recognized Kevin Shapiro as his supreme leader.

Kevin Shapiro was a good deal more than president of the student council. It was obvious why he had scorned that basically meaningless honor. Kevin Shapiro had become undisputed king of Himmler High. His word was law. Of course, he practically never said anything, but if he had said anything it would have been law.

Obviously he communicated to the Fanatical Praetorians. If Kevin Shapiro wanted to tell anybody anything, it was done through the Fanatical Praetorians. For example, if you were sitting in the lunchroom, a half-dozen Fanatical Praetorians might come over to you and say, "Kevin doesn't want you sitting there." So you'd move. Everybody was afraid of the Fanatical Praetorians.

They were little, but there were a lot of them. Also, they had learned to imitate Kevin's special way of being persuasive. "Look," they'd say, "we'll punch out your face, see?" It never failed to get results.

Big kids, who had formerly been known as bullies, cowered and cringed before the short kids in the Donald Duck hats. Some kids wanted to become Fanatical Praetorians, but they weren't short enough.

After school every day Kevin Shapiro would be escorted away from the school by a big crowd of Fanatical Praetorians. They even guarded him on weekends. Once I saw him leafing through comic books in a store downtown, while ten or eleven shrimps in sailor hats stood around him.

After a week or two, everybody was sufficiently afraid of the Fanatical Praetorians that they were obeyed even when they were alone. Even the teachers learned to respect them. In the Biology class taken by the Indiana Zephyr and Captain Colossal, there was only one Fanatical Praetorian, a kid named Shep Stoneman. It seems Shep Stoneman got into an argument with the teacher. The teacher wanted Shep to remove his sailor hat. Shep didn't want to. Finally, Shep told the entire class to get up and leave the room. They did it.

Mr. Winter and Mr. Gerstenblut were all over the building, dealing with problems caused by the Fanatical Praetorians. There were a great many comic books being circulated in the school because of the Heroic Realism movement, and there had been a number of tense moments between teachers and Fanatical Praetorians.

At one point, Mr. Winter outlawed the wearing of hats in school. The next day, by order of the Fanatical Praetorians, every kid in the school wore a hat of some kind all day, and a general strike was threatened. That is, all the kids wore hats except the Wild Dada Ducks.

This constituted a moral dilemma for us. Here was the breakdown of the normal un-Dada order, which we had all wished for, but we found we couldn't go along with the hats-on order which emanated from Kevin Shapiro—a hero we ourselves had created. We didn't exactly know why we felt we could not go along with it. There was something about Heroic Realism that made it impossible—but it was more than that. We had been nonconformists for so long that it just didn't feel right to go along with everyone else—and there was something else too, but we couldn't say what it was.

Of course, the hat-wearing was a complete success. What could Mr. Winter do? He couldn't very well call in the police. Nobody was doing anything destructive —they were wearing hats, that was all. He couldn't suspend everybody. He couldn't very well write to everyone's parents, and say that little Johnny had worn a hat on such-and-such a day and was therefore suspended. It was a clear victory for Kevin and his loyal followers. That was everybody but the Wild Dada Ducks.

Mr. Winter wriggled out of his defeat, ungracefully, by having all the homeroom teachers read something about how styles change, and how Himmler High students have always been models of good grooming and acceptable dress, and that if hats were "in" then the administration of the school wasn't about to spoil anybody's fun, and how Mr. Winter always kept up with the times, and had even personally been to a disco with his wife, and sometimes didn't wear a necktie.

It didn't fool anybody. The Fanatical Praetorians were running the place, and they obeyed nobody but Kevin Shapiro. It only remained to see what Kevin would decide to do next.

13

The Wild Dada Ducks were especially interested in what Kevin Shapiro would do next. Obviously, it had not gone unnoticed that we had been the only ones not to wear hats during the protest. The truth was, we were somewhat afraid of what the Fanatical Praetorians might do to us. One thing was certain, they would not do anything except on Kevin Shapiro's order.

The next thing Kevin Shapiro got interested in was making sure that everybody in the school ate Grape-Nuts. This project interested him so much that he actually spoke to the assembled kids in the lunchroom one day.

Kevin got up, and struck a pose indicating that he

was about to speak. Even without the shushing and fingers to lips of the Fanatical Praetorians, the room would have fallen silent in a hurry. This was to be the first public utterance of Kevin Shapiro since he had turned down the student council.

"Grape-Nuts is good!" he said.

After that no lunch at Himmler High School did not include a little carton of Grape-Nuts cereal with milk poured into the waxed paper liner. The school lunchroom didn't have enough in stock at first, and kids brought Grape-Nuts from home. Lunchtime became a symphony of crunching and slurping.

Fearing for our lives, and arguing that as Dadaists we had already approved of Grape-Nuts, the Wild Dada Ducks joined in the cereal eating. Secretly, we hoped that our failure to wear hats that day when everybody else wore them might be forgotten, especially since we were eating Grape-Nuts like the Heroic Realists.

And, in fact, in seemed that our act of disloyalty had been forgotten. In the days that followed, nothing special happened. Of course, the fulminations of the Heroic Realists annoyed us no end. Kids went on and on about the beauty of comic books, and our Dada sensibilities were continually offended by snatches of overheard conversation about Mouse-Man and Wonder Wombat—but in general, life was bearable at Himmler High School.

Kevin Shapiro's main concern seemed to be the continued eating of Grape-Nuts. Often at lunchtime, he could be seen contentedly surveying the spectacle of a great many kids, all working away at their little boxes of cereal.

The lunchroom at Himmler High is large, as is the school itself. While the room is not capable of containing the whole student population, a good thousand can eat there at once. Nowadays, they ate a good thousand boxes of Grape-Nuts at once.

Kevin Shapiro's concern about the cereal eating was such that he actually spoke again. This time he climbed up onto a table, and gestured for silence.

"Get 'em good and soggy," he said.

After this, people took considerably longer with their lunches. Under the ever-watchful eye of Kevin and his bodyguard, it became customary to let the milk and cereal sit uneaten for ten or fifteen minutes, the Grape-Nuts absorbing all the milk that did not run out the corners of the carton.

One day, a deputation of Fanatical Praetorians actually walked around the lunchroom, inspecting people's Grape-Nuts to see that they were good and soggy.

A couple of days after the Praetorian tour of inspection, Kevin Shapiro once again, and for the last time, addressed the assembled lunching students.

Again he stood upon a table, not too far from where the Wild Dada Ducks were sitting. He had his carton of well-sogged Grape-Nuts in his hand.

"Look!" said Kevin Shapiro. "Watch me!"

Kevin Shapiro turned the box over, and dumped the soggy contents into his cupped right hand.

"Down with Dada!" he shouted and hurled the

mess of dripping Grape-Nuts right into the face of the Honorable Venustiano Carranza (President of Mexico).

What followed was horrible. The Wild Dada Ducks were served at least one thousand portions of Grape-Nuts. They were thrown at us, poured over our heads, stuffed down our pants, and mushed into our hair. The massacre took place so quickly that we never had time to get out of our chairs. We sat there, stunned, and were turned into living, dripping statues.

When we left the lunchroom we squished as we walked, and left a sloppy trail of cereal.

14

Not long after the Grape-Nuts devastation, it seems Kevin Shapiro disbanded the invincible Fanatical Praetorians. Heroic Realism appeared to wane as an Art Movement, and conditions at the school returned entirely to normal.

Kevin Shapiro, refusing to do anything to exploit the total power he had over his fellow students, was gradually forgotten, and could be seen hunched over his Grape-Nuts at lunch, alone as before.

Whenever he saw any of the Wild Dada Ducks he laughed to himself.

The Wild Dada Ducks left him alone.

We also suspended our program of cultural improvement for our fellow students. We continued to meet after school every day in the Balkan Falcon Drug Company. There we pursued our discussions of Art and Philosophy.

For about a week we made no mention of our experience in the lunchroom with the Grape-Nuts. Finally, it seemed time to discuss its implications and historical importance.

"Does it seem possible," asked Igor, "that Kevin Shapiro seized control of the entire school, just so he could have us covered with wet breakfast cereal?"

No one was sure. It could have been planned from the start, or it could have just been an idea that occured to him at the moment.

"The important question," said Captain Colossal, "is what is the significance of Kevin's rise to power, and the Grape-Nuts attack? What does it mean in philosophical terms?"

"Yes," said the Indiana Zephyr, "what is the moral of the story?"

"It has no moral," said the Honorable Venustiano Carranza (President of Mexico), "it is a Dada story."

end